EVERYMAN'S LIBRARY

EVERYMAN,
I WILL GO WITH THEE,
AND BE THY GUIDE,
IN THY MOST NEED
TO GO BY THY SIDE

IRÈNE NÉMIROVSKY

DAVID GOLDER

THE BALL

SNOW IN AUTUMN

THE COURILOF AFFAIR

TRANSLATED FROM THE FRENCH
BY SANDRA SMITH

WITH AN INTRODUCTION BY
CLAIRE MESSUD

EVERYMAN'S LIBRARY
Alfred A. Knopf New York London Toronto
308

THIS IS A BORZOI BOOK
PUBLISHED BY ALFRED A. KNOPF

First included in Everyman's Library, 2008
David Golder Copyright © 1929 by Éditions Bernard Grasset
Le Bal (The Ball) Copyright © 1930 by Éditions Bernard Grasset
Les Mouches d'Automne (Snow in Autumn) Copyright © 1931 by Éditions
Bernard Grasset
L'Affaire Courilof (The Courilof Affair) Copyright © 1933 by Éditions
Bernard Grasset
English translations Copyright © 2007, 2008 by Sandra Smith
UK licence arranged by the French Publishers' Agency, New York
This edition published in the UK by arrangement with Chatto &
Windus, a division of the Random House Group Ltd.

Introduction Copyright © 2008 by Claire Messud
Chronology Copyright © 2008 by Everyman's Library
Typography by Peter B. Willberg

US website: www.randomhouse.com/everymans

ISBN: 978-0-307-26708-5 (US)
978-1-84159-308-1 (UK)

A CIP catalogue reference for this book is available from the
British Library

Book design by Barbara de Wilde and Carol Devine Carson

Typeset in the UK by AccComputing, North Barrow, Somerset

Printed and bound in Germany by GGP Media GmbH, Pössneck

IRÈNE NÉMIROVSKY

CONTENTS

INTRODUCTION

"Each of us has his weaknesses. Human nature is incomprehensible," muses the mysterious Léon M., narrator of Irène Némirovsky's 1933 novel, *The Courilof Affair*. "One cannot even say with certainty whether a man is good or evil, stupid or intelligent. There does not exist a good man who has not at some time in his life committed a cruel act, nor an evil man who has not done good...." The complicated, often murky ironies of human interaction are the stuff of Némirovsky's fictions: no matter what her subject—and her range was considerable—her work is unified in its unsparing examination of the desires and feelings that lie behind the most apparently clear-cut scenarios.

In *The Courilof Affair*, Léon M., in his retirement in Nice, pens his memories of his revolutionary days in Russia in the early years of the century and, in particular, of his assignment to assassinate the Tsar's Minister of Education, Valerian Alexandrovitch Courilof, known as "the Killer Whale," in 1903 (incidentally, the year of the author's birth). In preparation for the attack, Léon takes on the identity of Marcel Legrand, a Swiss doctor, and becomes the personal physician to Courilof. Over the course of their time together, he is moved by a growing understanding not simply of Courilof, but of human frailty. Compassion and revolutionary terrorism are not easily compatible, and his new knowledge threatens Léon's mission. As he recalls of Courilof and his politically problematic French wife (and former mistress), Margot, "It remains impossible for me to explain, even to myself, how I could... understand these two people.... For the first time, I saw human beings: unhappy people, with ambitions, faults, foolishness."

This capacity genuinely and fully to *see* human beings, to acknowledge the tender humanity of their flaws, is one of the supreme gifts of fiction, both for the writer and for the reader. Nobody knew this better than Irène Némirovsky, whose novels are fiercely preoccupied with the unveiling of her characters' foibles but who, through that unveiling, provides her readers with a bracing, unnerving, and often moving vision of ourselves as we really are. This is nowhere more true than in her unfinished masterpiece, *Suite Française*, the relatively recent discovery and publication of which have brought Némirovsky to the attention of a new generation of readers. Set in France under German occupation and written, extraordinarily, under the circumstances it describes, *Suite Française* moves between chilling satire of the petty selfishness of the bourgeoisie and a poignant evocation of the realities of village life under occupation—realities much like those of Léon M., in which to recognize the enemy's humanity is to compromise, or disable, a warrior's hatred. In reading that novel—or, more properly, those two novellas, since the remaining three segments that would have completed the masterpiece were never written—this reader, for one, gained an understanding of what it meant to live in France during the Second World War that I had not had before, steeped though I was in books and films on the subject.

Consistently through her work, Némirovsky's vision is neither easy nor comfortable; nor was her own life untainted by the moral complexities she captured so keenly in fiction. In its broadest outlines, of course, the tragic story of Irène Némirovsky's life is by now widely known: she was a refugee from the Russian Revolution who made France her home; she enjoyed literary acclaim and considerable privilege there during the '20s and '30s; and she mistakenly thought that privilege would protect her from the Nazis, an error that cost her her life. She was taken by the Germans in 1942 and died in Auschwitz of typhus not long after her arrival there. Her husband, Michel, left her final manuscript in the care of her two small daughters, who managed to salvage it in spite of their own tribulations during the war. They kept her notebook without reading it, for decades, and only in the 1990s did her older, surviving daughter, Denise Epstein, realize that these pages constituted not a diary but the fragments of a novel. It was published in France in 2004 and subsequently translated into English. The book has been an international best seller.

It may have seemed, to most English-language readers, that Némirovsky sprang into literary existence, fully formed, with the writing of *Suite Française*. In fact, however, she was in France a prolific, critically acclaimed, and popularly successful author, whose reputation long survived her. Her third novel, *David Golder* (the two first, *Le Malentendu* and *L'Ennemie*, were released in a monthly magazine, *Les Œuvres Libres*), was published when she was twenty-six, in 1929. The book made her name (and was made into a film and a play, both starring Harry Baur), and she was hailed by the *New York Times*, upon its 1930 translation into English, as a successor to Dostoevsky. In its wake she published a book almost every year until the Second World War. Her captivity and death, in this light, are all the more shocking: it is painful to think of the literary legacy that was lost.

Irène Némirovsky's ability to grasp life's contradictions was at least in part the result of the deeply contradictory facts of her own brief life. She was born in Kiev on February 11, 1903, the only child of Léon and Fanny (Margoulis) Némirovsky. Her father was a prosperous banker, allied with the Tsar's court, and as such the family enjoyed privileges rarely available to Jewish families. As for many White Russians, French was the lingua franca of their household. According to a recent biography by Olivier Philipponnat and Patrick Lienhardt, "she spoke a bookish Russian; so to speak, Russian was not her mother tongue," and possibly Némirovsky's closest early relationship was with her French governess, Marie, whom she called "Zézelle." But the political allegiances of the Némirovskys would cost them dearly, and the family fled their home, penniless, at the time of the Revolution, in January 1918, coming to France only after many peregrinations and a nearly yearlong stint in a village in Finland, just behind the Russian frontier. Once settled in Paris, Léon Némirovsky set about restoring the family fortunes, and as she reached adulthood, Irène moved in elite circles: largely politically conservative, generally Catholic (although she also contributed to left-wing journals such as *Marianne*). Her family was fully assimilated, and while she never denied her Jewishness (tellingly, she chose to marry a fellow Russian Jewish exile, Michel Epstein, whose history mirrored her own; and she asserted, in a 1935 interview, that "I never dreamed of hiding my origins. Whenever I had

IR È N E   N É M I R O V S K Y

the occasion, I protested that I was Jewish, I even proclaimed it!"), she also did not fully embrace it. In 1939, Némirovsky converted to Catholicism, a decision that has caused controversy in recent discussions of her life, work, and relation to her Jewish heritage. It has been asserted that she was herself anti-Semitic—her novel *David Golder*, in particular, has been held up as an example of this fact, as has her religious conversion—a claim that has threatened to cast a shadow upon her reputation.

The reality is, inevitably, more complicated. Certainly questions of social class play powerfully in Némirovsky's identity: in Russia, her family was set apart from other Jews not only by her father's occupation but by their situation in Kiev, where they lived among the wealthy in the hills high above the poverty-stricken Jewish ghetto of the inner city. Her unquestionably unsavory depictions of Jews (for example: "Golder looked with a kind of hatred at Fischl, as if at a cruel caricature. Fat little Jew...He calmly held in his killer's hands a porcelain bowl of fresh caviar against his chest.") reflect both some measure of self-loathing and a willed detachment from the Jew as "Other." As Irène Némirovsky puts it herself in her veiled autobiography, *The Wine of Solitude* (1935), "I spent my life fighting an odious blood, but it is inside of me." That these two positions seem initially paradoxical is, in truth, but an illusion, one of the many that we all harbor in the hope of parsing life more clearly, of making orderly sense of the world. Némirovsky—allied from birth with White Russians and hence against her own people, the Jews, and consequently most naturally affiliated, in France, with political conservatives, who were often anti-Semitic—did not have the luxury of such illusions; and she does not grant them to her characters. What she sees may not be attractive, but she is resolute in seeing clearly and has the courage to record her truths, however unappealing they may be. Therein lies her courage as a writer.

(It is worth noting, indeed, that while many of her supposed literary friends in Paris abandoned her at the outset of the war, it was Horace de Carbuccia, editor of the notably right-wing and often anti-Semitic journal *Gringoire*, who arranged to publish her work pseudonymously during the occupation and who thereby guaranteed Némirovsky's family some desperately needed income. This apparent irony would not have surprised her.)

David Golder is the remarkable, compelling, and at times painfully unsympathetic portrait of an aging Russian Jewish businessman and his entourage in 1920s France. It opens, significantly, with the word "No," as Golder denies his business partner, Simon Marcus, support in a venture pertaining to Russian oil wells. Golder's denial prompts Marcus's suicide and encourages others, including the reader, to see Golder as a ruthless, even heartless, entrepreneur. As the novel unfolds, however, our sympathies cleave to this brutal ruin of a man, preyed upon and exploited by his grasping wife, Gloria; her lover, Hoyos; and their friends; and by his beautiful, spoiled, and adored daughter, Joyce. Golder rages that "I'm just expected to pay, pay, and keep on paying... That's why I've been put on this earth"; and it seems he isn't wrong in this assessment. Joyce is his passion—"Every time he came back from a trip, he looked for her in the crowd, in spite of himself. She was never there, and yet he continued to expect her with the same humiliating, tenacious, and vain sense of hope"— and his Achilles' heel. To the last, in spite of all he learns about her, he can deny her nothing—even his life.

Central to our ultimate understanding of David Golder is the portrait of his old acquaintance and cardpartner, Soifer, of whom we are told that "his meanness bordered on madness.... For several years now, since he had lost all his teeth, he ate only cereal and puréed vegetables to avoid having to buy dentures." Soifer is, regrettably, a grotesque caricature of the greedy Jew; and surely he provided fine fodder for the growing number of anti-Semites in 1930s France. By 1935, Némirovsky said of the book, "If there had been Hitler [at the time], I would have greatly toned down *David Golder*, and I wouldn't have written it in the same fashion"; and again, three years later, "How could I write such a thing? If I were to write *David Golder* now, I would do it quite differently.... The climate is quite changed." But there is, nevertheless, in Némirovsky's portrayal, a strange tenderness even for Soifer: she writes of him, in a searing passage, "Much later, Soifer would die all alone, like a dog, without a friend, without a single wreath on his grave,

buried in the cheapest cemetery in Paris by his family who
hated him, and whom he had hated, but to whom he nevertheless left a fortune of some thirty million francs, thus fulfilling
till the end the incomprehensible destiny of every good Jew on
this earth."

This is an appalling indictment, not of Soifer himself but of
the warping force of the society around him. If it is an anti-
Semitic portrait, and crudely drawn, it is also a portrait of the
potential horror of any immigrant's life: if one were to substi-
tute the word "immigrant" for "Jew," Némirovsky's depiction
would carry the same force, with considerably less offense.
How many immigrants have been emotionally deformed by
their travails, have given everything for their families only to
be hopelessly misunderstood and even abandoned by their kin?
Is it not the fate of many in diasporas of different kinds, not
simply of Jews? Agonizing isolation—to be unknown, unac-
knowledged, unloved—is mercifully not every immigrant's
fate; but it is certainly a fate of immigrants, of the displaced,
more surely than of the rooted. As Némirovsky wrote in 1934,
"I continue to depict the society I know best, that is composed
of misfits, those who have been expelled from their milieu, the
place where they would normally have lived, and who do not
adapt to their new lives without clashes or suffering."

Unlike for Soifer, there is, for David Golder himself, a measure of grace. The novel concludes with his death, but not
before he has returned to his native Russia and embarked from
the port he knew as a youth, rendered by Némirovsky without
a hint of sentimentality: "The port. He recognized it as clearly
as if he had left the day before. The little customs building,
half in ruins. Beached boats buried in the black sand, which
was littered with bits of coal and rubbish; watermelon rind
and dead animals bobbing in the deep, muddy green water,
just as in the past." Golder is, at the last, relieved, at least
somewhat, of his lifelong deracination. Nor is he condemned
to die alone: he is accompanied, in his final voyage, by a young
Jew leaving Russia for the first time, to seek his fortune in the
West. To him, at the end, David Golder speaks, for the first
time in years, in his native Yiddish; and in the wake of their
communication, in his last moments Golder is granted a vision

of his own boyhood, and he hears the sound of his mother's voice.

The echo of Tolstoy's *Death of Ivan Ilyich* is strong in this novel, even if Golder's Gerasim is a young man on the make who will pocket the contents of Golder's wallet (with Golder's blessing) when he leaves. Némirovsky's vision is darker than her Russian forebear's; and her sense of her protagonist's fate is not rooted in a tradition of Christian redemption. But the debt is strong, and clear: from the novel's opening lines, Golder is learning how to approach death, and, very quickly, from his first heart attack onward, how to die. This is the matter of the book. Moreover, Golder's visit to Marcus's widow, early in the novel, echoes Peter Ivanovich's visit to Ivan Ilyich's widow in the opening pages of Tolstoy's masterpiece. And by the time Golder confronts death for the last time, in its absolute inexorability, he is both granted a Tolstoyan grace and must submit to a different, and mercilessly worldly, banality.

David Golder is not without flaws (not least of which is a lack of genuine complexity in all the characters besides Golder himself) nor, to a contemporary reader at least, without problematic elements. But it remains a remarkable novel. Némirovsky was only twenty-three when she wrote the first version of it; and yet none of her subsequent novels achieved comparable fame in her lifetime. The other early works gathered in this volume are perhaps less fully realized, and stand less firmly on their own merits, than *David Golder.* That said, each of them has distinct strengths, each moving the reader in a different way; and together they serve almost as instructive studies, or sketches, in Némirovsky's literary development, as she expands her range and sympathies, stretching toward the maturity that enabled the writing of *Suite Française.*

The Ball, first published in 1929 under the pseudonym "Nerey," is the slightest of these efforts, the story of a girl of fourteen, Antoinette Kampf, whose newly wealthy parents are preparing to throw a ball. Set in 1928, two years after Alfred Kampf's fantastic "killing on the stock market," the action is contained, and rather implausibly melodramatic. Antoinette, forbidden by her mother to attend the ball, wreaks her revenge by destroying all but one of the invitations when she is sent to post them, a sin masked by the fact that her English governess, Miss Betty—who was to have taken them to the post office but who was, instead, trysting with her boyfriend—maintains that she herself mailed the envelopes. As a result of Antoinette's vicious act, the single guest at the Kampfs' ball is their Cousin Isabelle, a resentful and impoverished music teacher to the aristocracy, who gloatingly witnesses the debacle. Madame Kampf, in whom the vanity of the socially aspirant is excruciatingly caught, is bitterly shamed by her apparent failure in society and turns to her despised daughter for consolation. It is somewhat difficult to suspend disbelief in this tale—Would the Kampfs really have expected their guests to appear, not having heard from any of them? Would they not have smelled a rat?—but the novella's strength lies in its portrait of the relationship between Antoinette and her mother.

Némirovsky, whose relations with her own mother were strained, repeatedly creates monstrously selfish middle-aged women in the maternal role, women who rage at the passing of their beauty and who see material compensation as their due and their only hope (Gloria Golder is another such character). The novella's interest lies, particularly, in the mind of young Antoinette, who sees herself and her parents more clearly than they possibly can, and yet whose immaturity prevents her from feeling any compassion: "No one loved her, no one in the whole world...But couldn't they see, blind idiots, that she was a thousand times more intelligent, more precious, more perceptive than all of them put together—these people who dared to bring her up, to teach her? These unsophisticated, crass nouveaux riches?" Antoinette is a dual creature, a living paradox, enacting at once her inevitable association with, and simultaneous detachment from, her parents: like Irène herself, she is caught between two worlds, one in which she can step back and condemn her parents as "unsophisticated, crass nouveaux riches," and another in which, at the novella's end, she eagerly accepts her mother's needy embrace. That this young woman is condemned to live this paradox, and that this paradox awakens in her a terrible and inevitable rage, is what makes *The Ball* more than a simple melodrama: there is here, albeit in embryo, a novelist's understanding of the intractable ironies of human nature of which Léon M. speaks so frankly in *The Courilof Affair*.

Snow in Autumn appeared a year after *The Ball*, in 1931, but is the definitive version of a tale published in 1924, "La Niania," a discreet homage to her grandmother, Rosa Margoulis, who had just fled from the USSR to France. It represents a departure of sorts for Némirovsky, in that it tackles the Russian émigrés' flight to France from a different angle, and also in its choice of a servant as the protagonist. The Karine family is aristocratic, and the novel opens on their Russian estate as their two sons, Youri and Cyrille, depart for war against the Bolsheviks. The story focuses on Tatiana Ivanovna, the household's nanny, who has been with the Karine family for fifty-one years and who sees anew, in the departure of these young men, the departure and loss of her earlier charges, generations before. The unraveling that ensues—the loss of one son, the family's retreat to Kiev and eventually to France, where they are forced to begin again with nothing—is painful to Tatiana Ivanovna chiefly as the loss of history. Long the repository of family lore and the keeper of family belongings, she carries the memory of the contents of every cupboard, of every piece of furniture, of every childhood incident on the lost Karine estate. But survival for the Karines requires a definitive break with their past, and Tatiana Ivanovna's role becomes painfully obsolete.

There is, as in *David Golder*, an intimation of the autobiographical in *Snow in Autumn*: the Némirovskys did not have a large country estate or the former serfs who would have remained on such properties; but their fraught removal to France, and the agonies of starting over, are at least somewhat reflected in the Karine family's trajectory. Loulou, the Karines' twenty-year-old daughter, is, like Joyce Golder, a hard, cold young woman, cynical and greedy for pleasure; but unlike Joyce, whose petulance is that of a spoiled child, Loulou's ferocity is born of all she has endured. At one point she breaks down, like a child, with her nanny: "Nianiouchka... I want to go home! Home, home!... Why have we been punished like this? We didn't do anything wrong!" The Karines are different from the Golders in genuinely having had a home, and in having lost it, rather than having left voluntarily in search of something better. The strangeness of Némirovsky's life is that she could identify with both the Golders and the Karines, and she could write their stories with equal authenticity. She could even inhabit the mind of Tatiana Ivanovna, for whom the loss of identity—an identity bound up in a place, and in things, and in a long life's history—proves insurmountable.

The Courilof Affair is a political novel; but its analysis of politics is ultimately, as another biographer, Jonathan Weiss writes, "a reflection on the moral corruption of all politics and ideology." Weiss further maintains, "It is clear that for Irène, the motivation for political action is not substantially different from the motivation of the businessman; in both cases, self-preservation and the willingness to sacrifice others for one's own profit take precedence over human kindness and generosity," but this reading is, I think, inaccurately harsh: the trajectory of Léon M.'s story records, in fact, a growth from unthinking political zeal into humanity and compassion, and thence into sorrowful cynicism, a recognition that it is possible fully to feel the agonies of the enemy and yet still to be forced, by history and circumstance, to show none of the mercy one feels. Léon says, "As long as we are on this earth, we have to play the game. I killed Courilof. I sent men to their deaths whom I realized, in a moment of lucidity, were like my brothers, like my very soul . . ."

The range of emotions that Léon experiences for Courilof anticipates, clearly, the emotions experienced by Lucile for her German soldier in "Dolce," the second section of *Suite Française*. Némirovsky could evoke, so effectively, the contradictory emotional ramifications of war, even in the midst of war, because she had already known those contradictions in the Russian Revolution: they defined her life and her work. *The Courilof Affair* is not a direct antecedent to *Suite Française*, but it anticipates many of its themes. And in our own time of political instability and terrorism, it offers both a window upon the revolutionary mindset and, powerfully, hope for an antidote to that mindset. It is a book that, rather like Dostoevsky's fiction, seems almost troublingly contemporary in its understanding of *ressentiment* and anomie.

Readers discovering Némirovsky in these pages for the first

time will thrill to her acuity and her frankness, and will marvel at her ability to evoke scenes, both externally and in their unspoken interiority. Even though she considered herself a French writer—and much about her work, formally and in its subject matter, is emphatically French—Némirovsky also remains a deeply Russian writer, whose gifts draw upon the examples of Tolstoy and Dostoevsky. She remains, as a woman and a writer, a contradiction who embraced her contradictions. F. Scott Fitzgerald famously said that "the test of a first-rate intelligence is the ability to hold two opposed ideas in mind at the same time and still retain the ability to function." Némirovsky's entire life and her literary output were about reality's duality, or multiplicity, and they constitute a stand—true, often beautiful, and in her own case, tragically doomed—against limitation, singleness, and impossibility. Fitzgerald went on to say, "One should, for example, be able to see that things are hopeless and yet be determined to make them otherwise." In the courage of her writing, Némirovsky undertook just that task. If, in our times, we need an example of why literature matters, even in the face of adversity and death, then Némirovsky stands as that example. Already in these early works, she reveals herself to be a writer of the utmost seriousness, and of considerable importance, whose clarity in the face of complexity enlarges our capacity for compassion and expands our humanity. You can't—in fiction or in life—ask for more than that.

Claire Messud

CHRONOLOGY

DATE	AUTHOR'S LIFE	LITERARY CONTEXT
1903	Irma Irina (Irène) Némirovsky is born in Kiev on February 11, the only child of Leonid (Léon) Némirovsky, a prosperous Jewish banker, and Anna (Fanny) Margoulis.	Balmont: *Let us be like the Sun.* Bryusov: *Urbi et Orbi.* Zola: *Vérité.* Huysmans: *L'Oblat.* First Prix Goncourt awarded (to *Force Ennemie* by J. A. Nau).
1904		Chekhov: *The Cherry Orchard.* Death of Chekhov. Bely: *Gold in Azure.*
1905	Anti-Jewish pogrom in Kiev (October 18). Irène is hidden by the family's cook, Macha.	Tolstoy: "Alyosha Gorshok"; "Fëdor Kuzmich." Kuprin: *The Duel.* Merezhkovsky completes trilogy, *Christ and Antichrist.* Blok: *Verses on the Beautiful Lady.*
1906	Attends the Carnival of Nice, on the French Riviera, which becomes her earliest memory. Travels regularly in the winter to France until the war: Paris, Vichy, Plombières, Cannes, Biarritz, etc. Summer holidays are spent in Yalta and Alushta, on the Ukrainian Riviera.	Tolstoy: "What For?" Andreev: "The Governor." Bryusov: *Stephanos.* Blok: *The Puppet Show.* Rolland: *Jean-Christophe* (to 1912). Claudel: *Partage de midi.*
1907		Gorky: *Mother.* Sologub: *The Petty Demon.* Conrad: *The Secret Agent.*

Russian Socialist Congress in London; schism between Bolsheviks and Mensheviks. Father Georgi Gapon forms Assembly of Russian Workers. In France, the Bloc Républicain, an alliance of left-wing and center parties, has been in power since 1899, providing stable government after the Dreyfus affair. First Tour de France. First powered flight of Wright brothers.

Russo-Japanese War: Japanese cripple Russian fleet off Port Arthur and defeat army at Liaoyang in China. Assassination of Plehve, Russian minister of the interior. Anglo-French Entente Cordiale. "La belle époque" in France.
Failed revolution in Russia. "Bloody Sunday" in St. Petersburg: troops fire on peaceful workers' procession led by Father Gapon (January). Widespread strikes and sporadic rioting follow. Universities closed (February). Union of Unions formed by professional classes, demanding constitutional reform (May). Mutiny on battleship *Potemkin* (June). After further Russian defeats, Peace of Portsmouth with Japan (September). General strike; first Soviet formed by workers in St. Petersburg, followed by 50 others; Witte appointed Russian premier, persuading Nicholas II to capitulate to demands for an elected assembly with legislative powers (October). Reactionary backlash: more than 600 pogroms around the country. Insurrection of workers in Moscow (December) brutally suppressed by military force. Completion of Trans-Siberian Railway (begun in 1891).
Separation of Church and State in France—culmination of a series of anti-clerical reforms. Withdrawal of socialists from the Bloc Républicain and creation of unified Socialist Party (SFIO). Until 1914 and mostly until 1940, France is governed by a series of centre coalitions, generally dominated by the Radicals, while the Socialists remain in opposition.
Fall of Witte (April). Fundamental Laws promulgated, restricting powers of first Duma which meets in May. Conservative Stolypin, new premier, institutes regime of courts-martial to suppress revolutionary terrorism and peasant disorders; hundreds executed 1906–7. Also introduces land reform enabling peasants to leave local communes and own private property (a quarter of the peasantry do so by 1917). Tsar dissolves Duma (July), after the majority party (the Kadets) passes a motion of no confidence in his government.
Dreyfus finally vindicated by a civilian court in France. Clemenceau becomes prime minister (to 1909). His program of social reform is blocked by parliament; industrial unrest is firmly suppressed.
Triple Entente of Great Britain, France and Russia. Second Duma proves as anti-Tsarist as the first and is again dissolved. Third Duma (1907–11) elected under a restricted franchise, producing a majority of moderate supporters for the government. Campaign against illiteracy in Russia—number of elementary schools doubles between 1908 and 1913. Cubism begins in Paris.

DATE	AUTHOR'S LIFE	LITERARY CONTEXT
1909		Gide: *La Porte étroite.*
1910		Death of Tolstoy. Bunin: *The Village.*
1911	Irène, dressed as Sarah Bernhardt, recites verses from *L'Aiglon* by Edmond Rostand for the military governor of Kiev, General Vladimir Soukhomlinov.	Hippius: *The Devil's Doll.* Conrad: *Under Western Eyes.*
1912		Remizov: *The Fifth Pestilence.* France: *Les Dieux ont soif.* Mann: *Death in Venice.* Wharton: *The Reef.*
1913	Léon Némirovsky moves with his family to St. Petersburg.	Gorky: *Childhood.* Mandelstam: *Stone.* Proust: *Du côté de chez Swann.* Alain-Fournier: *Le grand Meaulnes.*
1914	France and Russia are both at war. The Némirovskys remain in St. Petersburg.	Akhmatova: *Rosary.* Joyce: *A Portrait of the Artist as a Young Man* (to 1915).
1915		
1916		Bely: *Petersburg.*
1917	During the February Revolution, Irène witnesses the bread riots and attends the sham execution of her concierge, Ivan. In October, her French governess Marie commits suicide after being sent away by Fanny. The family flees to Moscow, then back to St. Petersburg.	Jean-Richard Bloch: *Et Compagnie.* Max Jacob: *Le cornet à dés.* Akhmatova: *White Flock.* Pasternak: *Above the Barriers.* Remizov: "Lay of the Ruin of the Russian Land."

CHRONOLOGY

DATE	AUTHOR'S LIFE	LITERARY CONTEXT
1918	The family escapes from Russia to Mustamäki, a Finnish village close to the Russian frontier (January). Irène writes her first poems in Russian.	Blok: *The Twelve.* Hippius: *Last Verses.* Merezhkovsky: *The Decembrists.* Apollinaire: *Calligrammes.* Cocteau: *Le Coq et l'arlequin.* Duhamel: *Civilisation.* Tzara: *Dada Manifesto.*
1919	In April, the Némirovskys flee Mustamäki for Helsinki, then Stockholm. Irène and her mother leave Sweden for France in June. They first settle in a furnished flat in Paris. Léon is able to continue as a banker and to rebuild the family fortunes.	Gide: *La Symphonie pastorale.* Roland Dorgelès: *Les Croix de bois.* Myriam Harry: *Siona à Paris.*
1920		Duhamel: *Vie et aventures de Salavin* (5 vols, to 1932). Aragon: *Feu de joie.* Mansfield: *Bliss.* Wharton: *The Age of Innocence.* Pound: *Hugh Selwyn Mauberley.*
1921	Studies French, Russian and Comparative Literature at the Sorbonne (to 1925). Forms lifelong friendship with Madeleine Avot. The Avots, a well-to-do Catholic provincial family, come to represent for Irène an ideal of French life that imbues her literary work. Publishes the first of her "petits contes drolatiques"—"Nonoche and the Super-lucid"—in the fortnightly magazine *Fantasio,* under the pseudonym "Topsy" (August).	Elissa Rhaïs: *Les Juifs ou la fille d'Eléazar.* André Spire: *Samaël.* Chardonne: *L'Epithalame.* Akhmatova: *Anno Domini MCMXXI; Plantain.* Tsvetaeva: *Mileposts.* Gumilyov: *The Pillar of Fire.* Zamyatin: *We.* Dos Passos: *Three Soldiers.*

CHRONOLOGY

Democratically elected Constituent Assembly meets and is dispersed by armed force. Lenin's cabinet brings Russian calendar in line with Western Europe and moves seat of government to Moscow (January); makes peace—on humiliating terms—with Central Powers at Brest-Litovsk (March). Assassination of Nicholas II and his family (July). "Red Terror": Soviet police force (Cheka) carry out brutal reprisals against pre-Revolutionary privileged classes. Civil war in Russia and Ukraine (to 1921). Large-scale exodus of refugees from Russia begins—many head for Berlin, Paris, Warsaw, Sofia, Belgrade, Tallin and Riga.

President Wilson's Fourteen Points for world peace (January). Armistice signed between Allies and Germany (November 11).

Versailles Peace Treaty (US refuses to ratify). Weimar Republic in Germany (to 1933). France regains Alsace and Lorraine. Clemenceau secures 8-hour day for workers in France, but further union reforms are blocked.

Postwar Jewish immigration to France swelled by arrivals from North Africa, Turkey, Greece and Eastern Europe (later from Germany and Austria). In 1914 there were an estimated 120,000 Jews in France; by 1939, c. 300,000. Workers from Poland and Algeria, later refugees from Italy, Armenia, Russia and Spain make France the most popular destination for immigrants in Europe.

Cocteau and "Les Six" frequenting the Gaya bar (soon to become "Le Boeuf sur le toit" after Milhaud's ballet of 1920, and one of Paris's most fashionable bohemian nightspots). Sylvia Beach opens bookshop Shakespeare & Company in Paris.

Vast program of reconstruction of devastated north-east France (to 1925). General election (November): huge majority to right-wing coalition (Bloc National), who rigorously enforce the terms of the peace treaty, maintain large standing army and seek to make military alliances with all Germany's neighbors. French mandate in Syria and Lebanon. Socialist Party splits at congress at Tours: foundation of French Communist Party (SFIC). League of Nations founded. Stravinsky: *Pulcinella*.

French resist British attempts to lower German war reparations. Start of regular radio bulletins from the Eiffel Tower. Tenth Party Conference: Lenin bans opposition within the Communist Party and introduces New Economic Policy (NEP). Famine in Russia (to 1922).

Paris in the 1920s viewed as the cultural capital of the Western world, attracting artists and intellectuals of many nationalities. Famous expatriates there include Picasso, Man Ray, Miró, Chirico, Stravinsky, Prokofiev, Ford, Joyce, Beckett, Durrell, and the "Lost Generation" of American writers, e.g. Hemingway, Pound, Williams, Stein, Dos Passos, Anderson and Fitzgerald.

Les Six: *L'Album des Six*; première of *Les Mariés de la Tour Eiffel* by the Ballets Suédois.

DATE	AUTHOR'S LIFE	LITERARY CONTEXT
1922	Her grandparents arrive from Russia. She writes "La Niania," a story set in Russia and Paris.	Martin du Gard: *Les Thibault* (10 vols, to 1940). Vignaud: *Nicky, roman de l'émigration russe.* Mandelstam: *Tristia.* Gorky: *My Universities.* Pasternak: *My Sister Life.* Joyce: *Ulysses.* Mansfield: *The Garden Party.* Eliot: *The Wasteland.* Cummings: *The Enormous Room.*
1923	Writes *L'Enfant génial* (The Genius Kid), a novella with a Russian setting and a Jewish protagonist (published in 1927). Moves to her own flat in the rue Boissière. Leads a wild life: jazz clubs, flirtations, late-night escapades, joyriding and "water cures" to soothe her asthma.	Edmond Fleg: *Anthologie juive.* Colette: *Le Blé en herbe.* Radiguet: *Le Diable au corps.* Alexei Tolstoy: *The Road to Calvary* (to 1945).
1924	"La Niania" appears in the daily *Le Matin* (May 9).	Breton's Surrealist Manifesto. Desnos: *Deuil pour deuil.* Bulgakov: *The White Guard.* Ehrenburg: *The Love of Jeanne Ney.* Mann: *The Magic Mountain.* Ford: *Parade's End* (to 1928).
1925	Last year in the Sorbonne University.	Gide: *Les Faux-monnayeurs.* Morand: *L'Europe galante.* Cendrars: *L'Or.* Bunin: "Mitya's Love." Nina Berberova: *The Billancourt Holidays* (to 1940). Kafka: *The Trial.* Fitzgerald: *The Great Gatsby.* Woolf: *Mrs. Dalloway.*
1926	Marries Michel Epstein, also a Russian Jew and the son of a well-known banker. Her first novel, *Le Malentendu* (The Misunderstanding), is published in the monthly *Les Œuvres Libres.* Writes the first version of *David Golder.*	Cendrars: *Moravagine.* Aragon: *Le Paysan de Paris.* Kessel: *Les Captifs; Makhno et sa Juive.* Edmond Fleg: *L'Enfant prophète.* Nabokov: *Mary.* Babel: *Red Cavalry.* Tsvetaeva: *The Ratcatcher.*

CHRONOLOGY

Stalin becomes Secretary of Communist Party Central Committee. Russia becomes USSR. Mussolini's march on Rome. British mandate in Palestine. Paris emerging as political and cultural centre of the Russian diaspora; Committee of the Zemstvos formed to set up schools and provide financial assistance for refugees. Forty Russian professors engaged by University of Paris. During the 1920s over a hundred Russian cabarets, restaurants and cafés open.

Hyper-inflation in Germany. Repeated German defaults on reparations lead Poincaré (French prime minister once again) to send troops into the Ruhr Valley. Hitler's Munich *putsch* fails. Matisse: *Odalisque aux bras levés*. *La Roue*—film directed by Abel Gance. Poulenc: *Les Biches* (ballet).

Dawes Plan ends reparation crisis. Poincaré's Bloc National beaten by a coalition of the left, the Cartel des Gauches. French financial crisis which a series of seven cabinets (to 1926) fails to resolve. France recognizes USSR. Death of Lenin. Russian conservatoire in Paris founded, the composer Rakhmaninov later becoming honorary chairman. League of Nations estimates number of Russian refugees living in France at 400,000. *Paris qui dort* (first science-fiction film) and *Entr'acte*, directed by René Clair.
Period of Franco-German reconciliation—*apaisement*—under foreign minister Briand (to 1930). Locarno Pact guarantees existing Franco-German frontier. French troops evacuate the Ruhr. Hitler: *Mein Kampf*. Society of Young Russian Writers and Poets holding regular literary evenings in Paris: lecturers include Zaitsev, Khodasevich, Shestov, Shmelyov, Berberova, Ivanov and Tsvetaeva. Russian artists working in Paris include Chagall, Bilibin and Goncharova. Picasso: *Les trois danseuses*. Bonnard: *La Fenêtre*, *Le Bain*. Paris International Exposition of Decorative Arts & Modern Industries. *La Peinture Surrealiste*—the first ever Surrealist exhibition, at Gallerie Pierre in Paris. Russian Orthodox church and Theological Institute opens in Paris. Josephine Baker makes her Paris debut in *La Revue nègre*.
Union Nationale forms government led by Poincaré, whose conservative policies (slashing government expenditure and raising taxes) stabilize the French economy. France sponsors Germany's entry into the League of Nations. Briand and Stresemann share Nobel Peace Prize. Trotsky dismissed from Politburo in USSR. Jean Renoir directs *Nana*. Chanel launches the "little black dress."

IRÈNE NÉMIROVSKY

DATE	AUTHOR'S LIFE	LITERARY CONTEXT
1926 *cont.*		Zaitsev: *The Golden Design.*
		Kafka: *The Castle.*
		Hemingway: *The Sun Also Rises.*
1927	*L'Enfant génial* is published in *Les Œuvres Libres.*	Proust: *A la recherche du temps perdu* (published in full, posthumously).
		Mauriac: *Thérèse Desqueyroux.*
		Khodasevich: *Collected Verse.*
		Bunin: "Sunstroke."
		Remizov: *Whirlwind Russia.*
		Heidegger: *Being and Time.*
1928	Her second novel, *L'Ennemie* (The Enemy), is published in *Les Œuvres Libres*, under the pseudonym "Nérey," an anagram of "Irène."	Colette: *La Naissance du jour.*
		Breton: *Nadja.*
		Yourcenar: *Alexis.*
		Malraux: *Les Conquérants.*
		Saint-Exupéry: *Courrier sud.*
		Kessel: *Belle de jour.*
		Nabokov: *King, Queen, Knave.*
		Ehrenburg: *The Stormy Life and Lazar Roitschwantz.*
		Shmelyov: *The Light of Reason.*
		Mayakovsky: *The Bedbug.*
1929	*Le Bal* (The Ball) appears in *Les Œuvres Libres* under the same pseudonym. Her daughter, Denise Epstein, is born in November. *David Golder* is published to great acclaim by Grasset in December, prompting comparisons with Tolstoy and Balzac. Irène dreams about writing the "script" of her own life.	Cocteau: *Les Enfants terribles.*
		Eluard: *L'Amour, la Poésie.*
		Giraudoux: *Amphitryon 38.*
		Edmond Fleg: *Pourquoi je suis juif.*
		Shmelyov: *Entering Paris: Tales of Emigré Russia.*
		Shestov: *In Job's Balances.*
		Zweig: *Buchmendel.*
		Hemingway: *A Farewell to Arms.*
1930	First polemic on the so-called anti-Semitic themes in *David Golder*, in both Jewish and anti-Semitic papers (spring). *Le Malentendu* is released as a book (Fayard), as is *Le Bal* (Grasset). *David Golder* is nominated for the Prix Goncourt. Première of the film version of *David Golder* by Julien Duvivier (December 17). First night of the less successful stage version by Fernand Nozière, at the Théâtre de la Porte Saint-Martin (December 26).	Albert Cohen: *Solal.*
		Nabokov: *The Defense*; *The Eye.*
		Berberova: *The First and the Last.*
		Cocteau: *La Voix humaine.*
		Freud: *Civilization and its Discontents.*
		Waugh: *Vile Bodies.*

CHRONOLOGY

Foundation of far-right Croix-de-feu league. Lindbergh's transatlantic flight. First "talkies." Trotsky expelled from Communist Party. Abel Gance directs 6-hour epic, *Napoléon*.

Devaluation of the franc to one fifth of its previous value. Kellogg-Briand Pact, outlawing war and providing for peaceful settlement of disputes (accepted by Germany 1929). First Five-Year Plan in USSR. Stalin *de facto* dictator and object of nationwide cult. First Stalinist show trials (to 1933). Fédération des Sociétés Juives de France (FSJF) established to care for needs of French Jewish community. Last performances of the Ballets Russes include Stravinsky's *Apollon musagète* (1928) and Prokofiev's *L'Enfant prodigue* (1929), starring Serge Lifar and with choreography by Balanchine. Ravel: *Boléro*.

Poincaré retires. Young Plan: revised war reparations agreement; Allies to evacuate Rhineland by June 1930. Wall Street crash. Sheltering behind a high-tariff barrier, France appears at first immune from the consequences of the Depression. Forcible collectivization of agriculture begins in USSR: around ten million peasants killed, sent to concentration camps or exiled in the process. Death of Diaghilev. Salvador Dali arrives in Paris, holding one-man show. Maurice Chevalier, "Louise."

The 1930s see increasingly unstable government in France, with 20 changes of premier. Construction of Maginot line begins (to 1939). Cocteau directs *Le Sang d'un poète*.

DATE	AUTHOR'S LIFE	LITERARY CONTEXT
1931	*Les Mouches d'automne* (The Flies of Autumn, English translation *Snow in Autumn*) is first published by Simon Kra (May), then Grasset (December). Première of film version of *Le Bal* by Wilhelm Thiele with the debutante actress Danièle Darrieux (September 11).	Claudel: *Le Soulier de satin.* Saint-Exupéry: *Vol de nuit.* Nizan: *Aden, Arabie.* Maurois' life of Turgenev. J.-R. Bloch: *Destin du siècle.* Mark Aldanov: *The Tenth Symphony.* Balmont: *Northern Lights* Ivanov: *Rozy.* Poplavsky: *Flags.* Woolf: *The Waves.*
1932	Death of her father from a pulmonary embolism. Though a rich man, he leaves Irène a paltry inheritance. She begins to publish short stories.	Céline: *Voyage au bout de la nuit.* Mauriac: *Le Noeud de vipères.* Romains: *Les Hommes de bonne volonté* (27 vols, to 1946). Chardonne: *L'Amour du prochain.* Nabokov: *Glory.* Roth: *The Radetzky March.* Huxley: *Brave New World.*
1933	*L'Affaire Courilof* (The Courilof Affair), a "terrorist" novel, published by Grasset. Financial troubles lead to an association with *Gringoire*, a high-circulation, right-wing weekly founded by Horace de Carbuccia in 1928, which from now on publishes the majority of her short stories.	Malraux: *La Condition humaine.* Duhamel: *Chronique des Pasquiers* (10 vols, to 1941). Nabokov: *Laughter in the Dark.* Stein: *The Autobiography of Alice B. Toklas.* Buck: *The Mother.*
1934	Irène changes publisher, moving from Grasset to Albin Michel for the publication of *Le Pion sur l'échiquier* (The Pawn on the Chessboard). Meets the author Paul Morand, who edits her compilation of four stories, *Films parlés* (Spoken Films) for Gallimard. Becomes theater critic for the daily newspaper *Aujourd'hui*.	Cocteau: *La Machine infernale.* Yourcenar: *Denier du rêve.* Brasillach: *L'Enfant de la nuit.* Berberova: *The Accompanist.* Fitzgerald: *Tender is the Night.* Cain: *The Postman Always Rings Twice* (Némirovsky writes preface to the French edition.)
1935	*Le Vin de solitude* (The Wine of Solitude), Albin Michel, a veiled autobiography. First appeal for naturalization as a French citizen. Moves to a new flat on avenue Constant-Coquelin (June). Becomes literary critic for the weekly *La Revue Hebdomadaire*.	Giraudoux: *La Guerre de Troie n'aura pas lieu.* Troyat: *Faux jour.* Tristan Bernard: *Robin des Bois.*

CHRONOLOGY

HISTORICAL EVENTS

Germany suspends payment of war reparations (suspended indefinitely by her creditors at Lausanne in 1932, and repudiated by Hitler in 1933). Depression hits France. Briand runs for president and is defeated. Geneva disarmament conference (to 1934). Roosevelt becomes US president. Trial of Mensheviks. René Clair: *Le Million*.

Right-wing parties lose control to Radicals; Herriot becomes prime minister; Franco-Soviet non-aggression pact. President Doumer murdered by a Russian émigré. First TV images broadcast in Paris.
Famine in Ukraine and elsewhere in USSR (to 1934), claiming some five million lives, though Soviet grain continues to be dumped on world markets.

Hitler becomes German Chancellor: proclaims Third Reich; opposition parties banned. Germany leaves the League of Nations. Daladier—another Radical—becomes French prime minister. Growth of Fascist movement in France. Second Five-Year Plan in USSR. Jean Renoir's film of *Madame Bovary*.

Stavisky Affair: financial scandal following the suicide of Russian émigré embezzler, Alexandre Stavisky, in which leading Radicals are implicated. A demonstration by far-right groups turns into a battle with police in which 15 people are killed and 1500 injured (February 6). Anti-Fascist general strike. Daladier resigns in favor of a National Union cabinet under Doumerge. King Alexander of Yugoslavia is asssinated in Marseilles.
Jean Vigo: *L'Atalante*. Hitler becomes German Führer. German rearmament commences. Stalin places national security under the soon-to-be notorious NKVD. Murder of Kirov, a protégé and potential rival of Stalin (December) prompts the start of the Great Terror the following year.
Premiership of Laval, whose unpopular attempts to combat the Depression lead to his downfall in 1936. Left-wing parties unite to form the Front Populaire. Mussolini invades Abyssinia. Nuremberg Laws in Germany debar Jews from public life. French-Soviet mutual assistance pact.

DATE	AUTHOR'S LIFE	LITERARY CONTEXT
1936	*Jézabel*, Albin Michel, a cruel portrait of her mother. One of her short stories, "Fraternité" (Brotherhood), is refused by *La Revue des Deux Mondes* on the grounds that it is anti-Semitic, although what Irène wanted to show was the "unassimilable nature" of emigrant Jews.	Louise Weiss: *Déliverance.* Céline: *Mort à crédit.* Bernanos: *Journal d'un curé de campagne.* Sartre: *L'Imagination.* Maritain: *Humanisme intégral.* J.-R. Bloch: *Naissance d'une culture.*
1937	Her second daughter, Elisabeth Epstein, born. Begins to write *Deux* (Both).	Breton: *L'Amour fou.* Bernanos: *Nouvelle Histoire de Mouchette.* Anouilh: *Le Voyageur sans bagage.* Camus: *L'Envers et l'endroit.* Drieu la Rochelle: *Rêveuse bourgeoisie.* Sartre: *La Transcendance de l'égo.* Maurois: *Histoire d'Angleterre.*
1938	*La Proie* (The Prayer), Albin Michel. Irène meets the priest Roger Bréchard, a model for abbé Philippe Péricand in *Suite française.* First stay in Issy-l'Evêque, a village in Burgundy. Her memories of 1917 are published in *Le Figaro* ("Naissance d'une révolution," June 4). She thinks of writing a novel based on the life of Léon Blum, Leon Trotsky or Alexandre Stavisky. Irène and Michel apply for French citizenship (November).	Sartre: *La Nausée.* Chardonne: *Le Bonheur de Barbezieux.* Queneau: *Les Enfants du Limon.* Albert Cohen: *Mangeclous.* Nabokov: *The Gift.*
1939	Still legally stateless, the family converts to Catholicism (February 2). Michel nearly dies from mumps and septicemia. Irène lectures on women writers on Radio Paris. *Deux* (Both) is published by Albin Michel. Though asked to re-produce documents already submitted (April), the Epsteins never receive an answer to their naturalization request. Final holiday in Hendaye, near the Spanish border (August). Irène sends the children to stay	Sartre: *Le Mur.* Saint-Exupéry: *Terre des hommes.* Drieu la Rochelle: *Gilles.* Brasillach: *Les Sept Couleurs.* Henry Bernstein: *Elvire.* Giraudoux: *Ondine.* Nathalie Sarraute: *Tropismes.* Anaïs Nin: *Un Hiver d'artifice.* Aldanov: *The Fifth Seal.* Joyce: *Finnegans Wake.*

CHRONOLOGY

General election in spring bitterly contested. The Front Populaire win a narrow majority of the vote but a large majority of seats. Communists refuse to participate in government. Léon Blum becomes first Socialist prime minister— an intellectual and the first French premier of Jewish origin. Blum persuades employers to increase wages, ending wave of strikes, and embarks on program of contraversial social reform. Spanish Civil War. Blum's alliance with the Radicals obliges him to opt for non-intervention though Spain has the only other Popular Front government in Europe. Hitler marches into demilitarized Rhineland. Three great Moscow show trials of leading Bolsheviks (to 1938). Unemployment in France remains high. Blum's cabinet falls over his efforts to improve exchange controls (June). Exposition universelle in Paris. Stalin liquidates millions—many of them Communisty Party members, mainly from educated and managerial classes and from the armed forces (to 1938). German air attack on Basque town of Guernica. Picasso: *Guernica*. Jean Renoir directs *La grande illusion*. Chevalier: *Paris en joie* (revue).

Disintegration of the Front Populaire. France returns to the usual center coalitions, with Socialists in opposition. Daladier becomes prime minister. His finance minister Reynaud suspends most of Blum's reforms. Hitler's troops enter Austria and part of Czechoslovakia. Munich Agreement: Britain and France appease Hitler. Kristallnacht—Nazis terrorize Jewish community (November 10). Third Five-Year Plan in USSR. Chagall: *La Crucifixion blanche*.

Hitler occupies the rest of Czechoslovakia (March). Madrid's surrender to General Franco ends Spanish Civil War (March). "Pact of Steel" between Italy and Germany (May). France and Britain press USSR to oppose Hitler but Nazi-Soviet pact signed (August). Germans invade Poland. France and Britain declare war on Germany (September 3). Soviet invasion of Eastern Poland and Finland. Jean Renoir directs *La Règle du jeu*.

DATE	AUTHOR'S LIFE	LITERARY CONTEXT
1939 *cont.*	with their nurse's family in Issy-Evêque on the outbreak of war. She embarks on a life of Chekhov (*La Vie de Tchekhov*).	
1940	*Les Chiens et les loups* (Dogs and Wolves), Albin Michel. *Les Echelles du Levant* (The Ports of Call of the Levant) is serialized in *Gringoire* (from May 18). Watching the exodus from Paris as the Germans advance, and recalling *The Rains Came* by Louis Bromfield (1937), Irène conceives the idea of a "choral novel," *Tempête en juin* (Storm in June), the first novel of her *Suite française*. Visits the children in Issy-l'Evêque (May) and decides to stay there, joined by Michel in June. Issy-l'Evêque is occupied by the Germans on June 18. First "Law on the Status of Jews" (October): Fayard reneges on contract to serialize her new novel, *Jeunes et vieux* (Young and Elderly) in his weekly, *Candide*. Michel is fired from the Banque du Nord.	Sartre: *L'Imaginaire*. Cocteau: *Le Bel Indifférent*. Maritain: *De la justice politique*. Troyat: *Dostoevsky*. Akhmatova: *From Six Books*. Koestler: *Darkness at Noon*. Hemingway: *For Whom the Bell Tolls*. Greene: *The Power and the Glory*.
1941	Publishes stories under various pseudonyms in *Gringoire*, Carbuccia, though a collaborator, being sympathetic to her situation. In April *Gringoire* begins serializing *Les Biens de ce monde* (The Goods of this World), a new title for *Jeunes et vieux*. Most of her so-called friends in the literary world and previous publishers turn aside from her. Albin Michel, however, offers financial and moral suport. Second "Law on the Status of Jews" (June). The German soldiers leave Issy-Evêque. Irène begins to write *Dolce* (July)—the second novel of *Suite française*.	Aragon: *Le Crève-coeur*. Mauriac: *Le Pharisienne*. Blanchot: *Thomas l'obscur*. Simone Weil starts writing the Cahiers which form the basis of *La Pesanteur et la Grâce*. Nabokov: *The Real Life of Sebastian Knight*. Brecht: *Mother Courage*.

CHRONOLOGY

Hitler's armies advance rapidly through the Netherlands and Belgium (May), breaking French defensive line near Sedan and entering Paris on June 14. Government leaves Paris (June 10) for Tours, then Bordeaux. Pétain, right-winger who favors surrender, gains control of cabinet. From London De Gaulle appeals to French patriots to continue the struggle. Armistice signed (June 22). France divided into an occupied zone (north and west coast) and an unoccupied southern zone. Daladier and others plan to set up a government-in-exile in Morocco but on Pétain's orders are arrested on arrival. Vichy parliament meets July 9–10, and votes itself out of existence on advice of Pétain and Laval, thus ending the Third Republic. Pétain dismisses Laval (December).

David Rapoport forms one of the first relief organizations for Jews in Paris at rue Amelot (June 15). Such organizations, run by both Jews and Christians, were to help many children to escape the Holocaust.

Germans order Jews in the occupied zone to register (September 27). The *Statut des Juifs*—first anti-Jewish legislation introduced by Vichy government (October 3). First "Otto List" (October 4) of prohibited books in France. Auschwitz concentration camp established (April). Warsaw ghetto opened (October).

Germany invades Norway and Denmark. Italy enters war. Dunkirk evacuation. Battle of Britain. USSR annexes Baltic states. Assassination of Trotsky.

German army invades USSR (June): Russia rallies under Stalin to embark on the Great Patriotic War. Hitler's demands for money, raw materials and food from France become heavier as the Eastern front develops. French resistance movement now strengthened by participation of Communists. De Gaulle claims status of legal government-in-exile for his Comité National Français. Vichy government establishes a Commissariat Général aux Questions Juives (April) to work with German authorities to "aryanize" Jewish businesses in the occupied zone. German edict denies Jews access to their bank accounts (May 8). Jews rounded up for the first time in Paris (May 14): 3700 foreign Jews arrested and sent to camps at Pithiviers and Beaune-la-Rolande. Second *Statut des juifs* (June 2). Arrests continue throughout the year: detention center opened at Drancy (August).

Siege of Leningrad begins (September). Japanese attack on Pearl Harbor: US enters the war (December).

DATE	AUTHOR'S LIFE	LITERARY CONTEXT
1942	Last short story published in *Gringoire* (February). Entrusts her chief editor, André Sabatier, with all her manuscripts (March). Begins to work on *Les Feux de l'automne* (Autumn Fires) and *Captivité* (Captivity), the third volume of *Suite française*. Arrested by French police on July 13, in pursuance of the latest Nazi decrees. Taken to a detainment camp at Pithiviers. Her last story, "Les Vierges" (The Virgins), is published in *Présent* on July 15: "Look at me. I am alone now, but my solitude was not chosen or wanted, it is the worst one, the humiliated, bitter solitude of abandonment and betrayal." Departs for Auschwitz on July 17. Dies in Auschwitz of typhus on August 19. Michel is arrested and gassed at Auschwitz on November 6. Their daughters Denise and Elisabeth live hidden until the Liberation of France in August 1944.	Camus: *Le Mythe de Sisyphe*; *L'Etranger*. Eluard: *Poésie et vérité*. Vercors: *Le Silence de la mer*. Queneau: *Pierrot mon ami*. Simone Weil writes essays and articles which are later assembled in *Attente de Dieu* and *Pensées sans ordre sur l'amour de Dieu*. Maritain: *Les droits de l'homme et la loi naturelle*.
1946	Posthumous publication of *La Vie de Tchekhov* (The Life of Chekhov), Albin Michel.	
1947	*Les Biens de ce monde* (The Goods of this World), Albin Michel.	
1957	*Les Feux d'automne* (Autumn Fires), Albin Michel.	
2004	*Suite française* (Denoël). (English translation published in 2006.)	
2005	*Le Maître des âmes* (Master of Souls), Denoël (formerly *Les Echelles du Levant*).	
2007	*Chaleur du sang* (Fire in the Blood), Denoël—a previously unpublished novel.	

CHRONOLOGY

Laval is restored, the result of German pressure (April). He agrees to conscription of French workers for German factories in return for the release of French POWs and undertakes to take action against the growing French underground movement.

A curfew imposed on Jews (February 7). First Jews from France deported to Poland and Germany (March). In total some 75,000 Jews are deported during the war, of whom only about 3 per cent survive.

Jews ordered to wear the yellow star of David (June 7). Second "Otto List" (July). "Opération Vent Printanier" (July): on the orders of the German authorities, French police undertake to arrest foreign Jews, targeting mainly Eastern European adults without French citizenship.

Fall of Singapore. German army reaches Stalingrad. Rommel defeated at El Alamein. Allied landings in French North Africa (November) to a short-lived resistance from Vichy troops in Morocco and Algeria. Hitler orders German troops to occupy the whole of France (November 11): Vichy government survives on suffrance.

Grateful acknowledgment is made to Olivier Philipponnat and Patrick Lienhardt, authors of *The Life of Irène Némirovsky*, who have provided the biographical details necessary for this chronology.

DAVID GOLDER

"NO," SAID GOLDER, tilting his desklamp so that the light shone directly into the face of Simon Marcus who was sitting opposite him on the other side of the table. For a moment Golder observed the wrinkles and lines that furrowed Marcus's swarthy face whenever he moved his lips or closed his eyes, like the ripples on dark water when the wind blows across it. But his hooded eyes with their Oriental languor remained calm, bored, and indifferent. A face as unyielding as a wall. Golder carefully lowered the lamp's flexible metal stem.

"A hundred, Golder? Think about it. It's a good price," said Marcus.

"No," Golder murmured again, then added, "I don't want to sell."

Marcus laughed. His long white teeth, capped in gold, gleamed eerily in the darkness.

"How much were your famous oil shares worth in 1920 when you first bought them?" he drawled; his voice was nasal, sarcastic.

"I bought them at four hundred. And if those Soviet pigs had given the nationalised land back to the oil companies, I would have made a lot of money. Lang and his group were backing me. In 1913, the daily output from the Teisk region was already ten thousand tons . . . seriously. After the Genoa Conference, I remember my shares fell from four hundred to one hundred and two . . . After that . . ." Golder made a vague gesture of frustration. "But I held on to them . . . Money was no object, in those days."

"Yes, but now, in 1926, don't you realise that your Russian oilfields aren't worth shit to you? Well? I mean, it's not as if you have either the means or the inclination to go and run them yourself, is it? All you can hope to do is shift them for a higher price on the Stock Market . . . A hundred is a good sum."

Golder slowly rubbed his eyes; the smoke that filled the room had irritated them.

"No, I don't want to sell." He spoke more quietly this time. "I'll sell after Tübingen Petroleum signs the agreement for the concession in Teisk. I think you know the one I'm talking about..."

Marcus mumbled what sounded like "Ah, yes..." and fell silent.

"You've been negotiating that deal behind my back since last year, Marcus," Golder said slowly. "You know you have ... I bet they offered you a good price for my shares once they closed the deal, didn't they?"

He said no more, for his heart was beating almost painfully, just as it always did when he claimed a victory. Marcus slowly stubbed out his cigar in the overflowing ashtray.

"If he suggests we go fifty-fifty," Golder thought suddenly, "it will all be over for him."

He leaned forward so he could hear what Marcus was about to say. There was a brief silence, then Marcus spoke.

"Why don't we go halves, Golder?"

Golder clenched his teeth. "Are you serious?"

"You know, Golder, you shouldn't make another enemy," Marcus murmured, lowering his eyes. "You've got enough already."

His hands were clutching the wooden table, and as they moved, his nails made short, sharp little scratching noises. Beneath the light of the lamp, his long fingers with their heavy rings shone against the mahogany of the Empire desk; they were trembling.

Golder smiled. "You're no longer very threatening, my friend..."

Marcus remained silent for a moment, carefully examining his manicured nails.

"Fifty-fifty, David! What do you say? We've been partners for twenty-six years. Let's wipe the slate clean and start again. If you'd been here in December when Tübingen spoke to me..."

Golder fiddled with the telephone wire, winding it around his wrists.

"In December," he repeated, frowning. "How good of you... only..."

He said no more. Marcus knew as well as he did that in December he had been in America looking for investors in Golmar, the company that had bound them together for so many years, like a ball and chain.

"David, there's still time..." Marcus continued. "Let's negotiate with the Soviets together, what do you say? It's a difficult business. We'll split everything down the middle—commissions, profits... How about it? That's fair, isn't it? David? Otherwise..."

He waited for some reply, an agreement, even an insult, but Golder's breathing was laboured and he said nothing.

"Listen," Marcus whispered, "Tübingen's not the only company in the world..." He touched Golder's unmoving arm as if to wake him. "There are other companies, newer ones, and..." he searched for the right words. "There are companies more willing to speculate, companies that didn't sign the 1922 Oil Agreement and who don't give a damn about who holds the old stock, you, for example... They could..."

"You mean Amrum Oil?" said Golder.

"Oh!" Marcus winced. "So you know about that as well? Well listen, my friend, I'm sorry, but the Russians are going to sign with Amrum. Since you're now refusing to play ball, you can keep your shares in Teisk till Judgement Day. You can take them with you to your grave..."

"The Russians aren't going to sign with Amrum."

"They've already signed," cried Marcus.

Golder waved his hand. "Yes, I know. A provisional agreement. But it was supposed to be ratified by Moscow within forty-five days. That was yesterday. Now it's all up in the air again, and you're worried, so you came to see what you could get out of me..." Golder started to cough. "Let me explain it all to you. Tübingen right? He wasn't too happy when Amrum whipped those Persian oilfields out from under his feet two years ago. So, this time, I suspect he'd rather die than lose the fight. Actually, it hasn't been that difficult so far: just a question of offering a bit more to that little Jew who has been helping you negotiate with the Soviets. Give them a call right now, if you don't believe me . . ."

"You're lying, you pig!" shouted Marcus in the strange, shrill voice of a hysterical woman.

"Give them a call. You'll see."

"And . . . what about Tübingen? Does the old man know?"

"Of course."

"This is all your doing, you bastard, you crook!"

"Well, what did you expect? Think about it . . . Last year there was that oil deal in Mexico, and three years ago the high octane deal. How many millions went from my pocket into yours? And what did I say about it? Nothing. And then . . ." Golder seemed to be looking for more proof, attempting to bring everything together in his mind, but then he brushed it all aside with a shrug of the shoulders.

"Business," was all he murmured, as if he were naming some terrifying god . . .

Marcus fell silent. He took a packet of cigarettes from the table, opened it, and carefully struck a match. "Why do you smoke these disgusting Gauloises, Golder, when you're as rich as you are?"

Golder watched Marcus's shaking hands as if he were contemplating the final death throes of a wounded animal.

"I need the money, David," Marcus suddenly said in a different tone of voice, the corner of his mouth contorting into a grimace. "I . . . I'm really desperate for money, David. Couldn't you . . . let me make just a little? Don't you think that . . ."

"No!"

Golder shook his fist in the air. He saw the pale hands clasp each other, the clenched fingers digging their nails into the flesh.

"You're ruining me," Marcus said finally, in an odd, hollow voice.

Golder said nothing, refusing to look up. Marcus hesitated, then quietly pushed back his chair.

"Good-bye, David," he said, and then shouted suddenly, "What was that?"

"Nothing," said Golder. "Good-bye."

GOLDER LIT A cigarette, but put it out when he started choking on the first puff. His shoulders were wracked by a nervous, asthmatic cough, which filled his mouth with bitter phlegm. Blood rushed to his face, normally deathly pale and waxy, with dark circles under the eyes. Golder was an enormous man in his late sixties. He had flabby arms and legs, piercing eyes the colour of water, thick white hair, and a ravaged face so hard it looked as if it had been hewn from stone by a rough, clumsy hand.

The room reeked of smoke and that smell of stale sweat that is particular to Parisian apartments in summer when they have been left empty for a long time.

Golder swivelled around in his chair and opened the window. For a long while, he looked out at the Eiffel Tower, all lit up. Its red glow streamed like blood down the cool dawn sky. He thought of Golmar. Six shimmering gold letters that tonight would be turning like suns in four of the world's greatest cities. GOLMAR: two names, his and Marcus's, merged together. He pursed his lips. "Golmar...David Golder, alone, from now on..."

He reached for the notepad beside him and read the letterhead:

GOLDER & MARCUS
Buyers and Sellers of Petroleum Products
Aviation Fuel. Unleaded, Leaded, and Premium Gasoline.
White-Spirit. Diesel. Lubricants.
New York, London, Paris, Berlin

Slowly he crossed out the first line and wrote, "David Golder," his heavy handwriting cutting into the paper. For he was finally on his own. "It's over, thank God," he thought with relief. "He'll go now..." Later on, after Teisk granted the concession to Tübingen, he would be part of the greatest oil company in the world, and then he would easily be able to rebuild Golmar.

Until then . . . He quickly scribbled down some figures. These past two years had been especially terrible. Lang's bankruptcy, the 1922 Agreement . . . At least he would no longer have to pay for Marcus's women, his rings, his debts . . . He had enough to pay for without him. How expensive this idiotic lifestyle was! His wife, his daughter, the houses in Biarritz and Paris . . . In Paris alone he was paying sixty thousand francs in rent, taxes. The furniture had cost more than a million when he'd bought it. For whom? No one lived there. Closed shutters, dust. He looked with a kind of hatred at certain objects he particularly detested: four lamps, Winged Victories in bronze with black marble bases; an enormous square inkstand, decorated with gilt bees—empty. It all had to be paid for, and where was he supposed to get the money?

"The fool," he growled angrily. " 'You're ruining me!' So what? I'm sixty-eight . . . Let *him* start over again. *I've* had to do it often enough . . . "

He turned his head sharply towards the large mirror above the cold fireplace, looking uneasily at his drawn features, at the mottled bluish patches on his pale skin, and the two folds sunk into the thick flesh around his mouth like the drooping jowls on an old dog. "I'm getting old," he grumbled bitterly. "Yes, I'm getting old . . . " For two or three years now he'd been getting tired more easily. "I absolutely must get away tomorrow," he thought. "A week or ten days relaxing in Biarritz where I can be left in peace, otherwise I'm going to collapse." He took his diary, propped it up on the table against a gold-framed photograph of a young girl and started leafing through it. It was full of names and dates, with 14 September underlined in ink. Tübingen was expecting him in London that day. That meant he could have barely a week in Biarritz . . . Then London, Moscow, London again, New York. He let out an irritated little moan, stared at his daughter's picture, sighed, then looked away and began rubbing his painful eyes, burning from weariness. He had got back from Berlin that day, and for a long time now he hadn't been able to sleep on the train as he used to.

He stood up to head for the club, as always, but then realised it was after three o'clock in the morning. "I'll just go to bed," he thought. "I'll be on the train again tomorrow . . ." He noticed a stack of letters that needed signing piled on the desk. He sat down again. Every evening he read over the letters his secretaries had prepared. They were a bunch of asses. But he preferred them that way. He thought of Marcus's secretary and smiled: Braun, a little Jew with fiery eyes, who had sold him the plans for the Amrum deal. He started to read, leaning very far forward under the lamp. His thick white hair used to be red, and a hint of that burning colour still remained at his temples and at the back of his neck, glowing, like a flame half hidden beneath the ashes.

THE TELEPHONE NEXT to Golder's bed broke the silence with its long, shrill, interminable ringing, but Golder didn't wake up: in the mornings, he slept as deeply and heavily as a dead man. Finally he opened his eyes with a low groan and grabbed the receiver.

"Hello, hello . . ."

He carried on shouting "Hello, hello," without recognising his secretary's voice, until he heard the words, "Dead, Monsieur Golder . . . Monsieur Marcus is dead . . ."

He said nothing. "Hello, can you hear me?" the voice continued. "Monsieur Marcus is dead."

"Dead," Golder repeated slowly, while a strange little shiver ran down his spine. "Dead . . . It isn't possible . . ."

"It happened last night, Monsieur . . . on the Rue Chabanais . . . Yes, in a brothel . . . He shot himself in the chest. They're saying that . . ."

Golder gently placed the receiver between the sheets and pressed the blanket over it, as if he wanted to smother the voice that he could still hear droning on like some enormous trapped fly.

Finally, there was silence.

Golder rang the bell. "Run me a bath," he said to the servant who came in with the post and breakfast tray, "a cold bath."

"Shall I pack your dinner jacket, Sir?"

Golder frowned nervously. "Pack? Oh, yes, Biarritz . . . I don't know. I may be going tomorrow, or perhaps the day after, I don't know . . ."

"I'll have to go to his house tomorrow," he muttered. "The funeral will be on Tuesday no doubt. Damn . . ." He swore quietly. The servant, in the adjoining room, was filling the bath. Golder swallowed a mouthful of hot tea, opened some letters at random, then threw the rest on the floor and stood up. He sat down in the bathroom, closed his dressing-gown over his knees and absent-mindedly twisted the tassels on his silk belt as he watched the flowing water with an engrossed, mournful look on his face.

"Dead . . . dead . . ."

Little by little, a feeling of anger grew within him. He shrugged his shoulders. "Dead . . . is death the answer? If it were me . . ." he muttered with hatred.

"Your bath is ready, Sir," said the servant.

Once alone, Golder went up to the bathtub, stretched his hand down into the water and left it there; all his movements were extraordinarily slow and hesitant, incomplete. The cold water froze his fingers, his arm, his shoulder, but he lowered his head and didn't move, staring dumbly at the reflection of the electric light bulb hanging from the ceiling as it shone and shimmered in the water.

"If it were me . . ." he said again.

Old, forgotten memories were resurfacing from deep within his mind. Dark, strange memories . . . A whole harsh lifetime of struggle . . . Today, riches, tomorrow, nothing. Then starting over . . . And starting over again . . . Oh yes, if he'd ever considered *that*, well, honestly, he would have been dead long ago. He sat up straight, absent-mindedly shook the water off his hand and leaned against the window, holding his freezing hands towards the warmth of the sun. He shook his head and said out loud, "Yes, honestly, in Moscow for example, or even in Chicago . . ." and his mind, unaccustomed to dreaming, conjured up the past in dry, brief little snapshots. Moscow . . . when he was nothing more than a thin little Jew with red hair, pale, piercing eyes, worn-out boots, and empty pockets . . . He used to sleep rough on benches, in the town squares, on dark autumn nights like these, so cold . . . Fifty years later, he could still feel in his bones the dampness of the thick white early morning fog, a fog that clung to his body, leaving a sort of stiff frost on his clothes . . . Snowstorms, and in March, the wind . . .

And Chicago . . . the small bar, the gramophone with its grating, tinny old-fashioned European Waltz, that feeling of all-consuming hunger as the warm smells from the kitchen wafted towards him. He closed his eyes and pictured in extraordinary detail the shiny, dark face of a black man, drunk or ill, slumped on a bench in the corner, who was hooting plaintively, like an owl. And then . . . His hands were burning now. He carefully held them flat against the glass, then took them away again, wiggled his fingers, and gently rubbed his hands together.

"Fool," he whispered, as if the dead man could hear him, "you fool . . . Why did you go and do it?"

GOLDER FUMBLED ABOUT at Marcus's door for some time before ringing the bell: his thick, cold hands couldn't find the buzzer and hit the wall instead. When he got inside, he looked around him in a kind of terror, as if he expected to see the dead man laid out, ready to be taken away. But there were only some rolls of black fabric on the floor of the entrance hall and bouquets of flowers on the armchairs; they were tied with purple silk inscribed with gold lettering, and the ribbons were so long and wide they trailed on to the carpet.

While Golder was standing in the hall, someone rang the bell and delivered an enormous, thick wreath of red chrysanthemums through the half-open door; the servant slipped it over his arm as if it were the handle of a basket.

"I must send some flowers," Golder thought.

Flowers for Marcus . . . He pictured the heavy face with its grimacing lips, and a bridal bouquet beside it . . .

"If you would care to wait for a moment in the drawing room, Sir," the servant whispered, "Madame is with . . ." He made a vague, embarrassed gesture. ". . . with Monsieur, with the body . . ."

He held out a chair for Golder and left. In the adjoining room, two voices were talking in a vague, mysterious whisper, as if at prayer; the voices grew gradually louder until Golder could hear them.

"The hearse decorated with Greek statues and a silver rail, in the Imperial style, with five plumes, with an ebony-panelled, silk-lined casket with eight carved, silver-gilt handles are included in the Superior Class. Then we have the Class A; that comes with a polished mahogany casket."

"How much?" a woman's voice whispered.

"Twenty thousand two hundred francs with the mahogany

casket. Twenty-nine thousand three hundred for the Superior Class."

"I don't think so. I only want to spend five or six thousand. If I had known how much you charged I would have gone elsewhere. The coffin can be made of ordinary oak if it's covered in large enough draperies..."

Golder got up abruptly; the voice was immediately lowered, softening once again to a solemn whisper.

Angrily, Golder grasped his handkerchief between his hands and absent-mindedly twisted and knotted it. "It's stupid, all this..." he muttered, "it's so stupid..."

He couldn't think of any other way to describe it. There wasn't any other way. It was stupid, just stupid... Yesterday Marcus was sitting opposite him, shouting, alive, and now... No one even used his name any more. The body... He breathed in the heavy, sickly smell that filled the room. "Is that him, already," he thought, horrified, "or these awful flowers? Why did he do it?" he muttered to himself in disgust. "Why kill yourself, at his age, over money like some little nobody..." How many times had he lost everything, and like everyone else just picked himself up and started again? That was how it was. "And as for this Teisk business," he said out loud, vehemently, as if he were imagining himself in Marcus's place, "he had a hundred to one chance it would come off, especially with Amrum involved, the fool!"

All sorts of ideas were buzzing angrily around in his mind. "You never know what's going to happen in business, you have to go with your instincts, change your tactics, try everything you can, but to choose death... How long are they going to make me wait?" he thought with disgust.

Marcus's wife came in. Her thin face, with its large, beaklike nose, had the sallow colour of antler-horn; her round, bright eyes glittered beneath her thin eyebrows, which sat very high on her forehead and looked oddly uneven.

She walked towards Golder with small hurried steps, took his hand, and seemed to be waiting for him to say something. But Golder had a lump in his throat and said nothing.

"Yes. You weren't expecting it..." she murmured with a bizarre little high-pitched squeal that sounded like a nervous laugh or stifled sob. "This madness, this humiliation, this scandal . . . I thank the good Lord for not having given us children. Do you know how he died? In a brothel, on the Rue Chabanais, with whores. As if going bankrupt weren't enough," she concluded, dabbing her eyes with her handkerchief.

Her sudden movement revealed beneath her black veil an enormous pearl necklace wound three times around her long, wrinkled neck which she jerked about like an old bird of prey.

"She must be very rich," thought Golder, "the old crow. It's always the same story: we kill ourselves working so that 'the women' can get richer . . ." He pictured his own wife quickly hiding her cheque-book whenever he came into the room, as if it were a packet of love letters.

"Would you like to see him?" she asked.

An icy wave flooded over Golder; he closed his eyes and replied in a shaky, colourless voice: "Of course, if I . . ."

Madame Marcus silently crossed the large drawing room and opened a door, but it led only to another, smaller room, where two women were sewing some black material. Eventually she said, "In here." Golder could see candles burning dimly. He stood motionless and silent for a moment, then made an effort to speak.

"Where is he?"

"Here," she said, pointing to a bed that was partly hidden beneath a great velvet canopy. "But I had to cover up his face to keep away the flies . . . The funeral is tomorrow."

It was only then that Golder thought he could make out the dead man's features beneath the sheet. He looked at him for a long time with strange emotion.

"My God, they're in such a hurry," he thought, overwhelmed by a confused feeling of anger and hurt. "Poor Marcus . . . How helpless we are when we die . . . It's disgusting . . ."

In the corner of the room stood a large American-style desk with its top open; papers and opened letters were scattered about the floor. "There must be some letters from me in there," he thought. He spotted a knife lying on the carpet. Its silver blade was all twisted. The drawers had been forced; there were no keys in the locks.

"He probably wasn't even dead when she rushed in to see what was left; she couldn't bear to wait, to try to find the keys..."

Madame Marcus caught the look on his face, but stared straight at him; all she did was to mutter curtly, "He left nothing." Then she added more quietly, in a different tone of voice, "I'm on my own."

"If I can help in any way..." Golder automatically replied.

She hesitated for a moment. "Well," she said finally, "what would you advise me to do with the Houillère shares?"

"I'll buy them from you at what they cost," said Golder. "You do know they'll never be worth anything? The company went bankrupt. But I'll also have to take some of these letters. I imagine you expected as much, didn't you?" he added in a hostile, sarcastic way that she appeared not to notice. She simply nodded and stepped back a bit. Golder began sifting through the papers in the half-empty drawer. But he couldn't manage to overcome a sudden feeling of sad, bitter indifference. My God, what's the point of it all, in the end?

"Why did he do it?" he asked abruptly.

"I don't know," said Madame Marcus.

"Was it over money? Just money?" He was thinking out loud. "It just isn't possible. Didn't he say anything at all before he died?"

"No. When they brought him back here, he was already unconscious. The bullet was lodged in his lung."

"I see," Golder said with a shudder, "I see."

"Later on, he tried to speak, but his mouth was full of foam and blood. He only said a few words, just before he died... He was almost peaceful, and I asked him, 'Why? How could you do such a thing to me?' He said something I could barely make out... Just one word that he kept repeating: 'Tired... I was... tired...' And then he died."

"Tired," thought Golder, who suddenly felt his age bearing down on him, like a heavy weight. "Yes."

A VIOLENT STORM was beating down on Paris the day of Marcus's funeral; everyone was in a hurry to bury the dead man deep within the wet earth and then leave.

Golder was holding his umbrella in front of his face, but when the coffin went past, balanced on the shoulders of the pall-bearers, he stared at it; the black fabric, embroidered with tear-shaped silver drops, had slipped away, revealing the cheap wood and tarnished metal handles. Golder turned sharply away.

Next to him, two men were talking loudly. One of them pointed to the hole being filled in.

"He came to see me," Golder could hear one of them saying, "and offered to pay me with a cheque drawn on the French Bank of America in New York, and I was foolish enough to agree. It was the night before he died, Saturday. As soon as I'd heard he'd killed himself, I cabled and only got a reply the following morning. Naturally, he'd cheated me. Insufficient funds. But I'm not going to let it drop, his widow will have to make it good . . ."

"Was it for a lot of money?" someone asked.

"Not to you perhaps, Monsieur Weille, not to you," the voice replied bitterly, "but to a poor man like me, it was an awful lot of money."

Golder looked at him. He was a small, hunched old man, rather shabbily dressed, who stood shaking in the wind, shivering and coughing. As no one said anything, he continued complaining in a low voice. Someone else started laughing.

"You'd be better off asking the madam at the Rue Chabanais, she's the one who's got your money."

Behind Golder, two young men were whispering behind an open umbrella: "The thing's a farce . . . You know they found him with some little girls? Only thirteen or fourteen years old . . . It's absolutely true, and on top of that . . ." He lowered his voice.

"Who would have guessed he had a taste for that . . ."

"Maybe he was just trying to satisfy a secret desire before dying, what do you think?"

"Trying to hide his predilections more likely . . ."

"Do you know why he killed himself?"

Golder automatically took a few steps forward, then stopped. He looked at the gleaming gravestones, the battered wreaths, whipped by the wind. He vaguely muttered something. The man next to him turned around.

"What were you saying, Golder?"

"What a mess, don't you think?" Golder said, suddenly sounding angry and oddly pained.

"Yes, when it's raining, a funeral in Paris is never much fun. But it will happen to all of us one day. Good old Marcus, even on the last day we'll ever have anything to do with him, he's arranged for all of us to die of pneumonia. If he can see us now plodding about in the mud, it will make him so happy . . . He was pretty tough, wasn't he? By the way, you'll never guess what I heard yesterday."

"What?"

"Well, I heard that the Alleman Company was going to bail out Mesopotamian Petroleum. Have you heard anything about that? You'd find that interesting, wouldn't you?"

He stopped speaking and pointed with satisfaction at the umbrellas that were beginning to move in front of them. "Ah! It's over at last, about time. Let's get going . . ."

With their collars up, the mourners pushed each other to escape the rain as quickly as possible. Some of them even ran over the graves. Like everyone else, Golder held his open umbrella with both hands and hurried away. The storm was pounding down on the trees and gravestones, beating them with a kind of futile, savage violence.

"How smug they all look, the lot of them," Golder thought. "One down, and now there's one enemy less . . . And how happy they'll all be when it's my turn."

They had to stop on the path for a moment to let a procession pass that was going in the opposite direction. Braun, Marcus's secretary, caught up with Golder.

"I have some more papers on the Russians and Amrum which will be of interest to you," he whispered. "Everyone seems to have been stabbing everyone in the back . . . Not a very nice business, Monsieur Golder."

"You think so, young man?" replied Golder, with a sarcastic look on his face. "No, not very nice. Well, bring everything to me at the train station at six o'clock, to the train for Biarritz."

"Are you going away, Monsieur Golder?"

Golder took a cigarette and crushed it between his fingers.

"Are we going to be here all night, for God's sake?"

The line of black cars was still filing past, relentless and slow, blocking the way.

"Yes, I'm going away."

"You'll have wonderful weather. How is Mademoiselle Joyce? She must be even more beautiful now . . . You'll be able to have a rest. You look nervous and tired."

"Nervous," grumbled Golder, suddenly furious, "no, thank God! Where do you get such rubbish? Now Marcus was another story . . . He was as jittery as a woman . . . And you can see where it got him . . ."

He pushed his way past two undertakers in shiny, dripping hats who were walking in the middle of the path, and fled, cutting through the funeral procession to get outside the gates.

It wasn't until he was in the car that he remembered he hadn't paid his respects to the widow. "Oh, she can go to hell!" He tried in vain to light his cigarette, but the rain had soaked it, so he spat the crushed tobacco out of the window. He huddled in the corner and closed his eyes as the car pulled away.

GOLDER DINED QUICKLY, drank some of the heavy Burgundy he liked, then smoked for a while in the corridor. A woman bumped into him as she passed by and smiled, but he looked away, indifferent. She was one of those little sluts from Biarritz... She disappeared. He went back into his compartment.

"I'm going to sleep well tonight," he thought. He suddenly felt exhausted; his legs were heavy and painful. He raised the blind and looked out blankly at the rain streaming down the dark windows. The drops of water ran into each other forming little, wind-whipped rivers, like tears... He undressed, got into bed, and buried his face deep in the pillow. He had never felt so exhausted. He stretched his arms out with difficulty; they were stiff, heavy... The berth was narrow... even narrower than usual, it seemed. "A bad choice of compartment, of course... the idiots," he thought vaguely. He could feel his body jolt as the wheels beneath him revolved with a heart-rending screech. The heat was suffocating. He turned over his pillow, then turned it again; he was burning up. He punched it down with his fist, angrily. It was so hot... It would be better to open the window. But the wind was blowing furiously. In a flash, all the letters and newspapers on the table flew into the air. He swore, closed the window again, pulled the blind down, switched off the light.

The air was heavy and smelled of coal mixed with a faint odour of eau de toilette. It made him feel sick. Instinctively, he tried to breathe more deeply, as if to force the heavy air into his lungs, but they rejected it, could not absorb it; it remained in his throat, choking him, like trying to force food into a nauseous stomach... He kept coughing. It was irritating... Worst of all, it was preventing him from sleeping. "And I'm so terribly tired," he murmured, as if complaining to some invisible companion.

He turned on to his back, then rolled slowly over on to his

side again, pushing himself up on his elbows. He gave a deliber-
ate, hard cough in an attempt to shrug off the unbearable feeling
of heaviness high in his chest, in his throat. It didn't work; he
felt even worse. He yawned with difficulty, but a sharp spasm
turned the yawn into a painful fit of choking. He stretched his
neck, moistened his lips. Perhaps his head was too low? He
reached for his overcoat, rolled it up, slipped it under the pillow,
then pulled himself into a sitting position. It was worse. His lungs
felt as if they were swelling up. And . . . it was strange . . . He had
pains . . . yes, pains in his chest, in his shoulder, around his
heart . . . Suddenly a shiver ran down his spine. "What's happening?" he whispered anxiously. Then he said bravely, "No, it's
nothing, it will stop. It's nothing . . ." and he realised he was
talking out loud, talking to himself. He braced himself, put all
his effort into inhaling deeply, but it was no use. He couldn't
breathe. He felt an invisible weight crushing his chest. He threw
off the covers, the sheet, opened his nightshirt. "What's going
on?" he panted. "What's wrong with me?" The thick, black
darkness bore down on him like a stone. That's what was
suffocating him, yes, that was it . . . He reached out his shaking
hand to turn on the light, but it fumbled along the wall in the
dark, trying in vain to find the little lamp set in the wall above
the bed. He sighed angrily, shuddered. The pain in his shoulder
was becoming sharper, more insistent . . . Cunningly lying in
wait, he thought, pacing about somewhere deep inside his body,
in the very core of his being, in his heart, waiting for him to
make the slightest movement and then it would strike. Slowly
he lowered his arm; it was as if he was forcing it down. Just
wait . . . don't move. Whatever happens, don't move . . . He was
breathing more and more heavily and quickly. The air entered
his lungs with a strange, grotesque sound, like steam hissing from
the lid of a cauldron; and when he breathed out, his entire chest
began to convulse, filled with a hoarse, choked wheezing, like a
moan, like a death-rattle.

The thick darkness flowed into his throat with soft, insistent
pressure, as if earth were being pushed into his mouth, as it was
into *his* . . . the dead man's . . . Marcus . . . And when he thought
finally of Marcus, when he finally allowed himself to be taken

over by the image, the memory of death, the cemetery, the yellow clay soaked with rain, the long roots clinging like serpents deep inside the grave, he suddenly felt such a tremendous need, such a desperate desire for light, to see familiar, ordinary things around him . . . his clothing swaying from the hook on the door . . . the newspapers on the little table . . . the bottle of mineral water . . . that he forgot about everything else. Angrily he stretched out his arm, and an excruciating pain, as sharp as a knife, like a bullet, deep and violent, shot through his chest, seemed to embed itself within his heart.

He had time to think "I'm dying," to feel he was being pushed, thrown over the edge of a precipice into a hole, a crater, as narrow and suffocating as a tomb. He could hear himself calling out, but his voice sounded as if it were coming from very far away, as if it were someone else's voice, separated from him by deep, murky water that swept over him and was dragging him down, lower and lower, into the wide, gaping hole. The pain was unbearable. Soon he fainted, which eased the pain a little, transforming it into a feeling of heaviness, suffocation, an exhausting and vain battle. Once again, he could hear someone calling in the distance, panting, shouting, struggling. He felt as if someone were holding his head under water and that it went on for centuries.

Finally, he came to.

The sharp pains had stopped. But his entire body felt wracked, as if all his bones had been broken, crushed beneath heavy wheels. And he was afraid to move, afraid to lift a single finger, afraid to call out. The slightest sound, the slightest movement would make it start all over again, he was sure of it . . . and this time, it would mean death. Death.

In the silence, he could hear his heart beating, hard and hollow; it seemed to tear at the muscles in his chest.

"I'm afraid," he thought desperately, "I'm afraid . . ."

Death. No, it wasn't possible, no! Couldn't anyone tell, sense that he was here, alone like a dog, abandoned, dying? "If I could only ring the bell, call someone. No, I just have to wait, wait . . . The night will soon pass." It had to be very late already, very late . . . He peered anxiously into the darkness that surrounded him; it was as thick and deep as before, without a glimmer of light, without even that vague halo that illuminates everything just before dawn. Nothing. Was it ten o'clock, eleven o'clock? To think that his watch was right there, the light was there, that he only had to reach out, stretch out his arm to press the alarm. It was worth the risk! But no, no . . . He was afraid to make a sound, afraid to breathe. If it happened again, if he felt his heart failing . . . and that horrible pain . . . No! The next time, he would surely die. "But what's happening, for God's sake? What is it? My heart. Yes." But he'd never had heart trouble. He'd never even been ill . . . A bit of asthma, perhaps . . . Especially recently. But at his age, everyone had something wrong. A bit of discomfort. It was nothing. Watch your diet, get some rest. But this! Oh, what difference if it was his heart or something else? They were only words, words that mean one thing: death, death, death. Who was it who'd said, "It will happen to all of us one day"? Oh, yes. All of us. And him. Those old Jews with their vicious faces who rubbed their hands together, sniggering . . . It would be worse for them! The dogs, the bastards! And the others . . . His wife . . . His daughter . . . Yes, even her, he was no fool. He was nothing more than a money machine . . . Good for nothing else . . . Just pay, pay, and then, drop down dead . . .

Good Lord, wouldn't this damned train ever stop? It had been hours, they'd been travelling for hours without a break! "Don't people sometimes make a mistake at stations and open the door of a compartment that's already occupied? My God, if only that would happen now!" He imagined hearing a sound in the corridor, the door banging open, people's faces . . . He would be taken away . . . It didn't matter where—to a hospital, a hotel . . . Anywhere, as long as they had a stretcher . . .

The sound of footsteps, human voices, some light, an open window . . .

But no, nothing . . . Nothing at all. The train was going faster. Long, piercing whistles filled the air, then faded away . . . There was the sound of wheels pounding the tracks in the darkness . . . a bridge . . . For a moment he thought that the train was slowing down. He listened hard, gasping for breath. Yes, they were going slower . . . slower . . . they'd stopped . . . A shrill whistle sounded, hung for a moment over the open countryside, and the train started moving again.

He shuddered. He had lost all hope. His mind was blank. He wasn't even suffering any more. There was nothing now but fear: "I'm afraid, I'm afraid, I'm afraid," and his racing, thundering heart.

Suddenly he thought he could make out something shining, faintly, through the thick blackness. It was opposite him. He strained to see. Barely a glimmer of light. Greyish, pale . . . But nevertheless something bright, distinct, in the darkness. He waited. It expanded, became clearer, spread, like a pool of water. It was the glass of the window, the window. It was dawn. The darkness was fading, becoming less dense, more fluid. He felt as if an enormous weight was lifting from his chest. He was breathing. This lighter air glided, flowed into his lungs. With infinite care, he moved his head. Cool air swept across his damp brow. Now he could make out shapes around him, outlines. His hat, for example, which had fallen on the floor . . . The water bottle . . . Maybe he could reach the glass, drink a bit? He stretched out his hand. He felt no pain, nothing. With beating heart, he moved his wrist. Still nothing. His hand felt its way to the table, held the glass. It had water in it, thank God; he never would have been able to lift the bottle. He raised his head slightly, put the glass to his lips, and drank. How wonderful it was . . . The flow of cool water across his lips, moistening his dry, swollen tongue, his throat. With the same care, he put the glass down, moved back a bit, waited. His chest still hurt. But less, a lot less, as each moment passed. It was more like a kind of neuralgia in his bones. Maybe it wasn't so serious after all . . .

Perhaps he could open the blind. All he had to do was press a button. Trembling, he stretched out his hand again. The blind suddenly sprang up. It was day. The air was white, cloudy and thick as milk. Slowly, with measured, methodical movements, he picked up his handkerchief, wiped his cheeks and lips. Then he put his face against the window. The cold of the glass felt wonderful as it ran through his whole body. He looked out at the hills where the grass was gradually recovering its greenness, at the trees . . . Far away in the distance he could see lights glowing faintly in the dawn fog. A railway station. Should he call some-one? It would be easy. But how strange that it should have gone away like that . . . Though it did prove that it wasn't anything serious, at least not as serious as he had feared. An anxiety attack perhaps? Still, he couldn't ignore it, he'd have to see a doctor. But it didn't have to be his heart. Asthma, maybe? No, he wouldn't call anyone. He looked at his watch. Five o'clock. Come on now, just wait a bit. No need to get all worked up like this. It was his nerves. Braun had been right, the little crook . . . Cautiously, he probed the spot beneath his breast as if it were an open wound. Nothing. His heart-beat, however, was strange, irregular. So what, it would pass. He was tired. If he could just sleep for a while, that would surely fix things. Just to be oblivious . . . No more thinking. No more remembering. He was absolutely exhausted. He closed his eyes.

He was already half asleep when, suddenly, he sat up. "That's it," he said out loud. "I see it now . . . It's Marcus. But why? Why?" At that moment he felt he could see within himself with extraordinary lucidity. Was it . . . a kind of remorse? "No, it's not my fault." Then he added more quietly, more angrily: "I have nothing to regret."

He fell asleep.

GOLDER SPOTTED THE chauffeur standing at the door of a new car; he suddenly remembered that his wife had sold the Hispano.

"It's a Rolls now, of course," he grumbled as he shot a look of hostility at the dazzling white car. "I wonder what she'll have to have next."

The chauffeur stepped forward to take his overcoat from him, but Golder stayed where he was, peering through the car's open window, trying to see if anyone was inside. Hadn't Joyce come? He took a few hesitant steps forward to take a final hopeful but humble look at the dark corner where he imagined he would see his daughter with her light dress, her golden hair. But the car was empty. He got in slowly, then shouted, "Get going, for God's sake. What are you waiting for?"

The car sped off. Golder sighed.

His daughter . . . Every time he came back from a trip, he looked for her in the crowd, in spite of himself. She was never there, and yet he continued to expect her with the same humiliating, tenacious, and vain sense of hope.

"She hasn't seen me in four months," he thought. He felt deeply hurt; he didn't deserve this, and yet his daughter so often aroused this very feeling within him. He felt it grasp his heart, as sharp and agonising as physical pain. "Children . . . They're all the same . . . and they're the reason we live. It's for them that we keep working. Not like my own father, no . . . At thirteen, get the hell out, fend for yourself . . . That's what they all deserve."

He took off his hat, slowly wiped his hand across his forehead to remove the dust and sweat, then stared out the window. But there were too many people, too much shouting, sun, wind. The short Rue Mazagran was so crowded that the car couldn't move; a young boy stuck his face against the car window as it passed by.

Golder moved back into the corner and pulled up the collar of his coat. Joyce . . . Where was she? Who was she with?

"I'm going to give her what for," he thought bitterly. "This time, I'm going to tell her off about it. 'Whenever you need money, it's "Dearest Dad, Daddy, Darling," but not the slightest sign of affection, of . . .' " He stopped himself with a weary gesture of his hand. He knew very well that he wouldn't say a thing . . . What was the point? And after all, she was still at the age when girls were silly and insensitive. A little smile played at the corners of his mouth, then quickly disappeared. She was only eighteen.

They had crossed Biarritz, passed the Hôtel du Palais. He gazed coldly at the sea; it was choppy, despite the fine weather, with enormous waves. The dazzling green hurt his eyes; he shaded them with his hand and turned away. It was only fifteen minutes later, when they were on the road past the golf course, that he finally leaned forward and looked at his house in the distance. He came here only between trips, to spend a week or so, as if he were a stranger, but every year he loved it more and more. "I'm making myself old. Before it wasn't a problem . . . hotels, sleeping compartments . . . But now it's all so tiring . . . It's a beautiful house . . . "

He had bought the property in 1916 for one million five hundred thousand. Now it was worth fifteen million. The house was made of stone, as white and heavy as marble. A beautiful, imposing house . . . When he saw its outline against the sky, with its balconies, its gardens—still slightly bare, for the sea winds prevented the young trees from growing quickly, but striking and magnificent nevertheless—a look of tenderness and pride spread across Golder's face. "A very good investment," he sighed deeply.

"Drive faster, Albert, faster," he shouted impatiently.

Down below, he had a clear view of the rose-covered arches, the tamarind trees, the rows of cedars leading down to the sea.

"The palm trees have grown . . . "

The car stopped in front of the steps, but only the servants came out to greet him. He recognised Joyce's little chambermaid who was smiling at him.

"Is there no one at home?" he asked.

"No, Monsieur, Mademoiselle will be coming home for lunch."

He didn't ask where she was. What was the point?

"Bring me the post," he said sharply.

He took the packet of letters and telegrams and began to read them as he climbed the stairs. On the landing, he hesitated for a moment between two identical doors. The servant, who had followed him with the suitcase, pointed to one of the bedrooms.

"Madame told me to put Monsieur in this room. His own room is being used."

"Fine," he said, indifferent.

Once in the room, he sat down on a chair, with the weary, blank look of a man who has just arrived at a hotel in some unfamiliar city.

"Is Monsieur going to have a rest?"

Golder shuddered and stood up with great effort.

"No, it's not worth it."

"If I go to bed," he was thinking, "I'll never get up again."

Nevertheless, when he'd washed and shaved, he felt better; there was just a slight, persistent trembling in his fingers. He looked at them. They were as white and swollen as a corpse.

"Are there many people staying?" he asked with difficulty.

"Monsieur Fischl, His Imperial Highness, and Count Hoyos..."

Golder silently bit his lip.

"Which Highness have they invented now? These damned women... And Fischl," he thought, annoyed, "why Fischl, in the name of... and Hoyos..."

But Hoyos was inevitable.

He went slowly downstairs and headed for the terrace. A large purple awning was stretched across it at the hottest time of the day. Golder stretched out on a chaise-longue and closed his eyes. But the sun penetrated the canvas and flooded the terrace with a strange red light. Golder fidgeted nervously.

"That colour..." he murmured, "it must be one of Gloria's idiotic ideas. What does it remind me of? Something terrifying.

Oh, yes . . . How had she put it, that old witch? 'His mouth was full of foam and blood.' " He shuddered. Sighing, he turned his painful head from side to side on the fine linen and lace cushions, which were already crumpled and damp from his sweat. Then, suddenly, he fell asleep.

WHEN GOLDER WOKE up it was already after two o'clock, but the house seemed empty.

"Nothing's changed," he thought.

With a kind of grim humour, he imagined Gloria coming towards him up the path as he had seen her so many times before: teetering because the heels on her shoes were too high, her hand shading her ageing painted face, her make-up melting in the dazzling sunlight . . . "Hello, David," she would say, "how's business?" and then "How are you?" but only the first question required a reply. Later on, the brilliant Biarritz crowd would invade the house. Those faces . . . It made him sick to think of them. All the crooks, the pimps, the old whores on earth . . . And he was the one paying for that lot to eat, drink, and get sloshed all night. The bunch of greedy dogs . . . He shrugged his shoulders. What could he do about it? In the past, he had found it amusing, flattering even. "The Duke of . . . Count . . . Yesterday, the Maharajah was at my house . . ." Filth. The older and sicker he got, the more tiresome he found people and the racket they made, the more tiresome his family and even life.

He sighed, knocked on the window behind him to call the butler who was laying the table, and gestured to him to raise the blinds. The sun blazed down on the garden and the sea. Someone called out: "Hello, Golder!"

He recognised Fischl's voice and slowly turned round without replying. Why did Gloria have to invite him of all people? Golder looked with a kind of hatred at Fischl, as if at a cruel caricature. Fat little Jew . . . He had a comical, vile, and slightly sinister air as he stood in the doorway with his red hair, ruddy complexion, and bright, knowing eyes behind thin gold spectacles. His stomach was fat, his legs short, skinny, and misshapen. He calmly held in his killer's hands a porcelain bowl of fresh caviar against his chest.

"Golder, my friend, are you staying long?"

Fischl walked over and took a chair, placing the half-empty bowl on the ground.

"Are you asleep, Golder?"

"No," Golder grumbled.

"How's business?"

"Bad."

"*I'm* doing very well," said Fischl, folding his arms around his stomach with difficulty. "I'm very happy."

"Oh, yes. That pearl fishing business in Monaco . . ." Golder sniggered. "I thought they'd thrown you in jail . . ."

Fischl gave a long, good-humoured laugh.

"Absolutely, I was taken to court . . . But, as you can see, it didn't end up as badly as usual. Austria, Russia, France . . ." He counted off on his fingers. "I've been in prison in three countries. I hope that's the end of it now, that they'll leave me in peace . . . They can all go to hell, I don't want to work any more. I'm old."

He lit a cigarette. "What was the Stock Market like yesterday?"

"Bad."

"Do you know what the Huanchaca shares were selling at?"

"One thousand three hundred and sixty-five," Golder said, rubbing his hands together. "You really got screwed there, didn't you?"

He wondered suddenly why he was so happy to see the man lose money. Fischl had never done anything to him. "It's strange how I can't bear him," he thought.

But Fischl just shrugged his shoulders. "*Iddische Glick*," he said in Yiddish.

"He must be rolling in it again, the pig," thought Golder. (He knew how to recognise the inimitable, telling little tremor in a man's voice that gives away his emotion even if his words appear indifferent.) "He doesn't give a damn . . ."

"What are you doing here?" he grumbled.

"Your wife invited me . . . Hey, listen . . ."

He walked over to Golder, automatically lowering his voice. "There's a business I know about that will interest you . . . Have you ever heard of the El Paso silver mines?"

"No, thank God," Golder interjected.

"There are millions to be made there."

"There are millions to be made everywhere, but you have to know how to make them."

"You're wrong to refuse to do business with me. We're made for each other. You're intelligent, but you lack daring, you're not willing to take chances, you're afraid of the law. Don't you think?"

He laughed, pleased with himself.

"As for me, I'm not interested in run-of-the-mill stuff—buying, selling . . . But to get something going, to create something—a mine in Peru, for example—when you don't even know where it is . . . Listen, I started something like that two years ago. When I bought the shares, they hadn't even turned over a shovelful of earth. Then the American investors jumped in. Whether you believe me or not, I'm telling you that within two weeks the land was worth ten times what I'd paid. I sold my shares for a huge profit. When business works like that, it's pure poetry."

Golder shrugged his shoulders. "Not really."

"Whatever you say. You'll regret it. There's nothing fishy about this one."

He smoked for a while in silence. "Tell me . . ."

"What?"

He looked at Golder, narrowing his eyes. "Marcus . . ."

But the aged face remained blank; there was a mere twitch of a muscle in one corner of his mouth. "Marcus? He's dead."

"I know," Fischl said quietly, "but why?" He lowered his voice even further. "What did you do to him, you old Cain?"

"What did I do to him?" Golder repeated. He looked away. "He wanted to cheat old man Golder," he said abruptly, angrily, as his hollow ashen cheeks blushed suddenly, "and that's dangerous . . ."

Fischl laughed. "You old Cain," he repeated smugly, "but you're right. As for me, well, I'm too nice."

He stopped speaking; he'd heard something.

"Here comes your daughter, Golder."

"IS DAD HERE?" shouted Joyce. Golder could hear her laughing. Instinctively he closed his eyes, as if to listen for longer. His daughter... What a lovely voice, what a radiant laugh she had. "Like gold," he thought, feeling indescribable pleasure.

Nevertheless, he didn't move, made not a single sign of going towards her, and when she appeared, leaping on to the terrace in that light, quick way she had that showed her knees beneath her short dress, all he did was to say ironically, "So you're home? I didn't expect you back so soon..."

She jumped on him and kissed him, then fell back on to the chaise-longue and stretched herself out, crossing her arms beneath her neck and laughing as she looked at him through the long lashes of her half-closed eyes.

Almost against his will, Golder slowly reached out his hand and placed it on her golden hair; it was moist, tangled from the sea. Though he seemed barely to be looking at her, his piercing eyes registered every change in her features, every line, every movement her face made. How she had grown... In just four months, she had become more beautiful, more of a woman. He was annoyed to see she was using more make-up. God knows she didn't need to, at eighteen, with her lovely fair skin and her delicate, flowerlike lips, which she painted a deep blood-red. Such a shame. "Foolish girl," he sighed, then added, "You're growing up..."

"And growing beautiful, I hope?" she exclaimed, sitting up abruptly then settling herself again with her legs tucked under her and her hands on her knees. She stared at him with her large, dark eyes; they sparkled with that haughty, arrogant look he so hated, the look of a woman who has been loved and desired her whole life. What was extraordinary was that, in spite of that look, in spite of make-up and the jewellery, she had retained the wild laughter of a little girl and the awkward, gauche, almost brutal gestures of extreme youth, with its light, intense grace. "It won't last," he thought.

"Get down, Joyce, you're annoying me . . ."

She lightly stroked his hand. "I'm happy to see you, Dad . . ."

"So you need money?"

She saw that he was smiling and nodded. "Always . . . I don't know where it goes. It seems to run through my fingers . . ." she spread her fingers out and laughed, "like water. It's not my fault . . ."

Two men were coming up from the garden. Hoyos and a very handsome boy of twenty with a thin, pale face; Golder didn't recognise him.

"That's Prince Alexis of . . ." Joyce quickly whispered in his ear, "You have to call him Your Imperial Highness."

She jumped down, then leapt on to the balustrade and straddled it, calling out, "Alec, come here! Where were you? I waited for you all morning, I was furious . . . This is Dad, Alec . . ."

The young man went up to Golder, greeted him with a kind of arrogant shyness, then went over to Joyce.

"And where did that little gigolo come from?" asked Golder as soon as he was out of earshot.

"He's good-looking, isn't he?" Hoyos murmured nonchalantly.

"Yes," grumbled Golder, then repeated impatiently, "I asked you where he came from."

"He's from a good family," Hoyos said, looking at him and smiling. "He's the son of that poor Pierre de Carèlu who was assassinated in 1918. He's the nephew of King Alexander, his sister's son."

"He looks like a gigolo," said Fischl.

"He probably is. Did anyone say he wasn't?"

"Anyway, he's with old Lady Rovenna."

"Just her? Such a nice young man? I'm surprised . . ."

Hoyos sat down and stretched out his long legs, carefully placing his pince-nez, fine handkerchief, newspaper, and books on the wicker table. The way in which his long fingers delicately touched each object, as if he were caressing it, irritated Golder deeply, and had done for years . . . Hoyos slowly lit a cigarette. It was only then that Golder noticed how the skin on the hand holding the gold lighter was all creased—soft and wrinkled like a withered flower. It was strange to think that even Hoyos, that handsome cavalier, had grown old. He must be almost sixty. But he was still as good-looking as ever, suave and slim, with his small, proud head, his silvery hair, his strong body, flawless face, and large, hooked nose. His nostrils flared with passion and life.

Fischl indicated Alec with a sullen shrug. "They say he prefers men. Is it true?"

"Not for the moment, in any case," murmured Hoyos. He stared at Joyce and Alec with a sardonic look on his face. "He's so young, people don't know what they like at that age . . . Say, Golder, you do realise that Joyce has got it into her head that she's going to marry him, don't you?"

Golder didn't reply. Hoyos gave a little snigger.

"What did you say?" asked Golder sharply.

"Nothing. I was just wondering . . . Would you let Joyce marry a boy like that who's as poor as a church mouse?"

Golder pursed his lips. "Why not?" he said finally.

"Why not?" Hoyos repeated, shrugging his shoulders.

"She'll be rich," Golder mused, "and anyway, she knows how to handle men. Just look at her . . ."

They both fell silent. Joyce, straddling the balustrade, was talking to Alec; she spoke quickly and softly. Every now and then, she slid her hands through her short hair, pushing it back nervously. It looked as if she was in a bad mood.

Hoyos got up and quietly walked towards them, winking. His dark, beautiful eyes were extraordinarily bright beneath his thick eyebrows, which were streaked with deep silver, like some rare fur. Joyce was whispering: "We could take the car if you like and go to Spain; I want to make love in Spain . . ."

Laughing, she brought her lips up close to Alec's mouth. "Would you like that? Well, would you?"

"And what about Lady Rovenna?" he objected, half-smiling.

Joyce clenched her fists. "That old woman of yours. I hate her! No, you'll go away with me, do you hear? You have no shame. Look . . ."

She leaned forward and discreetly showed him a little bruise just above her eyelid. "Look at what you did . . ."

She noticed Hoyos standing behind her.

He gently stroked her hair. "Listen, *chica*," he murmured:

Mama, I want to die of love,
She shouted and cried out loud.
That's because this is your very first love,
And the first is best, Madame.

Joyce clasped her beautiful arms together, laughed, and said, "Isn't love wonderful?"

WHEN GLORIA GOT home, it was nearly three o'clock in the afternoon. They were all there: Lady Rovenna, in a pink dress; Daphne Mannering, one of Joyce's friends, with her mother and the German gentleman who kept them; the Maharajah, his wife, his mistress, and his two daughters; Lady Rovenna's son; and Maria-Pia, a tall, dark-haired dancer from Argentina who had sallow skin as rough and scented as an orange.

The meal was served. It was drawn-out and magnificent. At five o'clock it finished, and more visitors arrived. Golder, Hoyos, Fischl, and a Japanese general started playing bridge.

They played until evening. It was eight o'clock when Gloria sent her chambermaid to tell Golder that they were invited out to dinner at the Miramar.

Golder hesitated, but he felt better; he went up to his room, changed, then, once he was ready, went in to see Gloria. She was standing in front of an enormous, three-panelled mirror finishing getting dressed; the chambermaid, kneeling in front of her, was having difficulty fitting her shoes. Slowly Gloria turned towards him; her ageing face was so covered in make-up it looked like an enamelled plate.

"David, I've hardly seen you for five minutes today," she murmured reproachfully. "Those cards . . . How do I look? I won't kiss you—my make-up's all done . . ." She stretched out her hand to him; it was petite and beautiful, weighed down by enormous diamonds. Then she carefully smoothed down her short red hair.

Her full cheeks looked as if they had been inflated from inside, and were faintly lined with broken veins; her exquisite blue eyes were pale and severe.

"I've lost weight, haven't I?" she said. She smiled, and he could see the gold fillings shining in the teeth at the back of her mouth.

"Well, David, haven't I?" she repeated.

She twirled around slowly, so he could see her better, proudly arching her body. It had remained very beautiful: her shoulders, arms, and high, firm breasts were extraordinarily striking, despite her age, and had retained the hard brilliance of marble. But her neck was lined, and her face sagged. This, together with her dark-pink rouge, which became purplish beneath the lights, gave her an air of decrepitude that was both sinister and comical.

"Can you see, David, how much slimmer I am? I lost five kilos in a month, didn't I, Jenny? I have a new masseur now. A black man, of course . . . They're the best. All the women here are mad about him. He made that fat old Alphand simply melt away. Do you remember her? She's become as svelte as a young girl. He's quite expensive though . . ."

She stopped talking: her lipstick had smudged at the corner of her mouth. Slowly she dabbed it away and patiently redrew on to her ageing, shapeless lips the pure, clean arch that the years had wiped away.

"You have to admit that I hardly look like an old woman," she said, with a little satisfied laugh. But he was gazing at her without actually seeing her. The chambermaid brought in a jewellery box. Gloria opened it and pulled out a tangle of bracelets that had lain jumbled together in the box like bits of thread snarled at the bottom of a sewing basket.

"Stop fiddling with that, David . . ." she continued, irritated. He was absent-mindedly toying with a magnificent shawl that was spread out on the settee, an enormous piece of gold and purple silk embroidered with scarlet birds and large flowers.

"David . . ."

"What?" said Golder grumpily.

"How's business?"

Her gaze suddenly changed as a piercing look flashed like lightning between her long eyelashes, heavy with mascara.

Golder shrugged his shoulders.

"So-so," he said finally.

"What do you mean 'so-so'? You mean, not good? David, I'm talking to you!"

"Not too bad," he said, half-heartedly.

"Darling, I need some money."

"Again?"

Gloria angrily tore off a bracelet that wasn't closing properly and threw it towards the table. It fell on the floor and she kicked it away. "What do you mean 'Again'?" she shouted. "You simply cannot imagine how much you annoy me when you say things like that. Come on, tell me. What do you mean? Don't you realise how expensive everything is? Your precious Joyce, for starters! Oh, money burns a hole in that girl's pocket . . . And do you know what she says to me when I dare to make the slightest criticism? 'Dad will pay.' And she's right—you've always got money for her! I'm the only one who doesn't matter. Do you think I can live on thin air, well, do you? What's gone wrong this time, is it Golmar?"

"Golmar! That went wrong long ago . . . If we were counting on Golmar . . . "

"But you do have something lucrative in the works?"

"Yes."

"What?"

"Oh, you really are tedious," Golder shouted. "This obsession you have with interrogating me about business! You never stop! You don't understand a thing about business and you know it, You women can all go to hell! What exactly are you worried about? I'm still here, aren't I?" He made an effort to calm down: "You have a new necklace, I see. Let's have a look."

She took the pearls and warmed them in her hands for a moment, as if they were wine.

"They're fabulous, aren't they? I know you're going to criticise me for spending too much money, but these days jewellery is the best investment. And it was a bargain. Guess how much they were? Eight hundred thousand, darling. That's nothing, right? Just look at the emerald on the clasp, that alone is worth a fortune, isn't it? Look at the colour, the size! And as for the pearls . . . OK, some of them are uneven, but what about those three at the front! You can get such amazing bargains. The sluts around here will sell anything for cash. If only you would give me more money . . . "

Golder bit his tongue.

"There was one young girl," she continued, "whose lover lost a fortune gambling; he was just a boy. She was going crazy; she wanted to sell me her fur coat, a magnificent chinchilla. When I tried to bargain with her she came here sobbing. I still said no. I was counting on her getting even more desperate so I'd have it for a better price, but I regret it now. Her lover killed himself. So of course she'll keep the coat. Oh, David! If you could just see what a beautiful necklace that mad old Lady Rovenna has bought herself! It's gorgeous. All diamonds . . . No one's wearing pearls this season, you know. I heard she paid five million. Can you believe it? I've had one of my old diamond necklaces reset. I'll have to buy five or six large diamonds to lengthen it. Needs must when you don't have the money. But God, Lady Rovenna has such amazing jewellery! And she's so old and ugly. She must be at least sixty-five!"

"You're a lot richer than I am now, aren't you, Gloria?" said Golder.

Gloria clenched her teeth with a little click, like a crocodile's jaws snapping shut on its prey.

"I detest jokes like that, and you know it!"

"Gloria," said Golder, hesitating a little, "you know, don't you, about Marcus?"

"No," said Gloria, vaguely; she had put some perfume on her finger and was dabbing it behind her ears and under the pearls. "No, what about Marcus?"

"Ah, so you don't know . . ." Golder sighed. "Well, he's dead. They've had the funeral."

Gloria stood still, her perfume bottle poised in mid-air in front of her.

"Oh!" she murmured in a softer tone of voice. She sounded pained, almost frightened. "How? How is it possible? He wasn't old . . . What did he die of?"

"He killed himself. He was bankrupt."

"What a coward!" exclaimed Gloria vehemently. "Don't you think that's cowardly? What about his wife? How delightful for her! Did you see her?"

"Yes," said Golder with a sarcastic laugh. "She was wearing a necklace with pearls as big as walnuts."

"And what would you have her do," Gloria asked bitterly, "give everything to him like a little fool, so he could lose it all again on the Stock Market or somewhere else, so he could kill himself two years later without leaving her a penny? Men are so selfish! That's what you would have wanted, isn't it?"

"*I* don't want anything," growled Golder. "I don't give a damn. Only, when I think how we work ourselves to death for you . . ." He stopped speaking, a strange look of hatred on his face.

Gloria shrugged.

"But my dear, men like you and Marcus don't work for their wives, do they? You work for yourselves . . . Yes, you do," she insisted. "In the end, business is a drug, just like morphine is. If you couldn't work, darling, you'd be as miserable as sin . . ."

Golder laughed nervously.

"Ah!" he said. "You've got it all worked out, my dear."

JOYCE'S CHAMBERMAID OPENED the door quietly.

"Mademoiselle sent me," she said to Gloria, who was looking at her with cold displeasure. "Mademoiselle is ready and would like Monsieur to come and see her gown."

Golder immediately stood up.

"That girl is so annoying," Gloria hissed, sounding hostile and irritated, "and you spoil her, you do, just like an old man in love. You are a fool."

But Golder was already on his way out.

She furtively shrugged her shoulders. "At least hurry her up, for heaven's sake! I wait in the car while she admires herself in the mirror. She's a real handful, I'm telling you . . . Have you seen how she behaves around men? You can warn her that if she's not ready in ten minutes, I'm going without her. And I mean it."

Golder said nothing and went out. On the landing, he stopped to breathe in Joyce's perfume with a smile; it was so intense and persistent that it filled the upstairs rooms with the scent of roses.

Joyce recognised the heavy footsteps that made the parquet floor creak. "Is that you, Dad?" she called out. "Come in."

She was standing in front of the large mirror in her brightly lit room, teasing Jill, her little golden Pekinese dog, with her foot. She smiled, tilting her pretty head to one side. "Do you like my dress, Dad?" she asked.

She was all in white and silver. Not considering his admiration to be sufficiently enthusiastic, she made a face and nodded towards her strong, flawless neck and beautiful shoulders.

"I'm not sure it's low-cut enough. What do you think?"

"Can I give you a kiss?" asked Golder.

She walked over to him, offered a delicately powdered cheek and the corner of her painted mouth.

"You wear too much make-up, Joy."

"I have to," she said nonchalantly. "My cheeks are totally white. I stay up too late, I smoke too much, I dance too much."

"Naturally . . . Women are idiots," grumbled Golder, "and as for you, well, you're mad to boot . . ."

"I love to dance so much," she murmured, half closing her eyes. Her beautiful lips were trembling.

She stood in front of him and stretched out her hands, but her large, sparkling eyes weren't looking at him; she was looking at herself in the mirror behind him. He smiled in spite of himself.

"Joyce! You're even vainer than before, my poor girl! Though, your mother did warn me . . ."

"She's much vainer than I am," she shouted crossly, "and she's got no excuse! She's old and ugly, not like me . . . I'm beautiful, aren't I, Dad?"

Golder pinched her cheek and laughed.

"I should hope so! I wouldn't like having an ugly daughter . . ." He stopped talking suddenly, went pale, and placed his hand over his heart; he panted, his eyes opening wide from a sudden sharp pain, then he sighed and let his arm drop . . . The pain had passed, but it had gone slowly, almost reluctantly. He pushed Joyce away, took out his handkerchief, carefully wiped his forehead and cold cheeks.

"Get me something to drink, Joyce."

She called the chambermaid in the adjoining room who brought in a glass of water; he drank eagerly. Joyce had picked up a mirror and was humming while arranging her hair.

"Daddy, what did you buy me?"

He didn't reply. She walked over to him and jumped on to his lap.

"Daddy, Daddy, look at me, come on, what's wrong? Answer me! Don't tease me . . ."

Automatically he took out his wallet and put a few thousand-franc notes into her hand.

"Is that all?"

"Yes. Isn't it enough?" he murmured, forcing himself to laugh.

"No. I want a new car."

"What? What's wrong with the car you've got?"

"It's boring, it's too small . . . I want a Bugatti. I want to go to Madrid with . . ."

She stopped suddenly.

"With whom?"

"Friends . . ."

He shrugged. "Don't talk nonsense."

"It isn't nonsense. I want a new car!"

"Well, you'll have to do without it."

"No, Daddy, Daddy darling . . . Get me a new car, get me one, say you will! I'll be a good girl . . . Daphne Mannering has a beautiful car that Behring gave her."

"Business is bad. Next year . . ."

"Why does everyone always say that to me! I couldn't care less, just buy it!"

"Enough! You're irritating me," Golder finally cried impatiently.

She stopped talking, sprang off his lap, then thought for a moment and came back to lean against him.

"But, Daddy . . . if you had a lot of money, would you buy one for me?"

"Buy what?"

"The car."

"Yes."

"When?"

"Right away. But I don't have any money. Stop pestering me."

Joyce let out a little squeal of delight.

"I know what we'll do! We'll go to the casino tonight . . . I'll see to it that you win. Hoyos always says I bring good luck. You can buy me the car tomorrow!"

Golder shook his head. "No. I'm coming home right after dinner. Don't you realise that I spent the night on the train?"

"So what?"

"I don't feel well today, Joy . . ."

"You? You're never ill!"

"Oh! Is that what you think?"

"Dad," she asked suddenly, "do you like Alec?"

"Alec?" Golder repeated. "Oh, that boy . . . He's nice . . ."

"Would you like to see me become a princess?"

"That depends . . ."

"I would be called 'Your Imperial Highness'!"

She went and stood beneath the bright chandelier, throwing back her fine golden hair.

"Take a good look at me, Dad. Do you think I'd make a good princess?"

"Yes," murmured Golder with a rush of secret pride that made his heart beat faster, almost painfully. "Yes, a very good one, Joyce."

"Would you pay a lot of money for that, Dad?"

"Is it expensive?" asked Golder, his rare, severe smile playing at the corner of his mouth. "I'd be amazed . . . These days, there are princes all over the place."

"Yes, but I'm in love with this one . . ." A profound, passionate expression swept across her face, making her grow pale.

"You know he has nothing, not a penny?"

"I know. But I'm rich."

"We'll see."

"Oh!" Joyce said suddenly. "It's just that I have to have everything on earth, otherwise I'd rather die! Everything! Everything!" she repeated with an imperious, feverish look in her eyes. "I don't know how the others do it! Daphne sleeps with old Behring for his money, but I need love, youth, everything the world has to offer . . ."

He sighed. "Money . . ."

She interrupted him with a happy, impetuous gesture. "Money . . . Money too, of course, or rather beautiful dresses, jewellery! Everything. I mean it, poor Dad! I'm so madly in love with all of it. I so want to be happy, if only you knew! Otherwise, I really would rather die, I swear . . . But I'm not worried. I've always had everything I've ever wanted . . ."

Golder lowered his head, then, forcing himself to smile, whispered, "My poor Joyce, you're mad . . . You've been in love with someone ever since you were twelve years old."

"Yes, but this time . . ." she gave him a hard, stubborn look, "I really love him . . . Give him to me, Dad."

"Like the car?" He smiled soberly. "Come on, let's go. Put on your coat and let's go downstairs..."

In the car, Hoyos and Gloria—covered in jewellery and as stiff and sparkling in the darkness as some heathen idol—were waiting for them.

IT WAS MIDNIGHT when Gloria suddenly leaned towards her husband who was sitting opposite her.

"You're as pale as a ghost, David, what's wrong? Are you that tired? We're going on to Cibourne, you know . . . It might be better if you went home."

Joyce had heard her. "Dad, that's an excellent idea," she called out. "Come on, I'll take you back. I'll meet you at Cibourne later, all right, Mummy? Daphne, I'm taking your car," she continued, turning towards the younger of the two Mannering women.

"Don't smash it up," Daphne warned in a voice made hoarse from opium and alcohol.

Golder motioned to the maître d': "The bill!"

He had said it automatically, but then remembered that, according to Gloria, someone else had invited them to the Miramar. Nevertheless, all the other men had quickly turned away; only Hoyos looked at him with a wry smile and said nothing. Golder shrugged his shoulders and paid.

"Let's go, Joy."

It was a beautiful night. They got into Daphne's small convertible. Joyce started the engine and set off like the wind. The poplar trees that lined the road fell away and disappeared as if into an abyss.

"Joyce, you're mad . . ." shouted Golder, who'd gone somewhat pale. "One night you're going to kill yourself on these roads."

She didn't reply but slowed down a little.

As they approached the town, she looked at him with wide, wild eyes. "Were you afraid, Dad?"

"You're going to kill yourself," he repeated.

She shrugged. "So what? It's a good way to die . . ."

She placed her lips against a scratch on her hand that was bleeding. "On a beautiful night . . . wearing a ball gown . . ." she said. "You just drive for a while . . . and then it's over."

"Be quiet!" he shouted, horrified.

She laughed. "Poor old Dad . . ." Then added, "Well, out you get, we're here."

Golder looked up. "What? But we're at the casino! Oh, I see now . . ."

"We'll leave right away if you want," she said.

She sat motionless, looking at him and smiling. She knew very well that, once he saw the brightly lit windows of the casino, the silhouettes of the gamblers walking back and forth behind them, and the small, narrow balcony that overlooked the sea, he wouldn't want to leave.

"All right then, but just for an hour . . ."

Ignoring the valets standing on the steps, Joyce let out a wild cry. "Oh, Dad, I do love you so! I just know you're going to win, you'll see!"

He laughed. "You won't have a penny of it, no matter what, I'm warning you, my girl."

They went into the casino; some of the young women who were wandering from table to table recognised Joyce and gave her a friendly smile.

"Oh, Dad," she sighed, "when will *I* be allowed to play? I do so want to . . ."

But he had already stopped listening to her, and instead was looking at his cards with trembling hands. She had to call him several times. Finally he turned round sharply and shouted, "What is it? What do you want? Stop bothering me!"

"I'll be over there," she said, pointing to a window seat by the wall, "all right?"

"Fine, go wherever you want, just leave me be!"

Joyce laughed, lit a cigarette, and sat down on the hard little velvet bench, tucking her legs under her and toying with her pearls. From where she was, all she could see were the crowds of people surrounding the tables: the men were silent and trembling, the women all eagerly reaching out their necks in the same bizarre way in order to see the cards, the money . . . Strange men

paced up and down in front of Joyce; now and again, to amuse
herself, she would lower her eyes and give one of them a long,
mysterious look—feminine, passionate, and seductive—that
would make him stop in his tracks, almost without realising it.
She would then burst out laughing, look away, and continue
waiting.

Once, when the crowd parted to let in some new players, she
had a clear view of Golder. The sudden, strange ageing of his
heavy, furrowed face, greenish beneath the harsh light, filled her
with vague anxiety.

"He's so pale . . . What's wrong with him? Is he losing?" she
wondered.

She raised herself up, eagerly straining to see, but the crowd
had already closed in around the tables.

"Damn! Damn!" she said to herself, frowning nervously.
"What if I went over to him? No, if you want someone to win,
you bring them bad luck."

She searched the room until her eyes alighted upon a young
man she didn't know who was walking past her with a beautiful,
half-naked young woman. She gestured to them urgently. "Tell
me, what's happening over there? That old man, Golder, is he
winning?"

"No, the other sly old fox is winning, Donovan," replied the
woman, naming a gambler who was famous in casinos all over
the world. Joyce threw down her cigarette in rage.

"He has to win, he has to," she murmured in despair. "I want
my car! I want . . . I want to go to Spain with Alec! Just the two
of us, free . . . I've never spent an entire night with him, sleeping
in his arms . . . My darling Alec . . . Oh, he has to win! Please,
God, let him win!"

The night passed. In spite of herself, Joyce let her head fall on
to her arms. The smoke was burning her eyes.

She vaguely heard, as if from the depths of a dream, someone
laugh as they pointed to her: "Look, there's little Joyce, sleeping.
Look how pretty she is . . ."

She smiled, stroked her pearls, then fell into a deep sleep. A
little later, she half opened her eyes; the windows of the casino
were becoming a paler shade of pink.

She lifted up her heavy head with difficulty and looked around. There were fewer people; Golder was still playing. "He's winning now," she heard someone say. "A while ago, he'd lost nearly a million . . ."

The sun was rising. Instinctively she turned her face towards the light, then went back to sleep. It was daytime when she felt someone shaking her; she woke up, held out her hands, then closed them over the crumpled banknotes that her father, standing over her, slid between her fingers. "Oh, Dad," she murmured joyously, "so it's true! You really did win?"

He didn't move; the stubble that had grown during the night covered his cheeks like thick ash.

"No," he said; he was having trouble articulating his words. "I lost more than a million, I think, then I won it back and fifty thousand francs more for you. That's all. Let's go."

He turned around and walked with difficulty towards the door. She followed him, still barely awake, dragging her large white velvet coat along the floor, her hands overflowing with banknotes. Suddenly, she thought she saw Golder stop, stagger.

"I must be dreaming . . ." she murmured. "Has he been drinking?" And at that very moment, his large body collapsed in a strange and terrifying way: he raised both arms in the air, waved them about, then fell to the floor with a deep, dull moan that seemed to rise up as if from the living roots of a falling tree that has been struck right through its heart.

"COULD YOU MOVE away from the window, Madame?" whispered the nurse. "You're in the doctor's way."

Gloria took a few steps back without removing her eyes from the bed. Golder's heavy head was thrown back and motionless; it made a deep impression in the pillow. "He looks dead," she thought, and shuddered.

He seemed completely unconscious. Although the doctor, leaning over his large, inert body, was feeling his pulse, listening to his heart, he didn't move a muscle, didn't even groan.

Nervously twisting her necklace in her hands, Gloria looked away. Was he going to die? "It's his own fault," she muttered angrily. "Why did he have to go and play cards? I bet you're happy now, you fool," she whispered, as if talking to him directly. "My God, think of all the money this is going to cost! Just let him get better . . . Just let it not go on for too long. I'll go mad! What a terrible night I've had . . ."

She recalled how she had spent the whole night in this bedroom, waiting for Dr. Ghédalia, wondering at every moment whether Golder was going to die, right there, right in front of her eyes . . . It had been horrible.

"Poor David . . . His eyes . . ."

He was staring at her again, with that lost look. He was afraid of death. She shrugged her shoulders. All the same, people don't die like that . . . "This is just what I needed!" she thought, secretly looking at herself in the mirror.

She made a sudden gesture of frustration and anger, then sat down, straight-backed and stiff, in an armchair.

Meanwhile, Ghédalia had pulled the sheet back up over Golder's chest and stood up. He let out a vague moan.

"Well? What is it?" Gloria asked anxiously. "Is it serious? Will he be well again soon? Will he be ill for a long time? Tell me the truth, I'm begging you, I can take it . . ."

The doctor leaned back against his chair, slowly stroked his black beard, and smiled.

"My dear Madame," he said in a melodious voice that flowed like milk, "I can see you're very upset. However, there's no reason to get in a state . . . Yes, I know, I know . . . His fainting like that frightened us, didn't it? Worried us somewhat . . . But that's only natural. After a week or ten days of rest, he'll be fine. He's just tired, overworked . . . Alas, we all grow a little older with each passing day, don't we, Monsieur? Our arteries aren't twenty years old any more. We can't stay young forever . . ."

"You see," Gloria exclaimed passionately, "I knew it all along. The least little thing and you think you're about to die. Look at him! Well, say something, speak, for goodness sake!"

"No," Ghédalia intervened, "no, he mustn't say a word, on the contrary! Rest, rest, and more rest! We'll give him a little injection to calm his nerves, and then, dear Madame, we shall leave him in peace."

"But how do you feel?" Gloria repeated impatiently. "Do you feel better? David?"

He made a weak gesture with his hands, and moved his lips; she saw rather than heard him say, "I'm in pain . . ."

"Come along, Madame, let's leave him alone," Ghédalia said once again. "He cannot speak, but he can hear us very well, isn't that so, Monsieur?" he added cheerfully, glancing furtively at the nurse.

He went out; Gloria joined him in the next room.

"It's nothing, is it?" she started to say. "Oh, he's so impressionable and nervous, it's awful . . . If you only knew what a terrible night I had with him!"

The doctor solemnly raised his small, white, chubby hand. "I must stop you there, Madame," he said in a completely different tone of voice. "My very first rule, which is un-wa-ver-ing, is never to allow my patients to have the slightest idea of what is wrong with them, when their illness is serious . . . But, alas, to their families I owe the truth, and my second rule is never to hide the truth from my patient's family . . . Never!" he repeated, emphatically.

"What are you saying? Is he going to die?"

The doctor gave a look that was both surprised and shrewd, as if to say, "I can see there's no point in putting on kid gloves here." He sat down, crossed his legs and, tilting his head slightly backwards, replied nonchalantly, "Not imminently, dear Madame . . ."

"What's wrong with him?"

"Angina pectoris." He hammered home the Latin words with obvious pleasure. "In simple words, a heart attack."

She said nothing. "He could live for a long time," he added. "Five, ten, even fifteen years, with a careful diet and the appropriate medical attention. Naturally, he will have to stop working. Nothing must upset him or fatigue him. He needs a calm life—peace, routine, no extremes of emotion. Complete rest. At all times . . . Then, and only then, can I give you my assurances that he will survive, insofar as it is possible to give any assurances whatsoever, for this is an illness, alas, that is full of sudden surprises. We aren't gods, after all . . ."

He smiled pleasantly. "Naturally, it is out of the question to talk to him about it now. You can see that for yourself, Madame, for he is in terrible pain . . . But in a week or ten days, we might be able to hope that the worst is over. That will be the time to give him the ultimatum."

"But it isn't possible for him to give up work . . ." Gloria murmured in a strained voice. "It just isn't possible . . ." Ghédalia said nothing. "It would kill him," Gloria concluded nervously.

"Madame," he replied, smiling, "believe me when I say I have seen many cases like this. Some of the most powerful men in the world are amongst my clientele, if I may say so . . . I once took care of a famous banker (for whom, I might add, my colleagues had unanimously declared there was no hope at all . . . but that's beside the point). That gentleman suffered from the very same illness as Monsieur Golder . . . And my verdict was exactly the same. His friends and family feared he wouldn't last long . . . Well, this great financier is still alive. It's been fifteen years! He became a passionate and highly knowledgeable collector of Renaissance silverware, and now owns a very great number of remarkable pieces, including a silver-gilt ewer believed to be the first creation of the great Cellini, a real masterpiece . . . I dare say that the contemplation of such beautiful, rare objects gives him pleasures he has never before experienced. You can be sure that, after the first few weeks of inevitable restlessness have passed, your husband will also discover his . . . how can I put it? . . . his hobby. Collecting enamels, gems, taking up more worldly pleasures, perhaps? Men are just big children . . ."

"You fool," thought Gloria. She was suddenly filled with bitter amusement at the idea of David spending his time with rare books, a medal collection, or other women . . . Good Lord, the man was an imbecile! And just how did he think they would live? Buy food? Clothes? Did he think that money grew on trees?

She stood up. "Thank you very much, Doctor," she said, nodding to him. "I'll think about what you've said . . ."

"Of course, I'll keep informed of my patient's progress," said Ghédalia, with a little smile, "and I think it would be better to let me be the one who explains everything to him later on. It takes a lot of tact, delicacy . . . We doctors, alas, are used to it. We heal the soul as well as the body."

He kissed her hand and left. She was alone.

Silently she paced the long, empty landing. She knew only too well—had always known—that he had never put aside a penny for her. Everything had been spent, gone into some business venture or other . . . So what now? "Millions on paper, of course, but cash in hand, nothing, not a penny," she hissed angrily between clenched teeth. "What are you worried about?" he had said. "I'm still here . . ." The fool! Surely, at sixty-eight, you should consider the possibility of death every day! Wasn't his first obligation to make sure he had left his wife a sufficient and decent amount of money? They had nothing. Once he gave up doing business, there would be nothing left. Business . . . a river of money that would dry up . . . "There might be a million," she thought, "maybe two, if we scraped the bottom of the barrel . . ." She shrugged her shoulders furiously. The way they lived, a million would last only six months. Six months . . . and to cap it all, she'd have to take care of him, a useless, bed-ridden man who was dying. "As if I need him to live another fifteen years!" she shouted out loud, hatred in her voice.

"Really . . . for all the happiness he's given me! No, no . . . " She detested him. He was mean, old, and ugly. All he really loved in this world was money, bloody money, and he wasn't even capable of holding on to it! He had never loved her . . . If he showered her with jewels, it was to make her a living symbol of his own wealth, a showcase, and ever since Joyce had started growing up, all that had been transferred to her . . . Joyce? Oh, he loved *her*, all right . . . Because she was beautiful, young, happy. Pride! He had nothing but pride and vanity in his heart! As for her, if she so much as asked for a diamond, a new ring, he would make such a scene, shouting, "Leave me alone! I haven't got any more money. Are you trying to kill me?" Other men worked as hard as he. *They* didn't consider themselves stronger or more intelligent than everyone else in the world, and at least, when they were old, when they died, they left their wives well provided for! Some women were so lucky, while she . . . The truth was he had never cared about her, never loved her. If he had, he wouldn't have had a moment's peace knowing that she had nothing . . . nothing except the pitiful little bit of money she had managed to put aside by making great sacrifices . . . "But that's my money, mine and mine alone! If he thinks that I'm going to support him with that! No thank you. I've had it with keeping men," she murmured, thinking of Hoyos. "No, let him sort himself out . . . " After all, why should she tell him the truth, for heaven's sake? She knew very well that, with his obsessive Jewish fear of death, he would give everything up in a flash. All he'd think about would be his precious health, his own life . . . The selfish coward. "Is it my fault that, after all these years, he hasn't been able to make enough money to die in peace? And right now, just when his business affairs are in such a horrible mess, it would be madness . . . Later on . . . I know what's happening now, I'll keep an eye on things. That deal he was talking about starting: 'something interesting,' he called it. After he's made the deal, that will be the time. It could even prove useful, to stop him from getting involved in some other mad project . . . There will be plenty of time . . . "

She hesitated, glanced at the door, walked over to a small writing desk in the corner.

Dear Doctor, I am beside myself with worry and so have decided,
after careful consideration, to have my dear patient taken to Paris
as a matter of urgency. Please find enclosed, with my sincerest
thanks . . .

She threw down the pen and quickly crossed the corridor to
Golder's bedroom. The nurse wasn't there. Golder seemed to be
asleep. His hands were trembling. She glanced in his direction,
then looked around until she saw his clothes lying over a chair.
Picking up his jacket, she reached into the pocket, pulled out his
wallet, and opened it. Inside was a single thousand-franc note,
folded in four; she hid it in her hand.

The nurse came in.

"He seems calmer," she said, nodding towards the patient.

Embarrassed, Gloria bent down and touched her husband's
cheek with her painted lips. Golder let out a moan and weakly
waved his hands about, as if trying to push away her cold pearls
from his chest. Gloria stood up and sighed.

"It's better if I go. He doesn't know who I am."

GHÉDALIA RETURNED TO the house that same evening.

"I couldn't let Monsieur Golder leave," he said, "without making it clear that I can accept no responsibility for him. You see, Madame, the fact is that your husband is in no condition to be moved. Perhaps I didn't explain myself well enough this morning..."

"On the contrary," murmured Gloria, "you frightened me in a way that was perhaps...excessive?"

She fell silent; they looked at each other for a moment without speaking. Ghédalia seemed to hesitate.

"Would you like me to examine the patient again, Madame? I'm having dinner at Blues Villa, Mrs. Mackay's house...I don't have to be there for another half hour. I would be only too happy, I promise you, to be able to make a less distressing diagnosis."

"Thank you," she replied grudgingly. She showed him into Golder's room, then went back into the drawing room and stood behind the closed door, listening; he was talking to the nurse in hushed tones. She moved away from the door, a dark look in her eyes, then went and leaned against the window.

Fifteen minutes later, he came in, rubbing his little white hands together.

"Well?"

"Well, my dear lady, there has been such an improvement that I am now inclined to believe that we are dealing with an attack brought about purely by nerves...That is to say, not by a coronary lesion...It is difficult to be absolutely certain, given our patient's state of exhaustion, but I can confirm that as far as the future is concerned, I can already say it is clearly possible to be entirely more optimistic. It certainly won't be necessary for Monsieur Golder to retire for many years to come..."

"Really?" said Gloria.

"Yes."

He remained silent, then said casually, "Still, I must reiterate that in his current condition, he must not be moved. However, you will have to do what you think best. My conscience is now clear and relieved, I must say, of a great burden."

"Oh, there's no question of moving him now, Doctor . . ."

She held out her hand to him, smiling. "I thank you from the bottom of my heart. I do hope you will agree to forget a very understandable moment of doubt and continue to care for my poor dear husband?"

He pretended to hesitate, hedged for a moment, and finally promised he would.

From then on, every day for nearly two weeks, his red and white car stopped in front of Golder's house. After that, Ghédalia suddenly disappeared. Golder's first conscious act, a little while later, was to sign a cheque for twenty thousand francs to pay for the doctor's services.

On that day, they had sat the patient up on his pillows for the first time. Gloria, her arm behind his shoulders, helped him to lean forward while she held the open cheque-book in her other hand. She looked at him surreptitiously. He'd changed so much. Especially his nose . . . It had never been that shape before, she thought: enormous and hooked, like the nose of an old Jewish moneylender. And his flabby, trembling flesh smelled of fever and sweat. She picked up the pen that his weak hand had let fall on to the bed, splattering ink over the sheets.

"Do you feel better now, David?"

He didn't reply. For nearly two weeks, all he had said was "I can't breathe" or "I'm in pain," mumbling in a strange, hoarse voice that only the nurse seemed to understand. He lay stretched out, eyes closed, his arms tight against his sides, as silent and still as a corpse. Nevertheless, when Ghédalia left, the nurse would lean over him to tuck in his sheets and whisper, "He was pleased . . ." and he would raise one quivering eyelid and fix her with a long, hard stare that contained a profound expression of pleading and distress. "He understands everything . . ." the nurse thought. And yet, even later on, when he was able to give orders, it was the same; he never asked her or anyone else what was wrong with him, how long it would last, when he could get out of bed. He seemed content with Gloria's vague assurances: "You'll be feeling better soon... You're overworked... You should give up smoking, you know... Tobacco is bad for you, David... No more gambling... You're not twenty any more..."

After Gloria left, he asked for some cards. He played patience for hours on end, a tray placed across his knees. His sight had deteriorated because of his illness; he wore his glasses all the time now, thick glasses with silver frames, so heavy that they were constantly slipping off on to the bed. He would fumble about looking for them, his trembling hands getting tangled in the folds of the sheets. When he had finished a game, he would shuffle the cards and start again.

That evening, the nurse had left the window and shutters open: it was very hot. It wasn't until much later, when night was falling, that she tried to put a shawl across Golder's shoulders; he pushed it away impatiently.

"There, there, you mustn't get angry, Monsieur Golder, there's a breeze coming in from the sea. You don't want to get ill again."

"Good Lord," Golder growled, his voice weak and breathless, hesitating on every word, "when will everyone leave me the hell alone? When will I finally be able to get out of bed?"

"The doctor said at the end of the week, if the weather's good."

Golder frowned. "The doctor... Why doesn't the doctor come to see me?"

"I think he's been called to Madrid for a consultation."

"Do... do you know him?"

She could see that anxious, eager look in his eyes. "Oh, yes, Monsieur Golder! Of course."

"Is he really... a good doctor?"

"Very good."

He leaned back against his cushions, lowered his eyes, then whispered, "I've been ill for a long time..."

"It's all over now."

"All over."

He felt his chest, raised his head, stared at the nurse. "Why does it hurt here?" he suddenly asked, his lips quivering.

"There? Oh . . ."

She gently took his hand and put it back down on the sheet.

"You know very well, don't you? You heard the doctor? It was an anxiety attack. Nothing serious."

"Nothing serious?" He sighed, automatically sitting up to start playing cards again.

"So it's not my . . . heart?"

He had spoken quietly and quickly, obviously very upset, and without looking at her.

"No, no," she replied, "come on now . . ."

Ghédalia had given her strict instructions not to tell him the truth. Still, he'd have to be told sooner or later . . . But that wasn't up to her. Poor man, he was so afraid of dying . . . She pointed to the cards.

"Look, you've made a mistake. You need the ace of clubs here, not the king. Let me see . . . put the nine there."

"What day is it?" he asked, without listening to her.

"Tuesday."

"Already? I should have been in London by now," he said quietly.

"Oh, you'll have to travel less now, Monsieur Golder . . ."

She saw him suddenly go completely white.

"Why?" he whispered in a broken voice. "Why? What are you saying, for God's sake? You must be mad! Have I been forbidden to travel . . . to leave here?"

"Not at all," she reassured him quickly. "Where did you get such an idea? I didn't say anything of the sort. It's just that you have to take care for a while. That's all."

She leaned over and wiped his face; great, heavy drops of sweat were running down his cheeks, like tears.

"She's lying," thought Golder. "I can hear it in her voice. What's wrong with me? My God, what's wrong with me? And why aren't they telling me the truth? I'm not a woman, for God's sake . . ."

Weakly, he pushed her aside and turned away. "Close the window, I'm cold."

"Would you like to get some sleep?" she asked, as she walked quietly across the room.

"Yes. Leave me in peace."

SHORTLY AFTER ELEVEN o'clock, the nurse was woken by Golder's voice in the next room. She rushed in and found him sitting on the bed, red-faced and waving his arms about.

"Write . . . I want to write . . ."

"He's got a high fever," she thought. She tried to get him back into bed, reasoning with him as if he were a child. "No, no, not now, it's too late. Tomorrow, Monsieur Golder, tomorrow . . . You have to get some sleep now."

Golder cursed her and repeated his order, trying to speak in a more lucid, calmer tone of voice.

She finally ended up bringing him his pen and a sheet of writing paper. But he could manage to scribble only a few letters. His hand was so heavy and painful, he could barely move it. He groaned and murmured, "You write . . ."

"To whom?"

"To Doctor Weber. You'll find his address in the Paris telephone directory, over there. 'Please come at once. Urgent.' Then my name and address. Understand?"

"Yes, Monsieur Golder."

He seemed appeased, asked for something to drink, then dropped back on to his pillows. "Open the windows and shutters," he said, "I can't breathe . . ."

"Do you want me to stay with you?"

"No. There's no point. I'll call if . . . The telegram, tomorrow, as soon as the post office opens, at seven o'clock . . ."

"Yes, yes. Don't worry. Get some sleep."

He dragged himself over on to his side; he was wheezing and it was agony to breathe; the pain wouldn't go away. He lay still, looking sadly out the window. The big white curtains were billowing in the breeze like balloons. For a long time, he just listened to the tide . . . One, two, three . . . The sound of the waves crashing against the rocks of the lighthouse in the distance; then the light, rhythmical lapping of the water as it flowed between the pebbles. Silence . . . The house seemed empty.

"What is it?" he thought again. "What's wrong with me? Is it my heart? My heart? They're lying. I know they are. You have to be able to face things . . ."

He paused, nervously wringing his hands. He was trembling. He didn't have the courage to say the word, or even think it clearly: death . . . He looked at the dark sky filling the window with a kind of horror. "I can't. No, not yet, no . . . There's still work to do. I can't . . . *Adenoï*," he whispered in despair, suddenly remembering the forgotten name of the Lord. "You know very well that I can't . . . But why aren't they telling me the truth? Why?"

It was so strange. While he was ill, he'd believed everything they'd wanted him to. Ghédalia . . . And Gloria. Still, he *was* getting better, that much was true. He was allowed to get up, go outside . . . But he didn't trust that Ghédalia. He could barely remember what he looked like. And as for his name . . . It was the name of a charlatan. Gloria couldn't do anything right. Why hadn't it occurred to her to call for Weber, the most highly esteemed doctor in France? When she'd had that attack of indigestion, she'd called him immediately, of course. Whereas for him . . . Golder . . . Anything would do for him, wouldn't it? He pictured Weber's face, his penetrating, weary eyes that seemed able to see straight into your heart. "I'll just say to him," he murmured, "that I have to know, I have my work, that's all there is to it. He'll understand."

And yet . . . What was the point, for God's sake? Why know in advance? It would happen in a flash, like when he'd fainted there in the casino. But forever, then, forever . . . My God . . .

"No, no! There's no illness that can't be cured! Come on . . . I keep saying, 'My heart, my heart,' like some sort of idiot, but even if it is . . . With medical attention, a diet, I don't know . . . Perhaps? Surely . . . Business . . . Yes, business . . . Well, that's the worst part. But I won't always be involved in business, not forever. There's the Teisk deal now, of course. That will have to be sorted out first. But that will only take six months, maybe a year," he thought, with the invincible optimism of a businessman. "Yes, a year at the most. And then, that will be that. I'll be able to rest, to live a quiet life. I'm old... Everyone has to stop someday. I don't want to work until the day I die. I want to enjoy life. I'll stop smoking... I'll give up drinking, I won't gamble any more... If it is my heart, I need peace and quiet. I'll have to stay calm, not get upset, or..." He gave a bitter laugh as a thought crossed his mind. "Business without stress! I'll die a hundred deaths before I finish the Teisk deal, a hundred deaths..."

Wincing, he turned over on to his back. He suddenly felt extremely weak and weary. He looked at the time. It was very late. Nearly four o'clock. He wanted something to drink. Feeling for the glass of lemonade that was left for him at night, he accidentally knocked it over on to the wooden table.

The nurse woke up with a start and peered into the room through the partially open door.

"Did you sleep a little?"

"Yes," he replied mechanically.

He drank greedily, handed her the glass, then suddenly stopped to listen to something. "Did you hear that? In the garden... What is it? Go and see."

The nurse leaned out of the window.

"It's Mademoiselle Joyce coming home, I think."

"Call her."

The nurse sighed and went out on to the landing; Joyce's high stiletto heels were clicking on the floor.

"What's wrong?" Golder heard his daughter say. "Is he worse?"

She ran into the room, flicked a switch, and light flooded down from the ceiling.

"I wonder how you can leave it so dark in here, Dad. It's so gloomy with just that old night light."

"Where have you been?" murmured Golder. "I haven't seen you in two days."

"Oh, I can't remember... I had things to do..."

"Where were you tonight?"

"Saint-Sébastien. Maria-Pia gave a wonderful ball. Look at my dress. Do you like it?"

She opened her large coat. Beneath it she appeared half-naked, the pink chiffon dress so low-cut that it barely covered her small, delicate breasts; she was wearing a pearl choker, and her golden hair was tousled by the wind. Golder looked at her for a long time without saying anything.

"Dad, you're acting so funny! What's wrong with you? Why aren't you answering me? Are you angry?"

She sprang up on the bed and knelt at his feet. "Dad, listen . . . I danced with the Prince of Wales tonight. I heard him tell Maria-Pia: 'She's the loveliest girl I've ever seen . . .' He asked her my name! Doesn't that make you happy?" she murmured with a joyous laugh that brought out two childlike dimples in her powdered cheeks. She leaned so far over the sick man's chest that the nurse, standing behind the bed, gestured for her to go away. But Golder, who usually felt suffocated by the weight of the sheets on his heart, let her rest her head and bare arms against him without saying a word.

"You're happy, dear old Dad, I knew it, I just knew it," cried Joy.

Golder's tired, closed lips grimaced in an attempt at a smile.

"You were cross because I left you to go out dancing, weren't you? But it's still me who made you smile for the first time. Say, Dad, did you hear? I bought the car! If you could only see how beautiful it is. It goes like the wind . . . You're such a dear, Dad."

She yawned and ran her fingers through her dishevelled golden hair.

"I'm going to bed, now. I'm exhausted . . . I didn't get home until six in the morning yesterday . . . I'm worn out, and tonight I danced and danced . . ."

She half closed her eyes and played with her bracelets and hummed softly, as if in a dream, "*Marquita—Marquita—your secret desires—shine in your eyes—when you dance* . . . Good night, Dad, sleep well. Sweet dreams . . ."

She leaned over and gently kissed his cheek.

"Off you go," he whispered. "Go to bed, Joy . . ."

She went out. He listened until the sound of her foot-steps faded, his face relaxing into an expression of peace. His daughter . . . her pink dress . . . She brought joy and life with her.

He felt calmer, stronger now. "Death," he thought. "I'm just letting myself get depressed, that's all. It's laughable. I'll have to work and keep on working. Even Tübingen is sixty-eight. For men like us, work is the only thing that keeps us alive."

The nurse had switched off the light and brewed some herbal tea over the small spirit lamp. He suddenly turned towards her. "The telegram," he murmured, "don't bother . . . Tear it up."

"Very well, Monsieur."

As soon as she left, he fell into a peaceful sleep.

BY THE TIME Golder had recovered, it was already the end of September, but the weather was better than in the middle of summer, without even the slightest breeze; the sky was bathed in a light as gold as honey.

That day, instead of going back upstairs to rest after lunch as he usually did, Golder sat on the terrace and had his cards brought to him. Gloria wasn't at home. A little later on, Hoyos appeared.

Golder peered at him over his glasses without saying anything. Hoyos adjusted one of the recliners so that its back nearly touched the ground, stretched out on it as if it were a bed, and let his fingertips contentedly graze the cold marble floor.

"It's beautiful out here," he murmured. "Not too hot. I detest the heat . . ."

"Would you happen to know," asked Golder, "where my daughter went for lunch?"

"Joyce? To the Mannerings', I suppose. Why?"

"No reason. Just that she's never here."

"It's like that at her age. Say, why did you get her that new car? She's like a woman possessed now . . ."

Hoyos raised himself up on his elbow and surveyed the garden. "Look, there's your Joy, over there!"

He went over to the balustrade and called out, "Hey, Joy! What's going on? Are you leaving? You're a mad little thing, you know!"

"What?" grumbled Golder.

Hoyos was laughing uncontrollably.

"She's so funny . . . My word, she's got her menagerie with her . . . Jill . . . Why not take your dolls with you too? No? But what about your little prince, eh? Aren't you taking him, my little beauty? Look at her, Golder, she's hilarious."

"What's that?" exclaimed Joyce. "Is Dad there? I've been looking everywhere for him."

She ran up on to the terrace. She was wearing her travelling coat, a little hat pulled down nearly over her eyes, and carried her dog under one arm.

"Where are you going?" asked Golder, standing up abruptly.

"Guess!"

"How do you expect me to know what's going on in your silly little head?" cried Golder, annoyed. "And answer when I speak to you, will you?"

Joy sat down, crossed her legs, looked at him defiantly and started laughing happily. "I'm going to Madrid."

"What?"

"Oh, you didn't know?" Hoyos interjected, "Yes, she's decided to drive to Madrid... All by herself... That's right, Joy, isn't it? You're going alone?" he murmured, smiling. "Of course, she'll probably get into an accident on the way, she drives so fast, but that's what she wants, there's nothing anyone can do. So, you didn't know?"

Golder stamped his foot angrily.

"Joyce! Are you out of your mind? What's all this about?"

"I told you ages ago that I'd be going to Madrid as soon as I had a new car... Why are you so surprised?"

"I forbid you to go, do you hear me?" Golder said slowly.

"I hear you. And?"

Golder made a sudden movement towards her, his hand raised. But Joyce continued laughing, her face just a little paler. "Dad! Now *you* want to slap me? Go ahead, I couldn't care less. But you'll pay dearly for it."

Golder lowered his arm, without touching her. "Go on then!" he said, the words barely audible through his clenched teeth. "Go wherever the hell you like . . ."

He sat down and went back to his cards.

"Come on, Dad," murmured Joyce, affectionately, "don't be cross. I could have left without saying anything, you know. And besides, why should it upset you?"

"You're going to smash up your pretty little face, my Joy," said Hoyos, stroking her hand. "You'll see . . ."

"That's my business. Come on, Dad, let's call a truce . . ."

She slipped her hands around his neck and gave him a hug. "Dad . . ."

"It's not your place to suggest a truce. Leave me alone! The way you speak to your father!" he said, pushing her away.

"Don't you think it's a little late to be teaching your pretty little girl manners?" Hoyos sniggered.

Golder banged his fist down on to the cards.

"Get the hell out of here!" he growled at Hoyos, "and as for you, Joyce, just go. Do you think I'm going to beg you?"

"Dad! You always spoil everything for me! Everything I like doing! Everything that makes me happy!" shouted Joyce, with tears of exasperation welling up in her eyes. "Leave me alone! Just leave me alone! Do you think it's been fun around here while you've been ill? I can't take it any more. 'Walk quietly, speak softly, don't laugh' . . . There's been nothing but sad old angry faces to look at. I want to get away from it all . . ."

"Go on then. Who's stopping you? So you're going alone . . ."

"Yes."

Golder spoke more quietly. "You don't imagine for a moment that I believe you, do you? You're taking that little gigolo. Slut. Do you think I'm blind? I know there's nothing I can do about it. What *can* I do about it?" he repeated, his voice quivering. "Just don't kid yourself that you're pulling the wool over my eyes. The person who can pull the wool over old Golder's eyes, my girl, hasn't been born yet, you hear me?"

Hoyos put his hands over his mouth and laughed quietly.

"You are tiresome, the two of you," he said. "Really, Golder, there's absolutely no point making a fuss. You simply don't understand women. The only thing to do is to give in. Come and give me a kiss, my lovely Joyce."

Joyce wasn't listening; she was rubbing her head against Golder's shoulder.

"Dad, my darling Dad . . ."

He pushed her away. "Get off, you're suffocating me . . . And get going quickly, otherwise you'll be leaving too late."

"Aren't you going to kiss me?"

"Kiss you? Of course . . ." He placed his lips against her cheek.

Joy watched him. He was laying out his cards; it was as if his clumsy fingers were slipping on the wood of the table.

"Dad . . ." she said, "you know I've run out of money?"

He didn't reply. "Come on, Dad," she continued, "give me a bit of cash, please?"

"Cash for what?" asked Golder in a dry tone of voice that Joyce had never heard before.

She tried to hide her impatience, but she couldn't help wringing her hands nervously as she replied, "For what? For my trip! What do you expect me to live on in Spain? My body?"

Golder suppressed a grimace.

"And you'll be needing a lot of money, will you?" he asked while slowly counting out the thirteen cards for the first row of his game of patience.

"Well, I don't know exactly how much. Look, you're being very tedious . . . It'll be a lot, naturally, just like always. Ten, twelve, twenty thousand . . ."

"Ah!"

She slipped her hand into Golder's jacket pocket and tried to take out his wallet.

"Oh, stop winding me up, Dad. Just give me the money now, will you! Give it to me!"

"No," said Golder.

"What?" cried Joyce. "What did you say?"

"I said no."

He tilted his head back and looked at her for a long while, smiling. He hadn't been able to say no this way for ages, with the clear, harsh tone of voice he'd used in the past. "No," he murmured again. He seemed to savour the shape of the word in his mouth, as if it were a piece of fruit. He slowly clasped his hands under his chin and stroked his lips with his forefinger several times.

"You seem surprised. You want to go. Go. But you've heard me, not a penny. Sort yourself out. Oh, you don't know me as well as you think, Joyce."

"I hate you!" she shouted.

He looked down and started quietly counting out his cards again. One, two, three, four . . . But when he came to the end of the row, he became confused and started repeating in a shaky voice, "One, two, three..." Then he stopped, as if he had no strength left, and sighed deeply.

"Well, you don't know me all that well, either," said Joyce. "I told you I wanted to go and I'm going. I don't need your bloody money!"

She whistled for her dog and left. A moment later, they heard the sound of the car shooting past on the road. Golder hadn't moved.

Hoyos shrugged his shoulders. "She'll manage, old boy..."

Since Golder didn't reply, Hoyos half closed his delicate, sleepy eyes and murmured with a smile, "You know nothing about women, old boy... You should have slapped her. It might have shocked her into staying. You never know with little creatures like that..."

Golder had taken his wallet out of his pocket; he turned it over and over in his hands. It was an old black leather wallet, worn out, like most of his personal belongings; the satin lining was torn, one of the gold corners was missing and an elastic band stopped the banknotes from falling out. Suddenly, Golder clenched his teeth and started banging it angrily against the table. Cards flew off in all directions. He continued pounding the wooden table, which resounded with each thump. Finally, he stopped, put the wallet back into his pocket, got up and walked past Hoyos, deliberately pushing into him with the full weight of his body.

"Now, there's a slap for you..." he said.

EVERY MORNING, GOLDER went down into the garden and walked along the tree-lined path for an hour. He moved slowly, in the shade of the great cedars, methodically counting his steps; at the fiftieth step, he would stop, lean against a tree-trunk, sniff through his pinched nostrils, and take a deep, painful breath, straining his trembling lips towards the sea breeze. Then he would start walking again, taking up the count where he left off and absent-mindedly pushing away the gravel with his cane. Wearing an old greatcoat, a woollen scarf around his neck, and a worn-out black hat, he looked strangely like some Jewish second-hand clothes merchant from a village in the Ukraine. As he walked, he would sometimes raise one shoulder, in a weary, mechanical movement, as if he were hoisting a heavy bundle of clothing or scrap iron on to his back.

On that day, he had gone out for a second time around three o'clock: it was a beautiful day. Sitting on a bench with a view of the sea, he loosened his scarf, unbuttoned the top of his coat, and cautiously breathed in. His heart was beating regularly, but there was still a continuous asthmatic wheezing as the air went in and out of his chest; the sound was sharp and faintly plaintive.

The bench was bathed in sunlight, and the garden basked in a yellowish glow, as transparent as fine oil.

The old man closed his eyes, let out a sigh that was a mixture of sadness and contentment, then stretched out his perpetually frozen hands and rubbed them gently against his knees. He liked the heat. No doubt, in Paris or London, the weather was awful... He was expecting a visit from the director of Golmar; he'd called the day before to say he would be coming... That meant, time was up; he would have to leave. God only knew where he would need to drag himself... It was a shame he had to go... It was such a beautiful day.

He heard the crunch of footsteps on the gravel path and turned around to see Loewe coming towards him. A short, pale man, with a grey, shy, weary face, he was weighed down by an enormous briefcase, crammed full of papers.

For a long time, Loewe had been a simple employee of Golmar. Even though he had now been its director for five years, one look from Golder was still enough to make him tremble. He hurried over, hunching his shoulders, laughing nervously. Golder couldn't help thinking of what Marcus used to say: "You think you're a great businessman, my friend, but you're nothing but a speculator. You don't know how to find or choose the right people. You'll be alone for as long as you live, surrounded by beggars or fools."

"So, tell me why you've come," he asked, interrupting Loewe's long, embroiled inquiry after his health.

Loewe stopped short, sat down on the edge of the bench, sighed, and opened his briefcase.

"I'm afraid . . . Let me explain . . . You'll have to listen carefully . . . But perhaps it will be too tiring for you? Do you prefer to wait? The news I have . . ."

"Is bad," interrupted Golder, annoyed. "Naturally. Stop making speeches, for the love of God. Say what you have to say, and clearly, if that's possible for you."

"Yes, Sir," replied Loewe quickly.

He was having difficulty balancing the enormous briefcase on his knees; he held it against his chest with both hands and started pulling out bundles of letters and papers that he let fall haphazardly on to the bench.

"I can't find the letter . . ." he murmured in desperation. "Oh, yes! Here it is . . . Shall I read it to you?"

"Give it to me . . ." Golder snatched the letter from him.

He was silent as he read it, but Loewe, who was watching his every move, noticed that his lips quivered slightly.

"You see," he said quietly, as if he were apologising.

He handed Golder some other papers.

"All the problems started at the same time, as usual . . . The New York Stock Exchange, the day before yesterday, was the final blow, so to speak. But it only aggravated things . . . You were expecting it, weren't you?"

Golder looked up sharply. "What? Yes," he murmured, absent-mindedly. "Where's the report from New York?"

Seeing Loewe begin riffling through his papers again, Golder angrily swept them away with his fist.

"Couldn't you have got them in order before, for God's sake?"

"I only just arrived . . . I didn't even stop at my hotel."

"I should think not," grumbled Golder.

"You see the letter from the Bank of England?" Loewe said, coughing nervously. "If the overdraft hasn't been paid off within a week, they're going to start selling your collateral."

"We'll see about that . . . The bastards! This is Weille's doing. But he won't get his hands on it for long, that I can promise you. My overdraft with them is about four million, isn't it?"

"Yes," said Loewe, nodding. "Everyone is very negative about Golmar at the moment, very negative. The most depressing rumours have been going around the Stock Market ever since poor Monsieur Marcus . . . And your own enemies have even gone so far as to spread the most malevolent lies about your illness, Monsieur Golder . . ."

Golder shrugged his shoulders. "Well . . ."

He wasn't surprised to hear it. Nor was he surprised at the effect Marcus's suicide had had. "That must have been of some consolation to him before he died," he mused.

"None of that," he said, "is anything to worry about. I'll have a word with Weille. The thing that worries me the most is New York . . . It is absolutely essential that I go to New York. Is there nothing from Tübingen?"

"Yes, there is. A telegram arrived just as I was leaving."

"Well, give it to me for heaven's sake!"

"WILL BE IN LONDON 28TH," he read and gave a sly smile. With Tübingen's help everything would be easy to sort out.

"Send a telegram at once to Tübingen, and tell him I'll be in London the morning of the twenty-ninth."

"Yes, Sir. Excuse me, but . . . is it true what certain people are saying?"

"What are they saying?"

"Well, er, that you're the one whom Tübingen has asked to negotiate an agreement with the Soviets for the Teisk concession, and that Tübingen is buying your shares and taking you into the company? Oh, that would be wonderful, a real coup, and we'll have no trouble getting credit once it's made public . . ."

"What day is it?" Golder interrupted, making rapid calculations. "Four o'clock . . . We could still leave today . . . No, there's no point travelling on a Saturday. I absolutely must see Weille in Paris. Tomorrow, then. Monday morning in Paris; I could leave by four o'clock and be in London on Tuesday. Then I could get a ship to New York on the first. If only I could avoid going to New York. No, impossible. Though I'm supposed to be in Moscow on the fifteenth, the twentieth at the latest. It's all very tricky."

He rubbed his hands together as if he were cracking walnuts between his closed palms.

"It's not easy. I have to be everywhere at once. Well, we'll see . . ."

He fell silent. Loewe handed him a sheet of paper covered in names and figures.

"What's this?"

"Would you please take a look? It's the salary increases for the employees. Perhaps you remember? We spoke to you and Monsieur Marcus about it last April."

Golder frowned and looked at the list.

"Lambert, Mathias, fine . . . Mademoiselle Wieilhomme? Oh yes, Marcus's typist . . . the little slut who couldn't even be bothered to type a letter properly! I don't think so! The other one, yes, the little hunchback one, what's her name?"

"Mademoiselle Gassion."

"Yes, that's fine . . . Chambers? Your son-in-law? Tell me, don't you think it was enough to hire that moron? He deigns to come to the office twice a week when he's got nothing better to do, and for all the work he does . . . Not a penny, you hear me, not a penny more!"

"But in April . . ."

"In April, I had money. Now, I don't. If I gave a raise to all the freeloaders, all the spoiled little rich kids you and Marcus crammed into the offices . . . Give me your pencil."

He angrily crossed out several names.

"What about Levine? His fifth child has just been born."

"I don't give a damn!"

"Come now, Monsieur Golder, you're not as hard as all that."

"I don't like people being generous with my money, Loewe. It's very nice making promises left, right, and centre . . . but then it's up to me to sort things out when there's not a penny left in the pot, isn't it?"

He suddenly stopped speaking. A train was passing. They could hear it clearly through the still air; it was getting louder, coming closer. Golder listened with lowered head.

"Won't you reconsider?" murmured Loewe. "Levine . . . It's difficult trying to feed five children on two thousand francs a month. You have to feel sorry for him."

The train was moving further and further away. Its long whistle hovered in the air like a plea, like a fearful question.

"Sorry!" shouted Golder, suddenly angry. "Why? No one ever feels sorry for me, do they? No one has ever felt sorry for me . . ."

"Oh, Monsieur Golder . . ."

"It's true. I'm just expected to pay, pay, and keep on paying . . . That's why I've been put on this earth!"

He breathed in with difficulty, then said quietly in a different voice, "Forget about the increases I crossed out, all right? And make those reservations. We'll leave tomorrow."

"I'M LEAVING TOMORROW," Golder said abruptly as he got up from the dining table.

Gloria trembled slightly. "Oh . . . Will you be gone long?"

"Yes."

"Are you . . . sure that's a good idea, David? You're still ill."

He burst out laughing.

"Why would that matter? *I* don't have the right to be ill like everyone else, do I?"

"Oh," hissed Gloria angrily, "that tone you take to make yourself sound like a martyr."

He walked out, slamming the door so hard behind him that the chandelier swayed, the glass tinkling in the silent room.

"He's nervous," said Hoyos softly.

"Yes. Are you going out tonight? Do you want the car?"

"No thanks, darling."

Gloria turned sharply towards the servant.

"I won't be needing the driver tonight."

"Very good, Madame."

He placed a silver tray with liqueurs and cigarettes on the table and went out.

Mosquitoes were buzzing around the lamps; Gloria nervously brushed them away.

"Goodness, how irritating . . . Would you like some coffee?"

"What about Joy? Have you heard from her?"

"No."

She said nothing for a moment, then continued in a sort of rage, "It's all David's fault! He spoils that girl like a mad fool, and he doesn't even love her! She just flatters his inflated ego! As if he has anything to be proud of. She behaves like a little slut! Do you know how much money he gave her the night he collapsed at the casino? Fifty thousand francs, my darling. Charming, just charming! I heard all about it. How she was practically walking in her sleep in that gambling joint, wads of notes stuffed into her hands, just like some prostitute who'd rolled an old man! But when it comes to me, it's always the same arguments, the same old story: business is bad, he's fed up with having to work for me, et cetera! Oh, I'm so unlucky! But where Joyce is concerned . . . "

"But still, she is a charming girl . . . "

"I know," Gloria cut in.

Hoyos stood up and went over to the window to breathe in the fresh evening air.

"It's such wonderful weather. Wouldn't you like to go down to the garden?"

"If you like."

They went out together. It was a beautiful, moonless night; the large white spotlights on the terrace cast an almost theatrical light over the gravel on the path, the branches of the trees.

"Smell how delicious it is," said Hoyos. "The wind is blowing in from Spain, there's cinnamon in the air, don't you think?"

"No," she replied, curtly.

She leaned against a bench. "Let's sit down. I find it tiring walking in the dark."

He sat down beside her and lit a cigarette. For a moment, his features were caught in the flare of the lighter: his delicate eyelids were like the withered petals of dead flowers; his perfectly shaped lips were still those of a young man, bursting with life.

"Well, now, what's going on? Are we alone tonight?"

"Were you expecting someone else?" she asked absent-mindedly.

"No, not especially. I'm just surprised. The house is usually as full as a country inn when there's a fair. Mind you, I'm not complaining. We're old, my darling, and we need people and noise around us. It wasn't like that in the past, but everything changes . . . "

"In the past," she repeated. "Do you know how many years it's been? It's terrifying . . . "

"Nearly twenty!"

"Nineteen O one. The carnival in Nice in 1901, my darling. Twenty-five years."

"Yes," he whispered. "You were just a little foreigner, aimlessly wandering the streets, in your simple dress and straw hat. But that soon changed."

"You were in love with me then. Now, all you care about is my money. I can sense it, you know. Without my money . . ."

He gently shrugged his shoulders.

"Hush, now . . . Don't get yourself in a state. Being angry ages you . . . and I'm feeling very sentimental tonight. Do you remember, Gloria, how everything looked silver and blue?"

"Yes."

They fell silent, as they both suddenly remembered a street in Nice, thronging on carnival night with people wearing masks and singing as they passed by; remembered the palm trees, the moon, and the shouts of the crowd in Place Masséna . . . remembered their youth . . . the beautiful night, as sensual and simple as an Italian love song.

Suddenly he threw away his cigarette. "Oh, my darling! Enough reminiscing; it makes me feel cold as death!"

"It's true," she said, unconsciously shivering. "When I think about the past . . . I so wanted to come to Europe. I can't remember any more how David managed to get the money to pay for my trip. I travelled third class. I watched from the deck as the other women danced, covered in jewels. Why do we have to wait until we're old to have such things? And, when I got here, I lived in a little family-run boarding house. If, at the end of the month, no money had come from America, I would stay in my room with nothing but an orange for supper. You never knew that, did you? I put on a brave face. God knows, it wasn't always easy. But what I wouldn't give now for those days, those nights . . ."

"It's Joyce's turn now. It's odd how that idea both annoys and consoles me at the same time. But that's not how you feel, is it?"

"No."

"I didn't think so," he murmured.

She could sense by the way he said it that he was smiling.

"There's something I'm worried about," she said suddenly. "You've often asked me what Ghédalia said about what was wrong with . . ."

"Yes. Go on."

"Well, it was a heart attack. He could die at any moment."

"Does he know?"

"No. I . . . I arranged things so that Ghédalia wouldn't say any-thing. He wanted to make him give up work. How would we have managed? He hasn't saved any money for me, nothing, not a penny. It's just that . . . well, I didn't think he would have to leave here so soon. And tonight he looked like death. So, really, I don't know what's best any more . . . "

Hoyos was quietly clicking his fingers; he looked annoyed. "Why did you do that?"

"I thought I was doing the right thing," she said angrily. "I was thinking of you, as usual. What would happen to you if David stopped earning money? You know very well, don't you, where my money goes?"

"Oh," he said, laughing, "I'd rather die than live to see the day when women stopped paying for me. There's something about being an old lover that I find wickedly appealing."

She shrugged her shoulders impatiently.

"Oh, do be quiet! Can't you tell how nervous I am! What should I do? What would happen if I told him the truth and he dropped everything? Don't tell me he wouldn't. You don't really know him. Right now, all he cares about is his health, he's obsessed with the idea of dying. Surely you've seen him every morning in the garden, wearing that old overcoat even in the sun? Oh, my God! If I had to watch him dragging on like that for years to come! I'd sooner see him die right now! If only . . . I swear, no one would miss him."

Hoyos bent down and picked a flower; he gently rubbed it between his fingers, then inhaled its perfume on his hand.

"How wonderful that smells," he murmured, "it's divine . . . The faint aroma of pepper . . . I think it's these lovely little white carnations that are planted along the edges of the flower-beds . . . You're unfair to your husband, my darling. He's a good man."

"A good man?" she scoffed. "Do you have any idea how many people he's ruined, how much misery he's caused, how many suicides? It's because of him that Marcus, his partner, his friend of twenty-six years, killed himself! You didn't know that, did you?"

"No," he replied with seeming indifference.

"Well," she continued, "what should I do?"

"Oh, there's only one thing you can do, my poor darling. Prepare him gently, as gently as possible, make him under-stand ... I don't think he'll give up the deal he's working on at the moment. Fischl told me a bit about it, but you know that I don't really understand much about business. As far as I could work out, your husband's business affairs are in a truly terrible state at the moment. He's counting on some negotiations with the Soviets to get him back on his feet. Something to do with oil, I think ... In any case, one thing is certain: given his current financial situation, if he suddenly dies now, you'll end up with nothing but a series of terrible debts, no money at all ..."

"It's true," she murmured, "his business is in chaos; I don't think even he realises how bad it is."

"Does anyone know?"

"Well, no," she said, angrily shrugging her shoulders. "I don't think he trusts anyone, and especially not me. His business! He hides it from me as if it were his mistress!"

"Well then, you see, if he knew, if he suspected that his life was in danger, he would make provisions, I'm sure. And of course, it would be an incentive to him, as well ..."

He laughed quietly.

"His last deal, his last chance ... Just imagine ... Yes, you have to make him understand."

Both of them turned around instinctively to look at the house. On the first floor, Golder's light was on.

"He's still awake."

"I don't want to see him," she whispered. "I ... He's never understood me, never loved me. Just money, money, for as long as he's lived. He's like a robot—no heart, no feelings, nothing. I've been in his bed, slept with him, for years, and he's always been exactly as he is now: hard, cold as ice. Money, business ... Never a smile, a caress, just shouting and endless scenes. Oh, I've been so unhappy!"

She fell silent. When she moved, the light from one of the

outside lamps hanging along the path made her diamond earrings sparkle.

Hoyos smiled.

"What a beautiful night," he said dreamily. "The flowers smell so divine, it's wonderful. Your perfume is too strong, Gloria, I've told you before. It overpowers these poor little autumn roses. What silence... It's extraordinary. You can hear the sound of the sea. How peaceful the night is. Listen, there are women singing on the road. Delightful, don't you think? Those clear, beautiful voices, the night... I love this place. I would be so upset, truly upset, if this house were sold."

"Are you mad?" she murmured. "What are you talking about?"

"My God, it could happen... This house isn't in your name, is it?"

She didn't reply.

"You've tried so many times," he continued, "remember? And what did he always say? Oh, the same old song: 'I'm still here...'"

"I really should speak to him, tonight..."

"Yes, that would be best, I think."

"Right away."

"That would be best," he repeated.

She slowly stood up.

"Oh, this whole business is so upsetting. Are you staying here?"

"Yes, it's so beautiful..."

WHEN SHE WENT into Golder's room, he was sitting on the bed working, propped up on piles of crumpled pillows; his shirt was open at the neck, the unbuttoned sleeves hanging from his bare arms. He had placed the lamp on the bed, on a tray with the remains of a half-empty cup of tea, a plate full of orange peel. Its light fell full on to his bent head, making his white hair gleam eerily.

He turned sharply when the door opened and looked at Gloria, before bending even further over his work and grumbling, "What is it? What do you want now?"

"I need to speak to you," she replied coldly.

He took off his glasses and slowly wiped his puffy eyes with the corner of his handkerchief. She sat down stiffly on the bed beside him, fidgeting nervously with her pearls.

"David, listen. I really must speak to you. You're going off tomorrow . . . You're not well, you're tired . . . Have you considered that, if anything happened to you, I'd be all alone in the world?"

He listened to her with a cold, gloomy expression, without moving, without saying a word.

"David . . ."

"What do you want from me?" he asked finally, staring at her in that harsh, fearful, stubborn way he reserved for her alone. "Leave me be, I have work to do."

"What I have to say is just as important to me as your work. You won't get rid of me that easily, I can assure you."

She clenched her teeth in cold fury.

"Why are you going away so suddenly?"

"Business."

"Well, I didn't think you were going off to meet one of your mistresses!" she cried, crossly shrugging her shoulders. "Oh, do be careful, David. Don't push me too far. Where are you going? Business is really bad, isn't it?"

"Not that bad," he murmured unconvincingly.

"David!"

She was shouting nervously, in spite of herself. She made a great effort to calm down. "I am your wife, it seems to me that I have the right to be concerned with matters that affect me as much as they do you."

"Up until now," Golder said slowly, "all you've said was, 'I want money, sort it out.' And I always have. And that's how it will be until the day I die."

"Yes, yes," she interrupted impatiently, with a hint of menace in her voice, "I know, I know. Always the same old story. Your work, your work! Meanwhile, what would *I* be left with if you suddenly died! You've really got it sorted, haven't you? So that the day you die, when all your creditors pounce on me, I'll have nothing, not a penny!"

"If I die! If I die! I'm not dead yet! Am I? Well, am I?" he shouted, trembling all over. "Shut up, do you hear me? Just shut up!"

"Yes, that's it," she scoffed. "You're like an ostrich with its head in the sand! You don't want to see or understand anything. Well, that's just too bad. You've had a heart attack, my dear. You could die at any moment. Why are you looking at me like that? Oh, you must be the biggest coward in the world. Call yourself a man? A man! Just look at this wimp. I think he's going to faint. Oh, really, don't look at me like that," she said with a shrug. "You could live another twenty years, the doctor said so. It's just, well, what can you do? You have to face such things. After all, we're all mortal. Remember Nicolas Lévy, Porjès, and all the others who juggled enormous fortunes, and when they died, what was left for their widows? An overdraft. Well, that's not what I want to happen to me, do you understand? Make some arrangements. To start with, put this house in my name. If you were a good husband, you would have made sure I had a proper fortune of my own long ago! I have nothing at all!"

She gave a sudden scream. Golder had punched the tray and

the lamp, knocking them to the ground. They shattered on the floor; the crash of glass broke the silence of the sleeping house.

"Brute! You brute! You beast!" Gloria exclaimed. "You haven't changed, have you? You haven't changed a bit. You're still the little Jew who sold rags and scrap metal in New York, from a sack on your back. Do you remember? Do you?"

"And what about you? Do you remember Kishinev, and that little shop of your moneylender father's in the Jewish quarter? You weren't called Gloria then, were you? Well? Havke! Havke!"

He hurled the Yiddish name at her like an insult, shaking his fist. She grabbed him by the shoulders, burying his head in her chest, to drown out his shouting.

"Shut up, shut up, shut up! You brute! You bastard! There are servants in the house ... the servants are listening! I will never forgive you! Shut up or I'll kill you!"

She let him go, shuddering: his old teeth were savagely biting into her flesh beneath her pearls. Golder's eyes were as fierce as a mad dog's. "How dare you," he shouted, "how dare you make demands! You have nothing? What about this? And that? And that?"

Furiously he grabbed at the heavy necklace, twisting it around his fingers. She dug her fingernails into his hands, but he held on. He was having difficulty breathing.

"That, my girl, that alone is worth a million! And what about your emeralds? Your necklaces? Your bracelets? Your rings? Everything you own, everything you wear, from head to toe ... And you have the nerve to say that I haven't provided you with a fortune? Just look at yourself, covered in jewels, weighed down with the money you extorted from me, stole from me! You, Havke! When I took you in, you were nothing but a penniless, miserable girl, remember? Remember? You were running through the snow, with holes in your shoes, your feet sticking out of your stockings, your hands red and swollen from the cold! Oh, my pretty, *I* remember! And I remember the boat we left on, and the immigrants' deck ... And now, you're Gloria Golder! With gowns, jewels, houses, cars, all paid for by me, by me, paid for with my health, with my life! You've taken everything from me, stolen everything from me! Do you think I didn't know that when this house was bought, you arranged to get a two-hundred-thousand-franc kickback, you and Hoyos? Pay, pay, pay... morning, noon, and night. All my life! Did you really think that I saw nothing, that I understood nothing, that I didn't see you getting richer, fattening up your bank account at my expense, and Joyce's? Stockpiling diamonds, stocks and bonds! You've been wealthier than me for years, do you hear me, do you?"

His cries were tearing at his chest; he grabbed his throat, overcome by a fit of coughing, a horrible cough that wracked his body like a gale. For a moment, Gloria thought he was going to die. But he still had enough strength left to hiss at her, a hiss that emerged with excruciating pain from the depths of his wracked chest.

"The house... you're not getting the house! Do you understand! Never..."

Then he fell to the floor and lay on his back, silent and motionless, eyes closed. He had forgotten she was there. All he could hear was the sound of his breathing, the cough that shook him and wouldn't stop, gathering in his throat like a huge wave, and his heart, his old, sick heart, pounding against his chest with deep, dull blows.

The attack lasted for a long time. Then, little by little, it subsided. The cough grew weaker and fainter. He turned to look at Gloria.

"Be happy with what you have," he whispered with effort, his voice breathless and exhausted, "because I swear to you that you will get nothing more from me ever again, nothing..."

She interrupted him, in spite of herself. "Don't try to speak. It's painful just listening to you."

"Leave me alone," he complained, pushing away the hand she had stretched out to him; he couldn't bear the feel of her cold rings, her cold hands on his body.

"Look. I want you to understand once and for all. As long as I live, everything will be fine. You are my wife, I've given you everything I could. But after I die, you won't get anything. Do you understand? Nothing, my dear, except everything you've already managed to amass ... and even that's too much. I've arranged things so that Joyce will get it all. And as for you? Not a penny. Not a cent. Nothing. Absolutely nothing. Do you hear? Do you understand what I'm saying?"

He could clearly see Gloria's cheeks turn white beneath her melting rouge.

"What are you saying?" she asked in a muffled voice. "Are you mad, David?"

He wiped away the sweat that was running down his face and looked darkly at Gloria.

"I want, I mean for Joyce to be free, rich ... As for you ... " He angrily clenched his teeth. "Not you, do you hear me, not you."

"But why?" she asked naively, without thinking.

"Why?" repeated Golder slowly. "Ah, so you really want me to tell you why? Very well then. Because I think I've already done enough for you. I've made you quite wealthy enough, you and your lovers ... "

"What?"

"That surprises you? I bet you understand better now, eh? Yes, your lovers ... all of them. That little Porjès, Lewis Wichmann, all the others ... and Hoyos ... especially Hoyos. *Him!* For twenty years I've watched him parading rings, clothing, even other women, paid for with my money. Well, enough is enough, understand?"

When she didn't reply, he repeated, "Understand? Oh, if you could only see your face. You're not even trying to pretend!"

"Why should I?" said Gloria in a kind of hiss that barely passed through her clenched lips. "Why should I? I've never been unfaithful to you. You can only be unfaithful to a husband ... to a man who actually sleeps with you ... who satisfies you. As for you! You've been a sick old man for years ... a wreck. Maybe you don't realise, or haven't been counting, but it's nearly eighteen years since you came near me. And before that?"

She burst out laughing. "And before that, David? Have you forgotten ... "

Blood rushed to Golder's ageing face, turning it almost purple, filling his eyes with tears. That laugh ... He hadn't heard it in years. Those nights when he'd tried to stifle it with his lips, in vain ...

"That was your fault," he whispered, as he had in the past. "You never loved me."

She laughed even harder. "Loved? You? David Golder? But could anyone love you? Do you want to leave your money to Joyce because you think she loves you, is that it? But she just loves your money, her as well, you fool! She's gone off, hasn't she, your Joyce? She's left you, old, sick, and alone! But while you were close to death, she was out dancing, do you remember? I at least had the decency to stay with you. As for her, she'll be dancing on your grave, you fool! Oh, yes, she loves you so much ..."

"I don't give a damn."

He was trying to shout, but his tormented voice stuck strangled and hoarse in his throat. "I don't give a damn. You don't have to tell me, I already know, I know. Make money for everyone else, and then die, that's why I was put on this filthy earth. Joyce is a little slut like you, I know that only too well, but she can't hurt me, not her. She's a part of me, she's my daughter, she's all I have in the world."

"Your daughter!"

Gloria fell back on to the bed, shaking with the shrill laughter of a madwoman.

"Your daughter! Are you sure about that? You don't know, do you, you who know so many things? Well, she's not yours, do you understand? Your daughter is not yours at all. She's Hoyos's daughter, you fool! Haven't you ever noticed how much she looks like him, how much she loves him? She guessed a long time ago, I'll bet on it. Haven't you ever noticed how we laugh when you kiss your Joyce, your precious daughter ..."

She stopped short. He wasn't moving, wasn't speaking. She leaned over him. He hid his face in his hands.

"David ... It isn't true ..." she whispered automatically. "Listen ..."

But he wasn't listening. He was crushing his face into his hands in shame. He didn't hear her stand up, didn't hear her pause for a moment at the door, didn't see how she was looking at him.

Finally, she went out.

SOME TIME LATER, he got up and dragged himself into the adjoining bathroom. He needed something to drink. He spent a while trying to find the jug of purified water that was left for him at night, but eventually gave up. Instead, he turned on the taps of the bathtub and wet his hands and mouth. He found it difficult to pull himself upright again; his legs were shaking like an old horse who has collapsed, half-dead, and can't get up, despite being urged on by the whip.

The cool night air blew in through the open window. Mechanically, he walked towards it and looked out. But he might as well have been blind: he saw nothing. He felt cold and went back into his room.

He stepped on some broken glass, let out a muffled curse, looked indifferently at the blood flowing from his bare feet, and got back into bed. He was shivering. He pulled the covers tightly around his body, over his head, pressing his forehead into the pillow. He was exhausted. "I'm going to fall asleep . . . to forget. I'll think about it tomorrow . . . tomorrow . . ." Why tomorrow? There was nothing he could do about it. Nothing. Hoyos . . . that filthy pimp . . . and Joyce . . . "It's true that she looks like him!" he cried out, despair in his voice. But almost immediately, he fell silent, his fists clenched. "She loves him so much," Gloria had said. "Haven't you noticed? She guessed a long time ago . . ." She knew, she was laughing at him, she was affectionate towards him only when she wanted money. "Little slut, little . . . I didn't deserve this," he murmured painfully, his lips dry.

He had loved her so much, been so proud of her. None of them had given a damn about him, none of them. A child of his own . . . What a fool he was! He had really believed he could possess something precious on this earth . . . To work all his life just to end up empty-handed, alone, and vulnerable, that was his fate. A child! Even at forty he'd been as old and cold as a corpse! It was Gloria's fault, she'd always hated him, mocked him, pushed him away...Her laugh...Because he was ugly, heavy, clumsy...And at the beginning, when they were poor, her fear, her terror at having a child... "David, be careful. David, listen, if you get me pregnant, I'll kill myself..." Wonderful nights of love they'd been! And then...He remembered now, he remembered it all quite clearly...He counted. It was in 1907. Nineteen years ago. She was in Europe, he was in America. A few months earlier, for the first time, he had earned some money, a lot of money in a construction deal. Then he had nothing again. Gloria was wandering about alone, somewhere in Italy. Now and again, she'd send short telegrams: "NEED MONEY." He always managed to get some for her. How? Ah, a Jewish husband always has to find a way...

A company was formed by some American financiers to construct a railway line in the West. A terrible region, vast empty spaces, swamps...Eighteen months later, all the money was gone. Everyone got out, one after the other, and he'd stepped in to take control of the business. He'd raised more capital, gone out there, stuck it out...Whenever he got his big, heavy hands on some deal, he didn't let go easily, no...

He'd lived alongside the workmen in a wooden hut made of rotting boards. It was the rainy season. Water dripped through the badly constructed roof and down the walls; when night fell, enormous mosquitoes from the swamp whined in the air. Every day, men died, burning with fever. They were buried at night so as not to interrupt the work. The coffins would sit waiting all day long under wet, shiny tarpaulins that rattled in the wind and rain.

And it was in that place that Gloria had arrived one fine day, with her fur coat, her painted nails, her high heels that stuck in the mud...

He remembered how she went into his room, how she forced open the small, filthy window. Outside the frogs were croaking. It was an autumn evening; the sky reflected in the swamps was deep red, almost brown...It was a pretty sight! A miserable little village...the smell of moss on wood, of mud, of damp...

"You're mad," he kept saying, "What are you doing here? You'll catch a fever . . . As if I need a woman to worry about . . . "

"I was bored, I wanted to see you. We're man and wife yet we live like strangers, at opposite ends of the world."

Later on, he asked, "Where will you sleep?" There was only one narrow, hard camp bed. He remembered how she had replied softly, "With you, David . . ." God knows he hadn't wanted anything to do with her that night. He was numb with exhaustion, work, lack of sleep, fever . . . He breathed in her perfume with a kind of fear; he'd almost forgotten. "You're mad," he kept saying, "you're mad . . ." as she pressed her burning body against his and whispered angrily through her clenched teeth, "Don't you feel anything? You're still a man, aren't you? Aren't you ashamed?" Had he really suspected nothing? He could no longer really remember. Sometimes, you close your eyes and turn away: you don't want to see. What's the point? When there's nothing you can do anyway? And afterwards, you forget . . . That night, she had pushed him aside, with that weary gesture of an animal who's had its fill. She'd fallen asleep where she lay, her arms crossed over her chest, her breathing heavy, as if she were having a nightmare. He had got up, started working, as he did every night. The kerosene lamp burned and went black, it was raining outside, the frogs were croaking beneath the windows.

A few days later she left. That same year, Joyce was born. Of course . . .

"Joy . . . Joy . . ." He said her name over and over again, with a kind of hoarse, dry sob, like the cry of an animal in pain. He had really loved her, his Joy, his daughter, his little girl . . . He had given her everything, and she couldn't care less about him. She had snuggled against him in the same way a slut caresses and kisses the sad old man who's in love with her. She knew very well that he wasn't her father. Money. Money was the only thing that mattered to her. Otherwise, why would she have gone away like that? And when he kissed her, she would turn away from him, saying, "Oh, Dad! You'll ruin my make-up." She was ashamed of him. He was heavy and clumsy, unsophisticated . . . A feeling of wild humiliation stabbed at his heart. One full, hot tear dropped from his swollen eyes on to his cheek. He wiped it away with a trembling hand. Cry over her? He, David Golder? Over that little slut? "She's gone off... she's left you, old, sick and alone ..." But at least she hadn't taken any of his money this time. He remembered with sharp, savage pleasure how she'd left without a penny. And Hoyos... how he'd said, "You should have slapped her." What was the point? Refusing her money had been the best revenge. They had forgotten that the money belonged to him, and that if he wanted, they would all die of hunger, all of them... He said "all of them," but he was really thinking only of Joyce. She'd get nothing more from him, not so much as, he harshly snapped his fingers, a penny. Ah, they had forgotten who he was. A sad, ill man, close to death, but still David Golder! In London, Paris, New York, when someone said the name David Golder, it evoked an old, hardened Jew, who all his life had been hated and feared, who had crushed anyone who wanted to do him harm. "The snakes..." he muttered, "the snakes. Oh, I'll teach them a lesson, before I die... since that's what she said: that I'm going to die ..." His trembling hands were clutching the sheets; he looked at his heavy fingers, shaking with fever, with a sort of hopeless sadness. "What have they done to me?" He closed his eyes, wincing in hatred. "Gloria." Her pearls had been as icy and slippery as a mass of slithering serpents... And as for the other one... that little whore ... "And what are they without me? Nothing, trash. I've worked, I've killed," he said suddenly, out loud, in a strange voice; he stopped. "Yes, I killed Simon Marcus," he said, slowly wringing his hands, "I know I did... Come on, you know very well, you did," he muttered darkly to himself, "and now... So they think I'm going to carry on working like a dog until I drop dead, well if that's what they think, they've got another think coming!" He let out a sharp, bizarre little laugh that sounded as if he were being strangled. "That mad old hag... and as for the other one, the ..." He swore in Yiddish, cursing her in a low voice. "No, my pretty one, it's over, I'm telling you, all over ..."

It was light now. He could hear someone at his door. "What is it?" he called out mechanically.

"It's a telegram, Sir."

"Come in."

The servant entered. "Are you ill, Sir?"

He didn't reply. He took the telegram and opened it.

"NEED MONEY. JOYCE."

"If you would like to reply, Sir," the servant said, looking at him oddly, "the messenger is still here . . ."

"What was that?" he said slowly. "No . . . There's no reply."

He got back into bed and lay there motionless, his eyes closed. That was how Loewe found him, a few hours later. He hadn't moved. He was breathing with great difficulty, his face contorted with pain, his head thrown back, his quivering lips colourless with fever and thirst.

He refused to get up, to speak; he uttered not a single order, not a word; he seemed half-dead, not of this world. Loewe put letters into his hands: letters with demands for money, delays, assistance, but he signed none of them; they just fell from his lifeless fingers. Loewe, terrified, left the same night.

Three days later, David Golder's crash on the Stock Market was over, dragging down many other fortunes along with his own, like a senseless tide.

JOYCE AND ALEC planned to spend the night near Ascain. They had left Madrid ten days earlier and were wandering through the Pyrenees, unable to tear themselves from each other's arms.

Joyce usually drove, while Alec and her dog, Jill, dozed, worn out by the heat of the sun. They would stop when it was dark and have dinner in the garden of some rural hotel where couples in love were serenaded by accordion players. The wistaria was in full bloom, and the trees hung with paper lanterns that sometimes caught light in a burst of golden flame that lapped at the leaves before turning to ash and falling to the ground. The young couple would sit at a wobbly wooden table caressing each other, while a girl with her hair tied back in a dark head-scarf served them chilled wine. Then they would go upstairs to spend the night in a sparsely furnished, cool bedroom, where they would make love, fall asleep, then leave the next day.

As evening fell, they were driving along a road near Ascain, in the mountains. The setting sun bathed the houses of the small village in a pale-pink light the colour of sugared almonds.

"Tomorrow," said Alec, "it's back to work...Lady Rovenna..."

"Oh!" muttered Joyce, angrily. "She's so ghastly, so ugly and mean..."

"We have to live," he said, then added, laughing, "When we're married, Joy, I'll only sleep with pretty young women." He placed a gentle hand on Joy's delicate neck and gave it a squeeze. "Joy, I really want you, you know that. Only you..."

"Of course I know," said Joy, glibly, her lovely painted lips in a triumphant little pout. "Of course I know."

It was getting darker. Deep within the Pyrenees, the peaceful little clouds that formed at night were beginning to slip down into the valleys where they would nestle until morning. Joyce stopped the car outside a hotel. A woman came out and opened the car door. "Monsieur, Madame. A single room with a large bed?" she asked with a smile, as soon as she saw them.

It was a very large room with a pale wood floor and an enormous, high bed. Joyce ran and threw herself down on the flowered quilt.

"Alec . . . come here . . ."

He leaned over her.

A little later, she gave a moan: "Mosquitoes . . . look . . ."

They were flying around the light on the ceiling. Alec quickly switched it off. Night had secretly, suddenly descended while they were kissing. Through the window, from the narrow garden full of sunflowers, came the sound of water flowing in a fountain.

"Where's the white wine we left to chill?" asked Alec, his eyes shining. "I'm hungry and thirsty . . ."

"What have we got to eat?"

"I ordered some crayfish and the wine," said Alec. "As for the rest, we'll have to make do with the dish of the day, my love. Do you realise we only have five hundred francs left? We've spent fifty thousand in ten days. If your father doesn't send you some money . . ."

"When I think of that man," said Joyce, bitterly, "how he let me leave without a penny! I'll never forgive him. If it hadn't been for old Fischl . . ."

"What exactly did old Fischl ask you to do for his fifty thousand francs?" asked Alec coyly.

"Nothing!" she shouted crossly, "I swear! Just the idea of him touching me with his ugly hands is enough to make me sick! You're the one who sleeps with old women like Lady Rovenna for money, you horrible little toad!"

She covered his mouth with hers and angrily bit his lip as if it were a piece of fruit.

Alec let out a cry. "Oh! I'm bleeding, you horrible little beast, look . . ."

She laughed in the darkness.

"Come on, let's go downstairs . . ."

They went out into the garden, Jill following close behind them. They were alone; the hotel seemed empty. In the clear evening sky, a large yellow moon hung suspended between the trees. Joy lifted the lid of the steaming hot soup tureen, breathing in its aroma with a little growl of pleasure.

"Oh, that smells good . . . Give me your bowl . . ."

She served him standing up; she looked so strange with her make-up, her bare arms, and her pearls flung behind her that he suddenly burst out laughing as he watched her.

"What's the matter?"

"Oh, nothing . . . It's funny . . . You don't look like a woman who . . ."

"A *young* woman," she interrupted, frowning.

"I can't picture you ever being a little girl . . . I bet you came into this world singing and dancing, with rings on your fingers and make-up on your eyes, didn't you? Do you know how to cut this bread? I want some."

"No, do you?"

"No."

They called the serving girl who cut the round, golden loaf, pressing it against her chest. Joy watched her with her head thrown back, lazily stretching out her bare arms. "When I was little, I was very beautiful . . . They would stroke me, tease me . . ."

"Who do you mean by *they*?"

"Men. Especially old men, of course . . ."

The servant took away the empty dishes and came back with an earthenware bowl of crayfish swimming in a steaming, delicious-smelling, spicy broth. They devoured them with great gusto. Joyce added even more pepper and then stuck out her tongue as if it were on fire. Alec slowly poured the chilled wine; it made the glasses turn misty.

"We'll have champagne in our room tonight, as we always do," murmured Joyce, slightly tipsy, while cracking an enormous crayfish between her teeth. "What kind of champagne do they have? I want some Clicquot, very dry."

She raised her glass between her cupped hands.

"Look . . . the wine is the same colour as the moon tonight, all golden . . ."

They drank together from the same glass, merging their moist, peppery lips, lips so young that nothing could change the way they tasted of ripe fruit.

With the chicken sautéed with olives and sweet pimentos, they drank a bottle of ruby Chambertin, full-bodied and warm, that left a wonderful taste in the mouth. Then Alec ordered some brandy and poured drops of it into two large glasses of champagne. Joyce drank. While they were having dessert, she started acting wild. With her dog on her lap, she threw back her head, looked up at the sky, then, with all her strength, pulled the golden locks of her short hair straight into the air.

"I want to sleep outdoors all night ... I want to spend my whole life here ... I want to spend my whole life making love ... What do you say?"

"I love your little breasts," said Alec. Then he fell silent.

He didn't speak much when he drank. He continued pouring the brandy into the golden champagne, drop by drop.

It was a peaceful night in the country; the mountains were bathed in moonlight; the cicadas were chirping.

"They think it's daytime," murmured Joyce, delighted. The little dog had fallen asleep in her arms; she didn't want to move. "Alec," she said, "put a cigarette in my mouth and light it for me."

Alec groped about in the dark, found a cigarette, and put it between her lips, then passionately grabbed the back of her neck and muttered something she couldn't understand.

When Joy suddenly uncrossed her legs, the little dog woke up, jumped down, stretched out on the grass, and nuzzled the moist, sweet-smelling September earth.

"Come, Joy," Alec urged quietly. "Come and play at love ... "

"Come on, Jill," Joyce said to her dog.

Jill looked up and seemed to hesitate. But the couple were already disappearing into the darkness, walking towards the house with slow, tottering steps, their young, intoxicated faces leaning towards each other. Jill got up with a throaty little noise that sounded like someone sighing and followed them, stopping every few steps to sniff the ground.

As usual, once inside the bedroom, the dog lay down facing the bed, and Joy repeated, as she did every night, "Jill, you naughty girl, we should make you pay to watch!"

The moon spread great puddles of silver over the floor. Joy undressed slowly, then went and stood naked in front of the window, wearing only her pearls; they shimmered in the cool moonlight.

"I'm beautiful, aren't I, Alec? Do you want me?"

"It's our last night together," Alec replied wistfully, like a child. "We have no more money, there's nothing left. We have to go back, we have to part . . . Until when?"

"My God, you're right . . ."

That night, for the first time, they didn't throw themselves hungrily into making love only to fall asleep afterwards, like wild young animals tired after doing battle; instead, with heavy hearts, they lay beneath the flower-covered quilt and, bathed in moonlight, cradled each other for a long time, wrapped in each other's arms, without speaking and almost without desire.

Then they felt cold and closed the shutters, pulling the heavy blue and pink curtains across the window. The electricity had been turned off, it was late; a burning candle on the edge of the table sent their shadows dancing to the ceiling. They could hear, very far away, the muffled sound of hooves hitting the ground.

"There's a farm nearby, most likely," said Alec, as Joy looked up. "The animals must be dreaming . . ."

Jill, still asleep, turned over with a great sigh, so weary and sad that Joy laughed and whispered, "Daddy sighs like that when he's lost on the Stock Market . . . Oh, Alec, your knees are so cold . . ."

On the white ceiling, their shadows mingled, forming an eerie knot, like a bouquet of flowers whose stems are entwined.

Joyce let her hands slide, slowly, down her trembling aching hips.

"Oh, Alec! I'm so in love with love . . ."

GOLDER RETURNED TO Paris alone. After the house in Biarritz had been sold, Gloria and Joyce went on a cruise on Behring's yacht, with Hoyos, Alec, and the Mannerings. It was not until December that Gloria returned to Paris; she immediately came round with an antiques dealer to arrange the sale of the furniture.

It was with a kind of sardonic pleasure that Golder watched the contents of the apartment being taken away: the table decorated with bronze sphinxes, the four-poster Louis XV bed, with its cupids, bows, and arrows. For a long while now, he'd been sleeping in the sitting room on a narrow, hard fold-out bed. Towards evening, when the final removal vans had gone, there remained nothing in the apartment except a few wicker chairs and a pine kitchen table. Wood shavings and old newspapers were scattered on the floor. Gloria came back. Golder hadn't moved. He was propped up on the bed, a black plaid blanket over his chest, looking with an expression of relief at the enormous bare windows, stripped of the damask curtains that had kept out the light and air.

The sound of Gloria's heavy footsteps was amplified by the bare wood floor. The noise seemed to surprise her; she shuddered nervously, stopped, then started walking again on tiptoe, trying to keep her balance, but the noise didn't stop. She sat down opposite Golder.

"David . . ."

They looked at each other in silence for a moment, their eyes hard. She was trying to smile, but, despite her efforts, her harsh, square jaw jutted forward with a voracious movement that made her face look carnivorous when she wasn't careful.

"Well," she said finally, nervously flicking the gloves she was holding, "are you satisfied, are you happy now?"

"Yes," he replied.

She clenched her teeth. "You're mad..." she hissed quietly. "You're a mad old fool..." Her voice was strange and sharp. "So you think I'm going to starve to death without you and your damned money, do you? Well, just look at me... I don't exactly look very poor, do I? Have you seen this?" She shook her wrist at him, making her new bracelet jingle. "Did you pay for that? No! So, what was this all about? What were you hoping to accomplish? You're the only one who's suffering, you fool... As for me, well, I'm managing... And everything that was here belongs to me, to me," she repeated, angrily striking the wooden chair, "and if you ever try to stop me from selling anything, however and whenever I want, you'll have to deal with me, you thief! You should be thrown into prison," she spat. "To leave your wife penniless after so many years of marriage... Answer me, say something," she shouted suddenly. "You know very well that I can see the truth! Well? Admit it! You did it so I'd have no money... You've bankrupted yourself and so many other poor souls just for that. You'd rather die between these four walls just to see me poor as well, is that it? Well? Is it?"

"I don't give a damn about you," said Golder. He closed his eyes. "I really don't give a damn about you, if you only knew..." he murmured, "not about you, your money, or anything to do with you... And don't think your money will last, my poor girl. Believe me, when you have no husband to keep topping up the cash, it goes very quickly..." There was no anger in his voice. He spoke in the low, measured tones of an old man, pulling up the collar of his jacket against the cold. An icy wind blew in from the street through the cracks in the bare window. "Yes, how quickly it goes... You've been playing the Stock Market, haven't you? They say that any stock you touch will go sky-high this year. But that won't last forever... And as for Hoyos..." He let out a surprising little laugh that made him sound almost young. "Oh, what a life you'll have in a year or two, you poor things!"

"And what about you? What about your life? You've buried yourself alive!"

"It's what I wanted to do," Golder said abruptly with a kind of haughty anger, "and I have always done what I wanted to do on this earth."

She fell silent and, very slowly, smoothed out her gloves.

"Are you going to stay here?"

"I don't know."

"So you have some money left, then?" she murmured. "You made sure you're all right..."

He nodded. "Yes," he said quietly, "but don't try to get any of it. Save yourself the trouble. I've made very sure..."

She gave a scornful laugh, nodding at the empty room.

"Oh! I'm happy to be rid of all of that," he said wearily, closing his eyes. "The sphinxes, the laurels... I don't need any of it."

Picking up her fox stole and her handbag, Gloria went and stood in front of the mirror above the fireplace. She began carefully to powder her face.

"I think Joyce will be coming to see you soon..."

When he didn't respond, she murmured, "She needs money..."

In the mirror, she could see a strange look pass over Golder's hard face.

"All this is because of Joyce," she said quietly and quickly, almost in spite of herself, "isn't it?"

She could clearly see his cheeks and hands quivering, as if overcome by a sudden chill.

"It's all because of Joyce. And yet Joyce hasn't done anything to you... How ironic."

She let out a little forced laugh, dry and bitter.

"You adore her... My God, you adore her... just like an old lover... It's grotesque..."

"That's enough," shouted Golder.

Her instinct was to recoil in fear, but she restrained herself.

"So," she whispered, raising her eyebrows, "are you starting at that again? Do you want me to have you locked up?"

"I wouldn't put it past you..." he sighed, sounding angry and tired. "Get out."

He seemed to be making a great effort to stay calm. Very slowly, he wiped away the sweat that was running down his face.

"Go. I'm asking you to go."

"Well, then, I suppose this is good-bye?"

Without replying, he stood up and went into the next room.

The thud of the door closing behind him echoed through the empty house. She remembered that he had always ended their quarrels like this. Then she realised that she would probably never see him again. This solitary life would undoubtedly finish him off, and soon . . . "To have lived so many years together to end up like this . . . And why? At our age . . . Over things that happen all the time . . . He made it happen . . . Well, it was his loss . . . But how ridiculous it was, by God . . . how ridiculous . . ."

She closed the door of the apartment and walked wearily down the stairs.

Golder was alone.

GOLDER WAS ON his own for a long time. At least his family wasn't bothering him any more.

The doctor came to see him every morning; quickly walking through the dark rooms, he would go into Golder's bedroom, place a stethoscope on his old chest and listen to the results of the night's heavy, laboured breathing. But Golder's heart condition was improving. The pain had subsided. And Golder too seemed to have subsided into a kind of slumber, a depressed stupor. He would get up and dress, trying to move as slowly as possible in order to save as much strength, as much of his life force as he could. Then he would walk around the apartment twice, aware of every movement of his muscles, every beat of his pulse and heart. After that, he would measure out his medicine himself, one gram at a time, on the kitchen scales, then boil an egg using his watch as a timer.

In the enormous kitchen, spacious enough for five servants in the past, there was now just one elderly maid, hunched over the stove, who prepared his meals. She watched with weary resignation as he paced back and forth, his hands clasped behind his back, in a dressing-gown he'd bought years before in London whose purple silk was so faded and torn that tufts of the white wool lining were sticking through the fabric.

Breakfast over, he would have an armchair and footstool placed by the sitting-room window, and he would sit there all day long, playing solitaire on a tray on his lap. If it was sunny, he would visit the chemist's in the next street, weigh himself, and walk slowly back home, leaning heavily on his walking stick and stopping every fifty paces to catch his breath, his left hand carefully holding closed the ends of his woollen scarf, which was wrapped twice around his neck and fastened with a pin.

Then, when night began to fall, Soifer would come round to

play cards. He was an old German Jew Golder had known in
Silesia; they'd lost touch but then run into each other a few
months earlier. Bankrupted by inflation, Soifer had played the
money markets and won everything back again. In spite of that,
he had retained a mistrust of money, and the way revolutions and
wars could transform it overnight into nothing but worthless
bits of paper. It was a mistrust that seemed to grow as the years
passed, and little by little, Soifer had invested his fortune in jewellery. He kept everything in a safe in London: diamonds, pearls,
emeralds—all so beautiful that even Gloria had never owned any
that could compare. Despite all this, his meanness bordered on
madness. He lived in a sordid little furnished room, in a dingy
street near Passy, and would never take taxis, even when a friend
offered to pay. "I do not wish," he would say, "to indulge in
luxuries that I can't afford myself." Instead, he would wait for
the bus in the rain, in winter, for hours at a time, letting them
go by one after the other if there was no room left in second
class. All his life, he had walked on tiptoe so his shoes would last
longer. For several years now, since he had lost all his teeth, he
ate only cereal and puréed vegetables to avoid having to buy
dentures.

His yellow skin, as dry and transparent as an autumn leaf, gave
him a look of pathetic nobility, the same kind of look that old
criminals sometimes have. His head was crowned with beautiful
tufts of silvery white hair. It was only his gaping, spluttering
mouth, buried in the deep ridges of his face, that inspired a feeling of revulsion and fear.

Every day, Golder would let him win twenty francs or so,
and listen to him talk about other people's business deals. Soifer
possessed a kind of dark sense of humour that was very similar
to Golder's and meant that they got along together well.

Much later, Soifer would die all alone, like a dog, without a
friend, without a single wreath on his grave, buried in the cheapest cemetery in Paris by his family who hated him, and whom
he had hated, but to whom he nevertheless left a fortune of some
thirty million francs, thus fulfilling till the end the incomprehensible destiny of every good Jew on this earth.

And so, at five o'clock every day, sitting at a pine table in front of the sitting-room window, Golder wearing his purple dressing-gown, Soifer with a woman's black wool shawl draped over his shoulders, the two men played cards. In the silent apartment, Golder's coughing fits echoed with a strange, hollow sound. Old Soifer moaned about his life in an annoyed, plaintive tone of voice.

Beside them, hot tea sat in two large, silver-bottomed glasses, part of a set that Golder, long ago, had ordered from Russia. Soifer would put his cards down on the table, automatically shielding them with his hand, take a sip of tea and say, "You know that sugar is going to go up again?" Then: "You know that the Banque Lalleman is going to finance the Franco-Algerian Mining Company?" And Golder would look up abruptly with an eager, lively expression, like a flame that flickers up from the ashes and then dies down again.

"That should be a pretty good deal," he replied wearily.

"The only good deal is to invest your money in something safe—if there is such a thing—then sit on it and protect it like an old hen. Your turn, Golder . . ."

They went back to playing cards.

"HAVE YOU HEARD?" said Soifer as he came in. "Have you heard what they've cooked up now?"

"Who?"

Soifer shook his fist at the window, indicating all of Paris.

"First it was income tax," he continued in a shrill, quivering voice, "soon there will be a tax on rent. Last week I spent forty-three francs on heating. Then my wife went and bought a new hat. Seventy-two francs! And it looks like a pot that's been turned upside down! I don't mind paying for something of quality, something that lasts, but that hat . . . It won't even last her two seasons. And at her age! What she could do with is a shroud! I would have paid for that with pleasure . . . Seventy-two francs! In my day, where we lived, we could buy a bearskin coat for that price. My God, if my son ever says he wants to get married, I'll strangle him with my bare hands. He'd be better off dead, the poor boy, than to have to keep paying for things his whole life, like you and me. And I heard just today that if I don't renew my identity card right away, I'll be deported. A miserable, sickly old man! I ask you, where would I go?"

"To Germany?"

"Oh, sure, to Germany," Soifer grumbled. "Germany can go to hell! You know what happened to me before in Germany, when I had that trouble over providing them with war supplies. No? You didn't know? Look, I've got to get going now, their office closes at four o'clock . . . And do you know how much it will cost me, for the pleasure? Three hundred francs, my dear Golder, three hundred francs plus their administrative costs, not to mention the time wasted and the twenty francs you always let me win, since we won't have time to play cards today. Oh, dear Lord! Why don't you come along with me? It will take your mind off things, it's nice out."

"Do you want me to come so I can pay for the taxi?" asked Golder with a smile that twisted his face like a sudden fit of coughing.

"Good heavens," said Soifer, "I was expecting to take the tram . . . And you know I never take taxis in order to avoid getting into bad habits . . . But today, my old legs feel as heavy as lead . . . And as long as *you* don't mind throwing your money out of the window?"

They went out together, each of them leaning on a walking stick. Golder listened quietly as his friend explained how a recent sugar deal had just ended in bankruptcy because of some sort of fraud. Soifer rubbed his trembling hands together in an expression of sheer delight as he reeled off figures and the names of the ruined shareholders.

When they left the police station, Golder felt like walking. It was still light; the final rays of the red winter sun lit up the Seine. They crossed the bridge, strolled up a street they chanced upon behind the Hôtel de Ville, then along another street that turned out to be the Rue Vieille-du-Temple.

Suddenly, Soifer stopped.

"Do you know where we are?"

"No," replied Golder, indifferent.

"Right over there, my friend, on the Rue des Rosiers, there's a little Jewish restaurant, the only one in Paris where they know how to make a good stuffed pike. Come and have dinner with me."

"You don't think I'm going to eat stuffed pike," Golder grumbled, "when I haven't touched fish or meat in six months?"

"No one's asking you to eat anything. Just come and pay. All right?"

"Go to hell."

Nevertheless, he followed Soifer who was limping painfully down the street, breathing in the smell of fish, dust, and rotting straw. Soifer turned round and put his arm through Golder's.

"A dirty Jewish neighbourhood, isn't it?" he said affectionately. "Does it remind you of anything?"

"Nothing good," Golder replied darkly.

He stopped and, for a moment, looked up at the houses, laundry hanging from their windows, without speaking. Some children rushed past his legs. He gently pushed them away with his cane and sighed. In the shops, there was hardly anything to buy except second-hand clothes or herring in tubs of brine. Soifer pointed to a small restaurant with a sign written in Hebrew.

"Here it is. Are you coming, Golder? You're happy to buy me dinner, aren't you? To make a poor old man happy?"

"Oh, go to hell!" repeated Golder. But he continued to follow Soifer. What difference did it make where he went? He felt more tired than usual.

The little restaurant seemed quite clean. It had brightly coloured paper table-cloths and a shiny brass kettle in one corner of the room. Not a soul in sight.

Soifer ordered a portion of stuffed pike and some horse-radish. With great reverence, he picked up the hot plate and lifted it to his nose. "It smells so good!"

"Oh, for goodness sake, just eat and leave me in peace," murmured Golder.

He turned round and lifted a corner of the heavy red and white checked curtain. Outside, two men had stopped and were leaning against the window, talking. He couldn't hear what they were saying, but Golder could understand by the way they gestured with their hands. One of them was Polish and wore an extraordinary, dilapidated fur hat with earflaps; he had an enormous curly, grey beard that he impatiently stroked, plaited, twirled, and untwisted endlessly, at great speed. The other one was a young boy with red hair that burst out in all directions, like flames.

"I wonder what they sell," thought Golder. "Hay and scrap iron, like in my day?"

He half closed his eyes. Now, as night began to fall and the tops of the houses were cloaked in shadow and the clatter and creak of a handcart drowned out the sound of the cars on the Rue Vieille-du-Temple, he felt as if he had been transported back in time to the old country, was seeing once again those familiar faces, but distorted, deformed, as in a dream . . .

"There are dreams like this," he thought vaguely, "where you see people who have died years before . . ."

"What are you looking at?" asked Soifer. He pushed away his plate, which still contained the remains of some fish and bits of mashed potato. "Ah, so this is what it's like to grow old . . . In the past, I would have happily eaten three portions like this! But now, my poor teeth . . . I have to swallow without chewing. It gives me heartburn here . . ." He pointed to his chest. "What are you thinking about?"

He stopped, watched Golder, and shook his head.

"Oy," he said suddenly, in his inimitable tone of voice that was plaintive and ironic at the same time, "Oy, Lord God! They're happier than we are, don't you think? Dirty and poor, all right, but does a Jew need much? Poverty preserves the Jews like brine preserves the herrings. I'd like to come here more often. If it weren't so far, and especially, so expensive—it's expensive everywhere nowadays—I'd come here every night to have a peaceful meal, without my family, who can all go to hell . . ."

"We should come here now and again," murmured Golder.

He stretched out his hands towards the glowing stove that had just been lit; it radiated a heavy smell of heat from its corner.

"At home," he thought, "a smell like that would make me choke . . ."

But he didn't feel sick. A kind of sensual warmth, something he'd never felt before, seeped deep into his old bones.

Outside, a man walked by carrying a long pole; he touched the street-lamp opposite the restaurant and a flame shot out, lighting up a narrow, dark window where washing was hanging above some empty old flower-pots. Golder suddenly remembered a little crooked window just like it, opposite the shop where he'd been born . . . remembered his street, in the wind and snow, as it sometimes appeared in his dreams.

"It's a long road," he said out loud.

"Yes," said Soifer, "long, hard, and pointless."

Both of them looked up and for a long while gazed, sighing, at the miserable window, the worn-out clothes beating against the panes of glass. A woman opened the window and leaned out to pull in the washing. She shook it out, then bent forward, took a little mirror out of her pocket, and used the light from the street-lamp to put on some lipstick.

Golder suddenly stood up.

"Let's go home . . . the smell from that oil stove is making me feel sick . . ."

THAT NIGHT HE dreamed of Joyce, her features mingling with those of the little Jewish woman he'd seen on the Rue des Rosiers. It was the first time in a long while. The memory of Joy lay dormant within him, like his pain . . .

He woke up, his legs shaking and as tired as if he had walked for miles. All day long he sat wrapped in blankets and shawls looking out of the window; his cards lay untouched. He was shivering; an insidious, icy chill seemed to pierce him, right down to his bones.

Soifer arrived later that evening, but he too felt unwell and melancholy and hardly spoke. He left earlier than usual, hurrying down the dark street, his umbrella clutched to his chest.

Golder ate dinner. Then, when the maid had gone up to bed, he walked around the apartment, locking all the doors. Gloria had had all the chandeliers taken away. In every room, an electric bulb hung from a long wire; they swayed in the draught and lit up Golder's reflection in the mirrors above the fireplaces. There he was, barefoot, holding his keys, with his wild, thick white hair and strikingly pale face, each day showing more and more of that bluish tint common amongst people with a heart condition.

The doorbell rang. Before answering it, Golder looked in surprise at the time. The evening papers had arrived long ago. Perhaps Soifer had had an accident . . .

"Is that you, Soifer?" he asked through the door. "Who is it?"

"Tübingen," a voice replied.

Golder, his face suddenly overwhelmed with emotion, unfastened the security chain. His hands were unsteady and he grew impatient with himself as he fumbled about, but Tübingen waited without saying a word. Golder knew that he could remain like that, motionless, for hours on end. "He hasn't changed a bit," he thought.

Finally, he managed to unlock the door. Tübingen came in.

"Hello," he said.

He took off his hat and coat, hanging them up himself, then opened his wet umbrella, set it in the corner, and shook Golder's hand.

His long head was oddly shaped, in such a way that his forehead looked too big and luminous. He had a puritanical, pale face, with thin lips.

"May I come in?" he asked, pointing to the sitting room.

"Yes, please do . . ."

Golder saw him glance around the bare rooms and lower his eyes, like someone who has intruded on a secret.

"My wife has left," he said.

"Biarritz?"

"I don't know."

"Ah," murmured Tübingen.

He sat down; Golder sat opposite him, breathing with difficulty.

"How's business?" he asked finally.

"The same as ever. Some good, some bad. You know that Amrum signed with the Russians?"

"What? For the Teisk shares?" Golder quickly asked, leaning forward suddenly as if he wanted to grasp a fleeting shadow. Then he let his hands drop back down and shrugged. "I didn't know," he said, sighing.

"Not for the Teisk shares. The contract stipulates the sale of a hundred thousand tons of Russian oil per year for five years, in Constantinople, Port Said, and Colombo."

"But . . . what about Teisk?" Golder muttered.

"Not mentioned."

"Ah."

"I knew that Amrum had sent agents to Moscow twice, but nothing came of it."

"Why?"

"Why? Perhaps because the Soviets wanted to get a loan of twenty-three million gold roubles from the United States and Amrum had to pay off three members of the government, including a senator. It was all too much. And they also made the mistake of letting the evidence get stolen, which blew up in the press."

"Oh, really?"

"Yes."

He nodded. "Amrum has paid dearly for our Persian oilfields, Golder."

"You've started up negotiations again?"

"Of course. Straight away. I wanted to own the whole of the Caucasus region. I wanted a monopoly on oil refinery and to become the sole distributor of Russian petroleum products in the world."

Golder smirked.

"You wanted too much, as you yourself just pointed out. They don't like giving foreigners such economic influence and consequently too much political power."

"The fools. I'm not interested in their politics. People can do what they want in their own country. Once I was there, they wouldn't have had their noses stuck into my business affairs, I can promise you that."

"If it had been me ..." Golder began musing out loud, "I would have started with Teisk and the Aroundgis. Then gradually, after a while," he opened his hand and quickly closed it, "I would have snapped it all up. All of it. All of the Caucasus, all the oil ..."

"That's why I've come to see you; I want you to handle the deal."

Golder shrugged his shoulders.

"No. I'm out of it now. I'm ill ... half dead."

"Did you keep your Teisk shares?"

"Yes," said Golder, hesitating, "I don't know why ... They were hardly worth anything. I could sell them as scrap paper ..."

"That's true enough, but only if Amrum wins the concession. Then I'll be damned if they're worth even that. But if *I* win ..."

He fell silent. Golder shook his head.

"No," he said, clenching his teeth, a look of suffering on his face. "No."

"Why not? I need you. And you need me."

"I know. But I don't want to work any more. I can't. I'm not well. My heart . . . I know that if I don't give up work entirely, and right away, I'm a dead man. I'm not interested. What for? I don't need much now, at my age. I just need to stay alive."

Tübingen shook his head.

"I'm seventy-two years old," he said. "In twenty or twenty-five years' time, when all the Teisk oil wells start producing, I'll have been dead a very long time. I think about that sometimes . . . when I'm signing a ninety-nine-year lease! By then, it won't just be me, but my son and my grandsons and their children who will all be in the hands of the Lord. But there will always be a Tübingen. And that's why I keep going."

"But I don't have anyone," said Golder, "so, what's the use?"

"You have children, like I do."

"I have no one," Golder repeated, angrily.

Tübingen closed his eyes. "There would still be something that you'd created."

He slowly opened his eyes and appeared to look straight through Golder.

"Something," he repeated eagerly in the deep voice of a man who is revealing the secret thing most dear to his heart, "something that you'd built, that was lasting . . ."

"And what is it that's lasting for me? Money? Oh, it's not worth the trouble . . . unless you could take it with you . . ."

"*The Lord giveth and the Lord taketh away. Blessed be the name of the Lord,*" Tübingen recited quietly, with the droning intonation of a puritan brought up on the Scriptures since childhood. "That's the law. There's nothing you can do."

Golder sighed deeply.

"No. Nothing."

"IT'S ME," SAID Joyce. She came so close that she was nearly touching him, but he didn't move.

"Anyone would think you didn't recognise me."

Then she cried out "Dad!" as she had in the past.

Only then did he shudder and close his eyes, as if blinded by a dazzling light. He stretched out his hand so weakly that it barely touched hers before it dropped down on to his knee; still he said nothing.

She pulled a footstool up to his armchair, sat down, and took off her hat, vigorously shaking her head in the way that was so familiar to him ... Then she waited, silently.

"You've changed," he whispered, in spite of himself.

"Yes," she said with a bitter laugh.

She was taller and thinner, with an indefinable look of weariness, distress, and resignation.

She was wearing a magnificent sable coat. She threw it down on the floor behind her, revealing her neck and, in place of the pearls Golder had given her, an emerald necklace, as green as grass, its stones so pure and enormous that Golder stared at it for a moment, speechless with disbelief. Finally, he laughed harshly.

"Ah, yes, I see now ... You've sorted yourself out too ... So why have you come then? I don't understand ..."

"It's a gift from my fiancé," she said quietly, with no emotion. "I have to get married soon."

"Ah ... Congratulations," he added, with difficulty.

She didn't reply.

He thought for a moment, wiped his forehead several times, then sighed, "Well then, I wish you ..." He hesitated. "So he's rich, is he? You should be happy ..."

"Happy!" She let out a cry of despair and turned towards him. "Happy? Do you know who I'm going to marry?"

He didn't answer.

"Old Fischl," she shouted, "that's who!"

"Fischl!"

"Yes, Fischl! What did you think I would do? I have no money now, do I? My mother gives me nothing, not a penny. You know her, she'd rather see me starve to death than give me any money, wouldn't she? So, what do you expect? It's lucky he wants to marry me . . . Otherwise I would have just had to sleep with him, wouldn't I? Although that might have been better, easier at least, one night with him from time to time . . . but that's not what he wants, you see? The horrible old pig wants to get his money's worth!" Her voice suddenly quivered with hatred. "Oh, I'd like to . . ." She stopped, ran her fingers through her hair and pulled it with all her might with a look of despair.

"I'd like to kill him," she said slowly.

Golder managed to laugh.

"But why? It's a very good idea, it's wonderful! Fischl . . . He's rich, you know, when he's not in prison, and you'll cheat on him with your young man . . . what was his name . . . your little gigolo? And you'll be very happy. Come on! This was how you were meant to end up, you little slut, it was written all over your face . . . Still . . . still, it's not what I used to dream of for you, Joyce . . ."

His face grew even paler. "Why should it matter to me, dear Lord?" he thought frantically. "Why should it matter to me? Let her sleep with whomever she likes, let her go wherever she pleases . . ."

But his proud heart was bleeding, as it had in the past.

"My daughter . . ." (in spite of everything, everyone thought she was Golder's daughter) "and Fischl!"

"I'm so unhappy, if you only knew . . ."

"You want too much, my girl. Money, love, you have to choose . . . But you've made your choice, haven't you?" He winced in pain. "No one's forcing you, are they? So, why are you whining? It's what you want."

"Oh, this is all your fault, all of it! It's all because of you! How am I supposed to live with no money? I've tried, I swear to you I've tried . . . If you could have seen me last winter . . . You remember how cold it was? Just like it always is, right? And there I was walking around in my little grey autumn coat . . . the last thing I bought for myself before you left. Wasn't I a pretty sight! But I can't, I just can't do it, I'm not cut out for it, I'm telling you! It's not my fault! Then I got into debt, had all sorts of financial troubles . . . So, to put an end to them, I did what I had to do, didn't I? If it hadn't been him, it would have been someone else. But Alec, Alec! You say I'll cheat on Fischl. Of course I will! But if you think he's going to make it easy for me, you're very wrong. Oh, you don't know him! Once he's paid for something, he watches over it, you know, he doesn't let it out of his sight. He's a dirty . . . a dirty old man! Oh, I just want to die, I'm so miserable, I'm so alone. I'm suffering, Dad. Help me. You're all I have!"

She clasped his hands and wrung them in despair.

"Speak to me!" she shouted. "Say something! Otherwise I'm going to walk out of here and kill myself. Remember Marcus? They say he killed himself because of you . . . Well, you'll have my death on your conscience too, do you hear me?"

Her shrill, childlike voice echoed eerily in the empty rooms. Golder clenched his teeth.

"So you think you can frighten me, do you? Don't think I'm a fool! And besides, I haven't got any more money. Just leave me alone. You mean nothing to me. You know very well . . . You've always known . . . You're not my daughter . . . You're . . . You're Hoyos's daughter and you know it! Well, go and see him. Let *him* protect you, let *him* look after you, let *him* work to support you. It's his turn now. As for me, well, I've done quite enough for you, you're no longer my problem. Go away, you mean nothing to me any more. Just get out!"

"Hoyos? Are you sure? Oh, Dad! If you only knew! Alec and I meet at his place . . . and we . . . with him right there . . ." She hid her face in her hands. He could see tears running through her fingers.

"Dad, you're all I have! I have no one else in the world!" she repeated, in despair. "I couldn't care less that you're not my father, you have to believe me . . . You're all I have! Help me, I'm begging you. I want so much to be happy. I'm young, I want to live, I want . . . I want to be happy!"

"You're not the only one, my poor darling . . . Leave me now, leave me . . ."

He made a vague gesture with his hand that simultaneously pushed her away and drew her closer. Then he gave a sudden shudder and allowed his fingers to stroke her neck, her bowed head, her short, golden, sweet-smelling hair . . . Oh, he had missed touching her so much, missed feeling beneath his hand that blossoming, urgent spark of life, as in the past . . . and . . .

"Oh, Joyce!" he whispered, his heart breaking. "Why did you come, Joyce? I was at peace . . ."

"My God, where else could I go?" She was nervously wringing her hands. "Oh, if you would . . . if only you would . . ."

Golder shrugged his shoulders. "What? You want me to give you Alec for life, buy him for you, like I used to buy you toys and jewellery? Is that it? But I can't do it now. It's too expensive. Did your mother tell you I still had money?"

"Yes."

"Look at how I live. I barely have enough to see me through until I die. But it would only last *you* a year."

"But why don't you do what you did before?" she begged desperately. "Get back into business, make money? It's so easy . . ."

"Really! Is that what you think?"

Once again, with a kind of fearful tenderness, he touched her fine golden hair. "Poor little Joyce . . ."

"It's funny," he thought, painfully. "I know exactly what will happen. In two months' time, she'll have had enough of sleeping with her Alec . . . or whoever else it is . . . and that will be that . . . But Fischl! Oh, if it were only someone else . . . anyone else! But Fischl!" He was filled with hatred. "The bastard will talk about 'Golder's daughter, whom I married even though she had nothing . . . nothing but the clothes on her back!' "

He leaned forward abruptly, took Joyce's face in both hands and raised it up, digging his old, hard nails into her delicate skin with a kind of urgency. "You . . . you . . . If you didn't need me, you'd have left me here to die all alone, wouldn't you? Well, wouldn't you?"

"Would you have sent for me?" she whispered.

She smiled. He looked helplessly at her tear-filled eyes and her beautiful, full red lips that opened slowly, like a flower.

"My little girl," he thought. "Perhaps, after all, she *is* mine, who knows? And anyway, what does it matter, for God's sake, what difference does it make?"

"You really know how to get what you want from your old man, eh, Joy?" he whispered passionately. "Your tears . . . and the idea of that pig being able to buy something that was mine, right? Right?" he repeated wildly, with a mixture of hatred and savage tenderness. "So then, you want me to try? You want me to make you some more money before I die? Are you prepared to wait a year? A year from now, you'll be richer than your mother ever was."

He let her go and stood up. He could feel the heat and energy of life coursing through his old, weary body once more—all the strength and passion he had felt in the past.

"Tell Fischl he can go to hell," he continued. His voice had become precise, matter-of-fact. "And if you weren't a complete fool, you'd send your Alec packing as well. No? If you let him spend all your money, what will you do after I'm gone? You don't care, is that it? You think you'll always be able to fall back on Fischl? Oh, I'm nothing but an old fool," he growled. He took Joyce by the chin, gripping it so tightly that she winced in pain. "You will do me the honour of signing the marriage contract I will have drawn up for you, and no questions asked. I'm not going to kill myself for your little gigolo. Understood? Do you want some money now?"

She nodded without replying. He let go of her, opened a drawer.

"Listen to me, Joy . . . Tomorrow you will go and see Seton, my lawyer. I'll instruct him to send you a hundred and fifty pounds every month . . ."

He quickly scribbled some figures in the margin of a newspaper that was lying on the table.

"That's just about what I used to give you. A bit less. But you'll have to make do with it for a while longer, my child, because it's all that I have left. Later on, after I get back, you can get married."

"But where are you going?"

He shrugged his shoulders angrily.

"Do you really care?"

He put his hand on her neck. "Joyce . . . If I die while I'm away, Seton will take care of everything to protect your interests. All you have to do is listen to him. Sign whatever he tells you to sign. Do you understand?"

She nodded.

He took a deep breath. "So . . . that's it then . . . "

"Daddy, darling . . . "

She had slipped on to his lap, buried her head in his shoulder, closed her eyes.

He looked at her with a faint smile—a mere quiver of the lips that he quickly repressed. "How loving people are when they're poor, eh? This is the first time I've seen you like this, my child . . . "

"And the last . . . " he thought, but he said nothing. He was happy simply to stroke her eyelids and neck. He did so for a long while, as if he were sculpting her features so he could remember them for a very long time to come.

"BOTH PARTIES AGREE to conclude the agreement regarding concessions within thirty days of the signature of this contract..."

The ten men sitting around the table all looked at Golder.

"Yes, go on," he murmured.

"In accordance with the following conditions..."

Golder fanned his face nervously with his hand in an attempt to dispel the cloud of smoke that threatened to choke him. The room was so thick with it that, from time to time, he could barely see the man opposite him who was reading: his pale, angular face and his black hole of a mouth became a mere patch of colour in the fog.

A strong odour of leather, sweat, and Russian tobacco hung in the air.

Since the night before, these ten men had not managed to agree on the final wording of the contract. And before that, their negotiations had lasted eighteen weeks.

He turned his wrist to check the time, but his watch had stopped. He glanced at the window. Through the dirty glass, he could see the sun rising over Moscow. It was a very beautiful August morning, yet already it held the icy, transparent purity of the first dawns of autumn.

"The Soviet government shall grant the Tübingen Petroleum Company a concession of up to fifty per cent of the oilfields located between the Teisk region and the area known as the Aroundgis, as described in the memorandum presented by the Tübingen Petroleum Company's representative, dated 2 December 1925. Each oilfield included in this concession shall be rectangular in shape, no larger than one hundred acres, and shall not be adjoining..."

Golder interrupted.

"Would you please read that last item again for me?" he asked, his lips closing tightly.

"Each oilfield . . . "

"So there it is," thought Golder in frustration. "No mention of that before . . . They wait until the very last minute to sneak in their dirty little ambiguous clauses that don't seem to mean anything precise, just to have an excuse to break the agreement later on, after we've advanced them the money for the initial expenses. I heard they did the same thing to Amrum . . . "

He remembered having read a copy of the Amrum contract, the one he'd found amongst Marcus's papers. Work was supposed to begin on a certain date. They had unofficially promised Amrum's representative that the date could be extended—then they claimed the contract had been broken. It had cost Amrum millions. "Bunch of pigs," he muttered.

He banged his fist down on the table angrily.

"You will cross that out right now!"

"No," someone shouted.

"Then I'm not signing."

"Oh, but my dear David Issakitch . . . " one of the men cried.

His warm, lyrical Russian accent and his soothing, considerate Slavonic expressions jarred strangely with the severe, narrow eyes set in his yellow face, and their intent, cruel stare.

"What do you mean, my dear friend?" he said, stretching out his arms as if he wanted to hug Golder. "Goloubtchik . . . you know very well that this clause doesn't mean anything significant. It is only there to appease the legitimate concerns of the proletariat who would not look favourably on having a part of Soviet territory pass into the hands of capitalists without some assurances . . . "

Golder brushed him away.

"Enough! What next! And what about Amrum, eh? In any case, I am not entitled to sign any clause that has not been read and approved by the company. Have I made myself clear, Simon Alexeevitch?"

Simon Alexeevitch closed his file. "Perfectly clear," he said, in a different tone of voice. "We'll wait then so the company has time to consider it and either accept or reject it."

"So that's it . . ." thought Golder. "They want to drag it out some more . . . Perhaps Amrum . . ."

He flung his chair aside and stood up. "There will be no more delays, do you understand? No more delays! This contract will be signed right now or not at all! You'd better be careful! It's yes or no, but right now! I refuse to spend even one extra hour in Moscow, let there be no misunderstandings! Come on, Valleys," he said, turning towards the secretary of the Tübingen Company, who hadn't slept in thirty-six hours and was looking at him in a kind of despair. Were they going to have to start all over again, my God, over something so insignificant? These endless negotiations, the shouting, Golder with his strangled, terrifying voice that at times seemed like nothing more than a kind of inarticulate babbling, like the sound of blood catching in your throat . . .

"How can he shout like that?" thought Valleys with an instinctive feeling of terror. "And the rest of them as well?"

They were now all huddled together at one end of the room, shouting wildly. Valleys could make out only certain words— "the interests of the proletariat," "the tyranny and exploitation of the capitalists"—which they hurled at each other in rapid fire as if they were punching each other in the face.

Golder, red with fury, was frantically hammering the table with his hand, sending papers flying in all directions. Every time he shouted, Valleys thought the old man's heart would explode.

"Valleys! For God's sake!"

Valleys shuddered and jumped to his feet.

Golder stormed past him, followed by the others who were screaming and waving their arms about. Valleys couldn't understand a word of it. He followed Golder as if he were in some kind of nightmare. They were already going down the stairs when a member of the commission, the only one who hadn't moved, got up and went over to Golder. He had a strange, almost Oriental face that was square and flat, and swarthy skin, like dried-out earth. He was a former convict. His nose was horribly scarred.

Golder seemed to calm down. The man whispered something in his ear. They went back into the room together and sat down. Simon Alexeevitch began reading again:

"On the annual production of oil estimated at approximately thirty thousand metric tons, the Soviet government will receive a commission of five per cent. For every ten thousand additional tons, a commission of zero point two five per cent will be added up to an annual yield of four hundred and thirty thousand tons, at which point the Soviet government will receive a commission of fifteen per cent. The Soviet treasury will also receive a fee equal to forty-five per cent of the petrol produced from the oil-fields and a fee on gas, on a sliding scale from ten per cent to thirty-five per cent, depending on the gasoline it contains . . ."

Golder was resting his hand on his cheek, eyes lowered, listening, without saying a word. Valleys thought he was sleeping: his face, with its deep furrows at the corners of his mouth and pinched nostrils, looked as pale and wan as a corpse.

Valleys looked up at the typed pages of the contract that Simon Alexeevitch still had in his hands. "We'll never get through all that in a day . . ." he thought dismally.

Golder suddenly leaned towards him. "Open that window behind you," he whispered, "quickly . . . I'm suffocating . . ."

He made Valleys jump. "Open it," ordered Golder again, almost without moving his lips.

Quickly Valleys pushed open the window, then went back to Golder, expecting to find him collapsed in the chair.

Meanwhile, Simon Alexeevitch was still reading:

"The Tübingen Petroleum Company may mine all its crude and refined products without paying a fee and without obtaining special authorisation. In the same way, it may import, duty free, any machinery, tools, or primary materials necessary to its operations, along with provisions for its employees . . ."

"Monsieur Golder," Valleys whispered, "I'm going to stop him. You're in no condition . . . you're as a white as a ghost . . ."

Golder angrily grabbed his wrist. "Be quiet! I can't hear what they're saying. Will you be quiet, for God's sake!"

"In exchange for these concessions, the company must make payments to the Soviet government, on a sliding scale from five per cent to fifteen per cent of the total yield from the oilfields, and from five per cent to forty per cent of the yield from the active oil wells . . ."

Golder groaned imperceptibly and slumped on to the table. Simon Alexeevitch stopped reading.

"I would like to point out to you that, as far as the active oil wells are concerned, the second subcommittee, whose report I have here, has estimated that . . ."

Valleys felt Golder's icy hand grab his own under the table and clutch it anxiously. Automatically, he squeezed Golder's fingers with all his might. He vaguely remembered how he had once held the fractured, bleeding jaw of a dying Irish setter in the same way. Why did this old Jew so often remind him of a sick dog, close to death, who still bares his teeth, growls wildly, and gives one last, powerful bite?

"Your remark regarding article twenty-seven . . ." said Golder. "We've hashed that over for three days now; we're not going to start all over again, are we? Go on . . ."

"The Tübingen Petroleum Company may construct any buildings, refineries, pipelines, and any other necessary structures. The agreed concessions will remain in force for a period of ninety-nine years . . ."

Golder had pulled his hand away from Valleys' and, with his head on the ink-stained oilcloth, tore open his shirt and began massaging his chest under the table, as if he were trying to expose his lungs to the fresh air. His trembling fingers clutched his heart with the wild, instinctive desperation of a sick animal who presses the injured part of his body to the ground. He was deathly pale. Valleys watched the sweat pour down his face, thick and heavy, like tears.

But the voice of Simon Alexeevitch had become louder, more solemn. He quietly rose from his chair to conclude:

"Article seventy-four. Final article. Once the term of this concession has expired, all the equipment and all the structures on the oilfields heretofore mentioned shall become the sole property of the Soviet government."

"It's over," sighed Valleys, in a kind of trance. Golder pulled himself up and gestured for someone to hand him a pen. The formality of signing the contract began. The ten men were all pale, silent, exhausted.

Eventually, Golder stood up and walked towards the door.

The members of the commission nodded reluctantly to him from their chairs. Only the Chinese representative was smiling. The others looked weary and furious. Golder gave a swift, mechanical nod in reply.

"Now he'll collapse," thought Valleys. "He's at death's door..."

But he didn't collapse. He walked down the stairs. It wasn't until he was out in the street that he seemed to be gripped by a kind of dizziness. He stopped, pressed his face against a wall, and stood there silently, his whole body shaking.

Valleys called a taxi and helped him into it. Every time they hit a bump in the road, Golder's head swayed and fell forward on to his chest as if he were dead. Gradually, however, the fresh air seemed to revive him. He breathed deeply, putting his hand to his wallet, which lay over his heart.

"Finally, it's over ... The pigs ..."

"When I think," said Valleys, "that we've been here for four and a half months! When will we be going home, Monsieur Golder? This country is horrible!" he concluded with feeling.

"Yes, it is. You'll leave tomorrow."

"But what about you?"

"Me ... I'm going to Teisk."

"Oh, Monsieur Golder," said Valleys, upset, "is that absolutely necessary?"

"Yes. Why?"

Valleys blushed. "Couldn't I go with you? I really wouldn't like to think you were alone in such a desolate place. You're not well."

Golder said nothing, then gave a vague, embarrassed shrug. "You must leave as soon as possible, Valleys."

"But couldn't you ... get someone else to go with you? It's not safe for you to travel alone in your condition ..."

"I'm used to it," Golder muttered sarcastically.

"ROOM SEVENTEEN, first on the left down the corridor," shouted the porter from below. A moment later, the lights went out. Golder continued climbing the stairs, stumbling on steps that seemed, as in a dream, to go on for ever.

His swollen arm was painful. He put down his suitcase, fumbled around in the dark for the banister, leaned over, called out. But no one replied. He swore in a quiet, breathless voice, climbed up two more steps then stopped, head back, bracing himself against the wall.

The suitcase wasn't really that heavy; all it had inside were his toiletries and a change of clothes. In certain Soviet backwaters there always came a time when you had to carry your own luggage—he'd realised that as soon as he'd left Moscow—but, even though his case was very light, he barely had the strength to lift it. He was exhausted.

He had left Teisk the night before. The journey had tired him so much that he'd had to make the driver stop along the way. "Twenty-two hours in a car!" he groaned. "Oh, my poor old body!" He'd been in a broken-down old Ford, and the roads through the mountains were almost impassable. He felt every bump and jolt shoot right through his bones. Towards evening, the car's horn had stopped working, so the driver had recruited a small boy from the village who climbed on to the running-board and, hanging on to the roof with one hand, kept two fingers of the other in his mouth and whistled continuously, from six o'clock until midnight. Even now, Golder could still hear him. He put his hands over his ears and frowned as if in pain. And the rattling the old Ford made, the noise of the windows that seemed about to shatter at every sharp corner . . . It was nearly one o'clock before they finally spotted some lights shimmering in the distance. It was the port, where Golder would go, the next day, to leave for Europe.

In the past, it had been one of the most important trading centres for grain. He knew it well. He'd come here when he was twenty. It was from this port that he had boarded a ship for the very first time.

Now only a few Greek steamers and Soviet cargo ships were anchored in the harbour. The town looked so pathetic and abandoned that it was heart-breaking. And his dingy, grubby hotel, with bullet holes in the walls, was inexpressibly sinister. Golder regretted not having left from Moscow as they had suggested at Teisk. These boats hardly ever carried anyone except the *schouroum-bouroum*—traders from the Levant who travelled all over the world with their bales of rugs and second-hand fur coats. But one night goes quickly. He was eager to leave Russia. The following day he'd be in Constantinople.

He had gone into his room. He let out a deep sigh, switched on the lights, and sat down in a corner on the first chair within reach; it was made of a hard, dark wood, and, with its severe straight back, it was extremely uncomfortable.

He was so exhausted that, the instant he closed his eyes, he lost consciousness and thought he'd fallen asleep. But it had been only a minute. He opened his eyes again and looked absent-mindedly around the room. The faint light that shone from the small electric bulb hanging from the ceiling was flickering as if it would go out at any moment, like a candle in the wind. It lit up some faded paintings: cupids, whose thighs were once rosy, the colour of fresh blood, but were now covered with a thick layer of dust. The high-ceilinged room was vast, with dark furniture covered in red velvet and a table in the middle on which stood an old oil lamp, whose glass shade was so full of dead flies it looked as if it had been coated in a thick layer of black jam.

There were bullet holes in the walls, of course. On one side in particular, the partition wall was riddled with enormous holes; cracks radiated from them like rays of the sun; the plaster was flaking off and crumbling like sand. Golder put his fist into one of the holes, then slowly rubbed his hands together and stood up. It was after three o'clock in the morning.

He took a few steps, then sat back down again to take off his shoes. As he leant forward, he suddenly froze, his arm outstretched. What was the point of getting undressed? He wouldn't be able to sleep. There was no water. He turned one of the taps on the sink. Nothing. It was stifling hot. Not a breath of air. The dust and sweat made his clothes stick to his skin. Whenever he moved, the damp material felt like ice against his shoulders. It sent a little shiver through his body, like a fever.

"Good Lord," he thought, "when will I ever get out of this place?"

He felt as if the night would never end. Three more hours to go. The boat was due to leave at dawn. But it would be delayed, naturally . . . Once at sea, he'd feel better. There'd be a bit of wind, a little fresh air. And then Constantinople. The Mediterranean. Paris. Paris? He felt a vague satisfaction at the thought of all those bastards at the Stock Exchange. He could just hear them: "Have you heard about Golder? . . . Well, who'd have believed it? . . . He really looked like he was finished . . ." Filthy bastards. What would the Teisk shares be worth now? He tried to work it out, but it was too difficult. Since Valleys had left, he'd had no news from Europe. All in good time . . . He let out a deep sigh. It was strange, he couldn't imagine what his life would be like when the journey was over. All in good time . . . Joy . . . He frowned slightly. Joy . . . Every now and then she would remember her old dad's existence, but only when she or her husband had lost money gambling, of course. Then she would come to see him, take some more money, and disappear again for months on end . . . He had expressly instructed Seton that she was not allowed to touch her capital. "Otherwise, from the day she gets married to the day I die . . ." He stopped himself. He had no illusions. "I've done everything I can," he said out loud, sadly.

He had taken off his shoes. He went and stretched out on the bed. But for some time now, he had been unable to lie down for long. He couldn't breathe. Sometimes he would fall asleep, but then he would immediately start suffocating and wake up to the distant sound of crying—strange, pitiful cries that came as if from some dream, and which seemed to him terrifying, incomprehensible, and threatening. He didn't realise that it was he who was crying out; the childlike sobs were his own.

Now, once more, as soon as he had lain down, he began to suffocate. With great difficulty, he pulled himself from the bed, dragged a chair over to the window, and opened it. Below was the port, dark water . . . Day was breaking.

Suddenly, he fell asleep.

AT FIVE O'CLOCK, the first blasts of the port sirens woke Golder.

He had difficulty picking up his shoes, and there was still no water when he tried the tap on the sink. He rang for the porter and waited a long time, but nobody came. Eventually, he found a little Eau de Cologne in a bottle in his suitcase and rubbed it on his hands and face. Then he got his things together and went downstairs.

Only once he was downstairs did he manage to get a cup of tea. He paid, then left.

Through habit, he started looking around for a taxi. But the town seemed deserted. A cloud of sand, carried inland by the sea breeze, obscured all the buildings. It lay so thick on the streets that there were deep footprints where people had walked past, as if through snow. Golder motioned to a young boy who was silently running barefoot along the middle of the street.

"Can you carry my suitcase to the port? Aren't there any taxis?"

The child seemed not to understand. But he took hold of the suitcase and walked on ahead.

The houses were all closed, their windows boarded up. There were banks, official buildings, but empty, deserted. On the walls, the outline of the Imperial Eagle remained etched into the stone, like a wound . . . Instinctively, Golder walked more quickly.

He vaguely recognised certain old, dark alley-ways, the houses made of rickety wood. But it was so silent . . . Suddenly, he stopped.

They weren't far from the port. The air had the strong smell of mud and salt. A small, dark shoemaker's shop, with its iron boot swinging in front of the window, creaking . . . On the corner opposite, his old lodging house, a place frequented by sailors and prostitutes . . . The shoemaker was one of his father's cousins who had settled in the town; Golder used to go and have a meal with him from time to time. He remembered the place well . . . He made an effort to try to recall what his cousin looked like. But all he could remember was the sound of his bitter, plaintive voice, probably because it was just like Soifer's: "Stay here, my boy . . . Do you think you're going to find gold on the streets somewhere else? Ha! Life is hard wherever you go."

Without thinking, Golder started to turn the door handle, then let his hand drop back down to his side. It had been forty-eight years! He shrugged his shoulders, kept walking.

"I wonder what would have happened if I'd stayed?" He laughed bitterly. "Who knows? Imagine Gloria doing the house-work and frying potato pancakes in goose fat on Friday night. Life . . . " he whispered softly. How odd it was that, after so many years, he should be brought back to this desolate place . . .

The port. He recognised it as clearly as if he had left the day before. The little customs building, half in ruins. Beached boats buried in the black sand, which was littered with bits of coal and rubbish; watermelon rind and dead animals bobbing in the deep, muddy green water, just as in the past.

He climbed on board a small Greek steamship that used to do the crossing between Batoum and Constantinople before the war. It must have been a passenger boat, for it seemed to have certain amenities. There was a sitting room, a piano. But since the Revolution, it had carried only merchandise—and strange merchandise at that. It was dirty and run-down.

"Thank goodness the crossing won't take long . . . " thought Golder.

On the bridge, a few *schouroum-bouroum* in their red skullcaps were sitting on the floor, playing cards. They looked up when Golder walked by. One of them waved a pink glass necklace that was hanging from his arm and smiled: "Buy something, good sir . . . " Golder shook his head and gently pushed them aside with his cane. How many times, during his first crossing—a crossing the memory of which clung to him with a strange, tenacious persistence—had he played cards with men just like these, at night, in some corner of the boat... That was so long ago... They moved back to let him pass. He went down into his cabin and looked with a sigh at the sea through the porthole. The boat was moving. He sat down on his berth, a plank of wood covered with a thin, prickly straw mattress. If the weather held, he would sleep on the bridge. But the wind was blowing fiercely and the boat was being tossed about. Golder looked at the sea with a kind of hatred. He was so weary of this endlessly changing world— the landscape rushing past train and car windows, these waves that roared like animals, the trails of smoke in the stormy autumn sky. If only the horizon could be still until he died... "I'm tired," he murmured. With that instinctive, nervous gesture of people with a heart condition, he pressed both hands against his chest. He massaged it gently as if it were a child or a dying animal—to encourage the worn-out, stubborn machine that beat so feebly in his old body.

Suddenly, after a particularly strong roll of the ship, he seemed to feel his heart falter, then start beating faster, too fast... At the same time, he was struck by an excruciating pain in his left shoulder. He went pale, sat with his head hanging forward, looking terrified, and waited for a long time. The sound of his breathing seemed to fill the cabin, drowning out the noise of the wind and the sea.

Little by little, the pain eased off, then stopped completely. "It was nothing," he said out loud, forcing himself to smile. "It's over."

He was having difficulty breathing. "Over..." he sighed more quietly.

He tried to stand. Outside, the sky and the sea had grown gradually darker. The cabin was as black as if it were the middle of the night. The only light came from the porthole, a strange green murky glow that was not really light at all. Golder fumbled about for his coat, put it on, then went out. He stretched out his hands in front of him, like a blind man. Each time the sea struck the boat, it shuddered, reeled, and plunged, as if it were about to disappear, dragged down into the water. He grasped the bottom of the little ladder that led to the bridge, and hauled himself up.

"Be careful, Comrade, there's a strong wind up there!" shouted one of the sailors who came running. Golder could smell the strong odour of alcohol on his breath.

"We're being tossed about, Comrade..."

"I'm used to it," Golder grumbled sarcastically.

But he had difficulty making it to the bridge. Great swells of water were crashing against the boat. In one corner, the *schouroum-bouroum* were huddled in a heap underneath a soaking wet tarpaulin, shivering like a mournful herd of frozen cattle. One of them saw Golder, looked up, and shouted a few words in a shrill, plaintive voice that was drowned out in the commotion. Golder gestured that he couldn't hear him. The man repeated what he'd said louder, tensing up his pale face and rolling his blazing eyes. Then suddenly he succumbed to a bout of seasickness, and fell back on to the deck; he lay motionless on his old sheepskin, amongst the bales of cargo and other men.

Golder walked past them.

Soon he had to stop. He stood still, bent over, like a tree yielding to a violent wind; his face was strained, and on his lips was the sharp, bitter taste of salt and the sea. He tried to open his eyes but couldn't; he was clutching a wet, icy-cold iron railing that was freezing his fingers.

As each wave crashed into the boat, it seemed to sink further, breaking under the weight of the sea; every now and then, a long, hollow, heart-rending groan rose up from its timbers, drowning out the harsh sound of the wind and the waves.

"Well," thought Golder, "this was all I needed..."

Nevertheless, he didn't move. With an odd sort of pleasure, he let the storm batter his old body. The sea water, mingling with the rain, soaked his cheeks, his lips; his eyelashes and hair were caked with salt.

Suddenly, he heard a voice shouting loudly, very close to him, but the wind drowned out the words. Struggling to look up, he vaguely made out the shape of a man, doubled over, hanging on to the rail with both arms.

A wave crashed into Golder, breaking at his feet. He could feel the water filling his eyes and mouth. He quickly jumped back. The other man followed him. With the storm knocking them against the wall with each step, they managed to stagger below deck.

"What horrible weather..." the man murmured in Russian, sounding terrified. "Dear God, what horrible weather..."

It was pitch black, and all Golder could see was a kind of long overcoat dragging along the floor, but he recognised the lilting accent all too well.

"Is this your first crossing?" he asked. "You're a Yid?"

The man laughed nervously but seemed cheered. "Yes," he murmured. "You too?"

"Me too," said Golder.

Golder had sat down on the old, tattered velvet settee fixed to the wall. The man remained standing in front of him. With numb hands, Golder fumbled in his jacket pocket for his cigarette case, opened it, and held it out. "Have one."

When he lit the match, he looked up for a moment and studied the face of the man bending towards him; he was young, barely more than a teenager, pale, with a long, sad nose, curly black woolly hair and enormous, anxious eyes.

"Where are you from?"

"Kremenets, Sir, in the Ukraine."

"I've been there," murmured Golder.

In the past, it had been a miserable village where black pigs had rolled about in the mud with Jewish children. It probably hadn't changed much.

"So, you're leaving? For good?"

"Oh, yes."

"Why are you leaving now? I know why we left in my day!"

"Ah, Sir," said the little Jew with an accent that was comical and tragic both at the same time, "do things ever change for people like us? I'm an honest young man, I am, Sir, and yet I just got out of prison two days ago. And why? Because an order came through to take some boxes of Montpensiers—you know, those candied fruits?—from the south to Moscow. It was summer and stifling hot; of course everything melted in the freight cars. When I got to Moscow they were dripping through the crates. But was that my fault? I spent eighteen months in prison for that. I'm free now. I want to go to Europe."

"How old are you?"

"Eighteen, Sir."

"Ah . . ." said Golder slowly. "About the same age as me, when I left."

"Are you from here?"

"Yes."

The young man fell silent. He smoked with obvious pleasure. In the darkness, Golder could see his hands, lit up by the cigarette; they were shaking.

"Your first crossing . . ." Golder said again. "So where are you going?"

"Paris, to start with. I have a cousin who's a tailor in Paris. He moved there before the war. But as soon as I have enough money, I'm going to New York! Yes, New York!" he repeated excitedly.

But Golder wasn't listening. Instead, he observed, with a kind of sad, poignant pleasure, the way the boy in front of him moved his hands and shoulders; the way his whole body trembled incessantly as he tripped over his words in his eagerness to speak. That feverish desire, that nervous energy . . . he too had once possessed them: the hungry exuberance so particular to young people of his race. All that was so long ago now . . .

"You know you're going to starve to death, don't you?" he said sharply.

"Oh, I'm used to that . . ."

"Yes . . . But over there, it's harder . . ."

"What's the difference? It won't be for long . . ."

Golder suddenly burst out laughing, a laugh as dry and sharp as a whip.

"So that's what you think, do you? Well, you're a fool! It lasts for years, years . . . And after that, to tell the truth, it's hardly any better . . ."

"After that . . ." the boy whispered passionately, "after that you get rich . . ."

"After that," replied Golder, "you die, alone, like a dog, the same way you lived . . ."

He stopped talking and threw back his head with a stifled moan. Once again he felt that excruciating pain around his shoulder, and his aching heart seemed to stop beating . . .

"You don't look well..." he heard the boy say. "Is it seasickness?"

"No," said Golder, his voice weak and stuttering. "No ... it's my heart..."

He was having trouble breathing; it hurt him to speak. But what did the past, *his* past, matter to this little fool anyway? Life was different now ... easier. Besides, he didn't really give a damn about this little Jew, for God's sake ...

"For someone who's been through as much as I have, my boy, seasickness and foolish things like that ... So, you want to get rich?"

He lowered his voice.

"Take a good look at me. Do you think it's worth it?"

He'd let his head fall forward on to his chest. For a moment, he felt as if the noise of the wind and the sea were fading away into the distance, merging into a kind of chant ... Then, suddenly, he heard the terrified voice of the boy shouting, "Help!" He stood up, staggered forward, then stretched both arms up, clutching at the air, the void. Then he collapsed on to the floor.

SOME TIME LATER he came round, as if pulled out of deep, dark water. He was semiconscious, stretched out on his cabin bed. Someone had opened his shirt and slipped a rolled-up overcoat underneath his head. At first, he thought he was alone. Then, when he began feverishly to look around the room, he heard the voice of the little Jew behind him.

"Sir..." he whispered.

Golder tried to raise his hand. The boy leaned towards him. "Oh, Sir! Are you feeling better?"

Golder moved his lips as if he had forgotten the shape and sound of human speech. Finally, he managed to murmur, "Light."

The light was switched on, and he sighed in pain. He moved, and gave a moan. Instinctively he reached for his chest, to touch his heart, but his heavy hands fell back down to his sides. He muttered a few confused words in a foreign language, and then seemed to come round completely. He opened his eyes. "Go and get the captain," he said, his voice strangely clear.

The boy went out. Golder was alone. He groaned slightly when a particularly strong wave hit the boat. But the rolling gradually subsided. Sunlight shone in through the porthole. Golder, exhausted, closed his eyes.

When the Greek captain, a large drunken man, came in, Golder appeared to be asleep.

"What's going on? Is he dead?" the captain asked, swearing.

Golder slowly turned his head towards the captain's hollow, pale face, with its pinched, white lips.

"Stop the boat..." he whispered.

When the captain didn't reply, he said it again, louder: "Stop. Do you understand?"

Golder's eyes, half hidden beneath his quivering eyelids,

burned so fiercely that the captain was confused; he shrugged his shoulders: "You're crazy."

"I'll pay you . . . I'll give you a thousand pounds."

"Mad," the captain growled. "He's on his way out . . . I'd bet my own life on it . . . What did I do to deserve a passenger like this?"

"Back to shore . . ." Golder mumbled, then, "Do you want me to die here all alone, like an animal? Bastard . . ." And then something no one could make out.

"Isn't there a doctor on board?" the boy asked. But the captain had already left. The young lad went over to Golder who was panting desperately.

"Try to be patient," he whispered softly. "We'll soon be in Constantinople . . . We're moving quickly now . . . The storm has stopped. Do you know anyone in Constantinople? Do you have any relatives there? Anyone at all?"

"What?" murmured Golder. "What was that?"

He finally seemed to understand, but all he kept saying was "What?" over and over again. Then he fell silent.

The boy continued whispering anxiously: "Constantinople . . . It's a big city . . . they can look after you there . . . you'll soon get well . . . Don't be afraid."

But at that moment, he realised that Golder was dying. For the first time, the hollow sound of death rose from his tortured chest.

It went on for nearly an hour. The boy was shivering. Even so, he didn't leave. He listened to the air reverberating in the dying man's throat with a deep, husky groan, like some mysterious force, as if an alien being had already taken over his body.

"It won't be long now," he thought. "Then it will all be over. I'll leave him then . . . I don't even know his name, for God's sake!"

Then he looked over at the wallet stuffed full of English money that had fallen to the floor when he had carried him over to the bed. He bent down, picked it up, looked inside, then sighed, and holding his breath, slipped it gently into Golder's open hand—a swollen, heavy, icy hand, the hand of a corpse.

"Who knows? That way . . . Maybe he'll come round for a

moment before he dies. He might want to give me this money . . .
Who knows? Who can know? I'm the one who's stayed with
him. He's all alone."

He began to wait. The sea grew calmer as night fell. The boat
glided calmly along. The wind had dropped. "It will be a beautiful night," the boy thought.

He stretched out his hand to touch the wrist dangling in front
of him; the heart was beating so faintly that the sound of the
watch, with its leather strap, almost drowned it out. Golder was
still alive, though. The body is reluctant to die. He was alive.
He opened his eyes. He said something. But the air was still
growling in his chest with a sinister, chilling sound, like flood
waters receding. The boy leant over him, listening intently.
Golder said a few words in Russian; then suddenly the forgotten
language of his childhood unexpectedly spilled from his lips, and
he started speaking Yiddish.

He spoke quickly, in a strange, mumbling voice that was interrupted now and again by long, hoarse wheezing. Sometimes he
would stop, slowly bringing his hands to his throat, as if to lift
some invisible weight. Half of his face was paralysed, the eye
already clouded over and staring. But the other eye was alive,
piercing. Sweat poured down his cheeks. The boy wanted to
wipe it away. "Never mind . . ." Golder groaned, "There's no
point . . . Listen. In Paris, you must go to Maître Seton, Rue
Albert, number twenty-eight. You must tell him that Golder is
dead. Say it. Say it again. Seton, Maître Seton, lawyer. Give him
everything in my suitcase and wallet. Tell him I want him to do
whatever he thinks best . . . for my daughter . . . Then you must
go to see Tübingen . . . Wait."

He was panting. His lips were moving, but the boy couldn't
understand what he was saying. He leaned so far over him that
he could smell the dying man's breath, the fever coming from
Golder's mouth.

"Hôtel Continental. Write it down," Golder finally whispered. "John Tübingen. Hôtel Continental."

The boy hurriedly took an old letter from his pocket, tore off
the back of the envelope, and wrote down the two addresses.

"You will tell him that Golder is dead," he ordered, his voice fading, "that I beg him to look after my daughter's interests . . . that I trust him and . . ."

He stopped. His eyes were darting about, their light edging towards darkness.

"And . . . No. Just that. That's all. Yes, that's fine."

He looked at the bit of paper that the young boy was holding in his hand.

"Give it to me . . . I'll sign it . . . That would be best . . ."

"I don't think you'll manage it," said the boy. Nevertheless, he took Golder's hand and slipped the pencil between his weak fingers.

"I don't think you'll manage it," he said again.

"Golder . . ." the dying man whispered, "David Golder . . ." with a kind of madness and terrified determination—the name, the syllables that formed it, sounding as incomprehensible to him as the words of some unknown language . . . Nevertheless, he managed to sign.

"I'll give you all the money I have with me," he whispered, "but you must swear to do everything exactly as I've said."

"Yes, I swear it."

"Before Almighty God," said Golder.

"Before Almighty God."

A sudden convulsion ran through his face, and blood started pouring from the corners of his mouth on to his hands. His rattled breathing eased.

"Sir, can you still hear me?" the boy asked fearfully.

The evening light pouring in from the porthole fell straight on to Golder's face. The boy shuddered. This time it really was the end. The wallet remained open in the outstretched hand. He grabbed it, counted the money, slipped it into his pocket, then put the envelope with the two addresses under his belt.

"Is he finally dead?" he thought.

He reached out towards Golder's open shirt, but his hands were shaking so violently that he couldn't manage to feel whether the heart was still beating.

He left him there. He walked backwards towards the door on tiptoe, as if he were afraid to waken him. Then, without looking back, he ran out.

142   IRÈNE NÉMIROVSKY

Golder was alone.

He had the still, frozen look of a corpse. But death had not claimed him all at once, like a wave. He had felt himself losing his voice, the heat of life, consciousness of the man he had once been. But right until the end, he could see. He watched as the light of the setting sun spilled over the sea, saw how the water sparkled.

And, deep from within his memory, until he drew his final breath, certain images continued to flash before him, fainter and more indistinct as death drew nearer. For a moment, he thought he was actually touching Joyce's hair, her skin. Then she seemed to pull away, to abandon him, as he plunged deeper into darkness. One last time, he thought he could hear her laugh, light and sweet, like a bell ringing in the distance. Then she was gone. He saw Marcus. Certain faces, vague shapes, as if carried along by the water at dusk, would swirl around for a moment, then disappear. And, as he reached the end, all he could see was a shop, lit up, on a dark street, a street from his childhood, a candle set behind an icy window, the night, snow falling, and himself... He could feel snowflakes on his lips, which melted with the taste of ice and water so familiar to him from the past. And he could hear someone calling: "David, David..." A voice hushed by the snow, the low, dark sky... A small voice that suddenly grew fainter and faded away, as if heading in a different direction. It was the last sound he was to hear on this earth.

THE BALL

I

MADAME KAMPF WALKED into the study and slammed the door behind her with such force that a gust of air made the crystal beads on the chandelier jingle with the pure, light sound of small bells. But Antoinette didn't stop reading; she was bent so far forward over her desk that her hair brushed the pages of her book. For a moment, Madame Kampf watched her daughter without saying anything; then she went to stand in front of her, arms crossed over her chest.

"You know, Antoinette, you could stop what you're doing when you see your mother," she barked. "Is your bottom glued to that chair? What refined manners you have! Where's Miss Betty?"

From the adjoining room came the sound of a sewing machine, punctuated by snatches of song, crooned in a youthful but rather poor voice: "What shall I do, what shall I do when you'll be gone away . . ."

"Miss Betty," Madame Kampf shouted, "come in here."

"Yes, Mrs. Kampf," the young woman replied in English, slipping through the half-open door. She had rosy cheeks and soft, frightened eyes; her hair was gathered in a honey-coloured bun that sat low on her neck, framing her small round head.

"I believe I hired you," Madame Kampf began harshly, "to look after and educate my daughter, and not so you could make yourself dresses. Does Antoinette not know she is meant to stand up when her mother comes into the room?"

"Oh, Ann-toinette! How can you?" said Miss Betty in a kind of sad twitter.

Antoinette was standing up now, balancing awkwardly on one leg. She was a tall, lacklustre girl of fourteen, with the pale face common to girls of her age—a face so thin and taut that it seems, to adults, like a round, featureless blotch. Dark circles were under her lowered eyelids, and her mouth was small and tight. The fourteen-year-old body . . . budding breasts that strain against the tight schoolgirl's uniform, that are painful and embarrassing to her delicate, childlike body; big feet and long arms like sticks of French bread that end in red hands and ink-stained fingers (and which one day, who knows, might turn into the most beautiful arms in the world); a spindly neck; short, dull hair that is dry and fine . . .

"Don't you see, Antoinette, that your manners are driving me to despair? Sit down again. I'm going to come back in, and this time you will do me the honour of standing up immediately, understand?"

Madame Kampf took a few steps out of the room and once again opened the door. Antoinette stood up so slowly and with such obvious reluctance that her mother clenched her teeth.

"Perhaps you can't be bothered, is that it, Miss?" she asked sharply, her voice threatening.

"No, Mama," replied Antoinette quietly.

"Well, then why have you got that look on your face?"

Antoinette attempted a smile, but with so little effort that it merely distorted her features into an unfortunate grimace. Sometimes she hated grown-ups so much that she could have killed them, mutilated them, or at least stamped her foot and shouted, "No! Just leave me alone!" But her parents frightened her. Ever since she was a tiny child, she'd been afraid of her parents.

When Antoinette was small, her mother had often held her on her lap, cuddled her, and kissed her. But Antoinette had forgotten all that. Instead she remembered what it was like to hear the roar of an angry voice above her head: "You're always under my feet, Antoinette . . ."; "Don't tell me you've dirtied my dress with your filthy shoes again! Go and stand in the corner, do you hear me? That will teach you, you little idiot!"; and one day on a street corner—the day when, for the first time, she had wanted to die—a shout so loud, during one of their scenes, that passers-by had turned round to stare: "Do you want me to smack you? Do you?" Deep in her heart she remembered how that slap burned her face. Right in the middle of the street! She had been eleven then, but big for her age. The passers-by, the grown-ups, she didn't care about them . . . But some boys had been coming out of school, and they'd laughed when they'd seen her: "Oh you poor thing!" Their sniggering had followed her as she walked, head down, along the dark autumn avenue, the street-lamps a blur through her tears. "Haven't you finished snivelling yet? You've got no character! You must know I punish you for your own good! And I'm warning you . . . You'd better not annoy me again, or else." People were horrible . . . And, even now, she was hounded from morning to night, as if deliberately to torment her, torture her, humiliate her: "Look at how you're holding your fork!" (in front of the servants, for God's sake); and "Stand up straight. Or at least try not to look like a hunchback." She was fourteen years old, a young lady—and, in her dreams, a woman who was beautiful, adored . . . She turned men's heads. They caressed her the way Andrea Sperelli caressed Elena and Maria in D'Annunzio's *Il Piacere*, the way Julien de Suberceaux caressed Maud de Rouvre. Love . . . She trembled at the thought of it.

"And if you think that I'm paying an English governess so you can have manners like that, you are very much mistaken, young lady!"

Madame Kampf lowered her voice.

"You keep forgetting that we're rich now, Antoinette," she said, pushing back a lock of hair that had fallen on to her daughter's face.

She turned to the Englishwoman.

"I have a lot of errands for you to run this week, Miss Betty. I'm holding a ball on the fifteenth . . ."

"A ball," murmured Antoinette, her eyes opening wide.

"Yes," said Madame Kampf, smiling, "a ball . . ."

She looked at Antoinette with pride, then frowned, indicating the Englishwoman with a slight twitch of the eyebrow.

"I don't suppose you've been talking, have you?"

"No, Mama, no," Antoinette quickly replied.

She knew all too well her mother's constant worry. At first—two years ago now, in 1926, when they'd left the Rue Favart after her father had made a killing on the Stock Market (first on the devaluation of the franc and then of the pound) and they'd become rich—Antoinette had been called into her parents' bedroom every morning. Her mother would be lying in bed polishing her nails; in the adjoining dressing room, her father, a dry little Jew with fiery eyes, would be shaving, washing, and getting dressed, all with the same break-neck speed that characterised his every action and which, in the past, had earned him the nickname "Feuer" amongst the German Jews, his friends at the Stock Market. For years Alfred Kampf had haunted the great steps of the Stock Market without getting anywhere. Antoinette knew that he used to be an employee of the Banque de Paris and, long before that, a doorman at the bank, wearing a blue uniform. Shortly before Antoinette was born, he'd married his mistress, Mademoiselle Rosine, the manager's secretary. For eleven years they had lived in a small, dingy apartment behind the Opéra Comique. Antoinette remembered how the maid would crash about in the kitchen washing the dishes while she sat at the dining-room table doing her homework, Madame Kampf reading novels beside her, leaning forward to catch the light from the large gas-lamp with the round frosted glass shade that hung above them. Now and again Madame Kampf would let out an angry sigh so loud and sudden that it made Antoinette jump. "What is it now?" Kampf would ask. And Rosine would reply, "It makes me feel sick when I think of how some people have such an easy life, how happy they are, while I'm stuck here, in this dirty hole, spending the best years of my life darning your socks..."

Kampf would simply shrug without saying anything. At this point Rosine would usually look at Antoinette and shout bad-temperedly, "And why are *you* listening? Is it any of your business what grown-ups are talking about?" rounding off the reprimand with, "Yes, that's it, girl. If you're waiting for your father to make his fortune like he's been promising to ever since we got married, you'll be waiting a very long time, you'll watch your whole life slip by ... You'll grow up, and you'll still be here, like your poor mother, waiting..." When she said the word "waiting," a certain look came over her tense, sullen features, an expression so pathetic, so deeply pained, that Antoinette was often moved, in spite of herself, to lean forward and kiss her mother on the cheek.

"My poor baby," Rosine would then say, stroking her daughter's face. But once she had shouted, "Oh, leave me alone, won't you! You're annoying me. You can be so irritating! Yes, you as well . . ." And never again had Antoinette given her mother a kiss, except in the morning and at night—the kind of kiss parents and children give each other automatically, like two strangers shaking hands.

Then, one fine day, they had suddenly become rich. Antoinette had never understood how. They had come to live in a vast white apartment, and her mother had suddenly appeared with her hair dyed blonde. Antoinette had glanced furtively, fearfully, at the flaming gold tresses which she hardly recognised.

"So tell me again, Antoinette," Madame Kampf would order from her bed each morning, "what do you answer if someone asks you where we lived last year?"

"You're an idiot," Kampf would say from the dressing room. "Who do you think is going to talk to her? She doesn't know anyone."

"I know what I'm talking about," Madame Kampf replied, raising her voice. "What about the servants?"

"If I catch her saying a single word to the servants, she'll have me to deal with," said Kampf, coming into the bedroom. "You understand, Antoinette? She knows she just has to keep her mouth shut and learn her lessons, and that's the end of it. We ask nothing more of her . . ." Turning to his wife, Kampf added, "She's not a fool, you know."

But as soon as he had left, Madame Kampf started in again.

"If anyone asks you, Antoinette, you're to say we lived in the Midi all last year. You don't need to go into detail as to whether it was in Cannes or Nice, just say the Midi . . . unless they ask for details, in which case it would be better to say Cannes, it's more sophisticated . . . But, of course, your father is right, it's best to say nothing at all. A little girl should speak as little as possible to grown-ups."

And she sent her away with a wave of her beautiful bare arm, a slightly thick arm, sparkling with the diamond bracelet her husband had just given her and which she only ever took off in the bath.

Antoinette was remembering all this when she heard her mother ask the Englishwoman, "Does Antoinette at least have nice handwriting?"

"Yes, Mrs. Kampf."

"Why?" Antoinette asked shyly.

"Because," explained Madame Kampf, "you can help me write out the envelopes this evening. You see, I'm sending nearly two hundred invitations. I'll never manage it alone . . . Miss Betty, I'm giving Antoinette permission to go to bed an hour later than usual tonight. You'd like that, wouldn't you?" she asked, turning towards her daughter.

But as Antoinette was once again lost in thought and said nothing, Madame Kampf shrugged her shoulders.

"That girl has always got her head in the clouds," she remarked quietly. "Doesn't it make you proud to think your parents are giving a ball?" she asked her daughter. "Well, doesn't it? I fear you don't have much feeling, my poor girl," she concluded with a sigh, as she turned and left the room.

II

ANTOINETTE WAS USUALLY put to bed by the English governess at nine o'clock precisely, but that evening, she stayed in the drawing room with her parents. She was so rarely allowed in there that she stared at the white panelling and gilt furniture as if she were visiting someone else's house. Her mother pointed to a small pedestal table laid out with ink, pens, and a packet of cards with envelopes.

"Sit down over there. I'll dictate the addresses to you," she said, then turned to her husband and asked loudly, "Will you be joining us, my dear?" The servant was clearing away the dishes in the adjoining room, and for several months now, the Kampfs had made a point of addressing each other with great formality in front of him. But as soon as Kampf got close enough, Rosine whispered, "For heaven's sake, get rid of that flunky, will you. He's so annoying..."

She noticed the look on Antoinette's face and blushed.

"Will you be much longer, Georges?" she asked imperiously. "You may go as soon as you've finished putting those things away."

The three of them then sat in silence, frozen to their chairs. When the servant had gone, Madame Kampf let out a sigh.

"I can't stand that Georges, I don't know why. As soon as I sense him behind me at dinner, I lose my appetite... And just what are you smirking about, Antoinette? Come on, let's get to work. Do you have the guest list, Alfred?"

"Yes," replied Kampf, "but first let me take off my jacket. I'm hot."

"Just make sure that you remember not to leave it lying around in here like the last time," said his wife. "I could tell from the looks on their faces that Georges and Lucie found it odd that you were in the drawing room in your shirt-sleeves..."

"I don't give a damn about the opinions of the servants," Kampf grumbled.

"Well, you're very wrong, my dear. It's the servants who make or break reputations, going from one place to another and talking . . . I would have never known that the baroness on the third floor . . ."

She lowered her voice and whispered something that Antoinette, despite all her efforts, failed to hear.

" . . . without Lucie who was with her for three years . . ."

Kampf reached into his pocket and pulled out a piece of paper covered with names, many of which were crossed out.

"Let's start with the people I know, all right, Rosine? Antoinette, you write. Monsieur and Madame Banyuls. I don't know their address, but you have the telephone directory there, so you can look up any addresses we need . . ."

"They're extremely rich, aren't they?" Rosine murmured with respect.

"Extremely."

"Do you think they'll want to come? I don't know Madame Banyuls."

"Neither do I. But I do business with her husband, so that's sufficient . . . I've heard his wife is charming, and besides, she doesn't receive many invitations from his circle since she was mixed up in that business . . . you know, the famous orgies in the Bois de Boulogne, two years ago . . ."

"Alfred, not in front of the child!"

"She doesn't understand. You just write, Antoinette . . . Nevertheless, she's a good person to start with . . ."

"Don't forget the Ostiers," Rosine said quickly. "It seems they give wonderful parties . . ."

"Monsieur and Madame Ostier d'Arrachon, number two . . . Antoinette . . . Well, my dear, I don't know about them. They're very prim and proper, very . . . The wife used to be . . ."

He made a gesture.

"No!"

"Yes. I know someone who used to see her in a brothel in Marseille . . . Yes, yes, I can assure you . . . But that was a long time ago, nearly twenty years. Her marriage completely transformed her. Now she receives very classy people, and she's extremely particular when it comes to her friends. As a general rule, all women with a past get like that after ten years."

"My God," sighed Madame Kampf, "it's so difficult . . ."

"We must be methodical, my dear. For a first party, invite anyone and everyone—as many of the sods as you can stand. When it comes to the second or third you can start to be selective. This time, we have to invite everyone in sight."

"But if we could at least be sure that everyone would come . . . If anyone refused, I think I'd die of shame . . ."

Kampf grimaced and stifled a laugh.

"If anyone refuses to come, then you'll invite them again the next time, and again the time after that. What do you want me to say? In the end, if you want to get ahead in society, you simply have to obey the Gospels religiously."

"What on earth do you mean?"

"If someone slaps you, turn the other cheek . . . Society is the best school in which to learn Christian humility."

"I do wonder," said Madame Kampf, somewhat shocked, "where you get all these stupid ideas, my dear."

Kampf smiled.

"Come on then, let's get on with it . . . Here's a piece of paper with some addresses on it. All you have to do is copy them, Antoinette . . ."

Madame Kampf leaned over her daughter's shoulder as she continued writing, her head lowered.

"It's true she has very nice handwriting, very neat . . . Tell me, Alfred, Monsieur Julien Nassan . . . Wasn't he the one who was in prison for fraud?"

"Nassan? Yes."

"Oh!" murmured Rosine, rather surprised.

"But why that look?" asked Kampf. "He's recovered his position, he's a charming young man, and a first-class businessman. What's more . . ."

"Monsieur Julien Nassan, 23A Avenue Hoche," Antoinette read out. "Who's next, Papa?"

"There are only twenty-five more," Madame Kampf groaned. "We'll never find two hundred people, Alfred!"

"Of course we will. Come now, don't start getting all upset. Where's your own list? All the people you met in Nice, Deauville, Chamonix last year..."

Madame Kampf took a notepad from the table.

"Count Moïssi, Monsieur and Madame Lévy de Brunelleschi, and the Marquis d'Itcharra: he's Madame Lévy's lover; they're always invited everywhere together..."

"Is there a husband, at least?" asked Kampf doubtfully.

"I understand that they are very respectable people. There are some more marquises, you know, five of them. The Marquis de Liguès y Hermosa, the Marquis... Tell me, Alfred, are we supposed to use their titles when we speak to them? I think we should, don't you? Not *Monsieur le Marquis* like the servants, of course, but *my dear Marquis, my dear Countess*... If we don't, the others won't even notice we're receiving the aristocracy."

"Maybe you'd like it if we pinned labels to their backs, eh?"

"Oh, you and your idiotic jokes! Come on, Antoinette, hurry up and copy those out, darling..."

Antoinette wrote for a moment, then read out loud: "The Baron and Baroness Levinstein-Lévy, the Count and Countess Poirier..."

"That's Abraham and Rebecca Birnbaum. They bought that title. Don't you think it's idiotic to call yourself Poirier, like a tree? If it was up to me, I'd choose..."

She drifted off into a deep dream.

"Just *Count and Countess Kampf*," she murmured. "That doesn't sound bad at all."

"Wait a while," Kampf suggested. "We've got at least ten years before that..."

Rosine was sorting through some visiting cards that had been thrown into a malachite bowl decorated with gilt Chinese dragons.

"Still, I'd really like to know who all these people are," she mused. "There's a whole batch of cards here I got at New Year... Loads from all those little gigolos I met in Deauville..."

"We need as many people as possible to fill the gaps. So long as they're dressed correctly..."

"Oh, my dear, you are joking. At least they're all counts,

marquises, viscounts . . . But I can't seem to match their faces to
their names . . . They all look alike. Still, it doesn't really matter,
in the end. You saw how it was done at the Rothwan de Fiesques'
party? You say exactly the same thing to everyone: 'So *pleased* to
see you . . .' and then, if you're forced to introduce two people,
you just mumble. No one can ever hear anything . . . Come on,
Antoinette darling, what you're doing isn't hard. The addresses
are on the cards . . ."

"But, Mama," Antoinette interrupted, "this one's the uphol-
sterer's card . . ."

"What are you talking about? Let me see. Good God, she's
right. I'm going out of my mind, Alfred, I really am . . . How
many is that, Antoinette?"

"One hundred and seventy-two, Mama."

"Well, that's not so bad!"

The Kampfs sighed with satisfaction and smiled at each other
with the same expression of weary triumph as two actors after
the third curtain call.

"We're doing well, aren't we?"

"Mademoiselle Isabelle Cossette . . . That's . . . that's not *my*
Mademoiselle Isabelle, is it?" Antoinette asked shyly.

"But of course . . ."

"But why are you inviting her?" exclaimed Antoinette, then
blushed violently, expecting a curt "What business is it of yours?"
from her mother. But Madame Kampf seemed awkward.

"She's a fine young woman . . . We have to be nice to people . . ."

"She's absolutely ghastly," Antoinette protested.

Mademoiselle Isabelle, a cousin of the Kampfs, was music
teacher to several families of rich Jewish stock-brokers. She was
a boring old maid, as stiff and upright as an umbrella; she taught
Antoinette piano and music theory. Extremely short-sighted but
refusing to wear glasses because she was proud of her rather pretty
eyes and thick eyelashes, she would lean over the piano and glue
her big pointed nose, bluish from rice powder, to the music.
Whenever Antoinette made a mistake, she would hit her fingers
sharply with an ebony ruler that was as hard and flat as she was.
She was as malicious and prying as a magpie. The night before
her music lessons, Antoinette would whisper a fervent prayer

(her father had converted when he got married; Antoinette had been raised a Catholic): "Please God, let Mademoiselle Isabelle die tonight."

"The child's right," Kampf remarked in surprise. "What's got into you to make you want to invite that old madwoman? You can't actually like her . . ."

Madame Kampf shrugged her shoulders angrily.

"Oh, you don't understand anything! How do you expect my family to hear about it otherwise? Can't you just picture the look on their faces? Aunt Loridon, who fell out with me because I married a Jew, and Julie Lacombe and Uncle Martial, and everyone in the family who looked down their noses at us because they had more money than us, remember? It's very simple: if we don't invite Isabelle, I can't be sure that the next day they'll all die of envy, and then it's not worth having the ball at all! Keep writing, Antoinette."

"Shall we have dancing in both reception rooms?"

"Of course, and in our hall . . . It's very beautiful, our hall . . . I'll hire great baskets of flowers. Just wait till you see how wonderful it will look filled with beautiful women in their most elegant dresses and best jewellery, the men in evening dress . . . It looked positively magical at the Lévy de Brunelleschis'. During the tangos, they switched off the electricity and left on two large alabaster lamps in the corners of the room that gave off a red light . . ."

"I don't care much for that idea. Makes it look like a dance hall . . ."

"But everyone seems to be doing it now. Women love letting men have a little feel to the music . . . The supper, naturally, on small tables . . ."

"How about having a bar to start off with?"

"That's a good idea . . . We need to warm them up when they arrive. We could set up the bar in Antoinette's room. She can sleep in the linen room or in the box room at the end of the corridor just for one night . . ."

Antoinette went pale and started trembling violently.

"Couldn't I stay for just a quarter of an hour?" she whispered, her words almost choking her.

A ball . . . My God, was it possible that there could take place—here, right under her nose—this splendid thing she vaguely imagined as a mixture of wild music, intoxicating perfumes, dazzling evening gowns, words of love whispered in some isolated alcove, as dark and cool as a hidden chamber . . . and that she could be sent to bed that night, like any other night, at nine o'clock, like a baby? Perhaps the men who knew the Kampfs had a daughter would ask where she was—and her mother would answer with her hateful little laugh, "Oh, but really, she's been asleep for hours . . ." And yet what harm would it do to her if Antoinette, yes, Antoinette as well, had a bit of happiness in this life? My God, to be able to dance, just once, wearing a pretty dress, like a real young lady, held tightly in a man's arms! She closed her eyes and repeated, "Just a quarter of an hour, can't I, Mama?" with a kind of bold despair, as if she were pointing a loaded revolver at her heart.

"What?" shouted Madame Kampf, stunned. "Don't you dare ask again . . ."

"You'll go to Monsieur Blanc's ball," said her father.

Madame Kampf shrugged her shoulders.

"I think this child must be mad . . ."

Antoinette's face suddenly contorted.

"Please, Mama, please, I'm begging you!" she shouted. "I'm fourteen, Mama, I'm not a little girl any more. I *know* girls come out at fifteen, but I look fifteen, and next year . . ."

Madame Kampf exploded.

"Well, honestly, how wonderful! Honestly!" she shouted, her voice hoarse with anger. "This kid, this snotty-nosed kid, coming to the ball! Can you just picture it? Just you wait, girl, I'll knock all those fancy ideas right out of you. You think you're going to 'come out' next year, eh? Who's been putting ideas like that in your head? You listen to me. I've only just begun to live, *me*, you hear, *me*, and I have no intention of rushing to lumber myself with having to marry off a daughter . . . I don't know why I shouldn't box your ears to teach you a lesson," she continued in the same tone of voice, while walking towards Antoinette.

Antoinette stepped back and went even whiter. The lost, desperate expression in her eyes caused Kampf to feel a kind of pity.

"Come on now, leave her be," he said, catching Rosine's raised arm. "The child's tired and upset, she doesn't know what she's saying . . . Go to bed, Antoinette."

Antoinette didn't move; her mother shoved her by the shoulders.

"Go on, out, and not a word. Move it, or I'm warning you . . ."

Antoinette was shaking from head to foot, but she walked slowly out of the room holding back her tears.

"Charming," said Madame Kampf after she'd gone. "That girl's going to be a handful . . . I was just the same at her age, though. But I'm not like my poor mother who never knew how to say no to me . . . I'll keep her in her place, I promise you that . . ."

"She'll calm down when she's had some sleep. She was tired. It's eleven o'clock already; she's not used to going to bed so late. That's why she got upset . . . Let's carry on with the list," said Kampf, "and forget about it."

III

IN THE MIDDLE of the night, Miss Betty was woken by the sound of sobbing in the next room. She switched on the light and listened for a moment through the wall. It was the first time she had heard the girl cry: usually when Madame Kampf scolded her, Antoinette managed to hold back her tears and say nothing.

"What's the matter with you, child? Are you ill?" she called through the wall.

The sobbing stopped.

"I suppose your mother scolded you. It's for your own good, you know, Antoinette... Tomorrow you'll apologise to her, you'll give each other a kiss, and it will be all over. It's late now, you should get some sleep. Would you like some herbal tea? No? You could answer me, you know, my dearest," she said, as Antoinette remained silent. "Dear, dear, a little girl sulking isn't a pretty sight. You're upsetting your guardian angel..."

Antoinette made a face and stretched out her clenched little fists towards the wall. Bloody woman. Bloody selfish hypocrites, the lot of them... They couldn't care less that she was crying all alone in the dark, so hard she could barely breathe... that she felt as miserable and lonely as a lost dog!

No one loved her, no one in the whole world... But couldn't they see, blind idiots, that she was a thousand times more intelligent, more precious, more perceptive than all of them put together—these people who dared to bring her up, to teach her? These unsophisticated, crass nouveaux riches? She had been laughing at them all evening, but of course they hadn't even realised... She could laugh or cry right under their noses and they wouldn't deign to notice... To them a fourteen-year-old was just a kid—to be pushed around like a dog! What right did they have to send her to bed, to punish her, to insult her? "Oh, I wish they were all dead," she exclaimed. Through the wall she could hear the Englishwoman breathing softly as she slept. Antoinette started crying again, but more quietly this time, tasting the tears that ran down her cheeks into the corners of her mouth and on to her lips. Suddenly, a strange pleasure flooded through her; for the first time in her life she was crying like a true woman—silently, without scowling or hiccoughing. Later on, she would cry the same tears over love . . . For a long time she listened to the sobs rising in her chest like the deep, low swell of the sea. Her mouth was moist with tears and tasted salty. She switched on the light and looked in the mirror with curiosity. Her eyes were swollen, her cheeks red and mottled. Like a little girl who's been beaten. She was ugly, ugly . . . She started sobbing again.

"I want to die! Dear God, please make me die . . . Dear God, sweet Holy Virgin, why did you make me their child? Punish them, I'm begging you . . . Punish them just once, and after that, I'll gladly die."

She stopped suddenly and said out loud, "Of course it's all a joke. The good Lord and the Virgin Mary are just a joke, like the good parents you read about in books and all that stuff about the happiest time of your life . . . "

The happiest time of your life, what a joke! She was biting her hands so hard that she could taste blood in her mouth. "Happiest . . . happiest . . . I'd rather be dead and buried . . . " she kept saying over and over again, furiously.

Day in, day out, doing the same things at the same times . . . It was slavery, prison! Getting up, getting dressed . . . Dull little dresses, heavy ankle-boots, ribbed stockings—all on purpose, on purpose so she'd look like a drudge, so that no one in the street would even glance at her, so that she'd be just some insignificant little girl walking by . . . "Fools! You'll never be young like me again, with skin as delicate as a flower, smooth, fresh, and lustrous eyelashes, and beautiful eyes—sometimes frightened, sometimes mischievous—which can entice, reject, desire . . . Never, never again!" But the desire . . . and these terrible feelings . . . Why did she feel this shameful, desperate envy eating away at her heart every time she saw two lovers walking by at dusk, kissing as they passed and teetering slightly, as if they were intoxicated? Why feel the hatred of a spinster at only fourteen? She would have her share eventually, she knew that. But it was so far off, so very far it seemed it would never come ... and, in the meantime, this harsh life of humiliation, lessons, strict discipline, shouting from her mother ...

"The woman dared to threaten me!" she said out loud. "She shouldn't have dared ..."

Then she remembered her mother's raised hand.

"If she had touched me, I would have scratched her, bitten her, and then ... But it's always possible to escape ... for ever ... There's the window," she thought feverishly.

She imagined herself lying on the street, covered in blood. No ball on the fifteenth ... "Couldn't the child have chosen another day to kill herself?" they'd say. As her mother had said, "*I* want to live, I, I ..." Perhaps, in the end, that's what hurt more than all the rest: never before had Antoinette seen in her mother's eyes that cold look, the look a woman would give to a rival.

"Dirty selfish pigs. *I'm* the one who wants to live, *me*! I'm young ... They're cheating me, they're stealing my share of happiness ... Oh, if only, by some miracle, I could go to the ball! To be the most beautiful, the most dazzling woman there, with all the men at my feet!"

She lowered her voice to a whisper.

"Do you know who she is? That's Mademoiselle Kampf. She's not pretty in the conventional sense, you know, but she is extraordinarily charming ... and so sophisticated. The others all pale by comparison, don't you agree? As for her mother, well, she looks like a kitchen maid compared to her daughter ..."

She laid her head on the tear-soaked pillow and closed her eyes; her weary limbs were overcome by a feeling of soft, gentle sensuality. She tenderly touched her body through her nightdress with light, respectful fingers. A beautiful body, ready for love ...

"Fifteen, O Romeo, that's how old Juliet was ..." she murmured.

Once she was fifteen, it would all be different; then she would savour life ...

IV

MADAME KAMPF SAID nothing about the previous night's argument to Antoinette, but all through lunch she let her daughter know she was in a bad mood by barking out the kind of curt reprimands at which she excelled when she was angry.

"What are you day-dreaming about with your mouth hanging open like that? Close it and breathe through your nose. How nice for parents to have a daughter who always has her head in the clouds! Will you pay attention to how you're eating? I bet you've stained the table-cloth . . . Can't you eat properly at your age? And don't look at me like that! You have to learn how to take criticism without making faces. Is it beneath you to answer? Cat got your tongue?

"That's it, here come the tears," she continued, standing up and throwing down her napkin. "Well, I'd rather leave the table than look at your stupid little face."

She went out, slamming the door behind her, and leaving Antoinette and her governess staring at the abandoned place setting opposite them.

"Finish your dessert now," Miss Betty whispered. "You'll be late for your German lesson."

Antoinette, her hands trembling, picked up a section of the orange she had just peeled. She always tried to eat slowly and calmly, so that the servant, standing motionless behind her chair, would think that she despised "that woman" and her constant nit-picking; but, in spite of herself, big, shiny tears fell from her swollen eyes on to her dress.

A little later, Madame Kampf came into the study; she was holding the packet of invitations.

"You're going to your piano lesson after tea, aren't you, Antoinette? You can give Isabelle her invitation, and, Miss Betty, you can put the rest in the post."

"Yes, Mrs. Kampf."

*

The post office was very crowded; Miss Betty looked at the clock.

"Oh, it's late! We don't have time . . . I'll come back during your lesson, dear," she said looking away, her cheeks redder than usual. "You don't . . . you don't mind, do you, dear?"

"No," murmured Antoinette.

She said no more; but when Miss Betty left her in front of Mademoiselle Isabelle's apartment building, urging her to hurry up and go in, Antoinette waited a moment, hidden behind the large doors leading to the courtyard. She saw the Englishwoman hurrying towards a taxi that was waiting at the corner. The car passed very close to Antoinette, who stood on tiptoe and looked inside, simultaneously curious and frightened. But she saw nothing. She stayed where she was for a while, watching the taxi disappear into the distance.

"I'd suspected she had a lover! They're probably kissing right now, like they do in books. Will he say, 'I love you'? And what about her? Is she his . . . mistress?"

Antoinette felt a sense of shame and disgust, mixed with a kind of vague suffering. To be free and alone with a man—how happy she must be! They'd be going to the woods, no doubt . . .

"How I wish Mother could see them," she whispered, clenching her fists. "Oh, I do! But no . . . People in love are always lucky! They're happy, they're together, they kiss . . . The whole world is full of men and women who love each other . . . Why not me?"

She was swinging her school bag in front of her. She looked at it with hate, then sighed, turned slowly, and crossed the courtyard. She was late. She could already hear Mademoiselle Isabelle: "Haven't you been taught that being on time is the most important obligation of a student towards her teachers, Antoinette?"

"She's stupid and old and ugly," thought Antoinette in exasperation.

To her face, she reeled out, "Hello, Mademoiselle, it's not my fault I'm late. It was Mother: she asked me to give you this . . ."

As she held out the envelope, an idea suddenly struck her.

". . . and she asked if you could let me leave five minutes earlier than usual."

That way she might be able to see Miss Betty coming back with her man.

But Mademoiselle Isabelle wasn't listening. She was reading Madame Kampf's invitation.

Antoinette saw the dry, dark skin of her pendulous cheeks suddenly flush red.

"What's this? A ball? Your mother is giving a ball?"

Mademoiselle Isabelle turned the invitation over, furtively brushing it against the back of her hand to see whether it was engraved or just printed. There was a difference of at least forty francs . . . As soon as she touched it, she knew it was engraved. She shrugged her shoulders angrily. Those Kampfs had always been insanely vain and extravagant! In the past, when Rosine had worked at the Banque de Paris (and, good God, it wasn't so very long ago), she'd spent all her wages on clothes. She wore silk lingerie, a different pair of gloves every week . . . But then again, she frequented, no doubt, the most disreputable places. It was only that kind of woman who found happiness. The others . . .

"Your mother has always been lucky," she muttered bitterly.

"She's furious," Antoinette said to herself. "But you'll definitely be coming, won't you?" she asked with a malicious little smile.

"I'll let you know. I'll do my very best because I'd really like to see your mother," said Mademoiselle Isabelle. "But, on the other hand, I don't know if I can . . . Some friends—the parents of one of my younger students, Monsieur and Madame Aristide Gros, the former cabinet private secretary (I'm sure your father has heard of him) . . . I've known them for years—they've invited me to the theatre, and I've already accepted . . . But I'll see what I can do," she added, without going into further detail. "In any case, tell your mother that I would be delighted, just delighted to see her . . ."

"I will, Mademoiselle."

"Now then, to work. Come along, sit down . . ."

Antoinette slowly adjusted the velour piano stool. She could have reproduced every stain, every rip in the material from memory. As she began her scales she stared mournfully at a yellow vase on the mantelpiece. It was full of dust inside, never a flower . . . And those hideous little shell boxes on the shelves. How ugly this dark little apartment was, how shabby and foreboding this place that, for years, she'd been forced to come to . . .

While Mademoiselle Isabelle arranged the sheet music, she cast a furtive look out the window. (It must be very beautiful in the woods, at dusk, with the bare, delicate trees and the winter sky as white as a pearl . . .) Three times a week, every week, for six years! Would it go on until she died?

"Antoinette, Antoinette, where are you putting your hands? Start again, please . . . Will there be many people going to your mother's ball?"

"I think Mama has invited two hundred people."

"Goodness! Does she think there will be enough room? Isn't she worried it will get terribly hot and crowded? Play louder, Antoinette, put some spirit into it. Your left hand is weak, my dear . . . This scale for next time and exercise eighteen in the third Czerny book . . ."

Scales, exercises . . . for months and months: Grieg's *Death of Ase*, Mendelssohn's *Songs without Words*, the "Barcarole" from the *Tales of Hoffmann* . . . Beneath her schoolgirl's fingers they all disintegrated into a harsh din . . .

Mademoiselle Isabelle banged out the beat with a rolled-up notebook.

"Why are you pressing the keys like that? *Staccato, staccato!* Do you think I can't see how you're holding your ring-finger and your little finger? Two hundred people, you say? Do you know them all?"

"No."

"Will your mother be wearing that new pink dress from Premet?"

Antoinette didn't answer.

"And what about you? You'll be going to the ball, I imagine? You're old enough . . ."

"I don't know," whispered Antoinette with a shiver.

"Faster, faster! This is how it should go: one, two, one, two, one, two . . . Come along, wake up, Antoinette! The next section, my dear . . ."

The next section . . . dotted with sharps to stumble over! In the next-door apartment a child was crying. Mademoiselle Isabelle switched on the lamp. Outside, the sky had grown dark . . . The clock struck four. Another hour had flowed through her fingers like water—lost, never to return. She wanted to be far away, or to die . . .

"Are you tired, Antoinette? Already? When I was your age, I used to practise for six hours a day. Now, wait a moment. Don't leave so fast—you're in such a hurry . . . What time should I come on the fifteenth?"

"It says on the invitation. Ten o'clock."

"Good. But I'll see you before then."

"Yes, Mademoiselle."

Outside, the street was empty. Antoinette huddled against the wall and waited. A moment later, she heard Miss Betty's footsteps, and saw her walking quickly towards her holding the arm of a young man. Antoinette lurched forward and bumped straight into the couple. Miss Betty let out a little cry.

"Miss Betty!" said Antoinette. "I've been waiting for you for at least fifteen minutes . . ."

Miss Betty's face was right up against hers; in a flash, her features were so changed that Antoinette stopped short, as if not recognising the person she was talking to. But she failed to notice her pitiful little mouth, gaping open, as bruised as a ravaged flower; she was staring at the man.

He was very young. A university student—maybe even still at school. His fresh lips were slightly swollen from shaving; his lovely eyes were mischievous. He was smoking. While Miss Betty stammered excuses, he said calmly and boldly, "Introduce me, cousin."

"Ann-toinette, this is my cousin," murmured Miss Betty.

Antoinette held out her hand. The boy gave a laugh, then said nothing; he seemed to think for a moment before suggesting, "Let me walk you home, all right?"

The three of them went down the dark, empty street in silence. The cool wind brushed against Antoinette's face; it was damp from the rain, as if misty with tears. She slowed down, watching the lovers in front of her, their bodies pressed together, neither of them speaking. How quickly they walked . . . She stopped. They didn't even turn round. "If I were hit by a car, would they even know?" she thought with bitterness. A man bumped into her as he passed by; she jumped back in fright. But it was only the lamp-lighter; she watched how each street-lamp burst into flame as he touched one after the other with his long stick. The lights shimmered and danced like candles in the wind . . . Suddenly, she felt afraid. She ran ahead as fast as she could.

She caught up with the lovers at the Alexandre III Bridge. They were standing close together, whispering to each other urgently. The boy looked impatient when he saw Antoinette. Miss Betty was flustered for a moment; then, struck by sudden inspiration, she opened her handbag and took out the packet of envelopes.

"Here, dear, take your mother's invitations. I haven't posted them yet. Run down to the little tobacconist's shop, over there, down that little street on the left . . . Can you see its light? You can put them in the letterbox. We'll wait for you here."

She thrust the packet of invitations into Antoinette's hand; then she quickly walked away. Antoinette saw her stop in the middle of the bridge and lower her head as she waited for the boy. They leaned against the parapet.

Antoinette hadn't moved. Because of the darkness, she could see only two shapeless shadows and the dark Seine reflecting the shimmering lights. Even when they kissed, she imagined rather than saw them leaning towards each other, their faces almost melting together. She began wringing her hands like a jealous woman. One of the envelopes slipped from her fingers and fell to the ground . . . She was frightened and quickly picked it up, but then she felt ashamed she'd been afraid. Was she always going to tremble like a little girl? Well, was she? She wasn't worthy of being a woman. And what about those two who were still kissing? Their lips were still pressed together! A kind of giddiness took hold of her: the wild need to do something outrageous and evil. She clenched her teeth, crumpled up all the invitations, tore them into little pieces and threw them into the Seine. For a long while, her heart pounding, she watched them floating, caught against one of the bridge's arches. And then the wind finally swept them deep into the water.

V

IT WAS NEARLY six o'clock and Antoinette was coming back from a walk with Miss Betty. As no one answered when they rang the bell, Miss Betty knocked. They could hear the sound of furniture being moved behind the door.

"They must be getting the cloakroom ready," said the governess. "The ball's tonight. I keep forgetting . . . and you, dear?"

She gave Antoinette a tender smile of complicity, but her face was anxious. She hadn't seen her young lover again in front of the girl, but ever since that encounter in the street, Antoinette had been so aloof that her silences, her looks, worried Miss Betty . . .

When the servant opened the door they were immediately greeted by a furious Madame Kampf, who was overseeing the electrician in the dining room.

"Couldn't you use the service entrance?" she shouted angrily. "You can see very well that we're setting up a cloakroom here. Now we'll have to start all over again. We'll never get it done," she concluded, grabbing hold of a table to help the concierge and Georges, who were setting up the room.

In the dining room and the long adjoining hallway, six waiters in white cotton jackets were preparing the tables for the supper. In the middle was the buffet, decorated with stunning flowers.

Antoinette wanted to go to her room; Madame Kampf again started shouting:

"Not that way, not that way . . . Your room is to be the bar, and yours, Miss Betty, is being used as well. Miss Betty will sleep in the linen room tonight, and you, Antoinette, in the little box room . . . It's at the other end of the apartment, so you'll be able to sleep. You won't even hear the music . . . What are you doing?" she said to the electrician, who was working unhurriedly and humming to himself. "Can't you see that this light bulb isn't working . . ."

"Give it time, lady . . ."

Rosine shrugged her shoulders, annoyed.

"Time!" she muttered to herself. "Time! He's been at it for an hour . . ."

She clenched her fists as she spoke, with a gesture so identical to the one Antoinette made when she was angry, that the girl, motionless at the doorway, began to tremble—like someone who unexpectedly finds herself standing in front of a mirror.

Madame Kampf was wearing a silk dressing-gown and slippers on her bare feet; her loose hair hung like writhing snakes around her fiery face. She caught sight of the florist, his arms full of roses, trying to make his way past Antoinette, who was leaning against the wall.

"Excuse me, young lady . . ."

"Get out of the way for goodness sake!" she screamed, so sharply that Antoinette lurched into the florist and knocked the petals off one of the roses with her elbow.

"You are unbearable," Madame Kampf continued, shouting so loudly that the glassware on the table started to vibrate. "Why are you here, getting in the way and bothering everyone? Get out, go on, go to your room—no, not to your room, to the linen room; go wherever you please but just get out of my sight! I don't want to see you or hear you."

Once Antoinette had gone, Madame Kampf rushed through the dining room and the butler's pantry—which was piled high with buckets of ice to chill the champagne—to her husband's office. Kampf was on the telephone.

"What are you doing?" she cried, the moment he'd hung up. "You haven't even shaved!"

"At six o'clock? You must be crazy!"

"First of all, it's six thirty, and secondly, there might be a few last-minute errands to do; so it's best to be ready."

"You're mad," he repeated impatiently. "We have servants for that . . ."

"Oh, it's just great when you start playing the aristocrat and gentleman!" she said with a shrug. "'We have servants for that . . .' Save your airs and graces for the guests."

"Don't get yourself in a state," Kampf replied, gritting his teeth.

"But how do you expect me..." cried Rosine, with tears in her voice, "how do you expect me not to get in a state? It's all going wrong! The bloody servants will never be ready on time. I have to be everywhere at once, supervising everything, and I haven't slept in three nights. I'm at the end of my rope. I think I'm going mad!"

She grabbed a small silver ashtray and threw it on the floor; but this outburst seemed to calm her down. She smiled, slightly embarrassed.

"It's not my fault, Alfred..."

Kampf shook his head and said nothing. As Rosine was leaving, he called her back.

"Listen, I've been meaning to ask you... Have you still not received any replies to the invitations?"

"No, why?"

"I don't know, it just seems odd to me... As if there's something going on. I wanted to ask Barthélemy if he'd received his invitation, but I haven't seen him at the Stock Market for over a week... Should I telephone him?"

"Now? That would be ridiculous."

"Still, it's very odd..." said Kampf.

"Well, people just don't bother replying, that's all!" interrupted his wife. "You either go or you don't... And do you know what? It even makes me happy. It means that no one wanted to let us down. Otherwise they would have sent their apologies, don't you think?"

Since her husband didn't reply, she asked him again, impatiently, "Well, don't you agree, Alfred? I'm right, aren't I? What do you think?"

Kampf spread out his arms.

"I have no idea... What do you want me to say? I don't know any more than you do..."

They looked at each other for a moment in silence. Rosine sighed and lowered her head.

"Oh, my God! We're finished, aren't we?"

"It'll be all right," said Kampf.

"I know, but in the meantime... Oh, if you knew how frightened I am! I wish it were over!"

"Don't get yourself upset," Kampf said again, rather un-convincingly.

He was absent-mindedly turning his paper knife over and over in his hands.

"Above all, say as little as possible . . . Just use the old clichés: 'So happy to see you! Do have something to eat! It's so warm! It's so cold . . .' "

"The introductions will be the worst," said Rosine anxiously. "Think about it! All these people I've only ever met once, whom I will barely recognise . . . and who don't know each other, who have nothing in common . . ."

"Oh for God's sake, you'll think of something. After all, every-one's been in our position. They all had to start somewhere."

"Do you remember our little apartment on the Rue Favart?" Rosine asked suddenly. "And how we hesitated before replacing the old, battered settee in the dining room? That was only four years ago, and now look . . ." she added, indicating the heavy gilt furniture all around them.

"Do you mean," he asked, "that in four years' time, we'll be receiving ambassadors and then we'll remember how we sat here tonight shaking with fear because a hundred or so pimps and old tarts were coming? Eh?"

She laughed and covered his mouth with her hand. "Well, really, do be quiet!"

As she was leaving the room, she bumped into the maître d', who was coming to warn her that the pretzels hadn't arrived with the champagne; and that the barman thought there wouldn't be enough gin for the cocktails.

Rosine put her hands to her head.

"Wonderful, that's all I need!" she shouted, starting her tirade all over again. "Couldn't you have told me before? Well, couldn't you? Where do you expect me to get gin at this time of night? Everything is closed . . . and the pretzels . . ."

"Send the driver, darling," Kampf suggested.

"The driver's gone to get his dinner," said Georges.

"Of course," screamed Rosine, beside herself, "of course he has! He doesn't give a damn . . ." She checked herself. "He doesn't *care in the least* whether we need him or not. He's off having his dinner! And he's not the only one I'll be firing tomorrow," she added, looking at Georges and sounding so furious that the manservant immediately pursed his long smooth lips.

"If Madame means me . . ." he began.

"No, no, my friend, don't be ridiculous . . ." said Rosine with a shrug. "It just slipped out. You can see very well that I'm upset . . . Take a taxi and buy whatever we need at Nicolas. Give him some money, Alfred . . ."

She hurried off to her room, straightening the flowers as she went and berating the waiters.

"This tray of *petits fours* is in the wrong place . . . Lift the pheasant's tail higher! Where are the caviar sandwiches? Don't put them out too soon: everyone will make a mad dash for them. And what about the *foie gras*? I bet they've forgotten the *foie gras*! If I don't do something myself . . ."

"We're just unwrapping it now, Madame," said the maître d', looking at her with ill-concealed contempt.

"I must seem ridiculous," Rosine thought suddenly, catching a glimpse of herself in the mirror with her purplish face, frightened eyes, trembling lips. But nevertheless—like an overtired child—she felt unable to stop the hysterics, no matter how hard she tried. She was utterly exhausted and on the verge of tears.

She went into her room.

Her maid was laying out her ball gown on the bed; it was silver lamé, decorated with heavy layers of pearls. Her shoes shone like jewels, her stockings were made of chiffon.

"Will Madame be wanting dinner now? We will serve it in here, of course, so as not to disturb the tables . . ."

"I'm not hungry," said Rosine angrily.

"As Madame wishes . . . But could I at least go and have my dinner now?" asked Lucie, gritting her teeth, for Madame Kampf had made her spend four hours re-stitching all the loose pearls on her dress. "May I remind Madame that it is nearly eight o'clock and that we are people, not animals."

"Go on then, off with you! Am I stopping you?" exclaimed Madame Kampf.

When she was alone, she threw herself down on the bed and closed her eyes. But the room was as cold as a cellar: they had shut off all the radiators in the apartment that morning. She got up and went over to the dressing table.

"I look such a fright . . ."

Carefully she began to apply her make-up; first a thick layer of face cream that she mixed in her hands, then the liquid rouge on her cheeks, the black mascara, the delicate little line to extend her eyelids towards her temples, the powder . . . She worked slowly, stopping every now and then to look more closely—passionately, anxiously devouring her face in the mirror, her expression both scornful and cunning. In a fit of pique she took hold of a single grey hair near her temple and pulled it out with exaggerated violence. How ironic life was. Oh, how lovely her face had been at twenty! Her cheeks so rosy! But she'd had darned stockings and patched underwear . . . And now— jewellery, gowns, but her first wrinkles too . . . all at the same time. My God, how you had to hurry up and live! Not leave it till too late to be attractive to men, to love . . . What good were money, elegant clothes, and beautiful cars if you didn't have a man in your life, a handsome young lover? A lover . . . how she had yearned for one. When she was still a poor girl she had gone with men who spoke to her of love, believed them just because they were well-dressed, with beautiful manicured hands . . . Boors, the lot of them! But she was still waiting . . . And now, this was her last chance, these final years before old age set in, true old age, impossible to fight, inevitable . . . She closed her eyes, imagined young lips, an eager, tender look, full of desire . . .

Hastily she threw off her silk robe, as if she were late for some lovers' tryst, and started dressing: she slipped on her stockings, her shoes, her gown, with the peculiar agility of women who have never in their life had a maid. Then the jewellery . . . She had a safe full of it. Kampf said it was the surest investment. She put on the double strand of pearls and all her rings; she covered both arms with bracelets made of enormous diamonds; then she pinned on a large brooch of sapphires, rubies, and emeralds. She sparkled and gleamed like a treasure trove. She took a few steps back, looked at herself with a joyous smile. Life was beginning at last, finally! Who knew? Perhaps tonight . . .

ANTOINETTE AND Miss Betty were finishing their dinner in the linen room; it had been served on an ironing board balanced across two chairs. Through the door they could hear the servants rushing about in the butler's pantry, and the sound of dishes clanking. Antoinette sat motionless, her hands tight around her knees. At nine o'clock, the governess looked at her watch.

"You have to go to bed right now, dear . . . You won't hear the music from your little room, so you should sleep well."

When Antoinette did not reply, Miss Betty laughed and clapped her hands.

"Come along, Antoinette, wake up, what's the matter?"

She took her to the dingy little box room where a fold-out bed and two chairs had been hastily set up. Across the court-yard were the brightly lit windows of the reception room and dining room.

"You can watch the people dancing from here," Miss Betty said jokingly. "There are no shutters."

After she left, Antoinette got up and pressed her face against the glass, partly in eagerness, partly in fear; a large section of wall was lit up by the golden light from the windows. Shadows passed back and forth behind the tulle curtains. The servants. Someone opened the bay-window, and Antoinette could clearly hear the sound of instruments being tuned at the end of the reception room. The musicians had already arrived. My God, it was after nine o'clock . . . All week long she had vaguely expected some catastrophe to wipe her from the face of the earth before anyone found out; but the evening had passed like any other. In a nearby apartment, the clock struck the half hour. Thirty, forty-five minutes to go, then . . . Nothing, nothing would happen. Of course it wouldn't. The moment they had come home from their walk that evening, Madame Kampf had leapt at Miss Betty and demanded, in that furious tone of voice that always made nervous people immediately lose their heads, "You did post the invitations, didn't you? You're quite sure you didn't lose any?" and Miss Betty had said, "Yes, Mrs. Kampf." Surely *she* was the one responsible, she alone . . . And if Miss Betty were dismissed, well, too bad, it would serve her right, it would teach her a lesson.

"I don't give a damn," Antoinette stammered. "I don't give a damn," biting her hands so hard that her young, sharp teeth made them bleed.

"And as for *her*, she can do what she likes to me, I'm not afraid, I don't give a damn!"

She looked out at the dark, deep courtyard below the window.

"I'll kill myself, and before I die, I'll say it's all because of *her*, and that will be the end of it," she murmured. "I'm not afraid of anything, I've already had my revenge . . ."

She went back to looking out of the window. Her breath was making the glass misty; angrily she wiped it and pressed her face against it once again. Finally, out of frustration, she threw open both sides of the window. The night was fine and cold. Now, with the piercing eyes of a fourteen-year-old, she could clearly see the chairs lined up along the wall, the musicians around the piano. She stood without moving for so long that she could no longer feel her cheeks or bare arms. For a moment, she almost convinced herself that nothing had happened, that the bridge, the dark water of the Seine, the torn-up invitations carried off by the wind had all been a dream, that the guests would miraculously appear and the ball begin. She heard the clock strike three quarters of an hour, then ten o'clock. Ten o'clock . . . She shuddered and slipped out of the room.

She walked towards the reception room, like an amateur assassin drawn back to the scene of the crime. In the corridor, two waiters, heads thrown back, were drinking champagne straight from the bottle. She went into the dining room. It was empty, waiting—the great table in the centre, with its Venetian-lace cloth and floral decorations, weighed down with game, fish in aspic, oysters on silver platters, and two identical pyramids of fruit. Pedestal tables with four or six place settings were scattered around the room, laid with dazzling crystal, fine porcelain, vermeil and silver. Looking back, Antoinette would never understand how she'd dared walk the entire length of that great room with its dazzling lights. At the door of the reception room, she hesitated for a moment, then noticed the large silk-upholstered settee in the adjoining antechamber. She dropped to her knees and crept between the back of the settee and the flowing drapes; there was just enough room for her if she hugged her knees to her chest, and, by leaning forward, she could see the reception room as if it were the stage of a theatre. She was trembling slightly, still frozen from her long vigil at the open window. At that moment, the apartment seemed silent, calm, asleep. The musicians were talking quietly. She could see a black man with brilliant white teeth, a woman in a silk dress, huge cymbals like at a fun fair, an enormous cello standing in the corner. The black man sighed, strumming a kind of guitar that gave off a low hum, like a moan.

"We start and finish later and later these days."

The pianist said a few words that Antoinette couldn't hear but that made the others laugh. Then Monsieur and Madame Kampf came in.

When Antoinette saw them, she instinctively flinched, as if trying to disappear into the floor. She crushed herself against the wall, buried her mouth in the fold of her bent arm, but she could hear their footsteps getting closer. They were standing right next to her. Kampf sat down in an armchair opposite Antoinette. Rosine walked around the room for a moment. She switched on the wall lights near the fireplace, then switched them off again. She was sparkling with diamonds.

"Sit down," Kampf said quietly. "It's idiotic to get yourself in such a state . . ."

Antoinette, who had opened her eyes and leaned forward so that her cheek was touching the wooden back of the settee, could see her mother standing in front of her. She was struck by the expression on her imperious face, an expression she had never seen before: a kind of humility—a mixture of eagerness and terror . . .

"Alfred, do you think everything will be all right?" she asked in a voice as quavering and innocent as a little girl's.

Alfred had no time to answer, for the sound of the doorbell ringing suddenly echoed throughout the apartment.

Rosine clasped her hands.

"Oh my God, it's beginning!" she whispered as if she were describing an earthquake.

The two of them rushed towards the open door of the reception room.

A moment later, Antoinette saw them come back, one on either side of Mademoiselle Isabelle, who was talking very loudly. Her voice was different from the one she normally used: it was oddly high-pitched and sharp, and interrupted by occasional peals of laughter that lit up her remarks like little sparks.

"I'd forgotten all about her," Antoinette thought in horror.

Madame Kampf, radiant now, continued talking. She had reverted to her self-satisfied, arrogant expression; she winked maliciously at her husband, secretly indicating Mademoiselle Isabelle's dress of yellow tulle and, around her long, dry neck, a feather boa that she flapped with both hands as if she were one of the ridiculous courtesans in a Molière play. A silver lorgnette hung from an orange velvet band around her wrist.

"Have you ever been in this room, Isabelle?"

"Well, no, it's very pretty. Who chose the furniture for you? Oh, look at these little vases, they're just delightful. So you still like the Japanese style, Rosine? *I'm* always standing up for it. Why, just the other day, I was defending it to the Block-Lévys, the Salomons, do you know them? They were criticising it as looking fake and typically 'nouveau riche,' to use their expression. 'Well, say what you like, I think it's cheerful, lively, and then, the fact that it's less expensive than the Louis XV style, for example, is hardly a defect, quite the contrary . . .'"

"You couldn't be more wrong, Isabelle," Rosine protested crossly. "Chinese and Japanese antiques are fetching ridiculously high prices . . . This period vase decorated with birds, for example . . ."

"Rather late in the period . . ."

"My husband paid ten thousand francs for it at the Drouot Auction House . . . What am I saying? Twelve thousand, not ten thousand, isn't that right, Alfred? Oh, I scolded him! But not for long. I myself have a passion for seeking out little ornaments. I just adore it."

"You'll have a glass of port, won't you, ladies?" interrupted Kampf, gesturing to the servant, who had just come in. "Georges, bring us three glasses of Sandeman port and some sandwiches, caviar sandwiches..."

Mademoiselle Isabelle had walked away; with the help of her lorgnette she was examining a golden Buddha embroidered on a velvet cushion.

"Sandwiches!" Madame Kampf whispered quickly. "Are you mad? You're not going to ruin my beautiful table just for her! Georges, just bring some plain biscuits from the china tray, do you understand, from the china tray."

"Yes, Madame."

He came back a moment later with the tray and Baccarat decanter. The three of them drank in silence. Then Madame Kampf and Mademoiselle Isabelle sat down on the settee where Antoinette was hiding. By reaching out her hand, she could have touched her mother's silver slippers and her teacher's yellow satin court shoes. Kampf was pacing up and down, glancing furtively at the clock.

"So tell me, who will be coming tonight?" asked Mademoiselle Isabelle.

"Oh," said Rosine, "some charming people, and some old fogeys too, like the Marquise de San Palacio, whose invitation I'm returning. But she does enjoy coming here so...I saw her yesterday. She was meant to be going away but she said to me, 'My dear, I have put off my trip to the Midi for a week because of your ball: everyone always has such a good time with you...'"

"Oh, so you've already given some balls?" Mademoiselle Isabelle asked, pursing her lips.

"No, no," Madame Kampf hastened to reply, "just some afternoon tea parties. I didn't invite you because I know how busy you are during the day..."

"Yes, I am. Actually, I'm considering giving some concerts next year..."

"Really? What an excellent idea!"

They fell silent. Mademoiselle Isabelle once again studied the walls of the room.

"It's charming, absolutely charming, such taste . . ."

Once again, silence. The two women coughed now and again. Rosine arranged her hair. Mademoiselle Isabelle carefully adjusted the skirt of her dress.

"Haven't we had beautiful weather these past few days?"

Kampf broke in. "Well really, are we going to sit around with our arms folded all night? People do come so late! You did put ten o'clock on the invitations, didn't you, Rosine?"

"I see I'm very early . . ."

"Not at all, my dear, what an idea. It's a terrible habit, arriving so late, it's deplorable . . ."

"Why don't we have a dance," said Kampf, clapping his hands cheerfully.

"Of course, what a very good idea! You may begin playing," shouted Madame Kampf to the orchestra. "A Charleston."

"Do you know how to Charleston, Isabelle?"

"Well, yes, a bit, like everyone . . ."

"Well, you won't be short of partners. The Marquis d'Itcharra, for example, a nephew of the Spanish ambassador. He wins all the competitions in Deauville, doesn't he, Rosine? While we're waiting, let's open the ball."

The two of them walked away from the settee, and the orchestra started playing in the empty drawing room. Antoinette saw Madame Kampf get up, rush to the window, and press her face— "Her as well," thought Antoinette—against the cold glass. The clock struck ten thirty.

"Good Lord, what are they doing?" whispered Madame Kampf impatiently. "I wish that old bag would go to hell," she added, almost loud enough to be heard, and then immediately gave a round of applause and called out, laughing, "Oh, how charming, just charming! I didn't know you could dance like that, Isabelle."

"She dances like Josephine Baker," Kampf replied from the other end of the drawing room.

When the dance was over, Kampf called out, "Rosine, I'm taking Isabelle over to the bar, don't be jealous now!"

"What about you, my dear, won't you join us?"

"In a minute. I just have to have a word with the servants and I'll be with you . . ."

"I warn you, Rosine, I'm going to flirt with Isabelle all night."

Madame Kampf found the strength to laugh and shake her finger at them; but she didn't say a word, and as soon as she was alone, she once again threw herself against the window. She could hear the sound of cars in the street below. When some of them slowed down in front of the building, Madame Kampf leaned out of the window and strained to look down into the dark winter street. But then the cars drove off, the sound of their engines growing fainter as they disappeared into the night. The later it got, however, the fewer cars there were, and many long minutes went by without a single sound coming from the street. It was as deserted as a country lane; there was only the noise of the nearby tramway, and the muted hooting of car horns, far away.

Rosine's teeth were chattering, as if she had a fever. Ten forty-five. Ten fifty. In the empty drawing room, a little clock struck the hour with a hurried little chime, like silvery bells; the one in the dining room gave an insistent reply, and from the other side of the street, the bell of a large clock on the front of a church rang slowly and solemnly, growing louder and louder as it marked the time that had passed.

"Nine, ten, eleven . . ." cried Madame Kampf in despair, raising her diamond-covered arms to heaven. "What's wrong? What's happened, dear sweet Jesus?"

Alfred came back with Isabelle; the three of them looked at each other without speaking.

Madame Kampf laughed nervously. "This is rather strange, isn't it? Unless something's happened . . ."

"Oh, my poor dear, perhaps there's been an earthquake," said Mademoiselle Isabelle, triumphantly.

But Madame Kampf was not prepared to give up just yet.

"Oh, it doesn't mean a thing. Just imagine that the other day, I was at the house of my friend, the Countess Brunelleschi: the first guests didn't start arriving until nearly midnight. So . . ."

Madame Kampf fiddled with her pearls. Her voice was full of anguish.

"It's very annoying for the lady of the house, very upsetting," Mademoiselle Isabelle murmured softly.

"Oh, it's ... it's just one of those things you have to get used to, isn't it?"

At that moment, the doorbell rang. Alfred and Rosine rushed to the doorway.

"Start playing," Rosine called out to the musicians.

They started playing a lively blues number. No one came in. Rosine could stand it no longer.

"Georges, Georges, someone rang the bell, didn't you hear it?"

"It was the ice cream being delivered from Rey's."

Madame Kampf couldn't contain herself.

"But I'm telling you, something terrible must have happened, an accident, a misunderstanding, a mistake in the date or the time, I don't know, something! Ten past eleven, it's ten past eleven," she said again in despair.

"Ten past eleven, already?" exclaimed Mademoiselle Isabelle. "So it is, but how right you are, time passes so quickly when you entertain, my compliments ... Why, I do believe it's a quarter past, can you hear the chimes?"

"Well, it won't be long now before people start arriving!" said Kampf loudly.

They all sat down again; no one said another word. They could hear the servants in fits of laughter in the butler's pantry.

"Go and tell them to be quiet, Alfred," Rosine said finally, her voice shaking with fury. "Go on!"

At eleven thirty, the pianist came in.

"Do you want us to wait a while longer, Madame?"

"No, just go away, all of you, just go!" Rosine roared. She seemed on the verge of a breakdown. "We'll pay you and then just go away! There won't be any ball, there won't be anything at all. It's an insult, a slap in the face, a plot by our enemies to humiliate us, to kill me! If anyone comes now, I won't see them, do you understand?" she continued, more and more violently. "You are to say that I'm not at home, that someone in the house is very ill, or dead, say whatever you like!"

"There, there, my dear," Mademoiselle Isabelle hastened to

say, "it isn't completely hopeless. Don't upset yourself like this, you'll make yourself ill . . . Of course, I understand how you must feel, my dear, my poor darling. But people can be so cruel, alas . . . You should say something to her, Alfred, look after her, console her . . ."

"What a farce!" Kampf hissed through clenched teeth, his face ashen. "Will you just shut up!"

"Now, now, Alfred, don't shout, you should be cuddling her . . ."

"Well, if she insists on making herself look ridiculous . . ."

He turned sharply on his heels and called out to the musicians, "What are you still doing here? How much do we owe you? Now get the hell out of here, for God's sake . . ."

Mademoiselle Isabelle slowly picked up her feather boa, her lorgnette, her handbag.

"It would be better if I left, Alfred, unless I can be of some help in any way, my poor dear . . ."

As he did not reply, she leant forward and kissed Rosine on the forehead, who remained motionless, her eyes dry and unblinking.

"Good-bye, my dear, please believe how sorry I am; I do feel for you," she whispered, mechanically, as if she were at a funeral. "No, Alfred, no, don't bother seeing me out; I'm going, I'm leaving, I'm already gone. Cry as much as you like, my poor Rosine, you'll feel better," she called out again at the top of her voice from the empty reception room.

As she walked through the dining room, Alfred and Rosine could hear her say to the servants, "Be careful not to make any noise. Madame is very upset, very distressed."

Then, finally, there was the hum of the lift and the dull thud of the doors in the courtyard opening and closing again.

"Horrible old bitch," murmured Kampf. "If at least . . ."

He stopped short. Rosine suddenly leapt to her feet, her face wet with tears, and shook her fist at him.

"It's all because of you," she shouted. "It's all your fault, you fool! You and your filthy vanity, wanting to show off . . . It's all because of you! The gentleman wishes to give a ball! To play host! What a farce! Do you think people don't know who you are, where you come from? *Nouveau riche!* They really screwed you, didn't they, your friends, your so-called friends. Thieves, crooks, the lot of them!"

"And what about yours? Your counts, your marquises, your pimps!"

They continued to shout at each other, a surge of angry, heated words that poured out like a flood. Then Kampf said more quietly, through clenched teeth, "When I picked you up out of the gutter, you'd already been around . . . God knows where! You think I was blind, that I didn't know? But I thought you were pretty and intelligent—that if one day I got rich, you'd make me proud of you . . . Well, I've been lucky, haven't I! Look where it's landed me: you've got the manners of a fishwife. You're nothing but an old woman with the manners of a fishwife!"

"Other men were happy with me . . ."

"I'm sure they were. But don't give me any details. You'll regret it tomorrow if you do . . ."

"Tomorrow? And what makes you think I'd spend another minute with you after the way you've spoken to me? You brute!"

"Leave then! Go to hell!"

He walked out, slamming the door.

"Alfred, come back!" Rosine called after him.

She waited, breathless, her face turned towards the reception room, but he was already long gone . . . He was taking the stairs. She could hear his furious voice in the street shouting, "Taxi, taxi . . ." then it grew fainter, disappearing around the corner.

The servants had gone upstairs, banging the doors and leaving all the lights on. Rosine, in her dazzling dress and pearls, collapsed into an armchair and sat there, motionless.

Suddenly she made a violent movement that was so abrupt and unexpected that Antoinette jumped and banged her head against the wall. Trembling, she made herself as small as she could; but her mother hadn't heard anything. She was pulling off her bracelets one by one and throwing them on to the floor. One of the bracelets was heavy and beautiful, decorated with enormous diamonds; it rolled under the settee and landed at Antoinette's feet. Antoinette, frozen to the spot, just stared.

She saw her mother's face—the tears streaming down her

cheeks, streaking her make-up. It was a wrinkled face, a face so distorted and scarlet, it looked childish, comical, pitiful . . . But Antoinette felt no pity; she felt nothing but a kind of contempt, a scornful indifference. One day, she would say to some young man, "Oh, I was a horrible little girl, you know. Why once I even . . ." Suddenly, she felt blessed because her future was full of promise, because she had all the strength of youth, because she was able to think, "How could anyone cry like that, just because of something like this . . . What about love, what about death? She's going to die one day. Has she forgotten about that?"

So, grown-ups also suffered over trivial things, did they? And she, Antoinette, had been afraid of them, had trembled because of their shouting, their anger, their vain, absurd threats . . . Ever so quietly, she slipped out of her hiding place. For a moment longer, still hidden in the shadows, she looked at her mother: she had stopped sobbing but remained huddled over, letting the tears flow down to her mouth without bothering to wipe them away. Then Antoinette stood up.

"Mother."

Madame Kampf leapt out of her chair.

"What are you doing here?" she shouted nervously. "Get out, get out at once! Leave me the hell alone! I can't even have a moment's peace in my own house any more!"

Antoinette, her face pale, stayed where she was, her head lowered. The shrill voice was still ringing in her ears, but it was distant and stripped of all its force, like the sound of false thunder in the theatre. One day, and soon, she would say to some young man, "Mother will make a fuss, but never mind . . ."

Slowly she stretched out her hand and began gently stroking her mother's hair with trembling fingers.

"Poor Mama, never mind . . ."

For a while, Rosine automatically continued to protest, pushing her away and shaking her contorted features. "Go away, I tell you. Leave me alone . . ."

Then a weak, defeated expression came over her face.

"Oh, my poor darling, my poor little Antoinette . . . You're so very lucky—yes, you really are—not to have yet seen how underhanded, how malicious, how unfair people can be . . . All those people who smiled at me, sent me invitations...They were just laughing at me behind my back! They despised me because I wasn't one of them. Nasty bitches...But you wouldn't understand, my poor darling. And your father! Oh, you're all I have! You're all I have, my poor darling..."

She threw her arms around her. Since Antoinette's silent face was pressed against her pearls, she couldn't see that her daughter was smiling.

"You're a good girl, Antoinette..." she said.

It was at this moment, this fleeting moment that their paths crossed "on life's journey." One of them was about to ascend, and the other to plunge downwards into darkness. But neither of them realised it.

"Poor Mama," Antoinette said softly. "Poor Mama..."

SNOW IN AUTUMN

CHAPTER I

SHE NODDED. "So we say good-bye, Yourotchka . . . Take good care of yourself, my darling boy," she said, as she had so often in the past.

How quickly time passed . . . When he was a child, leaving for school in Moscow in the autumn, he would come to say good-bye to her like this, in the very same room. That had been ten, twelve years ago.

She looked at his officer's uniform almost with surprise, a kind of sorrowful pride.

"Ah, Yourotchka, my boy, it seems like it was just yesterday."

She fell silent, gesturing wearily. She had been with the Karine family for fifty-one years. She was the nanny to Nicolas Alexandrovitch, Youri's father; after him, she had brought up his brothers and sisters, his children. She still remembered Alexandre Kirilovitch, killed in 1877 at thirty-nine in the war with Turkey. And now it was the children's turn: Cyrille, Youri, it was their turn to go off to war . . .

She sighed, making the sign of the cross over Youri.

"Go, and may God protect you, my darling boy."

"Of course, my dear."

He smiled, a resigned, mocking look on his face. He had the heavy, youthful features of a serf. He didn't look like the other Karines. He took the old woman's small hands in his own; they were as hard as bark, almost black. When he started to raise them to his lips, she blushed and quickly pulled them away.

"Are you mad? You don't think I'm some beautiful young lady, do you? Go on now, Yourotchka, go downstairs . . . They're still dancing down there."

"Good-bye, Nianiouchka, Tatiana Ivanovna," he said, sounding a bit lazy and slightly ironic. "Good-bye. I'll bring you back a silk shawl from Berlin, though I'd be surprised if I ended up there; but, in the meantime, I'll send you some nice fabric from Moscow as a New Year's present."

She forced herself to smile, pinching her lips even more; they had remained delicate, but were now tighter and pulled inwards, as if sucked into her mouth by her ageing jaw. She was seventy years old, very small and fragile-looking, with a smiling, lively face; her eyes were still piercing at times, and at others, calm and weary. She shook her head.

"You make many promises, and your brother's just the same. But you'll forget us once you're gone. Well, may it be God's will that it all ends soon, and that you'll both come back home. Do you think this wretched war will soon be over?"

"Definitely. It will end quickly and badly."

"You mustn't joke like that," she said crossly. "Everything is in the hands of God."

She walked away, kneeling down in front of the open trunk.

"You can tell Platochka and Piotre to come up and take whatever they want. Everything is ready. The fur coats are on the bottom with the tartan rugs. When are you leaving? It's midnight."

"We'll be all right as long as we get to Moscow by morning. The train leaves tomorrow at eleven o'clock."

She sighed, shaking her head in that familiar way.

"Ah, Lord Jesus, what a sad Christmas."

Downstairs someone was playing a light, lively waltz on the piano; she could hear the dancers moving across the old wooden floors and the metallic sound of the men's boots.

Youri waved. "Good-bye, I'm going downstairs, Nianiouchka."

"Go, my dear."

She was alone. "The boots . . . the things for the old overnight bag . . ." she mumbled as she folded the clothing, "they could still be useful at war . . . Have I forgotten anything? The fur coats are at the bottom . . ."

Thirty-nine years before, when Alexandre Kirilovitch had gone, she had packed his uniforms the very same way. Dear Lord, she remembered it well. The old chambermaid, Agafia, was still alive then . . . She herself was young . . . She closed her eyes, let out a deep sigh, clumsily got up.

"I'd really like to know where Platochka and Petka are, the scoundrels," she grumbled. "May God forgive me. Everyone's drunk today." She picked up the shawl that had fallen on the floor, wrapped it around her head and face, went downstairs. The children's wing had been built in the old part of the house. It was beautiful, with fine architecture and a large Greek pediment decorated with columns; the grounds stretched all the way to the next village, Soukharevo. Tatiana Ivanovna hadn't lived anywhere else in fifty-one years. She alone knew every cupboard, all the cellars, and the dark, deserted rooms on the ground floor that, in the past, had been the grand reception rooms, home to many generations.

She walked quickly through the sitting room. Cyrille saw her, laughingly called out: "Well, Tatiana Ivanovna. So your dear boys are leaving, are they?"

She frowned and smiled at the same time. "Now, now, it won't do you any harm to rough it a little, Kirilouchka . . ."

He and his sister Loulou had the beauty, the sparkling eyes, the contented and cruel features of the Karines before them. Loulou was waltzing in the arms of her younger cousin, Tchernichef, a schoolboy of fifteen. She was dazzling, with rosy cheeks, fiery red from the dancing; her thick, long black hair coiled around her small head, like a dark crown.

"Time," mused Tatiana Ivanovna. "Time . . . Ah, my God, you don't notice how quickly it goes, and then one day you realise that these little children are taller than you . . . Lulitchka, even she's become a young lady . . . My God, and it was only yesterday that I was telling her father: 'Don't cry, Kolinka, you'll feel better soon, my treasure.' He's an old man now."

He was standing in front of her with Hélène Vassilievna. He saw her, started, whispered: "Already, Tatianouchka? Are the horses ready?"

"Yes, it's time, Nicolas Alexandrovitch. I'll have the baggage put on the sleigh."

He lowered his head, gently biting his wide, pale lips.

"My God, already? Very well. What can you do? Come on then, come on."

He turned towards his wife, smiling faintly. "Children will

grow, and old people will fret," he said, his voice as weary and controlled as ever. "Isn't that so, Nelly? Come along, my dear, I really think it's time now."

They looked at each other without saying a word. She nervously threw her black lace scarf over her long, supple neck, the only part of her that had remained as beautiful as it had been in her youth, that and her green eyes that shimmered, like water.

"I'm coming with you, Tatiana."

"What for?" said the old woman, shrugging her shoulders. "You'll only get cold."

"It doesn't matter," she murmured impatiently.

Tatiana Ivanovna followed her in silence. They crossed an empty little room. In the past, Hélène Vassilievna was known as the Countess Eletzkaïa. On those summer nights, she would come to see Nicolas Karine, and they would walk through this little door to go into the sleeping house... It was here that she would sometimes run into the old nanny, Tatiana, in the morning. She could still picture her, pressed against the wall to let her pass as she made the sign of the cross. That all seemed long gone and past, like an eerie dream. When Eletzki died, she'd married Karine. At the beginning, Tatiana Ivanovna's hostility had upset and annoyed her, and often... She was young then. Now it was different. Now she took a kind of sad, ironic pleasure in watching the way the old woman looked at her, how she recoiled from her, how prudish she was, as if she was still that young adulteress running to meet her lover beneath the old lime trees... That, at least, she retained from her youth.

"You didn't forget anything, did you?" she asked out loud.

"Well, no, Hélène Vassilievna."

"There's so much snow. Have them put some more blankets on the sleigh."

"Try not to worry."

They pushed the terrace door open with great difficulty; it creaked beneath the weight of the snow. The icy-cold night was filled with the scent of frozen pine trees, and smoke, in the distance. Tatiana Ivanovna closed her shawl around her chin and ran out to the sleigh. She was still as straight and energetic as she had been in the past, when Cyrille and Youri were children and she would go to look for them at dusk. Hélène Vassilievna closed her eyes for a moment, picturing her two eldest sons, their faces, the games they played. Cyrille, her favourite. He was so handsome, so . . . happy . . . She feared more for him than for Youri. She loved them both passionately. But Cyrille . . . Oh, it was a sin to think such things . . . "My God, protect them, save them, grant us the blessing of growing old, surrounded by all our children . . . Hear me, Lord! Everything is in the hands of God," Tatiana Ivanovna always said.

Tatiana Ivanovna climbed up the steps of the terrace, shaking off the snowflakes that clung to her lace shawl.

They went back into the sitting room. The piano was silent. The young people were standing in the middle of the room, quietly talking amongst themselves.

"It's time, my children," said Hélène Vassilievna.

Cyrille motioned to her. "All right, Mama, in a second . . . One more drink, gentlemen."

They drank to the health of the Emperor, the Imperial Family, the allies, the defeat of Germany. After each toast, they threw their champagne flutes to the floor, and the servants silently cleared away the broken glass. The rest of the servants were waiting in the entrance hall.

When the officers passed in front of them, they all spoke at exactly the same time, as if they were reciting a mournful lesson they had learned by heart: "Well . . . Good-bye, Cyrille Nicolaévitch . . . Good-bye, Youri Nicolaévitch." It was only Antipe, the old chef, always slightly tipsy and sad, who leaned his large grey head on his shoulder and added automatically in his loud, hoarse voice: "May God keep you safe and sound."

"Times have changed," grumbled Tatiana Ivanovna. "In the past, when the Barines left . . . Times have changed, and so have people."

She followed Cyrille and Youri out on to the terrace. The snow was falling fast. The servants raised their lanterns, lighting up the ancient, frozen grounds, so still; and the statues at the foot of the drive, two Bellonas, goddesses of war who shimmered with frost and ice. One last time, Tatiana Ivanovna made the sign of the cross above the sleigh and the road; the young people called out to her, laughing as they leaned forward so she could kiss their cheeks, cheeks that were burning, whipped by the cold night air. "There, there, my dear, good-bye, look after yourself, we'll be back, don't worry." The driver took hold of the reins, made a strangely sharp whistlelike noise, and the horses started off. One of the servants put his lantern down on the ground, yawning.

"Are you staying here, Nianiouchka?"

The old woman didn't reply. The others went inside. She saw the lights on the terrace and in the entrance hall going out, one by one. In the house, Nicolas Alexandrovitch absent-mindedly took a bottle of champagne from one of the servants.

"Why aren't you drinking?" he murmured, with difficulty. "We should have a drink."

Carefully, he filled their glasses; his hands were shaking slightly. A large man with a dyed moustache, General Siédof, went over to him. "Try not to upset yourself, my friend," he whispered in his ear. "I spoke to His Highness. He'll look after them, don't worry."

Nicolas Alexandrovitch slowly shrugged his shoulders. He had gone to St. Petersburg as well. He'd been granted an audience and obtained letters. He had spoken to the grand duke. As if *he* could protect them from bullets, dysentery. "Once your children have grown up, all you can do is fold your arms and let life run its course . . . But you still get upset, rush about, imagine . . . Yes, you do . . . I'm getting old," he suddenly thought, "old and cowardly. War? . . . My God, why, twenty years ago I couldn't have imagined such luck."

Out loud, he said: "Thank you, Michel Mikaïlovitch. What can you do? They'll do what all the others do. May God grant us victory."

"God willing!" the old general said passionately. The others, the young men who had been at the front, said nothing. One of them instinctively opened the piano, played a few notes.

"Dance, my dears," said Nicolas Alexandrovitch.

He sat back down at the card-table, motioning to his wife.

"You should go and rest, Nelly. Look how pale you are."

"So are you," she whispered.

They silently squeezed each other's hand. Hélène Vassilievna left the room, and the elder Karine picked up the cards and started playing, fiddling absent-mindedly with the silver candelabra.

CHAPTER II

FOR QUITE A WHILE, Tatiana Ivanovna listened to the sound of the bells on the horse-drawn carriage growing fainter. "They're going quickly," she thought. She had remained in the middle of the path pressing her shawl tightly to her face. The snow, light and delicate, felt like powder against her eyelids; the moon had risen, and the deep trail left by the sleigh in the frozen ground sparkled with a fiery blue glow. The wind dropped and immediately the snow began falling heavily. The faint tinkle of the little bells had died away; the pine trees, laden with ice, creaked in the silence with the heavy groan of someone in pain.

The old woman slowly made her way back to the house. She thought of Cyrille, of Youri, with a kind of tender shock . . . War. She vaguely imagined a field and galloping horses, shells exploding like ripe pea pods . . . like a fleeting image . . . where had she seen that before? In a schoolbook, no doubt, one the children had coloured in. Which children? Cyrille and Youri, or Nicolas Alexandrovitch and his brothers? Sometimes, when she felt very weary, like tonight, they became confused in her mind. A long, confusing dream. Would she perhaps wake up, as she had in the past, to hear Kolinka crying in his old bedroom?

Fifty-one years . . . Before, she too had a husband, a child . . . They had died, both of them . . . It had happened so long ago that sometimes she could barely remember what they looked like. Yes, nothing lasted, everything was in the hands of God.

She went back upstairs to see André, the youngest Karine in her care. He still slept next to her, in the large corner room where Nicolas Alexandrovitch had slept, and then his brothers, his sisters. All of them had either died or gone to live far away. The room seemed too vast, the ceilings too high for the few pieces of furniture that remained: Tatiana Ivanovna's bed and André's, the white curtains and the little antique icon hanging over his cot. A toy chest, an old little wooden desk that had once been white but which the past forty years had worn so that it now looked a pale, glossy grey. Four bare windows, an old wooden floor. During the day, everything was bathed in a torrent of light and air. When night fell, with its eerie silence, Tatiana Ivanovna would say: "There should be more children by now."

She lit a candle, partially illuminating the ceiling's painted angels and their mischievous faces, then shaded the flame and walked over to André. He was in a deep sleep, his golden head nestled against the pillow; she stroked his forehead and his little hands that lay open over the sheets, then sat down next to him, as she always did. She would sit like this for hours, every night, half-asleep, knitting, drowsy from the heat given off by the wood-burning stove, dreaming of the past and the future: when Cyrille and Youri would get married, where new children would be sleeping there beside her. André would soon be gone. As soon as they were six, the boys went down to live on the floor below, with their tutors and governesses. But the old room had never remained empty for long. Cyrille? Or Youri? Or Loulou, perhaps? The burning candle crackled loudly, steadily, in the silence. She watched it, her hands slowly swaying, as if she were rocking a cradle. "I'll live to see other children, God willing," she whispered.

Someone knocked at the door. She stood up. "Is that you, Nicolas Alexandrovitch?" she asked quietly.

"Yes, Nianiouchka."

"Try not to make noise or you'll wake him up . . ."

He came into the room; she took a chair and quietly put it next to the stove.

"Are you tired? Would you like some tea? It will only take a moment to boil some water."

He stopped her. "No. It's fine. I don't want anything."

She picked her knitting up from the floor, sat down again, quickly clicking the shiny needles.

"It's been a long time since you came to see us."

He said nothing, stretched his hands out towards the crackling wood-burning stove.

"Are you cold, Nicolas Alexandrovitch?"

He crossed his arms over his chest and shivered slightly. "Have you caught a chill?" she cried, as she had in the past.

"No, not at all, my dear."

She shook her head crossly and said nothing. Nicolas Alexandrovitch looked over at André's bed. "Is he sleeping?"

"Yes. Do you want to see him?"

She stood up, took the candle and walked towards Nicolas Alexandrovitch. He didn't move. She leaned over, quickly tapped him on the shoulder. "Nicolas Alexandrovitch . . . Kolinka . . ."

"Leave me be," he murmured.

Silently, she looked away.

It was better to say nothing. And where could he cry freely, if not with her? Or Hélène Vassilievna . . . Yes, it was better to say nothing . . . She quietly retreated into the dark room. "Wait here, I'm going to make some tea, it will warm us both up."

When she got back, he seemed calmer; he was absent-mindedly turning the handle of the wood-burning stove; the plaster from the wall behind sounded like gently flowing sand.

"Look, Tatiana, how many times have I told you to plug up the hole behind the stove. Look, look over there," he said, pointing to a cockroach scuttling across the floor. "They're coming from that hole. Do you think that's healthy in a child's bedroom?"

"You know very well that cockroaches are a sign of a wealthy household," said Tatiana Ivanovna. "Thank God, we've always had them here, and you were brought up here and others before you." She handed him the glass of tea she had brought, stirred it. "Drink it while it's hot. Is there enough sugar?"

He didn't reply, took a sip with a weary, distant look on his face and, suddenly, stood up.

"Well, good night, and get that hole behind the stove fixed, understand?"

"If you say so."

"Bring the candle."

She picked it up, lighting his way to the door; she went down the first three steps leading to the room. They were made of reddish brick—loose, wobbly, and slanting to one side, as if pulled towards the earth by a heavy weight.

"Be careful. Will you be able to sleep now?"

"To sleep . . . I'm so sad, Tatiana, my soul is full of sadness."

"God will protect them, Nicolas Alexandrovitch. People die in their beds, and God protects Christians from bullets."

"I know, I know . . ."

"You must trust in God."

"I know," he repeated. "But it's not just that . . ."

"What else is wrong, Barine?"

"Nothing's going right, Tatiana, it's hard to explain."

She nodded.

"Yesterday, my great-nephew, the son of my niece in Sou-kharevo, was also conscripted for this cursed war. He's the only man in the family since his older brother was killed last spring. There's only his wife and a little girl the same age as our André . . . so who's going to work the farm? Everyone has his share of misery."

"Yes, we're living in sad times. I pray to God that . . ."

He stopped her. "Well, good night, Tatiana," he said quickly.

"Good night, Nicolas Alexandrovitch."

She stood silently, waiting until he had crossed the sitting room, listening to his footsteps creaking against the wooden floor. She opened the little window-pane. An icy wind was rageing so fiercely that it swept up her shawl and blew through her hair. The old woman smiled, closed her eyes. She had been born in a region in northern Russia, far from where the Karines lived, and there was never enough ice, never enough wind as far as she was concerned. "Where I come from," she said, "we used to break the ice with our bare feet, in the springtime, and I'd be happy to do it again."

She closed the little window; the whistling of the wind was blocked out. The only sounds that remained were the faint rustling of the plaster trickling down the old walls, like whispering sand, and the hollow, deep creaking of rats gnawing away at the antique wooden panelling.

Tatiana Ivanovna went back into her bedroom, prayed for a long while, and then got undressed. It was late. She blew out the candle, sighed, and said, "My God, my God," out loud, over and over again into the silence, then fell asleep.

CHAPTER III

WHEN TATIANA IVANOVNA had closed all the doors of the empty house, she went up to the little cupola set into the roof. It was a hushed May night, already sweet-smelling and warm. Soukharevo was burning; she could clearly see the flames in the air and hear the sound of people's screaming carried through the wind from far away.

The Karine family had fled five months earlier, in January 1918. Since then, every day, Tatiana Ivanovna had watched fires burning in the distant villages, the flames die down and then flare up again, as the Bolsheviks took the villages from the White Russians who in turn lost them again to the Bolsheviks. But the fires had never been as close as this evening; the flames lit up the abandoned grounds so clearly that she could see right down to the end of the long drive where the lilac trees had recently come into bloom. The birds, confused by the light, were flying to and fro as if it were daytime. Dogs were howling. Then the wind shifted, carrying away the sound and smell of the flames. The old, deserted grounds were calm and dark once more, and the perfume of the lilacs filled the air.

Tatiana Ivanovna waited a while, then sighed and went downstairs. In the downstairs rooms, they had taken down the carpets and draperies. The windows were boarded over and protected by iron bars. The family silver was hidden at the bottom of packing trunks, in the cellars; she'd buried the most valuable china in the old, deserted part of the orchard. Some of the serfs had helped her: they assumed that all this wealth would belong to them one day. These days, people cared about their neighbours only for their possessions. That's why they wouldn't say anything to the officials in Moscow, and later on, well, they'd wait and see . . . Without them, though, she wouldn't have been able to do anything. She was all alone, the other servants had left long ago. Antipe, the cook, the last one left, had stayed with her until March, when he'd died. He had the key to the wine cellar and wanted nothing more. "You're wrong not to have some wine, Tatiana," he would say, "it makes you forget all your troubles. Look, we're all alone, abandoned like dogs, and a curse on all the rest, I couldn't care less, just as long as I have some wine."

But she had never liked drinking. One evening, during those final stormy March days, the two of them had been sitting in the kitchen. He'd started rambling, remembering back to when he was a soldier. "They're not so stupid, these young people, with their revolution... It's their turn now... They've bled us enough, those bloody Barines, the dirty bastards." She hadn't replied. What was the use? He had threatened to burn down the house, sell the jewellery and the hidden icons. He had carried on like this, deliriously, for a while, then, suddenly began to shout plaintively: "Alexandre Kirilovitch, why have you abandoned us, Barine?" He'd started to vomit, a torrent of dark blood and alcohol poured from his mouth; he'd suffered until morning, then he'd died.

Tatiana Ivanovna fastened the iron chains on the sitting-room doors and went out on to the terrace through the little hidden door in the hallway. The statues were still in their wooden crates; they had been sealed away in September 1916 and left there, forgotten. She looked at the house; the delicate yellowish colour of the stonework was blackened by the thawing snow; beneath the acanthus leaves, the stucco was flaking off, revealing whitish marks, as if it had been struck by bullets. The windows in the greenhouse had been shattered by the wind. "If Nicolas Alexandrovitch could see all this..."

She took a few steps down the path and stopped still, clutching her hands to her heart. There was a man standing in front of her. She looked at him for a moment without realising who it was, without recognising the pale, exhausted face beneath the soldier's cap. "Is it you? Is it you, Yourotchka?" she finally asked, her voice shaking.

"Yes," he said; the look on his face was cold, hesitant and strange. "Will you hide me tonight?"

"Don't worry," she said, as she had in the past. They went into the house, into the empty kitchen. She lit a candle, held it up to see Youri's face.

"How you've changed, good Lord! Are you ill?"

"I had typhus," he said; his voice was slow, hoarse and husky. "And I've been as sick as a dog, not far from here, in Temnaïa. But I was afraid to get word to you. There's a death warrant out for me," he continued with the same steady, cold intonation. "I need something to drink . . ."

She gave him some water and knelt down to loosen the dirty, blood-soaked rags tied around his bare feet.

"I've been walking for a long time," he said.

She looked up. "Why did you come? The serfs have all gone mad around here," she said.

"Ah, it's the same everywhere. When I got out of prison, my parents had already left for Odessa. Where is there to go? People are fleeing everywhere, some to the north, others to the south . . ."

He shrugged his shoulders. "It's the same everywhere . . ." he repeated, apathetically.

"You were in prison?" she murmured, folding her hands.

"For six months."

"But why?"

"Lord only knows."

He fell silent, sat very still, continued with difficulty: "I got out of Moscow . . . One day, I found my way into a hospital train and the nurses hid me . . . I still had some money left . . . I travelled with them for ten days . . . Then I started walking . . . But I'd caught typhus fever. I collapsed in a field, near Temnaïa. Some people found me, took me in. I stayed with them for a while, but then the Bolsheviks were getting closer, so they were afraid, and I left."

"Where is Cyrille?"

"He was in prison with me. But he managed to get out and join the family in Odessa; someone gave me a letter from him while I was in prison . . . By the time I got out, they'd been gone for three weeks. I've never had any luck, my dear Nianiouchka," he said, smiling in his usual way, resigned and ironic. "Even in prison, Cyrille was in a cell with a beautiful young woman, a French actress, while I was locked up with some old Jew."

He laughed, then stopped, as even he was surprised by the broken, hollow sound of his voice. He held her hand to his cheek. "I'm so happy to be home, Nianiouchka," he sighed, and suddenly fell asleep.

He slept for several hours; she didn't move, she just sat there opposite him, watching him; tears flowed silently down her ageing, pale face. A while later, she woke him up, took him to the nursery, put him to bed. He was slightly delirious. He was talking out loud, sometimes reaching out to touch the calendar on the wall, still decorated with a colour portrait of the Tsar, or to grasp the rungs on the side of André's bed, where the icon was hanging, as if he were a child. He pointed to the page with the date: 18 May 1918, saying over and over again: "I don't understand, I don't understand."

Then he smiled as he looked at the window-shade billowing gently, and outside at the grounds, the trees lit up by the moon; and the spot, near the window, where the old wooden floor was slightly hollow. The pale moonlight washed over him, rocking him like a river of milk. How often had he got out of bed and sat right there, while his brother was asleep, listening to the coach-man's accordion, the stifled laughter of the servants . . . He had inhaled the strong perfume of the lilacs, like tonight . . . He strained to listen, unconsciously trying to hear the music from the accordion in the silence. But he heard nothing except an occa-sional soft, low rumbling. He sat up, saw Tatiana Ivanovna sitting next to him in the dark room, tapped her on the shoulder.

"What's that noise?"

"I don't know. It started yesterday. Maybe it's thunder, you sometimes get thunder in May."

"That?" he said. He laughed suddenly, staring at her with his wide eyes, eyes that looked pale but which burned with a feverish harsh light. "That's cannon fire, my poor dear! I thought it would happen . . . It was too good to be true."

His words were jumbled, confused, interspersed with laughter. Then he said quite clearly: "If I could just die peacefully in this bed, I'm so tired . . ."

By morning, his fever had broken; he wanted to get up, go out into the grounds, breathe in the spring air, warm and pure, as in the past. Everything else had changed... The deserted grounds, full of wild grass, looked pitiful and sad. He went into the little pavilion, stretched out on the ground, absent-mindedly feeling the broken shards as he looked at the house through the shattered coloured glass in the window. One night, in prison, when he was expecting to be executed at any moment, he had seen the house in a dream, just as he did today, from the window of the little pavilion; but the house had been open, the terrace full of flowers. In his dream, he had seen every detail, right down to the chimney sweeps walking along the rooftop. He had woken up with a start and had thought: "Tomorrow, I'll face death, that is certain. It is only just before dying that people have memories like this."

Death. He wasn't afraid of it. But to leave this earth in the turmoil of a revolution, forgotten by everyone, abandoned... It was all so absurd... Well, he hadn't died yet... Who knows? Perhaps he'd manage to escape. This house... He had truly thought he would never see it again, and here it was, and these windows with their coloured glass that the wind always shattered; he'd played with them as a child, picturing in his mind the vineyards of Italy... undoubtedly because of their purplish colour, like red wine and blood. Tatiana Ivanovna used to come in and say: "Your mother's calling you, my darling..."

Tatiana Ivanovna came in carrying a plate with some potatoes and bread.

"How have you managed to get any food?" he asked.

"At my age, you don't need much. I've always had enough potatoes and in the village, you can sometimes get bread... I've never wanted for anything."

She knelt down beside him, started feeding him, as if he were too weak to lift the food and drink to his lips.

"Youri... Don't you think you should leave right away?"

He frowned, looking at her without replying.

"You could walk to my nephew's house," she said. "He wouldn't harm you: if you have some money, he could help you find a horse and you could go to Odessa. Is it far?"

"Three or four days by train, ordinarily . . . Now . . . God only knows . . ."

"What can we do? God will help you. You could get to your family and give them this. I've never wanted to trust anyone else with it," she said, lifting the hem of her dress. "I have the big diamonds from your mother's necklace. Before leaving, she told me to hide them. They couldn't take anything with them, they left in the middle of the night when the Bolsheviks took Temnaïa, and they were afraid of being arrested. What kind of life must they have now?"

"Not a good one, I'm sure," he said, wearily shrugging his shoulders.

"Well, let's wait and see what happens tomorrow."

"Look, you're kidding yourself, it's the same everywhere. At least here, the serfs know me, I've never done them any harm."

"Who knows what they might secretly be thinking, those dogs?" she grumbled.

"Tomorrow, tomorrow," he repeated, closing his eyes. "We'll see what happens tomorrow. It's so peaceful here, my God."

And so the day passed. Towards evening, he headed back to the house. It was a beautiful dusk, clear and peaceful, like the evening before. He took a detour to walk by the ornamental lake; in autumn, the bushes were bare, yet the lake was still covered in a thick layer of dead leaves, frozen beneath the ice. The flowers from the lilac trees fell like light rain; he could scarcely make out the dark water, faintly shimmering through, here and there.

He went back into the house, up to the nursery. Tatiana Ivanovna had set a table beside the open window; he recognised one of the little delicate table-cloths of fine linen reserved especially for the children when they were ill and ate in their bedroom; and the fork as well, the antique silver knife, the old tarnished cup.

"Eat, drink, my darling. I've taken a bottle of wine from the cellars for you, and I know you used to like potatoes baked in embers."

"Not any more," he said laughing, "but thank you anyway, my treasure."

Night was falling. He lit a candle, setting it at the end of the table. Its flame burned tall and bright in the peaceful evening. It was so silent.

"Nianiouchka, why didn't you go with the family?" he asked.

"Well, someone had to stay and look after the house."

"You think so?" he said, sounding sadly ironic. "For whom, my God?"

They fell silent. "Wouldn't you like to go and join them?" he asked.

"I'll go if they call for me. I'll find my way there; I've never been shy or stupid, thank God . . . But what would happen to the house?"

She stopped suddenly, whispered: "Listen!"

Someone was downstairs, knocking at the door. They both stood up quickly.

"Hide, for the love of God, you have to hide, Youri!"

Youri went over to the window, cautiously looked outside. The moon was high. He recognised the boy who stood in the middle of the drive, stepping back to call out: "Youri Nicol-aévitch! It's me, Ignat!"

He was a young coachman who had been brought up in the Karine household. He and Youri had played together as children. He was the one who used to sing and play his accordion in the grounds on those summer nights. "If *he* wants to hurt me," Youri suddenly thought, "then everything be damned, and me with it!" He leaned out the window. "Come up, my friend," he shouted.

"I can't. The door is barricaded."

"Go down and open the door, Niania, he's alone."

"What have you done, you poor thing?" she whispered.

He made a weary gesture with his hand. "Whatever happens, happens. And anyway, he saw me . . . Go on, my darling, go and let him in."

She stood there motionless, trembling and silent. He walked towards the door. She stopped him, colour suddenly rushing back into her cheeks.

"What are you doing? It's not for you to go down to let in the coachman. Wait for me here."

He gently shrugged his shoulders and sat down again. When

she came back, followed by Ignat, he stood up and walked over to them.

"Hello, I'm happy to see you."

"So am I, Youri Nicolaévitch," said the boy, smiling. He had a big, full, rosy face.

"Have you had enough to eat?"

"God has helped me, Barine."

"Do you still play the accordion, like you used to?"

"Sometimes."

"I'd love to hear you play again . . . I'll be staying for a while."

Ignat did not reply; he kept smiling, showing his wide, shiny teeth.

"Would you like a drink? Bring another glass, Tatiana."

The old woman grudgingly obeyed. "To your good health, Youri Nicolaévitch." The young man drank.

They were silent. Tatiana Ivanovna walked over to them: "Fine. Get going now. The young Barine is tired."

"Even so, you must come with me to the village, Youri Nicolaévitch."

"Ah! Why?" Youri murmured, involuntarily lowering his voice. "Why, my friend?"

"You have to."

Suddenly Tatiana Ivanovna looked as if she were about to pounce. An expression so wild, so strange, passed over her pale, impassive face that Youri shuddered.

"Leave him be," he said almost despairingly to Tatiana. "Calm down. I beg of you. Leave him be, it doesn't matter . . ."

She was screaming, wouldn't listen to him, her thin, tense hands stretched out like claws: "Ah, you devil, you bloody bastard! You think I can't see what's in your eyes? And who do you think you are to be giving orders to your master?"

He turned towards her; his face had changed: his eyes were burning. Then he seemed to calm down, and said nonchalantly: "Be quiet, old woman. There are some people in the village who want to talk to Youri Nicolaévitch, that's all."

"Do you at least know what they want from me?" asked Youri. He suddenly felt exhausted, one sincere, deep desire remained in his heart: to go to bed and sleep for a very long time.

"They want to talk to you about dividing up the wine. We've received orders from Moscow."

"Ah! So that's it? I can see you enjoyed my wine. But you could have waited until tomorrow, you know."

He walked towards the door, with Ignat following behind. At the doorway, he stopped. For an instant, Ignat seemed to hesitate; then, suddenly, with the same swift movement he used in the past to grab the whip, he reached into his belt, pulled out a revolver and fired two shots. The first hit Youri between the shoulders; he screamed in amazement, shuddering. The second bullet went right through his neck, killing him instantly.

·

CHAPTER IV

ONE MONTH AFTER Youri's death, a cousin of the Karines came and spent a night with Tatiana Ivanovna. He was an old man, half dead from starvation and exhaustion, on his way from Odessa to Moscow to look for his wife, who had disappeared during the bombings in April. He brought her news of Nicolas Alexandrovitch and his family, and gave her their address. They were in good health, but were living in poverty. "Could you find a man you trust," he hesitated, "to bring them what they left here?"

The old woman left for Odessa, carrying the jewellery in the hem of her skirt. For three months, she travelled along the roads, as she had done when she was young, when she made the pilgrimage from Kiev, sometimes climbing on to trains full of starving people making the journey south. One September evening, she arrived at the Karines' home. They would never forget the moment when she knocked at the door, when they first saw her, looking haggard and calm, her bundle of old clothes on her back, the diamonds beating against her weary legs. They would never forget her pale face, completely drained of blood, nor the sound of her voice when she told them that Youri was dead.

They were living in a dark room near the port; sacks of potatoes had been hung from the window-panes to absorb the exploding bullets. Hélène Vassilievna lay on an old mattress on the floor; Loulou and André were playing cards by the light of a little stove, where three pieces of coal were nearly burnt out. It was already cold, and the wind whistled through the broken windows. Cyrille was sleeping in one corner of the room, and Nicolas Alexandrovitch began what was to later become the main activity of his life: pacing back and forth between their four walls, hands folded behind his back, thinking about a time that would never return.

"Why did they kill him?" asked Loulou. "Why, dear Lord, why?" Tears flowed down her face. She had changed, looked older.

"They were afraid he'd come back to claim his land. But they said he had always been a good Barine. They wanted to spare him the pain of a trial and execution, and that it was better to kill him that way . . ."

"The cowards," Cyrille suddenly shouted. "The bastards! Shooting him in the back! Bloody serfs . . . We should have been harder on you when we were your masters!" He shook his fist at the old woman with a kind of hatred. "Do you hear me? Do you?"

"I hear you," she replied, "but what's the use regretting that he died one way as opposed to another? God has received him in his sacraments, I could see it in his peaceful face. May God grant all of us such a peaceful end. He saw nothing, he didn't suffer."

"Ah! You don't understand."

"It was better that way," she repeated.

That was the last time she ever spoke Youri's name out loud; she seemed to have sealed her ageing lips over him, forever. When anyone else talked about him, she never replied; she sat silent and cold, staring into space with a kind of icy despair.

The winter was extremely harsh. They didn't have enough bread or clothes. Only the jewellery that Tatiana Ivanovna had smuggled back occasionally brought them some money. The city was burning; the snow fell softly, hiding the scorched beams of the ruined houses, dead bodies, and dismembered horses. At times, the city was different: provisions arrived, meat, fruit, caviar . . . God alone knew how . . . The cannon fire would stop, and life would begin again, intoxicating and precarious.

Intoxicating . . . Cyrille and Loulou were the ones who felt it, the only ones. Much later, they would remember certain nights—going for boat rides with other young people, the taste of kisses, the dawn breeze blowing on the stormy waves of the Black Sea—and this would never fade in their memories.

The long winter passed, another summer and another winter followed, when the famine was so bad that dead children were buried in sacks, in mass graves. The Karines survived. In May, they managed to get passage on the last French boat leaving Odessa, first to Constantinople, then to Marseille.

They stepped out on the port in Marseille on 28 May 1920. In Constantinople, they had sold their remaining jewellery; their money was sewn into their belts, out of habit. They were dressed in rags, their faces were strange and frightening, miserable, harsh. The children, in spite of everything, seemed happy; they laughed with a kind of solemn gentleness which made the older members of the family sense their own weariness even more.

The clear May air was full of the scent of flowers and pepper; the crowd moved slowly, stopping to look in the shop windows, laughing and talking loudly. Lights and music echoed from the cafés, all of it as bizarre as in a dream.

While Nicolas Alexandrovitch went to find some hotel rooms, the children and Tatiana Ivanovna stayed outside for a while. Loulou closed her eyes, lifted up her pale face to breathe in the fragrant evening air. Great round electric lights lit up the street with a bluish glow; clusters of delicate trees in bloom swayed their branches. Some sailors passed by, laughed as they looked at the pretty young girl, standing motionless. One of them gently threw her a sprig of mimosas. Loulou started laughing. "What a beautiful, charming place," she said. "It's like a dream, Nianiouchka, look . . ."

But the old woman had sat down on a bench and appeared to have dozed off, her head-scarf pulled tightly around her white hair and her hands crossed over her knees. Loulou saw that her eyes were wide open, staring straight in front of her. She touched her shoulder, called: "Nianiouchka, what's the matter?"

Tatiana Ivanovna suddenly shivered, stood up. At the same time, Nicolas Alexandrovitch waved to them.

They went inside and slowly crossed the entrance hall, feeling that everyone was looking at them oddly as they walked past. They were no longer used to thick carpets; they stuck to their shoes, like glue. An orchestra was playing in the restaurant. They stopped, listened to this jazz music for the very first time, with a vague sort of fear and mad delight. It was another world.

They went into their rooms and stood at the windows for a

long time, watching the cars go by in the street below. "Let's go out, let's go out," the children said over and over. "Let's go to a café, or the theatre . . ."

They had baths, brushed off their clothes, rushed to the door. Nicolas Alexandrovitch and his wife followed them more slowly, more hesitantly, but consumed, as well, by a longing for fresh air and freedom.

When he reached the door, Nicolas Alexandrovitch turned around. Loulou had switched off the lights. They had forgotten Tatiana Ivanovna, who was sitting at the window. The light from a gas street-lamp in front of the little balcony lit up her bent head. She sat motionless, as if waiting for something. "Are you coming with us, Nianiouchka?" asked Nicolas Alexandrovitch.

She didn't reply. "Aren't you hungry?" She shook her head, then suddenly got up, nervously twisting the fringes of her shawl. "Should I unpack the children's things? When will we be leaving?"

"But we've only just got here," said Nicolas Alexandrovitch. "Why do you want to go?"

"I don't know," she murmured, a blank, weary look on her face. "I just thought . . ."

She sighed, spread out her arms, then said quietly: "It's all right."

"Do you want to come with us?"

"No, thank you, Hélène Vassilievna," she said with difficulty. "No, really . . ."

They could hear the children running down the corridor. The adults looked at each other in silence, sighing; then Hélène Vassilievna made a weary gesture and went out, followed by Nicolas Alexandrovitch, who quietly closed the door.

CHAPTER V

THE KARINES ARRIVED in Paris at the beginning of summer and rented a small furnished apartment on the Rue de l'Arc de Triomphe. It was a time when Paris had been invaded by the first wave of Russian immigrants, all of whom piled into Passy and the area around the Arc de Triomphe, instinctively drawn to the nearby woods of the Bois de Boulogne. That summer the heat was unbearable.

The apartment was small, dark, stifling; it smelled of dust and old upholstery. The low ceilings seemed to weigh down on them; from the windows, you could see the courtyard, long and narrow, with its whitewashed walls shimmering cruelly beneath the July sun. Even in the morning, they had to close the windows and shutters. The Karines remained in these four dark rooms until evening, without going out, stunned by the noise in Paris, feeling slightly sick as they breathed in the smells from the kitchens and sinks that rose up from the courtyard. Back and forth they went, between their four walls, silently, like flies in autumn after the heat and light of summer had gone, barely able to fly, weary and angry, buzzing around the windows, trailing their broken wings behind them.

Tatiana Ivanovna sat all day long in a small laundry room, at the back of the apartment, mending clothes. The only servant, a young girl from Normandy with a fresh face and rosy cheeks, as lumbering as a work-horse, would sometimes open the door and shout, "Aren't you bored?" She thought the foreigner would understand her better if she spoke slowly and loudly, like when you speak to deaf people; her voice reverberated, making the china lampshade rattle.

Tatiana Ivanovna would vaguely shake her head, and the servant would go back to stirring her cooking.

André had been sent to boarding-school near the coast, in

Brittany. A while later, Cyrille left. He had found his prison cellmate, the French actress he'd been locked up with in St. Petersburg in 1918. She had a rich lover now. She was a pretty young blonde, generous, with a full, beautiful figure, and madly in love with Cyrille. It simplified his life. But sometimes, when he came home at dawn, he would look out the window down at the courtyard, wishing he were stretched out on the pink paving stones, and finished, forever, with all the complications of love and money.

Later, that feeling passed. He bought nice clothes. He drank. At the end of June, he went to Deauville with his mistress.

In Paris, when the heat broke towards evening, the Karines would go out to the Bois de Boulogne, to the Pavillon Dauphine. The adults would sit there, sadly listening to the orchestra playing, remembering the little islands and gardens in Moscow; Loulou, and the other young boys and girls, would walk along the shaded paths, reciting poetry, playing at being in love.

Loulou was twenty. She was no longer as beautiful as before; she was thin with angular movements like a boy, and rough, dark skin burned by the wind during their long sea crossing. On her face was a strange look, weary and cruel. She had so loved her active, dangerous, exciting life. Now, her very favourite thing was walking through Paris at dusk, and the long, silent evenings in the bistros, those popular little bars, with their smell of chalk and alcohol, and the sound of people playing billiards in the back room. Towards midnight, they would go back to one of their apartments and start drinking again, caressing each other in the darkened rooms. Everyone else was asleep; their parents only vaguely heard the sound of the gramophone playing until dawn. They saw nothing, or wanted to see nothing.

One night, Tatiana Ivanovna came out of her room to get some washing that was drying in the bathroom; she had to mend a pair of tights for Loulou, and the night before, she'd left them on the radiator. She often worked at night. She didn't need much sleep, and by four or five o'clock in the morning, she was up, silently wandering through the apartment; she never went into the sitting room.

On that night, she had heard footsteps and voices in the

entrance hall; the children had gone out ages ago, undoubtedly. She saw a faint light under the sitting-room door. "They forgot to switch off the lamp, again," she thought. She opened the door, and only then heard the gramophone playing, muffled by a pile of cushions; the low, breathless music sounded as if it were being played under water. The room was almost dark. Just one lamp, covered by a piece of red cloth, cast a shadow on the settee where Loulou was stretched out, apparently asleep, her blouse unbuttoned; in her arms was a young boy, his pale, delicate head thrown back. The old woman moved closer. They were actually asleep, their faces pressed against each other, their lips still touching. The smell of alcohol and thick smoke filled the room; all over the floor there were glasses, empty bottles, overflowing ashtrays, and cushions with the deep impressions made by their bodies.

Loulou woke up, stared at Tatiana Ivanovna, smiled; her dilated eyes, darkened by wine and passion, looked mockingly indifferent and extremely tired. "What do you want?" she whispered.

Her long, loose hair reached down to the carpet; she tried to move her head, then groaned; the boy's hand was caught in her tangled hair. She broke free suddenly, sat up.

"What is it?" she said again, impatiently.

Tatiana Ivanovna looked at the boy. She knew him well; she had seen him often at the Karines' home when he was a child. He was called Prince Georges Andronikof; she remembered his long blond curls, his lace collars. "Get him out of here, right now, do you hear me?" she said suddenly, gritting her teeth, her old face trembling and ashen.

Loulou shrugged her shoulders. "All right, be quiet . . . He's going."

"Lulitchka," the old woman murmured.

"Yes, yes, just be quiet, for God's sake."

She switched off the gramophone, lit a cigarette, put it out almost immediately. "Help me," she ordered curtly.

Silently, they tidied up the room, picking up cigarette butts and empty glasses. Loulou opened the shutters, greedily breathing in the cool air that wafted up from the cellars. "Isn't it hot?"

The old woman didn't reply, looking away with a kind of furious modesty.

Loulou sat down on the window-ledge, gently swaying and humming. She looked sober, ill; beneath her face-powder, smudged from kissing, white patches of her pale cheeks showed through. She had rings under her wide empty eyes and she stared straight ahead.

"What's the matter with you, Nianiouchka? We do the same thing every night," she finally said, her voice calm, hoarse from the wine and smoke. "And in Odessa, my God? On the boat? You never noticed?"

"You should be ashamed," murmured the old woman, sounding pained and disgusted. "You should be ashamed! And with your parents asleep right next door . . ."

"So what? Oh, so that's it, are you crazy, Niania? We weren't doing anything wrong. We have a few drinks, a few kisses, why is that so wrong? Do you think my parents didn't do the same thing when they were young?"

"No, my girl."

"Ah, so that's what you think, do you?"

"I was young once too, Lulitchka. It was a very long time ago, but I can still remember how my young blood burned through my body. Do you think anyone forgets that? And I remember your aunts when they were twenty, like you. It was in Karinova, in the spring . . . Oh! What beautiful weather we had that year. Every day we would go for walks through the forest, take boat rides on the little lake . . . And at night, there were always balls to go to, at home or at the neighbours' houses. Each young woman had someone they were in love with, and many times, they would all go out together, in the moonlight, in a troika. Your dead grandmother used to say: 'When *we* were young . . .' So what? They knew very well that certain things were allowed and others forbidden . . . Sometimes, in the morning, they would come into my room and tell me all about what this one or that one had said. And still, they got engaged one day, got married, lived their lives honestly, with their fair share of happiness and sorrow, until the day when God took them. They died young, as you know, one in childbirth, and the other five years later after a nasty fever. Oh, yes, I can remember . . . We had the most beautiful horses of all, and sometimes they would all ride out together, in a long line. Your father was a young man then; he and his friends, and your aunts, and some other young people, would ride into the forest, and the servants would carry the torches to light the way ahead . . ."

"Yes," said Loulou bitterly, pointing to the dingy little sitting room and the crude vodka that she was absent-mindedly swirling around at the bottom of her glass. "The decor has obviously changed."

"That's not all that's changed," grumbled the old woman. She looked sadly at Loulou.

"Forgive me, my darling . . . You shouldn't be ashamed, I've known you since you were born. You haven't sinned, have you? You're still innocent?"

"Of course I am, my poor old dear," said Loulou. She thought back to a night in Odessa, during the bombings, when she had slept in the home of Baron Rosenkranz, the former governor of the city; he was in prison and his son lived there, alone. The cannon fire had started so suddenly that she hadn't had time to get home, and she had spent the night in the empty palace, with Serge Rosenkranz. What had happened to him, to Serge? Dead, no doubt . . . Of typhus, starvation, a stray bullet, in prison . . . Take your pick. What a night that had been . . . The docks were in flames . . . They could see, from the bed where they were making love, walls of burning petrol engulfing the port . . .

She remembered the house, on the other side of the street, with its run-down façade and tulle curtains fluttering in the dark . . . That night . . . Death had come so close.

"Of course I am, Nianiouchka," she repeated automatically.

But Tatiana Ivanovna knew her only too well: she shook her head, silently pursed her lips.

Georges Andronikof groaned, turned over clumsily, then half woke up. "I'm utterly drunk," he said quietly.

He stumbled over to an armchair, hid his face in its cushions, and sat motionless.

"He works all day in a garage now, and he's starving. If he

couldn't drink ... and enjoy other things, well, what would be the point of living?"

"You're offending God, Loulou."

Suddenly the young girl hid her face in her hands and started sobbing violently.

"Nianiouchka ... I want to go home! Home, home!" she kept saying, twisting her fingers in a strange and nervous way that the old woman had never seen before. "Why have we been punished like this? We didn't do anything wrong!"

Tatiana Ivanovna gently stroked her dishevelled hair, heavy with the odour of wine and smoke. "It is God's holy will."

"Oh, you do irritate me, that's your answer to everything!"

She dried her eyes, angrily shrugging her shoulders.

"Go away, leave me alone! Just go ... I'm tired and upset. Don't say anything to my parents. What good would it do? You'd only upset them for nothing, and believe me, it wouldn't change anything. You're too old, you don't understand."

CHAPTER VI

ONE SUNDAY IN August, when Cyrille came home, the Karines paid for a Mass to be said for Youri's soul. They walked together to the Rue Daru. It was a beautiful day; the blue sky was sparkling. There was an outdoor fair on the Avenue des Ternes, frenzied music and clouds of dust; the passers-by looked curiously at Tatiana Ivanovna, with her long skirt and her black shawl covering her head.

On the Rue Daru, Mass was celebrated in the crypt of the church; the candles crackled softly. You could hear burning wax dripping on the flagstones during the silences between the responses. "May the soul of God's servant, Youri, rest in peace . . ." The priest, an old man with long trembling hands, spoke quietly, his voice sweet and muted. The Karines prayed in silence; they were no longer thinking of Youri, Youri was at peace, but for them, there was still such a long road to travel, a long, dark road. "My God, protect me . . . My God, forgive me . . ." they said. But Tatiana Ivanovna, kneeling in front of the icon that burned faintly in the darkness, touched her head to the cold flagstones and thought only of Youri, prayed only for him, for his salvation and eternal rest.

Once Mass was over, they started for home. They bought some baby roses from a young girl they passed; she had dishevelled hair and looked cheerful. They were beginning to like this city and its people. Once the sun came out, you could forget all your troubles on these streets, you felt light-hearted without quite understanding why . . .

Sunday was the servant's day off. The cold meal was laid out on the table. They ate hardly anything, then Loulou put the roses in front of an old picture of Youri, when he was a child.

"He had such a strange expression," said Loulou. "I'd never noticed before . . . It's an almost indifferent, weary look."

"I always saw the same look in pictures of people destined to die young or tragically," murmured Cyrille uncomfortably, "as if they somehow knew in advance and couldn't care less . . . Poor Youri, he was the best of all of us."

They silently studied the little picture; it had faded. "He's at peace now, free forever."

Loulou carefully arranged his flowers, lit two candles, placing one at each side of the picture, and they all stood motionless, forcing themselves to remember Youri. Now they felt only a kind of icy sadness, as if many long years had passed since his death. But it had been just two . . .

Hélène Vassilievna gently wiped the dust off the glass picture frame, without thinking, as if she were wiping tears from someone's face. Of all her children, Youri was the one she had understood the least, loved the least . . . "He is with God," she thought. "He is happier than the others."

They could hear the noise from the fair in the street.

"It's hot in here," said Loulou.

Hélène Vassilievna turned around. "Well, go out, my darlings, what can we do? Go and get some fresh air and look around the fair; when I was your age, I preferred the fairs in Moscow, on Palm Sunday, to the parties at court."

"I liked them too," said Loulou.

"Well, go on then," their mother said again, sounding weary.

Loulou and Cyrille went out. Nicolas Alexandrovitch stood in front of the window, looking at the white walls, seeing nothing. Hélène Vassilievna sighed. How he had changed . . . He hadn't shaved . . . He was wearing an old waistcoat, covered in stains . . . How handsome and charming he had been, before . . . And what about her? She secretly glanced at herself in the mirror; her face was pale, her skin sickly and puffy, her flannel dressing-gown old and worn. She was old, an old woman, my God!

"Nianiouchka," she said suddenly. She had never called her that. Tatiana Ivanovna, who was wandering silently between the furniture to tidy up wherever necessary, turned and looked at her with a strange, confused expression.

"Barinia?"

"We've grown old, my dear, haven't we? But you, you haven't

changed at all. It makes me feel better to look at you ... No, really, you're the same."

"The only time people change at my age is in the coffin," said Tatiana Ivanovna with a wry smile.

Hélène Vassilievna hesitated, then whispered softly, "You remember what it was like at home, don't you?"

The old woman blushed suddenly, raising her trembling hands to heaven. "Do I remember! My God! I could tell you where each and every thing was placed! I could walk through that house with my eyes shut! I remember every dress you ever wore, and the children's outfits, and the furniture, and the grounds, my God!"

"The sitting room with all the mirrors, my little pink sitting room ..."

"The settee, where you used to sit on winter evenings, when the children were brought down."

"And before that? Our wedding?"

"I can still see the dress you wore, the diamonds in your hair ... The dress was made of moiré silk, and the antique lace from the late princess ... Oh, my God, Lulitchka won't have anything to compare ..."

They both fell silent. Nicolas Alexandrovitch was staring out at the sombre courtyard; he could picture his wife, the way she looked the first time he'd seen her, at the ball, when she was still the Countess Eletzkaïa, in her white satin evening gown, and her golden hair ... He had loved her so much ... They were still together at the end of their lives ... That was something. If only these women would stop talking ... If only he didn't have all these memories in his heart, life would be bearable.

"What's the point?" he said, gritting his teeth without turning around. "What's the point? All that is over. We'll never get it back. Let other people hope if they want to ... It's over, over," he repeated angrily.

Hélène Vassilievna took his hand, raising his pale fingers to her lips, as she had done so often in the past.

"Sometimes it all surges up from the depths of my soul ... But there's nothing we can do ... It's God's will ... Kolia ... My dear ... My beloved ... We're together, and as for the rest ..."

She made a vague gesture; they looked at each other in silence, trying to find other features, other smiles on their aged faces, from long ago.

The room was dark and hot. "Why don't we take a taxi and go out tonight?" asked Hélène Vassilievna. "Would you like that? There used to be a little restaurant, near Ville d'Avray, by the lake; we went there in 1908, do you remember?"

"Yes."

"Maybe it's still there?"

"Maybe," he said, shrugging his shoulders. "We always assume that everything is being destroyed along with us, don't we? Let's go and see."

They stood up and switched on the lights. Tatiana Ivanovna was standing in the middle of the room, muttering something they couldn't make out.

"Are you staying here, Nianiouchka?" Nicolas Alexandrovitch asked her automatically.

She seemed to wake up; her trembling lips moved for a long time as if she were having difficulty speaking.

"And where would I go?" she finally said.

When she was alone, she went and sat down in front of Youri's picture. She stared at it, but other images arose from her memory, from long ago, forgotten by everyone else. The faces of the dead, dresses from fifty years before, empty rooms . . . She remembered the first sharp, plaintive little cry Youri made when he was born. "As if he knew what would happen to him," she thought. "The others didn't cry like that."

Then she sat down in front of the window and started to mend the stockings.

CHAPTER VII

DURING THOSE FIRST months in Paris, the Karines led a calm life. It was only in the autumn, when little André came back from Brittany, that they had to think about earning a living, as they were short of money. The last of the jewellery had been sold long ago. They had a little capital left, that might last two, maybe three years...And then? Some Russians had opened restaurants, night clubs, small shops. The Karines, like many others, used their remaining money to buy and furnish a boutique, at the back of a courtyard. They began selling lace, icons, whatever remained of the antique china they'd managed to bring with them.

At first no one bought anything. In October they had to pay the rent. Then they had to send André to Nice. The air in Paris was giving him asthma attacks. They thought about moving. They were offered an apartment near the Porte de Versailles that was brighter and less expensive, but it had only three rooms and a kitchen as narrow as a cupboard. Where would they put poor old Tatiana? It was out of the question to make her climb up six flights of stairs, with her bad legs. Meanwhile, each month was becoming more difficult than the previous one. A succession of maids came and went, unable to get used to these foreigners who slept during the day and—at night—ate, drank, and left their dirty dishes everywhere in the sitting room, scattered about the furniture until the next morning.

Tatiana Ivanovna tried to do bits and pieces, like the laundry, but she was getting weak, and her old arms were no longer strong enough to turn the heavy French mattresses or lift the wet washing.

The children, constantly weary and irritable now, bullied her, chased her away: "Leave it. Go away. You're getting everything mixed up. You ruin everything." She would go without saying a word. Actually, she didn't seem even to hear them. She sat for hours on end, motionless, her hands on her knees, silently staring into space. She was hunched over, nearly doubled up; her skin was white, like a corpse, with swollen blue veins at the corners of her eyes. Often when she was called, she didn't reply, content with shutting her hollow little mouth even more tightly. She wasn't deaf, though. Every time any one of them said the name of a place, even if they spoke quietly, or whispered, she would shudder and suddenly say in a weak, low voice: "Yes . . . on Easter Sunday, when the clock tower in Temnaïa burnt down, I remember that . . . " or "The pavilion . . . after you'd gone, the wind had already blown out the windows . . . I wonder what's happened to it all . . . "

She would fall silent again and look out the window at the white walls and the sky above the rooftops.

"When will winter finally come?" she would ask. "My God, it's been so long since we had any cold weather or frost. Autumn is very long here . . . In Karinova, it's already all white, of course, and the river will be frozen over . . . Do you remember, Nicolas Alexandrovitch, when you were three or four years old, and I, even I was young, and your poor late mother would say, 'Tatiana, you can tell you're from the north, my girl . . . The first time it snows, you go wild.' Do you remember?"

"No," murmured Nicolas Alexandrovitch wearily.

"Well, I remember," she grumbled, "and soon there won't be anyone but me who does."

The Karines didn't reply. Each one of them had enough of their own memories, their own fears and sadness. One day Nicolas Alexandrovitch said, "The winters here aren't like the ones at home."

She shuddered. "What do you mean, Nicolas Alexandrovitch?"

"You'll see soon enough," he murmured.

She stared at him for a moment in silence. The haggard, defiant, strange look in her eyes struck him for the first time.

"What's wrong, my poor old dear?" he asked softly.

She didn't reply. What was the point?

Every day, she looked at the calendar that told her it was the beginning of October, then stared at the rooftops for a long time, but still there was no snow. All she saw were dingy tiles, the rain, the withered autumn leaves, carried along by the wind.

She was alone all day long now. Nicolas Alexandrovitch scoured the city for antiques or jewellery for their little shop; he managed to sell a few old things and buy some others.

In the past, Nicolas Alexandrovitch owned a collection of precious porcelain china and ornate silver platters. Now, as he walked home along the Champs-Élysées at dusk, carrying a package under his arm, he would sometimes manage to forget that he had to work for his family, for himself. He walked quickly, breathing in the smells of Paris, watching the lights shining at dusk, almost happy, his heart sad yet peaceful.

Loulou was working as a model in a fashion house. Ever so gradually, life took shape. They got home late, tired, returning home with a kind of excitement from the streets, from their work. It spilled over into discussions, laughter, for a while, but the solemn attitude of the silent old woman gradually wore them down. They would eat supper quickly, go to their rooms, and fall into a dreamless sleep, exhausted by their gruelling day.

CHAPTER VIII

OCTOBER CAME AND went, and the November rains began. From morning until night, they could hear the downpour pounding the cobblestones in the courtyard. In the apartment, the air was warm, heavy. When the heaters were switched off, at night, the humidity from outside seeped in through the grooves in the floors. The harsh wind howled behind the iron covers of the cold fireplace.

For hours on end, Tatiana Ivanovna sat in the empty apartment, in front of the window, watching the rain fall. Its heavy drops flowed down the glass like a river of tears. In all the kitchens, above the identical little pantries with their washing lines nailed up between the walls, where the dust cloths were hung to dry, the servants exchanged pleasantries, or complained, in this language they spoke so quickly that she couldn't understand a word. Around four o'clock, the children came home from school. She could hear the noise of pianos all being played at the same time; and, on each table, in the dining rooms, identical lamps were switched on. They pulled the curtains closed, and then she would hear only the sound of the rain and muffled noises from the street.

How could they all live like this, shut up in these dark houses? When would the snows come?

November passed, then the first weeks of December, barely any colder. There were heavy fogs, smoke coming out of the chimneys, the last dead leaves, crushed, carried along by the wind. Then Christmas. On 24 December, after a light meal, eaten quickly at one end of the table, the Karines left to celebrate Christmas Eve at the home of some friends. Tatiana Ivanovna helped them dress. When they said good-bye to her, she felt a spark of joy seeing them all dressed up, as in the past, Nicolas Alexandrovitch in a tuxedo. She smiled as she looked at Loulou in her white dress, her long hair in curls over her neck.

"Go on, Lulitchka, you'll meet your fiancé tonight, God willing."

Loulou silently shrugged her shoulders, let herself be kissed without saying a word. They all left. André was spending the Christmas holidays in Paris. He was wearing the uniform from his school in Nice: a coat, short blue trousers, and cap; he looked taller and stronger. He had a quick, lively way of talking, the accent, gestures, and slang of a boy who'd been born and raised in France. That night he was going out in the evening with his parents for the first time. He was laughing, humming. Tatiana Ivanovna leaned out the window, watched him walk ahead, jumping over the puddles. The heavy doors of the courtyard slammed shut with a dull thud. Once again Tatiana Ivanovna was alone. She sighed. The wind, mild for the time of year, full of fine raindrops, blew against her face. She raised her head, looked blankly up at the sky. Between the rooftops she could barely make out the shadowy horizon; it was coloured an extraordinary red, as if burning with an internal fire. In the apartment building, gramophones were playing on the different floors, merging to form a discordant music.

"At home," Tatiana Ivanovna murmured, then fell silent. Why even think about it? That was over a long time ago . . . Everything was finished, dead.

She closed the window, went back into the apartment. She raised her head, breathed in the air with great effort, an irritated, worried look on her face. These low ceilings were suffocating her. Karinova . . . The large house with its immense windows, where the light and air washed over the terraces, the sitting rooms, the entrance halls, where fifty musicians could fit comfortably when they held balls in the evenings. She recalled the Christmas when Cyrille and Youri had left . . . She could almost hear the waltz they'd played that night . . . Four years had passed . . . She could picture the columns shimmering with ice in the moonlight. "If I weren't so old," she thought, "I'd be happy to make the journey back . . . But it wouldn't be the same. No, no," she muttered vaguely. "It wouldn't be the same." The snow . . . As soon as she saw the snow start to fall, she would be at peace . . . She would forget everything. She would go to bed and close her eyes, forever. "Will I live to see the snow?" she whispered.

She automatically picked up the clothing from the chairs and started folding it. For some time now, she thought she could see a very even, fine sprinkling of dust that fell from the ceiling and settled everywhere. It had begun in autumn, when it got dark earlier but they lit the street-lamps later, to save on electricity. She brushed and shook the fabric endlessly; the dust flew off, but only fell back down again a bit further away, like a cloud of fine ash.

She picked up the clothing, brushed it off, muttering, "What is this? What on earth is this?" with a painful, surprised look on her face.

Suddenly she stopped, looking around her. Sometimes she didn't understand why she was there, wandering through these narrow rooms. She placed her hands on her chest, sighed. The air was heavy, warm, and, unusually, the heaters were on, because it was a holiday; they gave off a smell of fresh paint. She wanted to switch them off, but she had never understood how to work them. She turned the little handle for a while in vain, then stopped. Once again she opened the window. The apartment on the other side of the courtyard was lit up and cast a rectangular swathe of bright light into the room.

"At home," she thought, "at home, at this time of year . . ." The forest would be frozen. She closed her eyes, pictured in extraordinary detail the deep snow, the fires in the village, shimmering in the distance; and the river and the grounds, sparkling and hard, like steel.

She stood motionless, leaning against the window-frame, pulling her shawl over her dishevelled hair, the way she always did. A fine, warm rain was falling; the bright raindrops, swept up in the sudden bursts of wind, wet her face. She shivered, pulled her old black shawl more tightly around her. Her ears were ringing; she felt as if a violent noise were beating through them, like a furious bell. Her head, her entire body, was aching.

She left the sitting room, made her way to her little room at the end of the hallway, and prepared for bed.

Before getting into bed, she knelt to say her prayers. She made the sign of the cross, then lowered her head to touch the wooden floor, as she did every night. But this evening her words were all confused; she stopped, stared at the little flame burning at the foot of the icon, almost in a trance.

She got into bed, closed her eyes. She couldn't fall asleep, so she just listened, in spite of herself, to the creaking furniture, the sound of the clock in the dining room, like a human sigh that announced the hour striking in the silence; and, above her, below her, the gramophones playing, this Christmas Eve. People were rushing up and down the stairs, crossing the courtyard, going out for the evening. She could hear people shouting constantly: "Open the door, please!" the muffled echo of the courtyard door opening then closing again, and footsteps disappearing into the empty street. Taxis sped by. A hoarse voice called out to the concierge in the courtyard.

Tatiana Ivanovna sighed and turned her heavy head over to the other side of the pillow. She heard the bells chime eleven o'clock, then midnight. She fell asleep several times, woke up again. Every time she dozed off, she dreamed of the house in Karinova, but the image kept fading, so she hurried to close her eyes again to try to recapture it. Each time it happened, some detail disappeared. Sometimes, the delicate yellow of the stone changed into the reddish colour of dried blood; or the house was solid, walled over, the windows gone. But still she heard the faint echo of the frozen branches on the pine trees, whipped by the wind, like the sound of shattered glass.

Suddenly the dream changed. She saw herself standing in front of the open, empty house. It was in autumn, at the time of day when the servants lit the wood-burning stoves. She was standing downstairs, alone. In her dream, she saw the abandoned house, the bare rooms, just as she had left them, with the carpets rolled up against the walls. She went upstairs, and all the doors slammed in the wind, with a strange, groaning noise. She walked quickly, hurrying, as if she were afraid of being late for something. She saw all the enormous rooms, wide open, empty, with bits of wrapping paper and old newspapers scattered about the floor, swept up now and again, hovering in the wind.

Finally she entered the nursery. It was bare like all the other

rooms, even André's bed was gone, and, in her dream, she felt a
kind of astonishment: she remembered having rolled up his
mattress and pushed it into a corner of the room herself. In front
of the window, sitting on the floor, was Youri: in his soldier's
uniform, pale and thin, just as he had been that last day, playing
with some old jacks, like he had as a child. She knew he was
dead, but still she felt such extraordinary joy at seeing him that
her aged, weary heart began to beat violently, almost painfully;
its deep, muffled rhythm pounded against her chest. She could
see herself running towards him, crossing the dusty wooden floor
that creaked beneath her weight, as it had in the past, but just as
she was about to reach out and touch him, she woke up.

It was late. Day was breaking.

CHAPTER IX

SHE WOKE WITH a moan and lay there motionless, stretched out on her back, staring at the bright windows, as if in a trance. A thick, white fog filled the courtyard; to her tired eyes, it looked like snow, like the first snows of autumn, thick and blinding, covering everything in a kind of mournful light, a harsh white glare.

She clasped her hands together. "The first snow..." she whispered.

She looked at it for a long time, an expression of delight on her face that was both childlike and frightening, a little deranged. The apartment was silent. No one would be home yet, of course. She got out of bed and dressed without taking her eyes from the window, imagining the snow falling, ever faster, streaking the sky with a feathery trail. At one point, she thought she heard a door closing. Perhaps the Karines were already back and had gone to bed? But she wasn't thinking about them. She imagined she could feel the snowflakes on her face, could taste their fire and ice. She took her coat, quickly tied her scarf around her head and fastened it under her chin with a pin. Automatically she felt around on the table, looking for the keys that she always took with her in Karinova, when she went out, her hand stretched out as if she were blind. She found nothing, but kept feeling around anxiously, forgetting exactly what she was looking for, impatiently sweeping away her spectacle case, the knitting she had just started, the picture of Youri as a child...

She felt as if someone was waiting for her. A strange fever burned in her soul.

She opened the wardrobe, leaving its door and the drawer open. A clothes hanger fell to the floor. She hesitated for a moment, then shrugged her shoulders, as if she had no time to lose, and quickly left the room. She crossed the apartment and hurried silently down the stairs.

Once outside, she stopped. The freezing fog covered the courtyard in a dense, white blanket that slowly rose from the ground, like smoke. Fine drops of rain stung her face, like the tips of snowflakes when they fall amidst a September rain, half-melted.

Behind her, two men in tuxedos came out of the building and looked at her oddly. She followed them, slipping through the half-open door, which slammed shut behind her back with a dull thud.

She was in the street, a dark, deserted street; a gas-lamp shone through the rain. The fog was clearing and a cold sharp drizzle had started to fall. The cobblestones and walls shimmered faintly. A man passed by, his soaked shoes leaking water; a dog rushed across the road, came up to the old woman, and sniffed her, then followed her, whimpering and moaning miserably. It stayed with her for a while, then wandered off.

She kept walking, saw a square, other streets. A taxi drove past so close that it splattered mud on to her face. She didn't seem to notice. She walked straight ahead, stumbling over the wet cobblestones. Now and again, she felt so utterly exhausted that her legs seemed to give way under the weight of her body and sink into the ground. She looked up, saw day breaking near the Seine, a patch of white sky at the end of the street. To her eyes, it was a blanket of snow, just like in Soukharevo. She walked faster, dazzled by the fine, burning rain that stung her eyelids. The sound of church bells rang in her ears.

Suddenly she had a moment of lucidity; she clearly saw the smoke and fog as it lifted; but then the moment passed. She started walking again, weary and anxious, her body bent over towards the ground. Finally she reached the quayside.

The Seine was so high that it had overflowed its banks; the sun was rising, and the horizon was a pure, luminous white. The old woman walked over to the parapet and stared intently at the dazzling stretch of sky. Below her, a small staircase had been carved out of stone; she took hold of the hand-rail, clutched it tightly with her cold, shivering hand, and started down. Water flowed over the last few steps. She didn't notice. "The river is frozen over," she thought. "It must be frozen over at this time of year."

She thought that all she had to do was cross the river and on the other side would be Karinova. She could see the lights from its terraces shimmering through the snow.

But when she reached the last step, the smell of the water finally hit her. She made a sudden movement of surprise and anger, stopped for a moment, then continued descending, despite the water that soaked through her shoes and weighed down her skirt. And it was only when she was waist-deep in the Seine that she came back to her senses. She felt freezing cold and tried to cry out, but had only enough time to make the sign of the cross before her hand fell back.

She was dead.

Her little body floated for a moment, like a bundle of rags, before disappearing from sight, swallowed up by the shadowy Seine.

THE COURILOF AFFAIR

PROLOGUE

TWO MEN SAT down separately at the empty tables on the terrace of a café in Nice, attracted by the red flames of a small brazier.

It was autumn, at dusk, on a day that felt cold for that part of the world. "It's like the sky in Paris ..." said a woman passing by, pointing to the yellowish clouds carried along by the wind. Within a few moments, it began to rain, enhancing the darkness of the deserted street where the lamps had not yet been lit; raindrops dripped down here and there through the soaked canvas awning stretched over the café.

The man who had followed Léon M. on to the terrace had secretly watched him ever since he'd sat down, trying to remember who he was; both men leaned forward towards the warm stove at the same moment.

From inside the café came the muddled sound of voices, people calling out; the crashing of billiard balls, trays banging down on the wooden tables, chess pieces being moved around the boards. Now and again, you could make out the hesitant, shrill fanfare of a small band, muffled by the other noise in the café.

Léon M. looked up, pulled his grey wool scarf more tightly around his neck; the man sitting opposite him said quietly: "Marcel Legrand?"

At the very same moment, the electric lights suddenly came on in the street, in the doorways, and outside the cafés. Surprised by the sudden brightness, Léon M. looked away for a moment.

"Marcel Legrand?" the man repeated.

There was a surge of electricity in the street-lights, no doubt, for they grew dimmer; the light flickered for a second, like the flame of a candle left outdoors; then it seemed to come back again, bathing Léon M.'s face, hunched shoulders, gaunt hands, and delicate wrists in a dazzling light.

"Weren't you in charge of the Courilof affair, in 1903?"

"In 1903?" M. repeated slowly.

He tilted his head to the side and whistled softly, with the weary, sarcastic look of a cautious old bird.

The man sitting opposite him was sixty-five; his face looked grey and tired; his upper lip twitched with a nervous tic, causing his big white moustache, once blond, to jump now and again, revealing his pale mouth, his bitter, anxious frown. His lively eyes, piercing and suspicious, quickly lit up and then almost immediately looked away.

"Sorry. I don't recognise you," M. finally said, shrugging his shoulders. "My memory isn't very good these days . . ."

"Do you remember the detective who used to be Courilof's bodyguard? The one who ran after you one night, in the Caucasus? . . ."

"The one who ran after me . . . unsuccessfully? I remember now," said M.

He gently rubbed his hands together; they were getting numb. He was about fifty years old, but he looked older and ill. He had a narrow chest, a dark, sarcastic expression, a beautiful but odd mouth, bad, broken teeth, greying locks of hair spilling over his forehead. His eyes, deeply set, shone with a dim flame.

"Cigarette?" he murmured.

"Do you live in Nice, Monsieur Legrand?"

"Yes."

"Withdrawn from active service, if I may put it that way?"

"You may."

M. took a puff of his cigarette, without inhaling, watched it burn in his fingers, and threw it down on the ground, slowly stubbing it out with his heel.

"That all happened a long time ago," he finally said, with a wry smile, "a very long time ago . . ."

"Yes . . . I was the one responsible for the inquiry, after your arrest, after the terrorist attack."

"Oh, were you?" M. murmured indifferently.

"I never managed to find out your real name. Not one of our secret agents knew who you were, either in Russia or abroad. Now that it doesn't matter any more, tell me something—you were one of the leaders of that terrorist group in Switzerland, before 1905, weren't you?"

"I was never one of the leaders of a terrorist group, just a subordinate."

"So?"

M. nodded, a weary little smile on his face.

"That's how it was, Monsieur."

"Really, and what about later on? In 1917 and after? I know I'm right, you were really . . ."

He paused, looking for the appropriate word; then he smiled, revealing long, sharp teeth gleaming between pale lips. "You were really in the thick of it," he said, tracing the shape of a big cauldron in the air. "I mean . . . at the top."

"Yes . . . at the top."

"The secret police? The Tcheka?"

"Well, my friend, I did a bit of everything. During those difficult times, everyone lent a hand."

He tapped out a tune on the marble table with his delicate, curved fingers.

"Won't you tell me your name?" the man said, laughing. "I swear I'm also peacefully retired now, like you. I ask out of simple curiosity, professional inquisitiveness, if you will."

M. slowly raised the collar of his raincoat and pulled his scarf tighter with the same cautious gesture he always used.

"I don't believe you," he said, laughing slightly and coughing at the same time. "People are always drawn back to their first love. And, besides, my name wouldn't tell you anything more now. Everyone forgot it a long time ago."

"Are you married?"

"No, I've kept some of the good old revolutionary traditions," said M., smiling again; he had a little mechanical smile that made deep ridges at the corner of his mouth. He picked up a piece of bread and ate it slowly. "What about you?" he asked, raising his eyebrows. "What's your name, Monsieur?"

"Oh, my name? No mystery there . . . Baranof . . . Ivan Ivan-itch . . . I was assigned to His Excellency, to Courilof, for ten years."

"Oh, really?"

For the first time, M.'s weary little smile faded; up until now, he'd been staring across at the harshly lit wax mannequins, the only items on display in the rain-drenched street, but he stopped staring, coughed slightly, looked straight at Baranof: "What about his family? Do you know what happened to them?"

"His wife was shot during the Revolution. The children must still be alive. Poor Courilof. We used to call him the Killer Whale. Do you remember?"

"Ferocious and voracious," said M.

He crumpled the remainder of his bread, started to get up, but it was still pouring; the rain bounced heavily off the pavement in bright sparks. He slowly sat down again.

"Well, you got him," said Baranof. "How many others did you personally bag, in total?"

"Then? Or afterwards?"

"In total," Baranof repeated.

M. shrugged his shoulders. "You know, you remind me of a young man who came to interview me once, in Russia, for an American magazine. He was very interested in the statistics, wanted to know how many men I'd killed since I'd come to power. When I hesitated, he innocently asked: 'Is it possible? Is it possible that you can't remember?' He was a rosy-cheeked little Jew by the name of Blumenthal, from the *Chicago Tribune*."

He motioned to the doorman who was walking between the tables outside: "Get me that cab."

The cab stopped in front of the café.

He stood up, extended his hand to Baranof.

"It's funny running into each other like this . . ."

"Terribly funny."

M. laughed suddenly. "And . . . actually . . ." he said in Russian, "how many people did die? 'In answer to our prayers'? With our help?"

"Huh!" said Baranof, shrugging his shoulders. "Well I, at least, was acting under orders. I don't give a damn."

"Fair enough," said M., his voice weary and indifferent. He carefully opened his large black umbrella and lit a cigarette on the brazier. The bright flame suddenly illuminated his face with its hollow cheeks that were the colour of earth, and his wide,

suspicious dark eyes. As usual, he didn't actually smoke his cigarette, just breathed in its aroma for a moment, half closed his
eyes, then threw it away. He gestured good-bye and left.

*Léon M. died in March 1932, in the house in Nice where he
had spent his final years.*

*Amongst his books was found a small black leather briefcase; it
contained several dozen typed pages clipped together. The first page
had written on it, in pencil, the words* THE COURILOF AFFAIR

CHAPTER 1

Nice, 1931

IN 1903, THE Revolutionary Committee gave me the responsibility of *liquidating* Courilof. That was the term they used at
the time. This affair was linked to the rest of my life only in a
minor sort of way, but as I am about to write my autobiography,
it stands out in my memory. It forms the beginnings of my life
as a revolutionary, even though I changed sides afterwards.

Fourteen years passed before I came to power, half of them
spent in prison, half in exile. Then came the October Revolution (*Sturm und Drang Period*) and another exile.

I have been alive for fifty years, years that have gone quickly
by, and I don't have much to complain about. But still the final
years seem long . . . the end is dragging on.

I was born in '81, on 12 March, in an isolated village in Siberia
near the Lena River; my mother and father were both in exile
for political reasons. Their names were well known in their
day, but are now forgotten: Victoria Saltykof and the terrorist
M. Maxime Davidovitch M.

I barely knew my father: prison and exile do not lend themselves to a close-knit family. He was a tall man, with shining,
narrow eyes, dark eyebrows, and large, bony hands with delicate
wrists. He rarely spoke. He had a sad, scathing little laugh. When
they came to arrest him the last time, I was still a child. He hugged
me, looked at me with a kind of ironic surprise, moved his lips
slightly in a tired way that could pass for a smile, went out of
the room, came back to get the cigarettes he'd forgotten, and
disappeared forever from my life. He died in prison, at about the
age I am now, in a cell in the Pierre et Paul Fortress, where the
waters from the Neva River had seeped in during the autumn
floods.

After his arrest, I went to live in Geneva with my mother.
I remember her better; she died in the spring of 1891. She was

a delicate, slight creature, with fair hair and a pince-nez—the intellectual type of the '80s. I also remember her in Siberia, when we were going back, after she was freed. I was six years old. My brother had just been born.

She was holding him in her arms, but away from her chest, with extraordinary clumsiness, as if she were offering him to the stones along the road; she shivered as she listened to his hungry cries. Whenever she changed him, I could see her hands shaking and getting tangled up in the nappy and pins. She had beautiful, delicate, long hands. When she was sixteen, she'd killed the head of the Viatka police at point-blank range; he'd been torturing an old woman right in front of her, a political prisoner, forcing her to walk in the fierce heat of the Russian sun, even though she was ill. At the height of summer, the Russian sun batters you to death.

She told me about it herself, as if she felt she had to hurry, but before I was old enough to really understand. I remember the strange feeling I had listening to her story. I remember her sounding resonant and shrill, different from the weary, patient tone of voice I was used to: "I expected to be executed," she said. "I considered my death to be the supreme protest against a world of tears and bloodshed."

She stopped for a moment. "Do you understand, Logna?" she said more quietly. Her face and gestures remained cool and calm; only her cheeks had gone slightly red. She didn't wait for me to answer. My brother was crying. She got up, sighing, and picked him up. She held him for a moment, like a heavy package, then left us alone, and went back to coding her letters.

In Geneva, she was in charge of one of the Swiss terrorist groups, the same one that took care of me and raised me after she died. We lived on an allowance from the Party and from money she earned giving English and Italian lessons; we wore our winter clothes in Mont-de-Piété in springtime; summer clothes in autumn . . . And so it went.

She was very tall and thin. She looked worn out at thirty, like an old woman; her hunched shoulders crushed her delicate chest. She suffered from tuberculosis, and her right lung was totally non-functional; but she would always say: "How could I get

medical care when the poor factory workers are coughing up
blood?" (The revolutionaries of that generation always talked
like that.) She didn't even send us away to live somewhere else:
weren't the children of the workers infected by their own sick
mothers?

However, I remember that she never kissed us. Besides, we
were morose, cold children, at least I was. Only now and again,
when she was very tired, would she stretch out her hand and
stroke our hair, just once, slowly, as she sighed.

Her face was long and pale, with yellowish teeth and weary
eyes that blinked behind her spectacles. She had delicate, clumsy
hands that always dropped things in the house, that couldn't
sew or cook, but wrote constantly, coding messages, forging
passports...I thought I had forgotten her features, what she
looked like (so many years have passed by since then), but here
they are, resurfacing once again in my memory.

Two or three nights a month, she would cross Lake Léman
from Switzerland into France, carrying bundles of pamphlets and
explosives. She would take me with her, perhaps to harden me
to the dangerous life that was to be mine in years to come, in a
kind of "revolutionary dynastic tradition," perhaps to inspire
trust in the customs officers, because I was so young, perhaps
because my two brothers were dead and she didn't want to leave
me alone in the hotel, the same way that middle-class mothers
might take their children with them to the cinema. I would fall
asleep on the deck. It was usually winter; the lake was deserted,
covered in a thick fog; the nights were freezing cold. Once in
France, my mother would leave me for a few hours with some
farmers, the Bauds, who lived in a house beside the lake. They
had six or seven children; I remember a group of little ruddy-
cheeked kids, very healthy but very stupid. There I drank piping
hot coffee. I ate warm bread with chestnuts. The Bauds' house—
with its fires, the delicious aroma of coffee, the screaming
children—was, to me, paradise on earth. They had a terrace, a
sort of large wooden balcony that looked out over the lake, and,
in winter, it was covered in snow and creaking ice.

I had two younger brothers; both had died. They'd also lived
alone in a hotel for a while, like me. One of them died when he

was two, the other at three. I can particularly recall the night when the second one died; he was a good-looking boy, big and blond.

My mother was standing up, at the foot of the bed, an old bed made of dark wood. She held a lit candle in her hand and was watching the dying child. I was sitting on the floor beside her, and I could see her exhausted face, lit from below by the candle's flame. The child had one or two little convulsions, looked up with a weary, astonished expression, and died. My mother didn't move; her hand covering the flame was the only thing that was obviously trembling. Finally, she noticed me and wanted to say something (undoubtedly something like "Logna, death is part of nature"), but she just clenched her lips sadly and said nothing. She placed the dead child on his pillow, took my hand and brought me to a neighbour's house. The silence, the darkness, and his pale face, his white nightshirt and long, fine blond hair—all this I remember as if it were a bewildering dream. Soon afterwards, she also died.

I was only ten years old then. I had inherited her predisposition to tuberculosis. The Revolutionary Committee lodged me at the home of Dr. Schwann. A naturalised Swiss citizen of Russian origin, he was one of the leaders of the Party. He owned a private clinic that had twenty beds in Monts, near Sierre, and it was there that I lived. Monts is a bleak village between Montana and Sierre, buried between dark fir trees and gloomy mountains, or perhaps that's just how it seemed to me.

For years on end, I lived glued to a chaise-longue, on a balcony, seeing nothing of the world except the tops of the fir trees and, on the other side of the lake, a glass cage similar to ours that reflected the rays of the setting sun.

Later on, I was able to go out, down into the village, meeting the other patients along the only usable road. They were wrapped up in shawls, and we all climbed back together, breathing with difficulty, stopping after every few steps, counting the fir trees along the road, one by one, staring with hatred at the circle of mountains that shut out the sky. I can still see them, after all these years, just as I can smell the sanatorium—that odour of disinfectant and new linoleum—just as I can hear, in my dreams, the sound of the *föhn*, the dry autumn wind, in the forest.

With Dr. Schwann, I studied foreign languages and medicine, which I particularly enjoyed. As soon as my health was better, I was given various assignments by the Revolutionary Committee in Switzerland and France.

I was a member of the Party by my very birth . . .

CHAPTER 2

I BEGAN WRITING these notes thinking I would eventually write my autobiography. There's so much time to fill. You have to do something at the end of your life, one way or another. But already, here I am, stopping. "A revolutionary education is difficult to explain in a way that is both sincere and instructive," I recall that brave Hertz once said. And my code name, "Léon M.," has its place in the iconography of the October Revolution, which no doubt should be left intact. The son of parents living in exile, brought up exclusively on revolutionary speeches, tracts, and models; and in spite of it all, I lacked strength and passion.

When I lived in Geneva, I would listen with envy as my friends talked about their youth. I recall a young man of thirty who had taken part in fourteen terrorist attacks—of which four had been successful; four of these murders had been carried out in vicious cold blood, in the middle of the street. He was a pale red-head with small, delicate, sweaty hands. One December evening after a meeting of the Committee, when we were coming back along the peaceful, frozen streets of Geneva, he told me how he had run away from home at the age of sixteen and wandered the streets of Moscow for eighteen days.

"What you never did," he said, smiling, "was to make your mother die of grief . . . or read illegal tracts by the light of a fire, like I did, when I was fifteen, at night, stretched out on the riverbank, in May . . ."

He spoke in a bizarre, rasping voice, in little rapid, breathless phrases, and sometimes, he would stop and say with a sigh: "The good old days . . ."

So true . . .

Later on, I also experienced exile, prison, the bunkers of the Pierre et Paul jail, the tiny cells, putrid-smelling in the summer heat, where twenty or thirty of us were locked up together; the vast, dark, freezing-cold prisons in the countryside and the fortress where those condemned to death were held and where it was possible, by pressing your ear to certain places in the wall, to hear the echo of revolutionary songs coming from the women's section.

But even now, I no longer appreciate the romantic side of the Revolution as much as I should.

An autobiography? Vanity. It would be better for me to remember certain things only for myself, as I did in the past. When I was in the state prisons they allowed us to write in note-books, but then they destroyed them as soon as they were full of stories and memories.

Would I even have had the time to finish an autobiography? So much has happened, so many years gone by . . . I feel death approaching with a sense of weariness, of indifference, that is unmistakable: the debates, the changes within the Party, every-thing I used to feel so passionate about—I'm tired of all of it. Even my body is tired. More and more often, I want to turn over to face the wall, close my eyes, and fall into the deepest, sweetest sleep, forever.

CHAPTER 3

AND SO I belonged to the Party through my birth, my childhood, through the conviction that a social revolution is inevitable, necessary, and fair, as fair as anything to do with human affairs could ever be. My love of power attracted me to it as much as my desire for a certain kind of human affection that I lacked, and it was the only place that I found it.

I like people, the masses. Here, near Nice, I live in Lourié's house. It is a cube made of white stone, in the middle of a garden where no tree grows higher than a broomstick; the house is between two roads, one leading to Monaco and the other to the sea; you breathe in a fine dust here that is full of petrol and is finishing off my poor old lungs. I live alone; in the morning, an old woman comes in to clean the four empty rooms that make up my house; she prepares my food and leaves. But the sounds of life continue to surround me, and that is what I love, that is what pleases me, people, cars, trams going by, quarrels, shouting, laughter . . . fleeting silhouettes, the faces of strangers, conversations . . . Below, behind the bare little garden, where six delicate, sinuous bushes have been planted that will grow into peach trees, almond trees, goodness knows what, there is a kind of little Italian bistro, with a player piano, and benches beneath an arbour. Working men—Italian, French—go there to drink.

At night, when they begin to walk up the twisting road that runs along the sea, I come out of the house; I sit down on the small low wall that separates the garden from the bistro; I listen to them. I watch them.

I can see the small square lit up by paper lanterns, the pale light reflected on their faces. They go home late. The rest of the night passes more quickly that way, thank goodness, for I cough and fall asleep only when it's morning. Why do I sit here looking at the flowers and the sea? I hate nature. I have only ever been happy in cities, those ugly, dirty cities with houses full of people, and on the streets in summer, when it's hot, where I walk by strange faces and weary bodies. These are the hours I wish to kill, when solitude and silence surge up, when the last of the cars are returning from Monte Carlo along the coast road. Since I became ill, I am overwhelmed by memories. Before, I used to work. But my work is finished now.

And so I began my life as a revolutionary at the age of eighteen; I was given several missions in the south of France; then I lived in Paris for a long time. In 1903, the Committee sent me to Russia. I was to kill the Minister of Education. It was after this event that I broke away from the terrorist section of the Party and joined T. After the Courilof affair I was condemned to death, but a few days before my execution, Alexis, the heir to the throne, was born, and I was saved by the amnesty granted. My sentence was commuted to hard labour for life. When I learned that I had been spared, I cannot recall feeling anything except profound indifference. In any case, I was ill, I was coughing up buckets of blood, and I was sure to die on the way to Siberia. But you should never count on death any more than you should count on life.

I lived and was cured in Siberia, in the penal colony. When I escaped, the Revolution of 1905 had started.

Even though I was so exhausted at night that I would collapse and fall asleep as if I were dying, I have happy memories of 1905 and those first months of the Revolution.

I would go with R. and L. to the factories, to the workers' meetings. I have always had a piercing, unpleasant-sounding voice, and my weak lungs prevented me from speaking out loud for long. As for the others, they would rant at the workers for hours on end. I would leave the platform and mix with the crowd, explaining whatever they found confusing, advising them, helping them. Amidst the heat and smoke in the room, their pale faces, their sparkling eyes, the shouts coming from their open mouths, their anger, even their stupidity, gave me the same feeling of euphoria you get from wine. And I liked the danger. I liked the sudden silences, how they held their breath in anticipation, the look of panic on their faces when they saw the *dvornik*, the informer who was in the pay of the police, walking past the window.

Into the dark night, those damp, freezing autumn nights in St. Petersburg, the workers would leave, one by one. They melted into the fog like shadows. We would disappear after they had gone; to throw the police off the trail, we would roam the streets until dawn, stopping only when we reached the dirty little *traktirs* where we hid.

I left Russia only to return on the eve of the October Revolution. I have described this period and the one that followed in my previous writings on politics and history.

After 1917, I became the Bolshevik, Léon M. In newspapers all over the world, they must have depicted me wearing a helmet on my head and with a knife between my teeth. I was given a job in the Tcheka Secret Police, where I remained for one year. But it requires fierce, personal hatred to carry out such terrible work without flinching. As for me . . .

What is truly strange is that I, who spared not only innocent lives but several guilty ones as well (for at certain moments I was overcome by a kind of indifference, and the prisoners reaped the benefits), I was hated even more than some of my comrades. For example, I was hated more than Nostrenko, the frenzied sailor who executed the prisoners himself; he was an extraordinary show-off who wore make-up and powder and left his shirt open, exposing a chest as smooth and white as a woman's. I can still see him, a combination of bad actor, drunkard, and pederast. Or Ladislas, the hunchback Pole, with his drooping, scarlet lip, slashed and scarred from an old wound.

I think the prisoners condemned to death vaguely consoled themselves with the idea that they were dealing with madmen or monsters; whereas I was an ordinary, sad little man who coughed, wore glasses, had a little snub nose and delicate hands.

When the policies of the leaders changed, I was sent into exile. Since then I have lived near Nice, supported by the modest income from books, newspaper articles, Party magazines. I ended up in Nice because I am living under the passport of a certain Jacques Lourié, who died of typhus in the Pierre et Paul Fortress, imprisoned for revolutionary conspiracy. He was a Jew from Latvia, a naturalised French citizen. He had no family, he was utterly alone, and he owned a small villa which I consequently inherited, as it were. The danger of running into his friends or neighbours pleased me somewhat. But everyone had forgotten Jacques Lourié. I live here, and will probably soon die here.

The house is small and not very comfortable, and Lourié, who was short of money, didn't have the walls surrounding it built high enough to stop people looking in.

On the left, there is a kind of enclosure, a piece of land for sale where goats come to graze on the thick sweet-smelling grass, between the abandoned bricks and stones. To the right, there is another little stone building, just like mine but painted pink, that is rented out to different couples each year. The road from Nice to Monte Carlo runs behind the house; below is the viaduct. The sea is far away. The house is cool and bright.

So this is how I live, and, sometimes, I don't know whether this tranquillity makes me happy or is killing me. Sometimes I feel I'd like to work again. At five o'clock, the time when my day used to begin in Russia, I wake with a start; or, if I haven't yet gone to sleep, I feel a profound sense of anguish. I pick up the odd thing: a book, a notebook. I write, as I am doing now. The weather is beautiful, the sun is rising, the roses smell wonderful. I would give it all, and my whole life, for that room where we all used to sleep, fifteen, twenty men, in 1917, when we came to power. It was a foggy night, snowing. You could hear the wind, the bombs, the faint sound of the Neva rising as it did every autumn. The telephone rang continuously. Sometimes I think: "If I were younger and stronger, I would go back to Russia, I would start again, and I would die happy and at peace . . . in one of those prison cells I know so well."

Power, the illusion of influencing human destiny, is as intoxicating as smoke, as wine. When you have none, you feel an astonishing sense of suffering, of painful uneasiness. At other times, as I've said, I feel nothing more than indifference and a sort of relief in remaining here and waiting for death to wash over me in a great wave. I am not suffering. It is only at night, when my fever rises, that a painful restlessness sweeps through my body, and the steady sound of my heart-beat echoes in my ears and tires me. By morning it has gone. I light the lamp, and I sit at my table, in front of the open window, and when the sun has finally risen, I fall asleep.

CHAPTER 4

THE EXECUTIVE COMMITTEE in Switzerland met once a year to examine a list of dignitaries, senior civil servants in the Russian Empire renowned for their cruelty and injustice, and to choose who was to die that year. My mother had belonged to this organisation which, in my day, was made up of about twenty people.

In 1903, the Russian Minister of Education was Valerian Alexandrovitch Courilof, who was universally despised. He was a reactionary from the Pobiedonostsef school; he had a reputation as a man who exercised brute, cold-blooded force. Though protected by Emperor Alexander III and Prince Nelrode, he didn't belong to the nobility and, as often happens, was "more of a royalist than the King"; he hated the Revolution and despised the ordinary people even more than the country's ruling classes.

He was tall and heavy, slow in his speech and movements; the students had nicknamed him the Killer Whale ("deadly and bloodthirsty"), for he was cruel, ambitious, and hungry for military honours. He was enormously feared.

The leaders of the Party wanted him to be assassinated in public, in the most grandiose manner possible, in order to catch the imagination of the people as much as possible. For this reason, this execution presented even greater difficulties than usual. Indeed, it was not enough to trust luck and throw a bomb, or shoot him, as we did, more or less, on most other occasions; in this case, we had to choose the right time and place. It was Dr. Schwann who first spoke to me about this man. Schwann, when I knew him, must have been about sixty years old; he was short, slim, frail, and as light as a ballerina; his woolly hair, frizzy, completely white as milk or the moon, spilled over his forehead. He had a small, angular face, a tight mouth with a narrow, cruel shape, a delicate nose, as pinched and curved as a beak. He was mad. He was declared so officially, so to speak, only after I left, and he died in an asylum in Lausanne. However, even at this earlier time, he already aroused within me an instinctive sense of foreboding and revulsion. He was something of a genius: he had been one of the first to experiment on pneumothorax in tuberculosis. He enjoyed destroying and healing in equal measures.

I can still picture him on my balcony, with me, a twelve-year-old child stretched out and wrapped up in my fur blanket, the moon illuminating the pine trees, the snow blue and thick, the frozen little lake sparkling in the shadows. The moonlight bathed Schwann's halo of white hair, his strange dressing-gown with its pink and baby-blue pattern, as he taught me the terrorist doctrine:

"Logna, you see a gentleman like that one over there, big, fat, who's bursting, feeding on the blood and sweat of the people . . . You laugh. You think: 'Wait, just you wait.' He doesn't know you. You are there, in the shadows. You start to move . . . like this . . . you raise your hand . . . a bomb isn't very big, you know; you can hide it in a shawl, in a bouquet of flowers . . . Whoosh! . . . It explodes! The gentleman is blown up, flesh and bones flying in all directions."

He spoke in a whisper, interspersed with laughter.

"And his soul will also fly away . . . *animula vagula, blandula* . . . little soul, wandering soul." (He was obsessed with Latin quotations, just like poor Courilof.)

He entwined his fingers in the most bizarre fashion, as if he were plaiting hair; his little hooked nose, his pinched mouth, were outlined with the sharpness of steel against the bluish, silvery background of the pine trees, the snow, and the moon.

One of the Party leaders sometimes gave him large sums of money, I've never understood how. Some people believe he'd also been an agent provocateur, but I don't think so.

He was the one who took me along to the Executive Committee meeting in 1903. It was a cold and glistening winter's night. We made our way to Lausanne on the little milk train that creaked as it descended the steep frozen fields, as hard and brittle as salt. We were alone in the compartment; Schwann was wrapped up in a shepherd's greatcoat, wearing no hat, as usual, despite the cold.

There, in his low murmur, he spoke to me again of the Killer Whale.

Twice already, the Committee had sent men to kill the minister, but both of them had been arrested and hanged. The Committee had recognised that it would be almost impossible for Russians to carry out the assassination. The police knew all the suspects; no matter how well disguised they might be, they couldn't hide their true identities for long; their arrests would compromise the work of the other Party members and would mean their death.

Moreover, for a while now, terrorist attacks had been kept secret; even the foreign press hardly mentioned them. This assassination had to take place audaciously, as I've already mentioned, where the people could see it with their own eyes. And insofar as possible, it had to be witnessed by the ambassadors of foreign governments, somewhere in public, during an official ceremony or on a public holiday, which made it ten times more difficult. As for me, well, nobody knew me, not the police, not the Russian revolutionaries. I spoke Russian, although with a heavy foreign accent, which was not necessarily a bad thing; it would therefore be easy to get me into the country with a Swiss passport.

I listened to Schwann speak, though it is difficult for me, with so many years' distance, to remember exactly what I felt. The Committee had a reputation for justice; it condemned only people who were guilty of crimes. And the conviction that I was risking my own life as much as the minister was risking his, this conviction was the justification for the murder and absolved me of it. Also, I was only twenty-two years old. I was nothing like the man I was to become. All I knew of life was a sanatorium and a dingy little room in Montrouge. I was eager, thirsty, for life; already I enjoyed the feeling of holding someone's life in my hands, the way you might hold a live bird.

I said nothing to Schwann. I tapped the window where the snow had stuck to it. I looked outside. Soon, we came to the plain where the fir trees grew scarcer; through the darkness you could see their branches sparkling, heavy with ice, lit up by the first log fires.

Finally, we arrived in Lausanne, where the Committee was meeting that night.

I knew all the Committee members, but it was the first time I'd ever seen them all together. There was Loudine and his wife, Roubakof, Brodsky, Dora Eisen, Leonidif, Hertz... Most of them, since then, have died violent deaths.

A few of them, on the other hand, gave up just in time. Hertz is still living here in France. When I came to Nice, I ran into him once on the Promenade des Anglais, strolling arm in arm with his wife, walking a little dog with curly white hair; he looked old and ill, but peaceful, just like a good little member of the French bourgeoisie.

He walked past without recognising me. It was on his orders that General Rimsky and Minister Bobrinof had been killed.

In 1907, he was supposed to blow up the Emperor's train, but he made a mistake and ordered the bomb to be thrown under the Petersburg–Yalta train, while the Emperor and his family were travelling in the opposite direction. It was a mistake that cost the lives of twenty-odd people (not counting the men who had followed his orders, thrown the bomb, and didn't have time to get away: such are the risks of the profession).

The meeting of the Committee in 1903 took place in Loudine's room; it lasted barely an hour. In order to confuse the neighbours, some wine bottles had been placed on a table, lit up by a lamp, opposite the window. Now and again, one of the women would get up and play some waltzes on an old piano in the corner of the room. I was given a passport in the name of Marcel Legrand, born in Geneva, a doctor of medicine, diplomas as proof of my qualifications, and some money. Then everyone went back home, while I checked into a hotel.

CHAPTER 5

I CAN REMEMBER in extraordinary detail the room where I spent that night. Through the old threadbare carpet, I could see floor-boards the colour of rope; I paced up and down all night as if in a trance. A small cloudy mirror, above the sink, reflected the image of the dark wooden furniture, the green wallpaper, and my pale, anxious face. I remember opening the window. I forced myself to look at a small, grey church, streaked with soft snow. Here and there, on the deserted street, gloomy lights were burning. I felt unspeakably exhausted and miserable. Throughout my entire life, just before I was about to do something essential to the fate of my Party—I'm not talking about my own life, which has never really been of much interest to me—I have always felt overwhelmed by deadly indifference. The clean, cold air finally brought me back to life. And, little by little, the secret exultation I had felt in the train won me over once again, the realisation that I was going to leave this lethal place, that I was cured, that the life of a revolutionary, with its passions and battles, was there waiting for me, and so many other things as well . . . I remained at the hotel for a few days.

Finally, one morning, 25 January 1903, I received my orders and left. I was to go to Kiev, and once there, my first order of business was to make myself known to a woman called Fanny Zart, who would follow me to St. Petersburg and help me. When I left Lausanne, something strange happened, something that struck me, and—even though it was insignificant and never had anything to do with my own life afterwards—I have never forgotten it. Even now, I still have dreams about it.

That day I had gone to Monts for one last meeting with Dr. Schwann and was returning to Lausanne on a little train, slowly puffing away, that stopped at each and every station. I was meant to reach Lausanne at midnight. We arrived in Vevey around ten o'clock in the evening. The station appeared deserted and you could even hear a little bell ringing in the total silence.

Suddenly, on the platform opposite me, I saw a man running towards a train that was pulling into the station. Schwann and I were walking by. The man looked like he wanted to throw himself under the train. A woman, standing next to me, let out a sharp little cry. All of a sudden, I saw him spin around, in a kind of circle, like a bird gliding downwards; he threw himself to the ground, then got up, started running again and fell over in exactly the same way—two or three times, he did this. Finally, he stayed on the ground, his body twitching.

The train had stopped; the passengers saw what was happening, jumped out, and helped the man up. I could see them lean over him, asking him questions, but he said nothing, just waved his arms in an astonished, feeble gesture, then began to sob uncontrollably.

They sat him down on a bench, stared at him for a moment, then left him there: the train was about to leave. I have carried the image of that man with me ever since: sitting, alone, in the deserted train station, on a cold January night, a big man in mourning, with a thick black moustache, a black felt hat, large hands clutching his knees in desperate resignation.

Afterwards, I often wondered why that incident made such a strong impression on me, for the face of that big man haunted me for years, it's true, and in my dreams, I watched his features merge with the Killer Whale's, after his murder. They looked a little like each other.

In Kiev, I found the address I'd been given for the medical student, Fanny Zart. She was a young woman of twenty, with a stocky build and black hair pulled forward over her cheeks like great sideburns; she had a long straight nose, a strong mouth whose lower lip drooped and gave her face an obstinate and scornful expression. Her eyes were unique to women in the Party, eyes whose harshness and determination were inhuman. (Only those of the second generation, nothing like the weary, short-sighted look of my mother.) She was the daughter of a watchmaker in Odessa and the sister of an extremely wealthy banker in St. Petersburg who financed her education and wanted nothing more to do with her. Because of this, her hatred of the wealthy classes took the concrete form of this little Jewish banker with his fat stomach. She had been a member of the Party for three years.

In Kiev, she lived in one large room on the top floor of a corner house; from her window, you could see both the market and the town square and, past the square, a long, deep road that ended at a charming gilded church. Afterwards, once we'd taken Kiev, I remembered that house: I had machine guns installed in it; when the people of Makhno came out of the church and filled the town square, pillaging and killing, we mowed them down.

She gave me a passport that belonged to one of her brothers: it had been agreed that the name Marcel Legrand would be used only in St. Petersburg, to cover my tracks as thoroughly as possible.

That very evening, I moved in with her. I was alone almost all day long. She was studying at the university, and when she got home at night she would make us something to eat, and we would talk; or rather, she would talk, going over and over the list of people to be assassinated.

Heavy snow fell over the frozen town square: you could see the policemen going home in pairs. Kiev was a small provincial town then, peaceful and dismal. Never have I seen, anywhere else, such beautiful sunsets, mournful and dazzling. The sky on the western side suddenly turned blood-red and hazy with purplish smoke. Endless flocks of crows flew about until nightfall, deafening us with their cries, with the beating of their wings. From our windows, we could see the houses all lit up, peaceful silhouettes behind the window-panes, the flickering light of paraffin lamps set on the floors in the shops, giving off a smoky glow all around them.

I saw no one but Fanny; according to the instructions I'd received, I was to meet no one else in the Party. Perhaps the leaders in Geneva were already beginning to suspect A. of being a traitor.

Finally, I left Kiev with Fanny. We arrived in St. Petersburg the day before Easter.

I WENT TO a boarding house she recommended to me; it was run by a Madame Schröder, a woman of German descent who had started out running a brothel that she later turned into a hotel with furnished rooms. She worked for both the revolutionaries and the police. Because of a kind of reciprocal tolerance, these types of places were the safest.

Streams of prostitutes went there; they were unknowingly our free informers. In the evening, before going back to the Nevsky River or the cabarets, they met up at Schröder's place; we'd put a pitcher of vodka or some tea on the table and they would give us, without even realising it, names and addresses better than any professional revolutionary could. They were kind creatures, sweet and totally penniless. They were reactionaries at heart, like most prostitutes usually are, and never suspected the role they were made to play by both sides. At least that was the case with most of them; certain amongst them knowingly betrayed others for money, out of jealousy or because they loved talking.

The next day was Easter Sunday. The very night we arrived, we decided to go to Saint Isaac's Cathedral, where, according to Fanny's informants, Courilof would be attending Mass. This way, I could see what the minister looked like in person, rather than from photos. Easter that year coincided with the commemoration of a saint whose name I have forgotten: for this reason, Courilof wouldn't sit in the ministers' chapel for Mass, as he ordinarily did.

Fanny was going to point him out to me and would then disappear. She was suspected by the police: her name had been mixed up in some secret typography business. That was why the Party had refused to entrust her with carrying out the assassination. She was an extraordinarily intelligent and sharp woman, driven by a kind of nervous passion, a constant tension I have seen, to that level, only in women, a tension that made it possible for them to perform miracles of endurance and energy. Then, suddenly, they would collapse, and either kill themselves or cross over to the other side, selling us to our enemies. Many of them, however, died courageously.

That same evening, Fanny had managed to get hold of some money and buy some second-hand peasant clothing so she could disguise herself. We took two large candles and *koulitch* cakes with us that could be blessed at church, and set off to take the longest route, so that Fanny could show me the ministerial palace where Courilof lived. St. Petersburg seemed extraordinarily beautiful to me. Easter had fallen very late that year; the nights were already light.

You could clearly see the red palaces, the quaysides, the dark granite houses. I stopped in front of the ministry, stared for a long time at the columns, the wrought-iron balconies; the stonework was the same deep red of the state buildings, the colour of dried blood. High gates surrounded a garden that was still bare; through the naked branches, I could see a sandy courtyard, a wide staircase of white marble.

We headed back to Saint Isaac's. The streets were full of poor people, like us, who were holding candles and cakes wrapped in white cloth napkins. They were being sold from tables set up amidst the biting wind. Cars passed slowly by. We got to the town square, where the crowd waited. I saw members of the diplomatic corps go inside—ministers, important dignitaries, women—then we went in with the ordinary people, crossing ourselves as they did.

Fanny made her way forward to a hidden corner of the church from where we could see the first pews. The scent of smoke from the incense was so strong that my head started pounding, and I felt as if I were looking through a haze at a crowd of people in evening dress, sparkling uniforms decorated with ribbons and stars. Their faces, in the candlelight, looked yellow, like the faces of corpses, their mouths surrounded by deep shadows. The clergymen, gleaming, chanted and swung their incense burners towards us.

"Third from the row on the left, between two women," said

Fanny. "One woman has a bird of paradise on her hat, the other's young, in a white dress."

I looked, and through the wafting incense, I could see a large man, heavy, whose hair and eyebrows were nearly white, with a square, unkempt beard and an expression that was callous, haughty, and stern. I studied him for a long time. He was as still as a stone. He raised his hand slowly to make the sign of the cross, but his enormous neck, his wide, powerful face, never moved; he didn't bat an eyelash. His wide, pale eyes stared straight ahead, fixed on the altar.

Fanny, holding a red handkerchief tightly to her chin, stared at him, her eyes burning. About a hundred policemen, some in uniform, some in civilian clothing but all unmistakable from their stiffness and their arrogant look of brutality, formed a barrier that separated this dazzling gathering of dignitaries and ministers from the masses.

The heat became so unbearable that I felt my temples throbbing; I could hear the muffled, wild beating of my heart. We knelt down like everyone around us, and the hymns seemed to crash down from the magnificent vaults above.

I couldn't see Courilof any more; I was overwhelmed by a feeling of feverish unreality; automatically, like the people around me, I bent down to touch my head to the floor. From the marble flagstones, a cold breeze, smelling frozen and damp, wafted upwards.

Finally, the service ended. We went outside; the police held the masses back; I saw Courilof get into a car, helped by a lackey in a black hat decorated with the official state emblem.

The clergy walked around the church three times; you could see the icons' long ribbons softly undulating in the clear night. Three times the priests passed by, holding up the sparkling cross, and their chants faded away into the distance.

We broke away from the crowd and followed the Nevsky River back to my house. Like everyone else, we were holding lit candles; the perfume from the wax filled the air; they burned with tall, high, transparent flames, for the night was very warm, without a hint of a breeze. "Symbol of peace, symbol of happiness," said some women behind us as they cupped their hands

around the bright flames. Above our heads, the sky began to
darken, but the horizon remained clear and pink, casting pale
shadows and shimmering reflections over the water in the canals.

Once again, we passed by the gates of the ministry; it was still
open, and cars were going inside to the gardens. We could clearly
see women in ball gowns through the windows and hear the faint
sound of music playing. The entire house was lit up from top to
bottom.

I don't know why, but walking along that street, feeling sick
(the smell of the incense and the heat in the church had made
me nauseous and feverish), I thought of the minister's impassive,
hostile face and felt, for the first time in my life, a kind of hatred.
My heart was filled with venom.

Curiously, Fanny seemed to sense how I felt.

"Well?" she said dryly, looking at me.

I shrugged my shoulders and didn't reply.

For the first time, this secretive and proud young woman told
me about herself, her life story. We were sitting on one of those
benches carved out of granite along the quayside. The wind from
the Neva River was blowing, still crisp and heavy with the smell
of ice; it blew out our candles.

Since then, I have heard many of our women tell the same
story; their lives were all similar with their wounded pride, their
yearning for freedom and vengeance. But there was something
affected and overly enthusiastic in her words and voice that
troubled me and froze me to the core. She was obviously upset;
her eyes sought mine with a kind of goodwill, the desire to move
me, to fill me with pity, admiration, and horror. I was barely
listening to her: that entire night was like a nightmare, and her
words merged into the surreal confusion of a feverish dream.

I SPENT A month keeping close watch at the villa, trying in vain to find a way to get inside. Little by little, I began to feel passionately excited; day and night I prowled around that house, questioning delivery men, the minister's lowliest employees, talkative shopkeepers in the neighbourhood. Within a short time, I knew Courilof's superficial life, his habits, the days and times he went to see the Emperor, the names of his friends, what ordinary people thought of him. Savage, ambitious: these words continually came up. I learned that he had lost his first wife, who came from an influential family protected by the Emperor's mother. She had favoured Courilof's rise to power; since Nicolas had ascended to the throne, Prince Alexander Alexandrovitch Nelrode had become the minister's protector.

Courilof had a son and a daughter from his first marriage, who lived with him; the boy was still a child and the girl was old enough to be married. About a year earlier, he had finally married his French mistress, Margot, a woman of dubious morals. Her real name was Marguerite Darcy; she was a former actress with a comic opera company and with whom Courilof had had a long-standing affair dating back to his youth.

One day, I saw this woman coming out of the house with the minister's daughter. I recognised the two women who had been sitting on either side of Courilof in the cathedral. The young woman was petite, with an extremely girlish face, almost childlike, with brown hair, pale, delicate, very pretty, and wide blue eyes; as for the woman . . . she was an extraordinary creature. She looked like an ageing bird of paradise: fading, losing its brilliant plumage, but still as dazzling as costume jewellery, the kind they wear in the theatre. She wore far too much make-up; the midday sun ruthlessly highlighted the pink stains on her cheeks, the fine but deep little wrinkles in her skin. Her face must have grown fuller with the passing years, but thanks to the pure lines of certain features, you could still see that she must have once been very beautiful.

She passed by so closely that she knocked into me, then gathered up the folds of her lace skirt and looked at me. Her eyes, so close to mine, astonished me with their beauty. Very dark, sparkling, edged with thin, black eyelashes, they had an intense, weary expression that struck me. She reminded me of an old prostitute I'd known at Schröder's, a complete wreck, who had that same intense, weary look.

She muttered a few words of apology in a strong French accent (her voice was affected and unpleasant) and kept walking. I followed her for a while. She had a ridiculous walk; she bounced like many old actresses do, as if they're afraid they'll make the floorboards of the stage creak because their legs have grown heavy with age.

"That woman," Fanny told me later, "lived with him openly for fourteen years. They held infamous orgies at their house in the Iles."

I avoided being there when the minister himself came out. I didn't want to attract the attention of his informers who, especially when he was going to see the Emperor, seemed to surface from every nook and cranny of the city and head for his house, as if their goal was to point out his presence to the whole neighbourhood. Later on, I found out that ministers who were somewhat in disfavour were kept under surveillance in this obviously tactless way; but at the time it surprised me.

Only once did I spot Courilof, and it was almost by accident. I was involuntarily drawn to his neighbourhood and house. I was walking past his front door when I saw, from the corner, that he was about to come out; the doorman and policemen were standing even more to attention than usual, their faces attentive and stern. Here and there, on the street corners, policemen in civilian clothing paced back and forth. (I'd learned how to recognise them: of all the inhabitants of St. Petersburg, they were the only ones who wore bowler hats and carried big rolled-up umbrellas, summer and winter alike.)

The door opened and Courilof headed for his car, followed by his secretary. He walked quickly and frowned, a sullen, dark expression on his face. I backed against a wall and watched him. Then, as strange as it may seem, he turned and looked at me, just as his wife had, but he seemed to look through me, without seeing me. It came to me in a flash that, to him, I was the living form Death had taken on this earth, and also—he was so fat, so impassive and solemn—I would take pleasure is seeing this superbly decorated mass, that harsh face explode into "flesh and bones flying in all directions." At that moment, I hated him— as I had hated Dr. Schwann in the past—with a feeling that was almost physical. I looked away and he walked past, continuing along. I went and sat down in a little cabaret where I had something to eat and remained for part of the night.

The next day, Fanny told me that sixty students had been arrested on charges of revolutionary activities at the insistence of the minister. One of the history professors had refused to answer their questions about the Paris Commune. These young people had protested in the only way they could, a stupid and childish way, smashing up their desks and singing revolutionary songs at the top of their voices (the "International" and the "Marseillaise" jumbled together), during the service in the chapel. Soldiers had cleared out the lecture halls.

I dined at Madame Schröder's place where she talked to me about Courilof's wife; she'd known her when she was twenty, "when she sang 'Giroflé-Girofla' in the little cabarets on the Iles. Afterwards, she became Prince Nelrode's mistress before meeting His Excellency."

"Does Courilof know that the prince received the lady's favours before him?" I asked.

But Madame Schröder told me that this circumstance, for some unknown reason, had made them even closer. She was still talking when Fanny came in, to tell us that in the city soldiers had opened fire and several young men and women had been wounded and killed. I have never seen, on a human face, a greater look of hatred than I saw on Fanny's face that day; her green eyes were blazing. Even I was deeply moved.

When we left, the city was utterly silent, as if it had been crushed. Several times since then I have experienced that extraordinary silence: it is the most definite sign that a revolution is about to begin. On that particular night, there were a few small revolts in the factories and textile works, immediately suppressed with extreme violence.

We walked through almost the entire city, hearing nothing except the sound of iron shutters quickly closing in front of the shops. Only a few remained open; a single lantern placed on the ground faintly lit them up.

The gates were closed in front of the great rectangular court-yard of the university, but just as we were arriving, a small group of men carrying stretchers went inside. We slipped in behind them and the gates shut again. The university buildings were as dark as night. Suddenly a light shone from one of the rooms; you could see it through the tall windows of the lecture halls shimmering faintly in the clear night. I don't know why, but it looked inexplicably sinister.

We hid behind the high columns and remained there, motion-less, spellbound, in spite of the very real danger, for the police continually rushed past us.

On the other side of the street, the houses were locked and dark. Just as we were about to leave, blending in with people who were coming and going, a car sped past and we recognised Courilof.

One of the guards went over to open the car door for him, but Courilof gestured that he wasn't getting out. They exchanged a few words; even though I was quite close to them, I couldn't make out anything. In the moonlight, as pure and clear as the rising sun, I could see the tall, motionless shape of the minister; his face was so cold and harsh that it didn't even look human.

At that moment, we heard footsteps coming from inside the courtyard and the men carrying the stretchers came out. There were eight of them, I think. As they passed in front of the car, they stopped and pulled back the sheets.

A man was standing next to Courilof; I can still picture him, short and pale with a big yellowish moustache and a nervous tic that made his upper lip twitch. He wrote down the names of the victims on a register as the stretcher bearers handed him note-books, identity papers, passports, all undoubtedly found in the victims' clothes.

For a second, I could see their young faces, their closed eyes, and that unforgettable look of secret, profound scorn that corpses have a few hours after they die, when the traces of suffering and terror have faded.

They were carried over to a parked black van and thrown in with a dull grunt, the kind porters make when they're lifting heavy trunks.

The minister made a gesture and the policemen stood back to let the car speed out. I had just enough time to see the minister lean back in the corner and pull his hat down over his eyes. I have never lost the impression of intense horror I felt at that sight.

CHAPTER 8

I HAD THOUGHT about trying to get myself into the minister's house by posing as a French valet, a tutor, or a doctor. It was this final choice that prevailed. One of our members in the Swiss delegation recommended me to his superior, who, in all innocence, recommended me to Courilof. Every year when Courilof went to stay in his house in the Iles, and then to the Caucasus, he took a young doctor, preferably foreign, along with him.

I went to the embassy and, with my false passport and letters of recommendation, I managed to achieve my goal more quickly than the real Marcel Legrand might have done. I obtained a letter from the Swiss minister, who guaranteed I was politically sound; the same day, I went to the ministry. There I was received by a secretary who examined my papers and kept them; then he asked me to come back the next day, which I did.

And so there I was the next day, waiting.

Courilof quickly lumbered across the room to shake my hand. I was struck by how different his features appeared when seen close up, compared with how I remembered them. He seemed older, and his face, which in public was as impassive as a block of marble, now looked flabbier, more mottled, softer, made of whitish fat; he had dark circles under his eyes.

I had noticed, the day when we crossed paths near his house, the way he had looked me in the eye without appearing to actually see me, as if he were looking for something behind a glass wall. His forehead and ears seemed enormous. Throughout the few seconds our meeting lasted, I could feel his weary blue eyes staring at me. Later on, I was told that it was a tic of Alexander III, this serious way of staring at someone without blinking. Undoubtedly, the minister was imitating him. But most significantly, he looked as if he were obsessed with one particular idea; beneath his distracted, fixed gaze, it wasn't fear that you felt, but rather annoyance and confusion.

He asked me a few questions, then asked if I could move into their house in the Iles the following Monday.

"I'll be there for the month of June," he said, "then in the Caucasus in autumn . . ."

I agreed. He gestured to the secretary, who accompanied me to the door. I left.

The following Monday, I was driven to the Iles. Courilof's house was built at the very edge, in a place called La Flèche, which looked out over the entire coast of Finland; here, the setting sun shimmered all night long during the month of May, bathing everything in its brilliant silvery light. Thin birch trees and miniature firs grew in the spongy soil, full of dark, stagnant water. Never have I seen so many mosquitoes. In the evening, a whitish mist settled around the houses as thick clouds of them flew in from the marshes.

The houses in the Iles were very beautiful. Sometimes, a villa in Nice reminds me of Courilof's villa, for it was built in the same Italian style, pompous and rococo, the stonework the colour of saffron with foundation walls painted sea green and adorned with great, bow-shaped balconies.

During the civil war, the entire villa was destroyed. I went back there once, I recall, during the 19 October battles against Youdenitch, when I was chief administrator of the army. Our Red Army was camping along the coast. I could find no trace of the house; it had been completely destroyed by the shells. It seemed to have been swallowed up by the earth; water had sprung up everywhere; it was virtually a pond, deep and calm, where you could hear the piercing buzz of those mosquitoes . . . Breathing in the smell of that water gave me a strange sensation.

I lived in that house for a while: it was me, Courilof's son Ivan, who was ten years old, and his Swiss tutor, Froelich. The minister had been delayed by the Emperor. Then Courilof's wife and daughter Ina (Irène Valerianovna) arrived, and finally the minister himself.

CHAPTER 9

VALERIAN ALEXANDROVITCH COURILOF arrived one night, quite late. I was already in bed. The sound of the car along the cobblestones in the courtyard woke me up.

I went over to the window. The servants were still holding the car door open as Courilof got out, helped by a secretary; he seemed to be having trouble walking and he crossed the courtyard with slow, heavy steps that pounded the ground. When he reached the stairs, he stopped, pointed to his luggage, and gave some orders I couldn't make out. I watched him. At that point in time, I never grew weary of watching him... I think that fishermen who have waited patiently for a very long time at the river's edge and finally feel their line bend and tremble in their hands, then reel in their salmon or sterlet, must have the same feeling as they contemplate their dazzling catch twitching and sparkling at their feet.

Courilof had been inside the house for a long time, yet I stood there for a long time, feverishly dreaming of the moment when I would see him dead by my hand.

That night, I didn't go back to bed; I was reading when a servant came in.

"Come downstairs at once," he said. "His Excellency isn't well."

I went down to the minister's bedroom. As I got closer to the door, I heard a voice barely recognisable as Courilof's, a kind of continuous cry, interspersed with groans and sighs: "My God! My God! My God! ..."

"Hurry up," the servant urged. "His Excellency is very bad."

I went in. The room was in total disorder. I saw Courilof stretched out on his bed, completely naked; a candle lit up his fat, yellowish body. He was thrashing around from side to side, undoubtedly trying to find a position that wasn't painful; but every movement caused him to cry out in anguish. When he saw me, he started to speak but suddenly a flood of dark vomit shot out of his mouth. I looked at his yellow cheekbones, the harsh circles under his narrowed eyes. He pointed to the region near his liver; his hand was shaking as he watched me, his large eyes wide open. I tried to examine it, but his abdominal wall was covered in fat; nevertheless, I noticed the abnormal thinness of his rib-cage and legs in contrast to his enormous stomach.

His wife, kneeling behind him, was holding his head in both hands.

"His liver?" I asked.

She nodded towards a syringe of morphine on the table that had been prepared for him.

"Professor Langenberg normally looks after His Excellency, but he's away," she murmured.

I injected the morphine and put hot compresses over the area around his liver. Courilof fell into a fitful sleep, interspersed with groans.

I kept changing the compresses for nearly an hour. He had stopped groaning, but sighed deeply every now and then. There was no hair at all on his body, but it was covered in a whitish fat, like wax. I noticed a little gold icon on his chest, hanging from his neck on a silk ribbon. The entire room—very large and dark, irregularly shaped, with dark green, almost black carpeting— was covered from top to bottom in images of the Virgin and saints, like a chapel. An enormous icon in a gold frame took up one entire corner of the room; it contained a statue of the Black Madonna—her hair was studded with gemstones, her face sorrowful and unattractive. The tapestries were lit up in places by little shimmering lights cast by the lamps in the icons; I counted three of them above the bed, lined up one on top of the other, in the folds of a billowing curtain.

His wife hadn't moved; she continued holding his rigid, yellowish head ever so carefully, as if he were a sleeping child. I told her she should leave him, as he was unconscious. She didn't reply, didn't even seem to hear me, just clasped his tilted head even more tightly. He was breathing with difficulty, his mouth open and nostrils dilated, his wide pale eyes burning beneath his lowered eyelids.

"Valia... my love; Valia, my darling..." she whispered.

I watched her closely. She looked exhausted; her face, free of make-up, was the face of an old woman... but she must have been beautiful once. She possessed an extraordinary mixture of the ridiculous and the pathetic. Her hair was arranged in little gold ringlets, like a child's; her mouth, lined with deep, fine wrinkles, looked like the tiny cracks found on paintings. Circles around her eyes formed a kind of dark ring near the sockets; perhaps it was this that gave her such a deep, weary expression.

"Do you think he's cold?" she murmured. "When he's in pain like this, he can't even stand the feel of sheets on his body."

I went to get a blanket and covered his naked body; he was starting to shake with cold and fever. I was being very gentle, but I couldn't help brushing against the area around his liver. He let out a kind of bestial moan, and, though I don't know why, it moved me.

"There, there," I said. "It's gone now."

I put my hand on his forehead and wiped away the perspiration. My hands were cold and his forehead was burning hot. I knew it must have felt good to him. I slowly stroked his head and face again; I looked at him.

"Are you feeling better, Valia, my darling?" his wife said quietly.

"Leave him," I said again. "He's sleeping."

She raised his head and carefully put it down on the pillow. I took a flask of vinegar, wet my hands, started stroking his face again. He lay stretched out in front of me; despite his suffering, his pale face retained its cold, harsh expression.

The servant had remained in the room, standing in a corner, dozing off. "Should I go back and get Professor Langenberg?" he asked quietly.

"Yes, do," said Madame Courilof quickly. "Hurry, hurry up."

I went over to the open window and sat down on the ledge where I could smoke and breathe more comfortably. It was already morning and the first cars were driving past.

A while later, Courilof sat up and gestured for me to come over.

"They've gone to get Professor Langenberg," I said.

"Thank you. You did a good job. You seem to know what you're doing."

He spoke to me in French, in a gentle, emotional tone of voice. He must have been suffering horribly; his face was grey and he had dark circles under his eyes. His wife leaned over him; she stroked his cheek gently and remained standing next to his bed, watching him carefully.

He told me I could examine him; I did so very gently and when he asked me questions, I told him I thought he'd been working too hard. I was struck by the terrible condition in which I found almost all of his organs. He looked as if he were made of steel, and his demeanour—his girth, his height—made him look like a giant. However, his lungs were congested, his heart-beat irregular and quick; there wasn't a single muscle beneath this mass of flesh.

I carefully returned to the area around his liver; I thought I could feel an abnormal growth, but he stopped me, growing even paler: "Don't, please," he said.

He pointed to the right side of his body. "Here, over here. There's a sharp pain, like someone's cutting me with a razor."

The way he'd moved had obviously caused him more pain. He groaned, angrily clenching his teeth: he was so accustomed to controlling everything with certain gestures, a certain look, that he unconsciously used the same methods when dealing with illness and death.

A little while later, he seemed calmer and started talking again. He spoke quietly, said his life was difficult and that he felt very tired. He sighed several times, waving his large hand about. It was shaking slightly.

"You don't understand, you don't know this country, but we're going through hard times," he said. "Everyone's authority has been weakened. People loyal to the Emperor have a heavy burden to bear."

The longer he spoke, the more he began to use pompous and affected language. There was a strange contrast between his moralistic words and the old, weary expression on his face, where you could still see tears in his eyes from the pain he was suffering.

He stopped talking. "Go and get some rest, Marguerite," he whispered to his wife.

She gave him a long kiss on the forehead and went out.

I followed her, and as I walked past her, I looked at her face with curiosity.

"He has a problem with his liver ... doesn't he?" she asked with a look of fear and anguish on her exhausted face.

"Undoubtedly."

She hesitated, then said quietly: "You'll see, that Langenberg ... These doctors, these Russians, I don't trust them ... If he weren't a minister, things would certainly be very different! But they hide behind each other so no one takes any responsibility. They're afraid, they're never around when you need them!"

She spoke quickly, in a guttural Parisian accent, half swallowing her words. She shook her odd-looking golden hair, staring at me with wide, tired eyes. "Are you French?"

"No, Swiss."

"Ah!" she said. "That's a shame." She thought for a moment in silence. "But ... you do know Paris?" she finally asked.

"Yes."

"I'm from Paris," she said, looking at me with pride. And her eyes and teeth automatically lit up with a dazzling smile. "I'm a Parisian!"

We'd reached the staircase. I stood back to let her pass; she gathered up her flowing robe, placed her foot on the first step— it was still pretty, shapely with a high arch, and she was wearing gold, high-heeled slippers. She was about to go up the stairs when a servant, who was walking through the hallway, dropped a tray full of porcelain.

I could clearly hear the shatter of crockery and the young girl's nervous, shrill scream. Madame Courilof, stiff and white as a sheet, seemed frozen to the spot. I tried to reassure her but she wasn't listening to me; she just stood there, pale and motionless. Only her lips quivered, turning her face into a grotesque grimace that was horrible to behold.

I opened the sitting-room door, pointed to the servant kneeling on the floor, cleaning up the shards. Only then did a bit of colour return to her cheeks.

She sighed deeply and went upstairs without saying a word. On the landing, as we were parting, she forced herself to smile. "I live under the constant threat of a terrorist attack," she said to me. "My husband is well respected by the people ... but ... "

She didn't finish her sentence, just lowered her head and walked quickly away. Later on, every time the minister was late, I would see her lean out the window, undoubtedly expecting to see a stretcher with a dead body on it being carried down the path. The sound of any unfamiliar footsteps or voices in the house made her start in the same way; a deathly pallor would come over her face—the miserable expression of a hunted animal waiting for the deadly blow, but not knowing how or when it would come.

After the minister was assassinated, I can recall with perfect clarity hiding in the room next to where his body was laid out. When she came in, she looked almost at peace; her eyes were dry. She seemed free at last.

CHAPTER 10

THE NEXT DAY, Courilof called me in while Langenberg was there.

Langenberg was a large man, Germanic looking and blond, with a sharp, square beard and a cold, ironic, piercing expression behind his spectacles. His cold, damp hands made Courilof's body shiver nervously when he touched him; I could see it from where I sat at the foot of the bed.

Langenberg seemed to enjoy Courilof's reaction; he examined his fat, trembling body, turning it over with a smug look on his face that annoyed me.

"It's all right, it's all right."

"Do I have to stay in bed?"

"Just for a few days . . . not for too long. Do you have a lot to do at the moment?"

"My line of work doesn't allow for breaks," said Courilof, frowning.

As he was leaving, Langenberg took me aside. "When you examined him, did you feel a growth?" he said.

I told him I had no doubt about it. He nodded several times. "Yes, yes."

"It's cancerous," I said.

"Well," he replied, shrugging his shoulders, "I don't know . . . It's certainly a small tumour, that's for sure . . . If it weren't Courilof, if it were some ordinary person . . . *ein Kerl* . . . I could operate and remove it, which would give him a few more years to live . . . But Courilof! The idea of taking on such responsibility!"

We walked up and down the bright little entrance hall in front of the bedroom.

"Does he know?"

"Of course not," he replied. "What good would that do? He's consulted any number of doctors, all of whom suspect the same thing but refuse to operate on him. Courilof!" he repeated. "You don't understand, my boy, you don't know this country!"

He prescribed a diet and some treatments and left.

The attack lasted about ten days, and I slept in a room adjoining Courilof's, so I could hear him if he called for me. This part of the house was constantly full of the minister's staff, secretaries who brought him files and letters. I watched them wait their turn, shudder and walk over to the closed door; I could hear as they questioned each other in hushed voices: "What kind of a mood is he in today?"

One of them, a low-ranking staff member whose duties required him to see the minister several times a day, surreptitiously crossed himself when he went into the bedroom. He was rather old, as I recall, dignified and well groomed, with a pale face, tense with anxiety. Courilof, however, almost always spoke in the same tone of voice, measured and polite, cold and curt, hardly moving his lips. He was rarely impatient, but when he was, his voice was barely recognisable from where I waited in the next room. He would hurl abuse in a harsh, breathless voice, then stop suddenly, sigh, and wave them away, exclaiming: "Get out! Go to hell!"

One day, I was standing in the doorway when Madame Courilof noticed a female visitor I'd seen on several occasions. She had one of those pale, ordinary faces that are attractive and hold your attention because of certain clear-cut features; her deep-set eyes had a tragic look about them. She stood as straight as a steel beam, and her hair had white streaks in it and rippled over her forehead; she had large teeth, wore a grey cloth dress with a stiff triple collar decorated with lace, all of which gave her a strange and striking appearance. I didn't know her name, but I'd seen her treated with the utmost respect.

When she saw her, Madame Courilof seemed extraordinarily upset; she hesitated for a moment, then made a deep curtsey. The woman looked at her, studying first her golden hair, then her powdered cheeks, then her mouth. She sighed softly, then raised her eyebrows, shaping her pale lips into a sarcastic little smile.

"Is His Excellency feeling better?" she finally murmured angrily.

"My husband is feeling better, yes, Your Highness," Madame Courilof replied.

There was a brief silence, and the visitor went into the bedroom. Madame Courilof stood in the middle of the room for a moment, not knowing what to do, then slowly walked away. As she passed by me, she smiled sadly, shrugged her shoulders and whispered, "How oddly these women dress, don't you think?"

When I looked at her closely, I noticed that she looked exhausted and tears had welled up in her eyes.

On another occasion, I met an elderly man in the minister's bedroom who was wearing a white summer uniform. I subsequently learned that it was Prince Nelrode. When Courilof spoke to the prince, his voice changed, becoming as deep and soft as velvet.

When I went in, I saw Courilof half sitting in bed; he'd raised himself up with difficulty, so his features looked strained and pale, but he smiled while nodding his head seriously, with a sort of respectful affection. As soon as he noticed me, his expression changed; he let his head fall grandly back on to the pillow and said under his breath: "In just a moment, Monsieur Legrand, just a moment . . ."

I showed him the injection I had prepared.

The visitor gestured. "I'll leave you now, my dear friend."

He looked at me with curiosity, raising his pince-nez to his eyes, then letting them drop down again.

"Yes, Langenberg told me you had a new doctor."

"A very skilful one," Courilof said graciously. But then immediately, he gave me a haughty, weary look. "Off you go, Monsieur Legrand, I'll call for you."

I was becoming familiar with how Courilof behaved—with his inferiors, his peers, with people he respected or needed. And all his little gestures, his expressions, the words he used—they were all classic, predictable to a certain extent. But every evening when I went into his room and found him alone with his wife, I realised how human nature is truly bizarre.

At night, I would sleep in the same room as he, stretched out on a chaise-longue next to the alcove. I would go up to bed

late. The house was usually filled with the sound of footsteps, voices—but hushed, muted, out of a sense of deferential
fear, but still audible, like the humming of a beehive. In the evening, everything was silent. It was cold, as it often is in St.
Petersburg at the end of spring, when the icy winds run down
from the north along the Neva River. I remember going into
the bedroom where all you could hear was the crackling and
spitting of logs in the wood-burning stove. A pink lamp burned
in the corner of the room. Next to the bed, sitting on a small,
low armchair, Madame Courilof held her husband's hands.
When she saw me, she exclaimed in her shrill little birdlike voice:
"Eleven o'clock already? Time for you to get some rest, my
darling."

I would sit down with a book by the window. Within a few
minutes, they would forget I was there and quietly continue their
conversation.

Gradually I would look up and, in the darkened room, study
their faces. They seemed different. He would listen to her endlessly, pressing her hand against his forehead, a faint smile hovering at the corner of his lips (those stony lips that hardly seemed
designed to smile). Sometimes even I enjoyed listening to her.
Not that she was intelligent, far from it, but she had a way of
rambling on that was fascinating, almost as if she couldn't stop
herself; it was as relaxing as the steady sound of a brook, or a bird
singing. However, she knew when to be silent, how to be still,
how to anticipate his every desire, like an old, wise pussycat.
Beneath the pinkish light, half hidden in shadow, what stood out
were her beautiful eyes and golden hair, its colour fading. Every
so often she would give a little cry, shrug her shoulders with the
inimitable sound of a woman who has seen all there is to see of
life. Sometimes she would let out a kind of involuntary sigh, a
cry of: "Oh! My God, the things I've seen!" and then she would
gently stroke Courilof's hand.

"My darling, my poor darling . . ."

For they would forget I was there and would speak to each
other endearingly; she would call him "my sweetheart . . . my
love . . . my darling . . ." Such words spoken to Courilof, to the
"ferocious, voracious Killer Whale," moved me.

"Oh!" she said one day. "Do you think I don't know? I never should have listened to you. What was the point of getting married? We were happy as we were."

Suddenly, she fell silent: she had undoubtedly remembered I was there. But I sat totally still.

She sighed. "Valia, do you remember?" she said softly. "Do you remember how it used to be?"

"Yes," he replied curtly.

She hesitated, then whispered with a note of fear and hope in her voice, "What if they get their way . . . Who knows? If you weren't a minister any more, we could leave the country, we could go and live in France, the two of us."

When she said that, I saw Courilof's face change, tense up. Something harsh and inhuman came over his features, a look in his eyes.

"Ah!" he said, his voice pompous and solemn, gradually growing louder as he spoke. "Do you actually think I want to stay in power? It's a burden. But as long as the Emperor needs me, I will carry out my duties to the end."

She bowed her head sadly. He was starting to get restless, tossing and turning in the bed.

"I'll leave you alone," she murmured.

He hesitated, then opened his eyes and looked at her. "Sing me a little song before you go, anything . . ." he asked sweetly.

She sang French love songs, old arias from operettas, swinging her legs, swaying her body, moving her head as if she were in the spotlight, undoubtedly as she had been in the past, in the little cabarets in the Iles. And yet, her voice was still beautiful. I turned away so I couldn't see her, so I could just hear her sweet, sonorous song. Looking at her was horrible; she made me feel pity and scorn. But how did *he* feel when he looked at her? I wondered if she had really once been so beautiful that . . . There wasn't a single picture of her in the house.

He watched her without moving, lost in some vague, passionate dream. "Ah! No one sings like that any more!"

I remember he took her hands, almost stroking them, with an affectionate kind of indifference, as if they were the hands of a friend, a child, a wife of many years. But his eyes were closed, and, little by little, memories from the past surely came back to him. I could see him press her hands more tightly, forcing the blood to rush away from her fingers. She smiled, a bitter, melancholy little grimace on her face.

"The good times are all in the past, my darling."

He sighed. "Life passes quickly," he said, sounding troubled and anxious.

"It's slow enough now. It's youth that goes so quickly." She whispered a few words to him that I couldn't make out, then shrugged her shoulders. "Really?" she said.

Her words and gesture must have surely had some special meaning for them both in the past, for she started to laugh, but sadly, as if she were implying *Do you remember? I was young then* . . .

And he imitated her tone of voice and said again: "Really? What was that? Really? My darling little one."

When he laughed, his chin trembled and the expression in his eyes became clear and soft.

Then Courilof's children came in: Ina and the boy, Ivan, who was fat and weak, just like Courilof, with pale cheeks, big ears, easily short of breath.

Courilof spoke to the boy with deep affection. He hugged him, stroked him, held him to him for a long time while sighing, "Ah! This is my son, my heir." He gently stroked his hair, his arms.

"Look, Monsieur Legrand, he's anaemic," he added.

And I still remember how he would lower the boy's pale lips and eyelids for me to see.

The girl said nothing, her face was cold and impassive. Nevertheless, she looked like Courilof; she had his mannerisms and voice. She constantly fiddled with a gold necklace she was wearing. Courilof displayed such coldness towards her that he was virtually hostile. He hissed at her when he spoke, looked at her with an expression of annoyance and anger.

The children kissed his hand. He made the sign of the cross on their bowed heads, as well as on the powdered face of his ageing mistress.

Finally, all three of them left.

CHAPTER 11

COURILOF AND HIS wife were in the habit of writing to each other from their bedrooms; the servants would carry books or fruit from one end of the house to the other until very late at night, with little notes written in pencil.

I sometimes read them out to him, at his request, for he was proud of his wife; he enjoyed having me see her handwriting and style. She wrote in a rambling fashion, teasing and melancholy, that was actually similar to the way she spoke and was quite charming. She often reminded him to ask me about his medicines, treatments, or diet, along with endearments like:

"Good night, my one and only darling! Your old, devoted Marguerite."

Or: "I cannot wait until tomorrow: a new day is always precious at our age, and tomorrow means I will be able to see you again."

Once, I read: "My darling, would you please see an elderly woman, for my sake. She's the widow Aarontchik, who has come a long way from the provinces to seek justice from you. In the past, and long before I had the joy of knowing you, this woman was my lodger in Lodz, and she looked after me devotedly when . . ."

Then followed a series of initials that I read out to Courilof, without understanding what they meant. He frowned and his face took on that sad, sour look I was beginning to know so well.

He let out a deep sigh. "File it."

That same night he thought for a moment, then asked me, "Don't you find that French women have an innately graceful and elegant sense of style?"

He didn't wait for my reply but continued, "Ah! If only you could have seen Marguerite Eduardovna in *La Périchole*, when I first met her!"

"Was that a long time ago?" I asked.

He always seemed upset and surprised when I asked him a question, like someone who blushes in embarrassment for a rude person. I recall one day, during the Revolution, when I was interrogating one of the grand dukes. Which one was he? I've forgotten his name, but he was elderly. He'd been in prison in the Kresty jail for more than a year and was dying of hunger when he was brought to me. But he remained cool and calm, treating his guards with meticulous, ironic politeness, seeming to bear his misfortunes with extraordinary stoicism. Right up until the moment when I came into the room. I hadn't slept in thirty-six hours, and I sat down opposite him without the customary formalities. This man—whose face had been half smashed by one of the guards—blushed, not out of anger, but rather out of embarrassment, as if I had taken all my clothes off in front of him. Poor Courilof had also picked up certain mannerisms from Alexander III; he too sometimes looked like a dictator.

I waited while he stared at me for a moment with a haughty, anxious look in his pale, wide eyes.

"It's been fourteen years," Courilof said at last. He thought for a moment, then added, "I was young then too . . . A lot of water has gone under the bridge since then."

At night, as I have already mentioned, I slept in his room. He was patient and never complained. He often couldn't sleep, and I would hear him quietly tossing and turning, moaning as he tried to pick something up from the table.

I remember certain nights in Switzerland, sleepless nights when you listened for every sound, the blood rushing through your veins, the quick pulse at your temples, times when you could smell death oozing from your body, when you were so very weary . . . and at those times, life seemed so wonderful and the nights so long.

"Can't you sleep?" I once asked.

I'd been listening to him for nearly an hour, turning his pillow over and over, no doubt unable to find a cool place on the pillow-case. I knew that feeling very well. He seemed unbelievably happy to hear the sound of my voice. I pulled back the screen that separated the chaise-longue where I slept in the alcove from the rest of the bedroom. He sighed softly.

"Good Lord, I'm in so much pain," he said, his voice breathless and trembling. "It feels like a razor's cutting into me."

"That's usually what it feels like when you have your attacks," I said. "It will pass."

He nodded several times with visible difficulty.

"You're brave," I said.

I had already noticed that this man had a pathological, childish need to be praised. He blushed slightly, sat up, leaned against his pillow and pointed to a chair next to his bed where I should sit down.

"I am extremely religious, Monsieur Legrand; I know that young people today lean more towards rationalism. But the courage you are kind enough to recognise in me, and that even my enemies acknowledge as indisputable, comes from my trust in God. Not a single hair falls from anyone's head without his permission."

He fell silent and we watched the mosquitoes buzzing around, attracted by the light of the lamp. Even now, in summer, whenever I see mosquitoes flying about and twitching their greedy noses, my thoughts return to those nights in the Iles. I can still hear the metallic, lyrical hum of their delicate wings above the water.

I closed the window, saw he was burning up with fever; he didn't seem able to sleep. I offered to read to him. He accepted, thanking me. I took a book down from the shelf. After a few pages, he stopped me.

"Monsieur Legrand, aren't you sleepy? Really?"

I said that I slept badly when the nights were light like this.

"Would you help me?" he said. "I have a lot of work to catch up on. I'm very worried about it. Don't say anything to Langenberg," he continued, forcing a smile.

I brought him the stack of letters he pointed out; I passed them to him one at a time, and he scribbled notes in the margins in different coloured pencils that he chose with the utmost care. I furtively glanced at the letters as I handed them to him: they were letters from strangers, for the most part, full of suggestions about suppressing revolutionary ideas in the secondary schools and universities; and an unbelievable number of denunciations, by teachers of students, students of other students. Secondary school students, university students, head teachers, schoolmasters: it seemed as if everyone in Russia spent their lives spying and denouncing each other.

Then came the reports. One of them described serious disruptions in the university in one of the provincial cities (Kharkov, I think); the minister asked me to take down his reply; it was the text of an order he was planning.

He was sitting up against his pillows; the more he dictated, the more severe and cold his face became. He spoke each word individually, with an air of dignity, punctuating them with the same wave of his hand. He ordered them to cancel the lectures. Then he thought for a while, and a grim smile hovered over his lips and in the corners of his half-closed eyes.

"Write this down, Monsieur Legrand: 'The time wasted in useless political discussions will be made up during the forthcoming holidays: these will be shortened by the duration of the disruptions. If, in spite of this, the disruptions continue into the autumn, the exam results will be null and void; all the students, whatever their grades may have been, will be required to start their course over again from the beginning.'"

Once he'd hissed that out, he looked at me smugly.

"That will make them think twice," he said, sounding threatening and scornful. "The next one, please, Monsieur Legrand."

For this one he dictated a memo intended for school-teachers:

"During Russian Literature and History lessons, you must take advantage of every opportunity to use the facts in order to awaken in the tender souls of your young students a passionate love for HM the Emperor and the Imperial Family, as well as an indissoluble attachment to the sacred traditions and institutions of the Monarchy. In addition, the words and actions of all the teachers will be designed to be an example of Christian humility and true orthodox charity to your students. It goes without saying that any statements, reading, and, in general, any subversive actions you have the opportunity of noting amongst the students entrusted to your care, must, as always, be punished most severely."

Next there were requests for appointments. I saw a letter signed by Sarah Aarontchik, begging His Excellency to arrest someone called Mazourtchik, who was guilty of having "corrupted" her sixteen-year-old son by making him read Karl Marx. Valerian Alexandrovitch, who seemed transformed from the minute he was dealing with his correspondence, made a gesture. His eyes were gleaming behind his glasses; his wide, shiny forehead shone bizarrely, lit up by the lamp.

"Wait a moment. Pass me that note from my wife."

He re-read it closely, placing it in a coloured folder where various other papers were organised. Then he took out fifteen or so documents and requests for appointments and spread them out on the bed.

"This is the batch for tomorrow and the next day," he said with pride.

I continued passing him the letters I held in my hand. Finally he stopped me, saying he was tired. He lay there, stretched out, his eyes closed, and sighed. A severe, weary expression came over his face, an expression I knew very well. The night when they had brought the bodies for him to see, in the courtyard of the university, he had had the same nervous tension in his lips, the same rigidity of his features.

"Is it true that the army killed six students last month?" I asked suddenly. "What did they do?"

He frowned. "Who told you about that?" he asked quickly, his voice dry and suspicious.

I gave him the vaguest reply I could. He looked straight at me and suddenly spoke most passionately. "Those poor children ... just imagine ... and from good families. They had chased their history professor out of the lecture hall, thrown stones at him! Nothing important." He sighed sarcastically. "It was all because of the instigators, professional revolutionaries, a diabolical lot who will end up destroying everything that is good and noble in Russia. I was forced by public outrage and general indignation to clamp down ... I ordered the leaders arrested and the lecture rooms emptied and called in the troops to evacuate the university. Six of these unfortunate fanatics barricaded themselves up inside the empty classrooms. A shot was fired. By whom? I don't know any more than you do. But a soldier was wounded. In spite of my express orders, the colonel opened fire. Six unfortunate youngsters were killed. Not a single weapon was found on any of them. What can you do! Whose fault was it? The colonel was inconsolable; the soldiers had simply obeyed orders. These youngsters had been rash, presumptuous, I had to clamp down. There are some inexplicable contradictions. Someone said afterwards: 'The shot was fired by an agent provocateur.' All this comes under the jurisdiction of my colleague at the Home Office, but he's denying everything and landing me with all the responsibility. But the people who are truly guilty are those vultures, the revolutionaries," he said, stressing each and every syllable. "Wherever they go, they bring chaos and death."

He fell silent. I noticed he'd been mumbling as if he were delirious. I was careful not to interrupt him.

"No one wanted the sinner to die," he continued, "but misfortunes happen. Nevertheless, when it is one's duty to lead, one cannot stop at that. *Dura lex, sed lex:* the law is hard, but it is the law. Such things have always happened and will always happen," he said passionately.

As he talked, I could see his face changing, growing paler, taking on a look of slyness and anguish. I said nothing.

"You see, Monsieur Legrand," he continued, "the whole country is defended against revolution by an extremely complex system, a Wall of China made of restrictions, prejudices, superstitions, traditions, you might even call them, but they are extremely sturdy, for the pressure of the enemy is much stronger than you could ever imagine. And at the slightest hint of weakness, the slightest crack, the enemy will make sure that everything comes crashing down. This is what Prince Alexander Alexandrovitch Nelrode, my friend, has said himself, and it is gospel. He is a true statesman, Monsieur Legrand, and a true gentleman."

He pronounced this word with touching, comical solemnity and the slightly sibilant affected accent of a pure-bred Englishman.

It was nearly morning. I switched off the lamp. He had become greatly agitated as he spoke and was burning with fever; even a few steps away from him, I could feel the heat coming from his body. I changed the hot compresses and gave him something to drink. He was struggling to breathe and the swollen area around his liver was rising and falling like a balloon.

"Why is it," he asked in a softer, fainter, shaky voice, "why do I feel such a terrible pain on my right side, as if a crab is digging into my flesh with its claws?"

I said nothing. In any case, he didn't really seem to see me.

"God! I'm not afraid of death!" he said suddenly. "It is a great joy to die a Christian, with a clear conscience, having served my religion and my Emperor."

Suddenly his pompous, solemn tone changed once again, became anxious, full of a kind of zeal and goodwill. "I haven't touched a single penny of the money entrusted to me by the state. I will leave empty-handed, just as I arrived when I came to power."

He sighed weakly, finally seeming to recognise me. "Thank you, Monsieur Legrand. Would you be kind enough to give me something to drink?"

I handed him a glass and he drank the cold tea, panting like a dog quenching its thirst. I left him alone and went to lie down. The heat in the room and the stench of fever made me drowsy. I finally fell asleep, feeling I was being tossed from one nightmare to the next.

CHAPTER 12

COURILOF RECOVERED; at least, Langenberg allowed him to go and present his report to the Emperor, and from that day on, I no longer saw my Killer Whale. Our paths would sometimes cross in the rooms on the lower floor, next to the office. He would nod at me as he passed by, and say in his pompous, mocking voice: "Are you getting used to the climate of the Palmyra of the North, my dear Monsieur Legrand?"

And, without waiting for my reply, he would nod his wide smooth forehead several times and murmur: "Yes, yes, of course." And with an absent-minded, kindly wave of the hand, he would keep going.

Whenever I asked him about his health, he would smile and say, "*Nil desperandum*," slightly raising his voice, undoubtedly to arouse the admiration of all the scroungers gathered around him. "I have never had a tendency towards hypochondria, thank God! Work, now that's the true fountain of youth!"

At that time, I became close to Froelich, with the goal of finding out details regarding the minister's first wife. Utterly pointless but I was curious! Froelich had known her well; he had raised the Courilofs' nephew, Hippolyte Nicolaévitch, who, at present, held an important post at the ministry under Courilof. (He was called "Little Courilof" or "Courilof the Thief" to distinguish him from his uncle.)

Froelich had been his tutor for fifteen years, right up until the death of the first Madame Courilof. In response to my questions, he hesitated slightly, then said, "You are familiar with the reputation of Her Majesty the Empress Alexandra? Mysticism bordering on madness. The first wife of His Excellency was the same. By the end of her life, she was completely mad." He replied touching his finger to his forehead. "His Excellency's private life has not been easy . . . "

"And now?" I asked.

Froelich gave a little whistle of delight; he had thin, tight lips, an anxious look in his eyes; he rubbed his hands together, glanced nervously around him. "The beautiful Margot," he said quickly, "will ruin His Excellency's career. The only reason he hasn't already fallen out of favour by now is that Prince Nelrode is his friend and has protected him. And, truthfully, isn't it scandalous that the Minister of Education, whose main function is to protect Russian youth from the path of evil, gives them instead, by this marriage, an example of loose morals?"

He fidgeted with his pince-nez for a moment. "It appears she was once very beautiful," he observed, with regret.

A few days later, Prince Nelrode came to lunch at the Iles. I recognised the elderly man with the weary, delicate eyes I'd once met in the minister's room when he'd been ill. In 1888, Prince Nelrode had narrowly survived a terrorist attack. His assailant, someone named Grégoire Semenof, aged seventeen, had easily been overcome by the prince's soldiers. And the prince arranged for a rather barbaric, though efficient, execution; his men kicked Semenof in the head until he was dead.

There was another story about Nelrode. During one of the uprisings in Poland, when the town square was covered in dead bodies, he had a thin layer of dirt scattered over them and instructed his squadrons to carry out manoeuvres there, crushing and levelling the earth for six hours, until there remained nothing of these fallen men but a bit of dust.

The other guests were Langenberg, Baron Dahl, his son Anatole, and the Minister of Foreign Affairs (one of the three such ministers who had been labelled "foreign to foreign affairs," a nickname that was an instant success). Unbelievably old and pale, hunched up like a compass and as light as a dead leaf, his head constantly shaking, smelling of violets, he took a quarter of an hour to cross the terrace, leaning on Courilof's arm. In his hazy eyes, he had the dreamy, sad look of a very ancient horse dying of old age in his stable. His conversation, in the purest, most classical French, was so dotted with circumlocutions, euphemisms, allusions to events of a former age long forgotten by everyone, that he seemed unintelligible, not only to me but to his colleagues as well. It was obvious, however, that they happily listened to him, as if he were speaking a classical language that was mysterious and poetic.

I looked at Dahl with curiosity: I knew from Froelich that he was the sworn enemy of Courilof and his eventual successor at the Ministry of Education. He was fat, of average height; his neck was short and thick, his head shaved in the German style. His eyelashes, eyebrows, and moustache were a faded blond that blended into his greyish pale face. He had bulging cold eyes, like certain fish, very wide nostrils that breathed in deeply, and a look on his face that was simultaneously arrogant and nervous, the kind of expression you see on certain international criminals. Froelich told me that, in his youth, Dahl had been a notorious pederast (Froelich called it "dubious morals"), but now Dahl seemed to have settled down, desiring only the pursuit of a brilliant career.

Marguerite Eduardovna sat at the place of honour. Wearing make-up and powder, with pearls around her neck and her body poured into her long, tight corset and lace bodice, she said nothing. She seemed not even to hear the men's conversation, just stared sadly out into space.

Almost immediately, the conversation turned to the Emperor and the Imperial Family. The expressions they used to discuss them—"His Majesty deigned to grant me the immense honour of allowing me an audience with him . . . When I had the profound pleasure of seeing our beloved sovereign . . ."—were spoken with such mockery and scorn that the words took on a tone of intentional farce. Nelrode, in particular, excelled at it. He looked at the gold-framed portrait of the Emperor on the wall opposite him and a smile fluttered across his lips, a spark of intelligence flared in his delicate, weary eyes.

"You all appreciate the goodness, the magnificent soul, the angelic innocence of our dearly beloved sovereign, don't you?" Courilof gave a little ironic sigh and fell silent. The others nodded, and the same amused twinkle lit up their eyes. What he really meant was: "You all know that Emperor Nicolas is hardly intelligent"; everyone understood what he was saying, and each of them believed himself the only one to understand. Courilof was obviously attempting this sarcastic, nonchalant tone. But he couldn't quite manage it; a hatred he could barely disguise made his voice quiver the moment he said the Emperor's name. Dahl stopped eating and drinking for a moment, then looked at Courilof for a long time, his eyes half closed yet staring at him ironically, as if he were watching Courilof performing on a tightrope.

Sometimes one of the guests would secretly glance over towards the end of the table where Courilof's daughter sat next to Dahl's son, Baron Anatole, a large, pale young man of twenty. His mouth gaped open, his cheeks were puffy, his eyelashes white: the spitting image of the suckling pig you eat at Easter. He listened to no one and spoke in a sharp, monotonous voice that now and again shot through the noise of the conversation like a plane in a tailspin.

"The ball that Princess Barbe gave was all in all more successful, *a grander affair*, than Princess Anastasie's ball . . ."

Dahl and Courilof both frowned and made a point of looking away. A long discussion about censorship followed. It was late, nearly four o'clock, and still no one thought of leaving the table. It was a beautiful, sunny day; the rose bushes in the gardens swayed in the wind; beyond the treetops, you could see St. Petersburg in the distance, like a dark cloud topped in gold.

Censorship of personal correspondence was a tradition that the elderly Minister of Foreign Affairs deemed appropriate, "having proved its worth." But the prince thought it dangerous.

"A statesman should not allow himself to feel personal animosity," he said, "and the practice of reading the correspondence of one's enemies can only lead to such feelings. When I read that our dear Ivan Petrovitch refers to me as a blood-thirsty tiger, it makes no difference that I am hardened by fifty years of service to the Imperial Court of Holy Russia, for my sins, it still upsets me. I am only human . . . What's the point of knowing too much? It is always better, always wiser, to close one's eyes."

"Excellent advice for certain husbands," said the elderly minister.

After he said this, he laughed; his false teeth rattled several times in his empty mouth, and he looked squarely at Marguerite

Eduardovna, with the dreamy, sad expression of a melancholy old horse who chews its cud and stares blankly out in space. Courilof took the insult without saying a word, without flinching, but he frowned slightly, and his face appeared paler and harsher.

The conversation continued, turning to the appointment of a new governor general in P . . . and he replied to Dahl in a steady voice. It was only several moments later, when no one was looking as Nelrode told some anecdote about a civil servant accused of misappropriation of public funds and theft, that my Courilof sighed softly, cautiously, and let his head drop heavily down.

The prince lifted the glass of wine in front of him to his lips, smelled it without drinking it, as if it were a bouquet of flowers. He put it down again, shrugged his shoulders in his familiar way, and said: "Who hasn't His Majesty Emperor Nicolas appointed as governor general! *O tempora! O mores!* It's exactly the same with the Saint George Cross. It's handed out like candy these days! Now when His Majesty Alexander III was Emperor . . ."

He stopped for a moment, sighed, thought for a while, then murmured: "Sad, such a very sad day for Russia when that sovereign died!"

"Definitely," said Courilof enthusiastically. "*Juvenile consilium, latens odium, privatum odium, haec tria omnia regna perdiderunt.* (Childish advice, envious conspiracy, and private hatred have brought down kingdoms.) Nevertheless, no one reveres and, dare I say, adores His Majesty Emperor Nicolas more than I do, but it is unfortunately true that a certain softness, a certain nobility of character, doesn't quite fit with exercising absolute power."

"But it is very kind to be noble and sensitive, like His Majesty," said the prince, slightly sneering, his tone unmistakably filled with respectful scorn. "That is how he recently granted Emperor William a commercial treaty that is very advantageous to Germany but infinitely less so for Russia . . . His Majesty, our dearly beloved Emperor Nicolas, couldn't refuse Emperor William anything; he was the Emperor's guest at the time, as he did me the honour of telling me himself."

"*Tamen, semper talis*. . . Still, and always, the same," murmured Courilof.

"I have noticed throughout my very long life," the elderly Minister of Foreign Affairs said slowly, "that princes are too inclined to follow the noble instincts of their magnanimous hearts. It falls to their ministers to balance such tendencies with practical realities and economic necessity."

He smiled and suddenly seemed to me infinitely less stupid and inoffensive than I'd thought; a gleam suddenly illuminated his lifeless eyes. At that very moment, he looked at me. I was bathed in sunlight; this was the reason, without a doubt, that my face stood out in the dimness and caught his near-blind glance from amongst everyone else. He nodded towards me.

"Monsieur is getting an education," he said in a voice that was kindly, mocking, and scornful all at once, the same tone my Courilof tried to imitate without managing it.

Marguerite Eduardovna saw her husband give her a look and stood up to leave; I was about to go with her when Courilof called me back. "Stay. The prince would like you to recommend something for his asthma."

I sat down again and, after some time, they forgot about me. I'd stopped listening to them. I was bored and tired. They were smoking and speaking more loudly. I heard Dahl's sudden laughter, the Killer Whale's voice, and the prince. I remember thinking about Fanny, about the Party leaders in Geneva. I looked at the sun over the grounds and started to automatically recite the months . . . July, August, September . . . "Ceremonies and public holidays don't really start until the autumn . . ." I felt a vague sense of sadness. At that very moment, I was struck by Nelrode's voice (they were going on about the run-up to the Russo-Japanese War):

"No one wants war. Not the sovereign, not the ministers. In fact, no one ever wants war or any other sort of crime, but that doesn't stop it. Because the people in power are weak human beings, not blood-thirsty monsters, as everyone imagines them to be. *Lord*, wouldn't that be preferable!"

He took the elderly Minister for Foreign Affairs by the arm.

"It just makes my blood boil! These children, these incompetents... Still! All that will pass very quickly! As we will... So what?" he said. He shrugged his shoulders wearily, closed his eyes and began reciting:

"*So what if your life went entirely according to your wishes?*

"*So what if you'd read the Book of Life straight to the end?*

"Good Lord! What are we doing in this hell? We're not greedy animals, yet we're wasting our lives in vain pursuits, seeking favour and friendship from the sovereign."

"You are still young," said the elderly minister bitterly. "Wait until you have reached the very end of your days, as I have, and see the coldness and hostility of the princes replace the trust and goodwill they have bestowed upon you before!... Do you know that since last Christmas, I've been prevented from having private meals with the sovereigns? I feel," he suddenly exclaimed with extraordinary vehemence, a despairing tone of the betrayed lover in his voice that made me smile, "I truly feel that you can't recover the past! I cannot sacrifice the little time I have left to these ungrateful rulers. It's killing me, I say it openly, it's slowly killing me!"

He stopped, and I thought I saw tears glistening in his eyes. I turned around to look at him more closely. I was right; from his cloudy eyes, the vacant eyes of a very old animal, a single tear-drop fell. I felt a mixture of scorn and pity.

Courilof, however, had taken some pornographic Japanese prints out of a locked cabinet, and they were all leaning towards him, laughing nervously, their hands shaking. A long time afterwards, they started talking about women. I watched Courilof. He was a different man, his eyes sparkling, his voice husky, his fingers trembling.

"There's a new singer," said the prince, "at the Villa Rodé, a fifteen-year-old girl, still thin and plain, but with the most beautiful hair in the world, and her voice. Pieces of gold thrown against a crystal platter wouldn't make such a pure, brilliant sound."

"Villa Rodé," said Dahl.

He deliberately stopped himself, looked at Courilof, his eyes half closed.

"No one really knows how to sing any more, now that Marguerite Eduardovna has left!" said Dahl.

Courilof frowned and suddenly the excitement was gone from his face; he went pale, became anxious and sombre once more.

"Well, gentlemen," he said, "let's go out into the garden, shall we."

CHAPTER 13

ON THE TERRACE, I could hear Langenberg finishing a conversation he'd started with Dahl. "We should create a secret society with the purpose of exterminating all these damned socialists, revolutionaries, communists, free thinkers, and all the Jews, of course. We could recruit former thieves, common criminals, in exchange for sparing their lives. These revolutionary thugs deserve no more pity than mad dogs," he said.

Courilof and the prince had stopped and were smiling as they listened to him talk.

"Damn it! My boy," said the prince, "how you do go on. But we're far from that point, unfortunately!"

They went down into the garden. Dahl, Langenberg, and the elderly Minister of Foreign Affairs soon left. Courilof and the prince were alone.

"How can you and I prevent ourselves from leaning towards the liberalism we're reproached for at court?" I heard Courilof say. "When one hears such stupidity, it's heart-breaking."

The elderly prince stopped. He'd asked permission to put on his cap, for it was very hot for the season. He was standing in the middle of the path lined with white roses. I was walking behind them, but they took no notice of me. He carefully put on an English cap that had a large peak lined in green silk, pulled it down over his eyes, and said, in French, his voice deep and weary, "Sticks and stones." He struck the ground sharply with his cane.

"I will never regret having been humane," he said. "At my age especially, Valerian Alexandrovitch, you'll see, it is a great consolation."

He had long, pale hands; I can still picture them. I vividly imagined that morning in Poland when he'd launched the squadron into the little town square covered in blood and dead bodies.

At the time, I listened to him with ironic disbelief. Later on—

when I had taken their place—I understood there had not been an ounce of hypocrisy in what these men said. They simply had a short memory, as we all do.

They talked about the assassination attempts of the revolutionaries. They were sitting on a bench, at a place called the Rond Pont des Muses. I can still picture the yew trees trimmed into bizarre shapes, and the scent of the box trees. I had slipped behind the hedge. I was so close that I could have stretched out my hand and touched them. I listened to them speak with passionate curiosity.

"I'm often warned," said the prince, "that assassinations are being planned, and people write to me or have me told: 'Don't go here, or there.' I never listen to them. But I have to admit, when I'm at home at night, going to bed, knowing that the next day I have to go somewhere, I'm frightened. But as soon as I get into my car, it's all right."

"Well," said Courilof, "I say my prayers every morning when I wake up. I take each new day as the last day of my life. When I get home in the evening, I thank God for having granted me one more day."

He fell silent. He had spoken in the tone of banal solemnity that I knew so well, but his voice was shaking.

"Ah! Yes," said the prince, in his inimitable way, "you believe in God . . ." He let out a weary little laugh. "Well, as for me," he murmured, "I do my best to believe, but I swear I don't know why. I get a certain personal satisfaction out of it, not a feeling of contentment at having fulfilled my obligations, Valerian Alexandrovitch, but the bitter satisfaction of seeing, once again, how very stupid people are. As for posterity and all that nonsense, I'm not interested. Think of how much noise they made over what happened to that anarchist Semenof! I spared him months of suffering, you know, the anguish and fear of being executed, and, at the same time, avoided a trial that would only have encouraged ideas in people we'd then have to fight. It was the same in Poland. Having the horses trample dead bodies couldn't do them any more harm, you have to admit that, and inspiring terror did them good; it stopped the insurrection dead and so saved human lives. The more I see, the more value I place on human life . . . and less on what they like to call 'ideas,' " he continued as if in a dream. "In a word, I behaved rationally. And that is what people cannot forgive."

"Well, I have faith in posterity," murmured Courilof. "Russia will forget my enemies, but she will not forget me. It's all very hard, very difficult," he kept saying with a sigh. "They say you have to be capable of shedding blood, and it's true."

He stopped for a moment, then added quietly: "For a just cause."

"I don't believe in just causes much either," sighed the prince. "But I'm a good deal older than you, it's true; you still have illusions."

"It's hard; life is difficult," the minister said again, sadly. He fell silent for a moment, then said quietly: "I have so many problems."

I leaned forward even more. This was my first really dangerous move since I'd been in the minister's house. But I was gripped by intense curiosity.

The prince gave a little cough, then turned and looked at Courilof. I could see the two of them, a few metres from me, through the break in the hedge. I held my breath.

Courilof began complaining: he was overworked, ill, surrounded by enemies who plotted against him.

"Why didn't I listen to you? Why did I get married?" he said over and over again, bitterly. "A statesman must be invulnerable. *They* know," he said, strongly stressing each word. "*They* know where it hurts the most, and every time I get ahead, that's where *they* strike. My life has become a living hell. If you only knew what filth, what crass lies are told every day about my wife!"

"I know, my poor friend, I know," the prince said softly.

"For Ina's twentieth birthday," Courilof continued, "I was planning to give a ball, as is our tradition. You know that Their Majesties have never set foot in my house since the day my wife died. Well, just imagine," he exclaimed, his voice shaking, "that our sovereigns let it be known to me that if they were to attend the ball, it would be better if Marguerite Eduardovna were not there! And I was forced to smile, to take the insult in silence. It is inconceivable that a man in my position, who strikes fear into the hearts of thousands of people, should be forced to bow before this crowd, this mass of lazy louts who make up the court. Ah! I'm tired of being in power! But I am fulfilling my obligation by remaining." He said this several times, passionately.

"It is true that if Marguerite Eduardovna could leave Russia for a while . . ." the prince began.

"No," said Courilof. "Personally, I would rather end it once and for all and leave as well. She is my wife before God. She bears my name. And anyway, why should they drag up the past? Do they even know what happened then? When they called her a 'loose woman,' they said it all. I'm not talking about love; I'm not talking about the early years; but as for the devotion she has shown me, the comfort, the help she has been to me for fourteen years, only I can be the judge of that. My life! My miserable life! My poor first wife, you know the lengths I went to care for her; no one, not even you, can know how much I have . . ."

He wanted to say "suffered," but the word refused to cross his proud lips. He stood up taller, making a weary gesture with his hand. "She's dead. Her poor soul is with God! But didn't *I* have the right to rebuild my life as I saw fit? I can see now that the private life of a statesman belongs to the public, like his work. As soon as you try to keep a little piece of your life for yourself, that's exactly where your enemies strike."

"Margot," the elderly prince said, as if in a dream. "Even today, though she's older, less beautiful, she still has an inexplicable charm. Without a doubt, the same kind of charm we find in people whom we have greatly loved."

"As for me," said Courilof, sounding so sincere that I was struck by it, "I loved her long ago; you know how many mad things I did for her, but none of that compares with how I feel about her now. I am alone in life, Alexander Alexandrovitch, we are all alone. The higher our positions, the more complete our solitude. In her, God has given me a friend. I have many faults— man is but a mass of faults and misery—but I am loyal. I do not abandon my friends."

"Be careful of Dahl," said the prince. "He wants your post, and in my opinion, they are only waiting for you to make a false move to give it to him. And Dahl was a former colleague of yours at the ministry. Who else would set us up if not our colleagues? Why don't you marry off your daughter to his imbecile of a son? A rich dowry would appease him. He only wants power for the money it will bring."

Courilof hesitated. "Ina is disgusted by the very idea of such a marriage," he said. "And in any case, I'm afraid it wouldn't solve anything. Dahl is one of those insatiable dogs who not only eat the meat off the bone, but the bone as well."

"You've heard, haven't you," asked the prince, "about his latest masterpiece? You know that the pet subject at court for some time now is *Russia for the Russians*. In order to get a contract for the railways, for example, you have to have a name that ends in *of*. The baron dug up a poor little penniless prince from somewhere or other who has a traditional name. He's using it to get contracts for mines or railways that he then sells on to Jews or Germans, after taking a fair commission for himself. Two thousand roubles for the prince, and presto! Amusing, don't you think?"

"Every now and again I am staggered by the extraordinary greed of these people," said Courilof. "An ordinary man has the right to be greedy, because he knows that otherwise he would starve to death. But these people who have everything—money, friends in high places, property—they never have enough! I just don't understand it."

"Each of us has his weaknesses. Human nature is incomprehensible. One cannot even say with certainty whether a man is good or evil, stupid or intelligent. There does not exist a good man who has not at some time in his life committed a cruel act, nor an evil man who has not done good, nor an intelligent man who has never been foolish, nor a fool who has never acted intelligently! Still, that's what gives life its diversity, its surprises. I find that idea rather amusing."

They had stood up as they talked and walked away from the Rond Pont. I waited for a while and then left as well.

CHAPTER 14

THEY STAYED IN the garden for the rest of the day, along with Vania, Courilof's son, who listened to them, looking bored.

"For him," said the minister, "life will be better."

I could hear everything they said; their words carried through the calm summer air.

"We're going through difficult times, but if public opinion were only on our side, I am convinced that we would get back on our feet."

"As for me," said Courilof, "you could never know how much it comforts me when people are sympathetic towards me. Society is weary of flirting with the idea of a revolution. I think we have ten or twelve hard years ahead. But the future is marvellous."

"My dear boy . . ." the prince murmured, sounding sceptical. But he said no more.

Courilof, lost in thought, caressed his son's hair. The boy yawned furtively, nervously, but he couldn't stop his entire body from trembling, a sign of the instinctive repugnance that children feel when touched by elderly hands.

I imagined Courilof's secret thoughts very well. "Her Imperial Highness seems distressed by the birth of Grand Duchess Anastasia," he said, as if speaking them out loud. "This fourth disappointment is difficult. Their Majesties are still young, it's true . . ."

There was a long silence. Then the prince shook the ash off his cigarette.

"Yesterday I saw His Royal Highness the Grand Duke Michael," he said, pouting. "He really is the spitting image of his noble father."

Both of them were now looking at the little boy and smiling, as if, through him, they could see the shape of the future: the Emperor dying without an heir; his brother, the Grand Duke Michael, succeeding him on the throne, an era of peace and happiness for Russia. At least, that's what I was sure Courilof was thinking. The prince's thoughts were more difficult to work out . . . Yes, I remember that day very well indeed.

Finally the prince remembered me and called me over to ask for a remedy for his painful chronic cough. I pointed to his cigarette and told him he should stop smoking.

He began to laugh.

"Youth always goes to extremes. You can take away a man's life, but not his passions."

He had a precise way of speaking and a brilliantly dry way of expressing himself. I suggested he take a sedative. He agreed, thanking me. I left. I remained in my room for a long time, musing and wondering whose dreams and speculations about the future—ours or theirs—were fair. I was extremely sad and tired, but filled with feelings of blissful savagery, feelings that surprised even me.

When I returned to the garden, it was late and dusk was falling, the sort of dusk you get in springtime. The sky was clear and brilliant, like deep, transparent, rose crystal. At moments like these, the Iles were truly beautiful. The little lagoons formed by the water, between two strips of land, shimmered faintly and reflected the sky.

The prince's carriage had pulled up; he was sitting in the back with a fur blanket over his legs. He held some fresh white roses, cut especially for him, and was stroking them.

I gave him the prescription for the sedative.

"Are you French, Monsieur?" he asked me.

"Swiss."

He nodded.

"A beautiful country . . . I'm going to spend a month in Vevey this summer."

He signalled the driver with a little kick, and the door closed. The carriage set off.

On the road back to St. Petersburg, near the city gates, a

woman—the former fiancée of Grégoire Semenof, who had been waiting for this moment for fifteen years—threw a bomb into the prince's carriage. They were all blown to bits: the horses, the driver, the elderly man who was peacefully smelling his roses, along with the assassin herself.

CHAPTER 15

COURILOF LEARNED OF the assassination that same evening. We were at dinner. One of the officers in the prince's entourage came in. As soon as Courilof heard the sound of the sabre striking the paving stones, he seemed to guess something terrible had happened. He jumped in fright, so suddenly that he dropped the glass of wine he was holding; it crashed against the leg of the table. But almost immediately, he regained control of himself, stood up and went out without saying a word. Marguerite Eduardovna followed him.

That night I could clearly see his window from my room. His lights were on, and I watched him pace slowly back and forth until morning. I saw his shadow go over to the windows, peer out, turn slowly around, disappear into the other side of the room, then come back into view.

The next day, when he saw me, he just murmured weakly, "Have you heard . . ."

"Yes."

He brought his hand to his head, looking at me with his wide, pale eyes.

"I knew him for thirty years," he finally said.

That was all. Then he quickly turned away and made a weary gesture.

"Well, there you have it . . . It's over."

The next day I received a message from Fanny, which both surprised and worried me, for she was not supposed to take such risks, and it had been agreed she would contact me only to set the date for Courilof's assassination.

She asked me to meet her in Pavlovsk, about an hour outside St. Petersburg, in front of the Kursaal Concert Hall.

There was a piano and violin recital in Pavlovsk. We met in the entrance, where a great crowd of people were silently listening to music by Schumann. I can still remember those bright, rapid chords.

Fanny had once again disguised herself as a kind of peasant. I told her rather angrily that we were involved in a game that was theatrical and distasteful enough without making it even more complicated and dangerous with elaborate costumes. Afterwards, in fact, my long experience as a revolutionary taught me that nothing is more likely to destroy a mission than excessive precautions. Beneath her red head-scarf, her long Jewish nose and thick lips would have betrayed her more surely than her real passport. But there was a large crowd; no one saw her, or they thought she was a servant.

We went out into the grounds, where the mist, at dusk, was as thick as a cloud. We sat down on a bench. The fog surrounded us like a dense wall: two steps away, a yew tree was half hidden by a damp, thick, white haze, like the milky sap that comes out of certain types of plants when you cut their stems. Even the air had the sweet scent of foliage, a sickly smell that irritated my throat.

I was coughing. Fanny, annoyed, removed the red scarf from her head.

"Bad news, comrade. Lydie Frankel, who was keeping the dynamite in her house, was killed in an explosion. In Geneva, they decided to hand over that part of the mission to me. I'll get hold of the bombs when we need them. The assassination will probably be set for autumn. I have some letters for you from Switzerland."

I took the letters, automatically putting them into my pocket.

Fanny laughed nervously. "Are you really going to keep those letters in your overcoat so they can fall into the hands of the informers? Read them, then burn them."

I read them; they contained nothing of consequence. Nevertheless, I set fire to them with my cigarette and scattered the ashes about. Fanny leaned towards me.

"Is it true," she asked eagerly, "is it true, comrade, that you saw Prince Nelrode a few hours before he died?"

"It's true."

She questioned me in a low, muffled voice. A savage, doleful flame lit up her green eyes. I said I'd heard the prince and the minister talking to each other.

She listened to me in silence, but I could see what she was thinking in her eyes. She had come closer and was staring at me.

"What?" she finally said.

She stopped; she seemed unable to find words to express her horror.

"What did they say?"

She drew back nervously. By then, the fog had become so dense that Fanny's face was half hidden in the mist. I could hear her voice quivering with passion and hatred. As for me, I was tired and annoyed. She pressed me to answer her questions. I angrily told her that in my opinion, they had said a few reasonable things but also talked a lot of nonsense. Yet I could see it was useless to explain to her how these two politicians, who were feared and hated—with their faults, their insensitivity, and their dreams—had seemed as imperfect and unhappy as anyone, including me. She would have read an obscure, secret meaning into my words that they didn't contain.

Meanwhile, the music had stopped; the crowd came out of the concert hall and slowly dispersed along the paths through the grounds. We went our separate ways.

CHAPTER 16

IT JUST SO happened that the day the widow Aarontchik—the elderly Jewess recommended by Marguerite Eduardovna—came to visit, I was in Courilof's room. He wasn't feeling well; his wife asked me to firmly cut the interview short if I thought he was getting weak or tired. Four days had passed since the assassination. No business had been carried out since then. Courilof spent half of each day at the prince's residence, beside the coffin that contained his mangled remains, with priests who recited prayers imploring peace for the dead man's soul; the rest of the time, Courilof went to church.

Finally, on the fifth day, the funeral took place.

Several supposed accomplices of the female assassin had been arrested. Courilof wanted to be present when these "monsters, these wolves in sheep's clothing," as he called them, were all interrogated. Afterwards, two of them were hanged.

Courilof came home exhausted; he said nothing, except when he was shouting at the servants or employees at the ministry. Only with me did he remain patient and courteous. He seemed to actually feel a kind of sympathy towards me.

The audience granted to the widow Aarontchik had been delayed like all the others. Courilof received her in an enormous room I'd never been in before, full of portraits of the Emperor and mementos of Pobiedonostsef and Alexander III, all in glass frames and labelled like jars in a pharmacy. A dazzling light came in through the half-closed, enormous scarlet curtains; they looked stained with fresh blood. He made a savage picture that was striking to behold: his pale, motionless face above the white linen jacket of his uniform, decorations around its collar, others pinned at the side; his hand rested on the table with its heavy gold wedding band, adorned with a red stone that caught the light.

A small, thin woman was shown in; she was shaking. She had white hair, a bony, angular face, a nose like a beak. She was dressed in mourning clothes that looked tarnished in the sunlight. She took three steps forward, then stopped, dumbstruck.

The minister spoke to her in a deep, low, quiet voice, the one he sometimes used with inferiors who'd been recommended to him.

"You are the widow Sarah Aarontchik," he asked, "of the Jewish faith?"

"Yes," she whispered.

Her hands were visibly shaking; she clasped them in front of her and stood motionless.

"Come closer."

She didn't seem to understand; she looked up at him, blinking, her eyes full of resignation and a kind of holy terror.

His eyes were lowered, his head thrown back; he was absent-mindedly tapping an open letter on the table, waiting for her to speak.

She remained silent.

"Come now, Madame," he called out. "You did ask for an audience, didn't you? You wanted to speak to me. What did you want to say?"

"Your Excellency," she murmured, "I met your wife, Marguerite Eduardovna . . ."

"Yes, yes," he interrupted curtly. "That has nothing to do with the business that brings you here, I presume?"

"No," she stammered.

"Well then, get to the point, Madame. My time is precious."

"The Jacques Aarontchik case, Your Excellency."

He gestured that he knew all about it.

As she said no more, he sighed, picked up a file, leafed through it for a moment and quickly read out loud: "I, the undersigned . . . denounce Pierre Mazourtchik, junior supervisor . . . Hmm! . . . Hmm! . . . Guilty of having corrupted my son . . ."

He smiled faintly, took another statement from the table and read out loud:

" 'I, the undersigned, Vladimirenko, teacher in the secondary school at . . . denounce one Jacques Aarontchik, of Jewish faith, aged sixteen, guilty of having incited revolution and subversive acts in his classmates.' Do you accept these facts as true?"

"Your Excellency, my unfortunate child was the victim of an agent provocateur. I thought I had done the right thing, I denounced his tutor, Mazourtchik, who was making him read these books and things... I'm just a widow, a poor woman. I didn't know, I couldn't know..."

"No one is reproaching you for anything," said Courilof; his icy, haughty tone stopped the woman dead. "What is it that you want?"

"I didn't know I was dealing with one of Your Excellency's agents. He also denounced my son. I am just a poor widow."

I looked at her hands clasped in front of her; they were dirty, with furrows as deep as wounds. It made a horrible impression, and I saw that Courilof was also looking at them, shuddering, but somewhat fascinated. Her hands weren't marked by some rare disease, but by doing the washing, the housework, by boiling water, by old age.

The minister frowned, and I watched his heavy, impatient hands pushing the files about on the table.

"Your son has been expelled," he said at last. "I will look into the matter to see if there is reason to believe in his sincere repentance, and I will authorise him to continue his studies, if he proves himself worthy. Up until now, he was the best student at the school, as I can see from his reports, and given his young age... In any case, you have made this great journey, despite being elderly and all alone; if you will be responsible for your son, for his political opinions..." he said, his voice becoming more and more dry and nervous.

She said nothing. He nodded, indicating that the audience was over.

Then, for the first time, she looked at him.

"Your Excellency, excuse me, but he's dead now."

"Who's dead?" asked Courilof.

"He is... my little... Jacques..."

"What? Your son?"

"He killed himself, two months ago, Your Excellency, out of de... despair," she mumbled.

And suddenly, she began to cry. She cried in a humble, vile way, with a snorting sound that made you feel sick. Her tiny face, dark red, was suddenly covered in tears; her shrivelled, trembling mouth was wet, gaping, hanging open on one side from the violence of her sobbing.

The more she cried, the more Courilof's face grew heavier, paler.

"When did he die?" he finally asked in his harsh, ringing voice, even though the woman had already told him; but he seemed confused. He spoke automatically, rapidly.

"Two months ago," she said again.

"Well then, why have you come to see me?"

"To ask for help. He was going to help me, he was about to finish school. He was already earning fifteen roubles a month. Now, I'm all alone. I still have three young children to raise, Your Excellency. Jacques killed himself because he was expelled from school over a mistake. I've brought a letter with me from the head teacher, saying it was clearly a mistake, that the papers and books taken from my son's room had been planted there by Mazourtchik . . . by Your Excellency's agent, because we couldn't pay him the hundred roubles he was demanding. I have all the facts here, the dates, the confession of the guilty party."

She offered the papers to the minister, who held them in two fingers as if they were rags, then threw them down on the table without even looking at them.

"If I have understood correctly, you are accusing me of your son's death."

"Your Excellency, I'm just asking for help. He was only sixteen. You are a father, Your Excellency."

She was shaking and panting so violently that she could barely get the words out of her mouth.

"But why the hell have you come to me?" he suddenly shouted. "Because of your son? Is there anything I can do about your son? He's dead, God has his soul! There you have it. Get out of here, you have no right coming here and bothering me with your sad story, do you understand?" he thundered. "Get out of here!"

He was shouting, beside himself, his eyes filled with a kind of terror; he struck everything on the table so hard that the letters fell to the floor.

The elderly Jewess turned very pale. She started to move, then suddenly, we heard her humble, persistent voice once again: "Just a little help, Your Excellency; you're a father..."

I looked at Courilof and saw him wave her away. "Go," he said. "Leave your address at the ministry. I'll send you some money."

Suddenly he threw his head back against the chair and started to laugh. "Go!"

She left. He continued laughing; a sad, nervous laugh that echoed strangely.

"Vile old woman, old fool," he kept saying, trembling with anger and disgust. "So then, we're going to pay her for her son...Do such creatures deserve any pity?"

I didn't reply and he closed his eyes, as he often did, weary all of a sudden.

I tried to imagine his thoughts. But when he opened his eyes, his face was impenetrable once more. I remember thinking about the elderly Jewess; her absurd gesture had revealed such depths of despair, ignorance, and poverty. And on that day, I don't know why, but for the first time the idea of murdering this pompous fool filled me with horror.

CHAPTER 17

A FEW DAYS passed, and the story of the elderly Jewess began to bear bitter fruit. I don't know if it was because Courilof's sadness over the death of the prince was magnified by his anxiety over his own fate. I don't think so: he was too wrapped up in himself to realise how very useful the elderly man had been to him, how the prestige of Nelrode's name was enough to put an end to certain conspiracies against him. Nevertheless, around that time, on several occasions he would say: "He was faithful to his friends. He was a loyal man, you could count on his word. That is very rare in life, young man . . . You'll see."

If he still had any illusions, however, the arrival of the first anonymous letters quickly made them vanish.

Up until then, Dahl's fears of displeasing the prince had kept him from campaigning against the minister, whose post he desired for himself. With the prince gone, the game began.

Dahl rushed to tell everyone at court that the Minister of Education had been threatened by an elderly Jewess from Lodz with scandalous revelations about "the beautiful Margot's past."

"She used to live in Lodz, when she was a second-rate actress in a touring company," Dahl said. "This woman, a former midwife, had secretly given her an abortion, and after learning of Margot's excellent marriage, she had come to St. Petersburg to blackmail the minister." As proof, he pointed to the sum of money that Courilof had, in fact, sent to the old Jewess. Suddenly all the old stories about Marguerite Eduardovna resurfaced; they had been discreetly whispered around the city at the time of her marriage, and now they were openly discussed. Without a doubt, some of them were true, based entirely on fact; no one could deny her youthful indiscretions or her affair with Nelrode. Public opinion deemed it scandalous.

"An ugly, filthy business," said Dahl in disgust.

They were saying that she still had lovers, protected by Courilof, as he himself had been protected by his predecessor: "It's her good nature. She happily uses her great influence over her husband to protect her former lovers and numerous admirers in the two most prestigious regiments in the army, the Horse-guards and the Preobrazhensky Guards."

That, however, was partly true. But they also accused her of being the mistress of Hippolyte, Courilof's nephew, whom she couldn't stand; and, finally, of procuring young girls for her elderly husband, because she was "a loving wife." That was just as absurd as the rumour Fanny spread about "the infamous orgies in the house at the Iles."

I was truly astonished that anyone who actually knew the minister could believe such idle gossip. Poor Courilof—pious, conscientious, cowardly, and prudent—was entirely incapable of carrying out such deeds. Nevertheless, he wasn't a man of "flaw-less morals," as Froelich would have put it. Courilof's private life was as uneventful as any ordinary Swiss citizen's, but it probably hadn't always been that way. He was hot-blooded and extremely passionate. These days he no longer indulged himself, and hadn't for many years—undoubtedly due to religious scruples and because he had to be prudent. But he found it particularly odious to see his enemies guessing the secret weaknesses he forced him-self to overcome. I was never able to understand one element of his character: a mixture of sincere puritanism and deceitfulness. As for the rest—well, I found him quite transparent.

After a while, the press got hold of the widow Aarontchik's story. The extreme right accused Courilof of "liberalism," of "giving in to revolutionary ideas," because he had given money to the mother of a suspicious Jew. On the other hand, revolution-ary newspapers edited abroad reported that this woman's son had been murdered by policemen, agents provocateurs paid by Courilof, in order to destroy papers that might compromise the careers of certain highly placed members of the teaching profession.

The Emperor allowed it to continue. He hated Courilof, as much as such a weak man could experience any strong feelings. He'd heard details of certain unfortunate things his minister had said; he guessed that Courilof wished to one day see Grand Duke Michael, the Emperor's brother, on the throne. (Prince Alexis, heir to the throne, hadn't been born yet, but the Emperor and Empress had an unshakable belief that they would one day have a son.)

Finally, owing to Courilof's regular tactlessness, he had a falling out with his colleague from the Home Office as well; its director could not forgive Courilof for having criticised one of his men. Morning, noon, and night, masses of letters and newspapers from varying political affiliations landed on Courilof's desk; all of them hostile to him.

Marguerite Eduardovna did her best to remove them, but by some strange fate, despite all the precautions she took, every one landed in her husband's hands. He never read them in front of us and, sometimes, openly threw them away. But he couldn't prevent his gaze from immediately moving towards the title of the item underlined in blue pencil. He would gesture for one of the servants and say, "Burn this filth."

And as they collected up the scattered papers, he stared at the pages with burning curiosity. His large, pale eyes almost popping out of his head, he looked like an animal strangled by two strong hands, being choked to death. Finally, when the servant left, carrying away the stack of letters, Courilof would turn towards us and say: "Dinner's ready! Come along!"

The children spoke quietly, but he remained silent, looking at each of us absent-mindedly, without actually seeing us; sometimes, he couldn't control the way his lips trembled slightly. He then spoke quickly, enunciating each word in a hateful, scornful manner, his voice growing more and more scathing and shrill. At other times, he fell into a deep dream, sighed, gently reached out to his son who sat at his side, and stroked his hair.

On those days, he was more patient and in a better mood than usual. He resigned himself to putting up with the boiling hot compresses that Langenberg had ordered me to place on his liver. It was as if he were offering his physical pain up to God and asking in return that he quash his enemies.

CHAPTER 18

I WENT INTO his room every morning to treat him, as soon as he was awake. He was stretched out on a chaise-longue in front of the open window, wearing a scarlet silk dressing-gown that made his cheeks look pale and puffy. For some time now, his wild beard had been going grey. The yellowish colour of his skin, the deep purple bags under his eyes, and the two delicate bruises that appeared at the sides of his nose were evidence of the progress of his disease. He had lost weight, he was melting away; his heavy, yellowish flesh hung on him like a piece of oversized clothing. This was obvious only when he was naked; once he was dressed, his uniform, with its decorations across his chest, became a kind of imaginary breast-plate.

It was obvious that Langenberg's hot compresses had about as much effect on his cancer as they would on a corpse.

Every morning, his son came to see him. He would hold the boy, stroke him, gently place his large hand on the boy's forehead, push his hair back, lightly pull his long ears. He treated him with deep and unique tenderness; he seemed afraid of hurting him, of touching him too roughly. But then he would say, "Just look at how strong he is, don't you think, Monsieur Legrand? Off you go, my boy . . ."

With his daughter, the public Courilof re-emerged: cold, impassive, giving orders without raising his voice. In spite of myself, I felt an aversion to Irène Valerianovna. But I liked the married couple, the Killer Whale and his old tart; they moved me, I don't know why.

Now, as I write, I walk back and forth, remembering; it remains impossible for me to explain, even to myself, how I could intimately understand these two people. Could it be because I lived in an abstract world all my life, in a "glass cage"? For the first time, I saw human beings: unhappy people with ambitions, faults, foolishness. But I haven't got time to think about those things! I just want to concentrate on what happened back then, that moment buried in my memory . . . Anything is better than sitting and doing nothing, waiting to die. Look at the work done by the Party: what Karl Marx brought to the workers, the translations of Lenin's writings, the Communist Doctrine, all doled out in instalments to the local Bolshevik middle classes! I did what I could. But I'm ill, I'm tired of it all. These old memories are less tiring. They numb me, preventing my memory from lingering on futile recollections of war and conquest, on everything that will never again return—at least, not for me.

I recall that Courilof went to the court one day around that time, when some foreign sovereign or other notable was there to be received. Courilof could hardly stand up: two servants dressed him, flitting around him and pinning his decorations on his chest, stuffing him into his dress uniform. He wore a kind of corset that tied at the back, to support the diseased portion of his body underneath his clothes. I was in the next room and could hear him panting in pain as they tightened the corset.

He got into the carriage, looking stiff and pompous, sparkling with gold. They left.

He came back around dusk; when I heard Marguerite Eduardovna scream, I immediately rushed out. I thought he'd passed out. He didn't get out of the car himself but rather was carried out by servants and brought to the house. To my great surprise, this relatively calm and patient man flew into a rage when one of the servants accidentally knocked against his arm, started swearing and hitting him.

The servant, who had a simple, kind face beneath the cap of his uniform, went white with terror and stood motionless, as if he were at attention, looking straight ahead. His wide, horrified eyes fixed on his master, with the same dumbfounded look you see in cattle.

Courilof seemed struck himself at the sound of his own slap. He stopped. I could see his lips moving, as the look on the valet's face rekindled his fury. He shook his fist, shouted "Get out of here, you good-for-nothing bastard!," let out a thunderous curse in Russian, then collapsed; he didn't actually faint, he just fell into a heap like an animal dying of rabies. His neck moved like a bull's does when it's trying to shake off the sharp spears digging into its flanks. He got up with great difficulty. Pushing us away, he staggered up the stairs. Marguerite Eduardovna and I followed him up to his room. He tore off his collar. He couldn't stop whimpering. It wasn't until he was in bed and his wife was stroking his forehead that he began to calm down. I left them like that: she sat at his bedside, talking to him quietly; he had his eyes closed, his entire face twitching nervously.

I thought he would want me to stay that night to keep an eye on him, as he always did when he was ill; but he seemed afraid he might say something he shouldn't. He didn't send for me. Only his wife stayed by his side.

When I saw her the next day, I asked about the minister's health. She made an effort to smile. "Oh! It was nothing," she said over and over again. "It was nothing, nothing at all . . ."

She shook her head, her lips trembling, then looked straight at me with her deep, wide eyes. "If only he could rest for a few months . . . We could go and live in Paris for a while . . . Paris, in the spring, when the chestnut trees are in bloom . . . Don't you think! Do you know Paris?"

She fell silent.

"Men are ambitious," she said suddenly, with a sigh.

Later, I found out what happened when Courilof saw the Emperor at court; at least, I heard what Courilof's enemies were saying. The Emperor had received his minister while nervously fiddling with the pencils on his desk. This was how people close to him knew they had fallen from favour. When they arrived, before saying a word to them and without looking up, Nicolas II would start automatically arranging the files and other items on his desk.

Rumour had it that the Emperor had said, word for word: "You know that I do not meddle in your private life, but you could at least try to avoid scandals."

Later on, it occurred to me that the Emperor wouldn't have needed to say even that much; his disapproval would have been infinitely more subtle, less obvious, perhaps barely visible to the naked eye, a hint of coldness in his voice, the Empress looking away . . .

The next day, someone mentioned the visit of the foreign sovereign in front of me.

"His Majesty deigned to forget I was there," Courilof said bitterly. "He failed to introduce me to the king."

There was a silence. Everyone understood what that meant. In fact, for some time now, the Killer Whale's position had been precarious. A strange joy ran through me.

"Well, to hell with it!" I thought. "Let him go away, let him give up his job as minister and live in peace until the cancer kills him!"

The idea of killing this man filled me with repulsion and horror. He was a blind creature already living in the shadow of death; his face looked ghostly, yet he was still preoccupied with vain dreams and futile ambitions. How many times during that period did he say over and over again: "Russia will forget my enemies, but she will not forget me."

It seemed strange, grotesque even, to think that he had already forgotten about the men who owed their deaths to his inability to give lucid orders in time; or to the system of espionage he had instituted. He still believed posterity would judge him by his good deeds, that posterity would be forced to choose between him, that bastard Dahl, and the rest of the other idiots!

I remember . . . We were sitting on a bench in the garden: Courilof, his wife, and his daughter, who listened to him without really paying attention, her delicate, childlike face closed and impenetrable. You could tell she was very far away for the moment, in a day-dreaming world where worries about her father had no place. When he'd stopped talking, she continued to play absent-mindedly with the long gold necklace she wore. He turned, looked at her, and frowned sadly in annoyance. Little Ivan was running about, calling the dogs; you could hear him panting; he was fat and easily became short of breath.

I watched thick clouds of mosquitoes rise above the dark waters in the bay. Everyone around me seemed just like those mosquitoes; they hovered over the marshes, restless in the wind, tormenting people, only to disappear, the devil knows why!

CHAPTER 19

IRÈNE VALERIANOVNA'S BIRTHDAY was in June. Towards the middle of the month, they began to prepare for the ball at Courilof's house. The minister wanted to invite the Emperor and Empress in order to show his enemies that in spite of everything, he was solidly established in his post and loved at court. No one was completely blind to his scheme, but it did, nevertheless, make a good impression.

The Emperor's coldness had not yet been followed by any hostile acts towards his minister. A large sum of money had silenced the reactionary press a bit; as for the liberal newspapers, they continued moaning, but to Courilof, they were of no consequence.

I thought that Marguerite Eduardovna was going to leave St. Petersburg before the ball. Every day I expected to see her go; but no, she stayed, though not to take care of the arrangements. It was the minister himself who took care of all the preparations. His complexion was pale; he looked at everyone and everything anxiously, with a harsh and defiant expression on his face.

One day I took a chance and again followed Dahl and the Killer Whale into the garden, where they were talking. Dahl looked his most evil self. He watched Courilof in silence, a smirk on his thin, tight lips.

At one point I think they heard me behind them: the gravel was crunching beneath my feet. Courilof seemed impatient. But as soon as they were sitting down, I hid behind the manicured hedges and kept still. They forgot about me.

"My dear Valerian Alexandrovitch," I heard Dahl say. "Since you do not wish to offend your family and acquaintances by excluding them, and as it would be unacceptable, on the other hand, to expect Their Majesties to mingle with your relatives and friends, why don't you organise an entertainment in the

Malachite Room, just for the princes, the very high aristocracy, and the ladies?"

"Do you think so?" the Killer Whale said, sounding doubtful.

"Yes I do."

"Perhaps . . . Yes, it's an ingenious solution . . . Perhaps."

They fell silent.

"My dear friend," Courilof began.

Dahl nodded, smiling. "I am completely at your service, my friend."

"You know that Their Majesties have not come to my house since my first wife died."

"Since your second marriage, yes, I know, my friend."

"To invite them, now, I feel . . . would be rather difficult. I . . . Who could I send to put out feelers? What do you think? I have a list of women who specialise in this type of mission. On the other hand, I've heard that Her Imperial Highness hardly ever goes out at present; it would be very painful, as you can imagine, to suffer a refusal."

He read the names on his list to Dahl. At each one, Dahl interrupted him with a little snigger, gently touching his arm: "No . . . no . . . not her . . . Her behaviour . . . His Majesty expressed disapproval of her . . . That one is divorced, and the suggestion of immorality in her actions, even though she might have been wrongly accused, has upset Her Imperial Highness. You simply would not believe, my friend, the extent to which the court is leaning towards a sense of austerity that borders on puritanism. Do you understand?"

"I understand."

The baron said no more and looked at the Killer Whale with an expression that was both severe and mocking.

"It's the trend, my friend." He shrugged his shoulders. Each of his looks seemed to say: *You do see what I mean*; his smile looked as though it meant: *You can guess, I suppose, to whom I am referring, to the fragility of your position.*

Carefully lowering their voices, they started talking about Courilof's daughter as a possible wife for the young Anatole Dahl.

"An alliance between us would be valuable," said Courilof,

sounding sly and frightened. "I like your son... Of course, they're still children."

"Yes," said Dahl, coldly. "He's a good boy. But he's very young and so innocent! He needs some time to experience life, to sow his wild oats." He said this last bit in French, forcing a little laugh.

"Of course, of course," murmured Courilof. "Nevertheless..."

His words were measured, full of tact and paternal dignity; but how much fear, how much impatience made him shudder inside. He was, quite simply, offering Dahl his daughter as if she were a sacrifice to the angry gods. I knew that the young woman was extremely wealthy: the first Madame Courilof had left her entire fortune to her children; and the minister too had handed over his own portion to them when he had married Marguerite Eduardovna. I have never known anyone as clumsy in his generosity.

Dahl's unexpected reservations about a potential marriage confirmed to me that his attitude towards Courilof was firmly entrenched, even more so than Courilof thought. I remember that I was listening attentively when suddenly, I threw my head back and looked out at the peaceful bay, up at the sky. I felt an extraordinary hunger for an insignificant, bourgeois, peaceful life, far from the rest of the world.

Nevertheless, Dahl and the Killer Whale finally agreed on the name of some woman or other, a friend of the Empress.

"She's a good woman and is experienced at such missions," said Dahl.

Courilof sighed. "Do you really think Their Majesties will deign to come?"

"I'll see what I can do," Dahl promised, wearily and rather regally shaking his head.

"Alas! I do not have the good fortune of being in favour with my venerable Empress."

"Of course you do, of course you do," the baron muttered. "Her Majesty is a woman, after all" (he seemed to be apologising, by a slight hesitation in his voice, for attaching such a common word to the sacred name of the Empress); "she is highly strung, with a very Germanic frankness, unable to keep her thoughts to herself. She has a good heart: too good, perhaps, too noble, for the petty concerns of our times."

"Of course," Courilof replied warmly. "No one, if I may say so" (this way of expressing himself seemed to please him), "no one in the world adores and reveres Her Imperial Majesty as I do. Nevertheless, Mathieu Iliitch, I do believe that she does not like me. I must have offended her, without meaning to, I assure you, or perhaps hurt her feelings. Being a queen does not make her less of a woman, as you have so rightly said."

"Sometimes, it's even regrettable," Dahl hissed, his voice full of insinuation.

Then they began to exchange views on various members of the court and the sovereigns. The conversation lasted rather a long time.

"Mathieu Iliitch," Courilof suddenly said, "you are the one whom Her Majesty has judged worthy of reporting certain of her thoughts to me, regarding the presence of my wife at the ball. Would you please be so kind as to tell her . . ."

He stopped for a moment and I could hear his voice breaking, a tremor of fear and courage beneath his pompous statements.

"Please could you tell her that Marguerite Eduardovna, that *my wife*, will not be leaving St. Petersburg and that she will not do so until she has paid her respects to her sovereigns?"

Dahl hesitated for a split second. "Absolutely, my dear friend."

"I'm tired of all this uncertainty. I wish *my wife*" (once again, he stressed the words), "*my wife* to be treated by everyone with the respect that my own name should guarantee her. I have thought about this for a long time, Mathieu Iliitch. If I give in this time, it will start all over again in some other way. I know very well that the persecution from which I am suffering began the day when I insisted on presenting my wife at court. I know that . . . But I wish the situation to be clear. If the Emperor refuses to come, I will know that it is impossible for me to remain in my post. I would happily resign; I'm ill, I'm tired."

A long silence followed.

"All right, my dear friend," Dahl said again.

Then they parted. Dahl left; Courilof remained sitting on the bench, two feet away from me. I could see him perfectly clearly.

It was a hot, hazy day; those small flies you get in summer were buzzing around. Courilof's face was pale and still. At one point he let out a long, deep sigh that sounded as if it came truly from the very depths of his heart. I watched him for a long time. Finally, he stood up. He walked slowly to the end of the small path, flicking at the gravel in front of him with the end of his cane; he looked weary and pensive. But as soon as he came to the wide, straight road that led to the house, my Courilof stood up tall, stuck out his chest, and continued along with a stiff, pompous stride. It was the posture of a man accustomed to walking through two rows of people as they bowed down.

CHAPTER 20

OVER THE NEXT few days, the house began to resemble a buzzing hive. Partitions were knocked down, wall hangings nailed up.

As far as I can remember, the Empress made everyone wait a long time for a response. Courilof became more and more nervous. From morning until night, he paced back and forth through the house, his heavy footsteps resonating against the parquet flooring. He was impatient, behaved harshly towards his secretaries and servants. I especially recall his hostility and indifference when he spoke to his daughter. Sometimes he furtively watched Marguerite Eduardovna. I imagined he was contemplating the importance of his political ambitions, comparing them to his love for her. Each time, he wore a kind of resigned smile, an expression of profound gentleness; then he would turn away and sigh.

Meanwhile, Fanny waited for me every night at the little gate to the grounds and told me about the harassment in the universities, the disturbances crushed with unbelievable violence, the students who'd been arrested and deported. I remember a strange feeling: her voice shook with hatred while Courilof's pale face haunted me. There was no difference. The students were right; so was Courilof. Every human insect thought only of himself: of his pathetic, threatened existence, hated and scorned by everyone else. It was legitimate . . . but I understood them all too well. There were no rules any more. God demands blind faith from his creations.

More time passed and still the Empress did not reply. Nevertheless, there was a continual rush of florists and upholsterers to the house. For some time, they had discussed organising a celebration at night in the gardens.

As I said, the grounds in front of the house led down to the water, a sad little northern bay, surrounded by pine trees and brambles. Courilof, it seemed, wanted to build a stage and have costumed musicians performing. But all these niceties were completely alien to his nature. His nephew, Hippolyte Courilof, was helping him. Courilof never knew his nephew's reputation, nor how badly it reflected on him. He did his best to help the boy advance in his career. It was mainly because of him that Courilof was accused of nepotism, to the detriment of the state.

"*He* doesn't steal," people said, "but it's us ordinary people who lose out. He gets posts for all his close relatives, his cousins, his brothers, and *they* all steal!"

The first Madame Courilof had raised the boy, who'd been orphaned very young, and the minister scrupulously continued to carry out all his dead wife's former wishes. In his first wife's room, which remained intact, was an enormous portrait of Hippolyte Courilof as a child, his long, pallid face framed by a mass of golden curls. It was part of the minister's character, this foolish loyalty, his unswerving honesty; such actions eased his conscience, but also led him to commit masses of blunders that caused enormous fiascos.

Every evening, he and the minister would go down to the riverbank together, to measure the land, discuss where the musicians should set up, or the colour of the paper lanterns.

Hippolyte Nicolaévitch ran along the water's edge, waving his arms, pointing to the bay.

"Just picture it, Uncle, the sea in the distance, lit up in the moonlight, the delicious perfume of the flowers, the music, muted by the water, the women in their beautiful dresses, a true Watteau painting!"

He pronounced the letter "r" deeply, as they do in French, raising his chubby white hands up high. He was a hunchback without the hump; his chest was extremely round and his long, pale face sat low on his neck.

"It will be very expensive, of course," he added casually. "Leave it to me."

Dusk was extraordinarily desolate in these sad islands. I remember the falling rain splashing against the calm surface of the bay. The setting sun hovered above the horizon until morning, a circle of dull, smoky red, engulfed in mist.

Courilof listened gloomily and often called out to me: "What do you think, Monsieur Legrand? You don't say much, but you have good taste. What colour do you think the paper lanterns should be? Green?"

He didn't listen to what I said, though; he just stood there watching the still water and then walked back, sighing.

Finally, Courilof decided to go and ask for the Emperor's reply himself and give him the guest list for approval, if he agreed to attend. I accompanied the minister to the Winter Palace that day. When he got into the carriage, he saw all the people who'd come to ask favours waiting in the courtyard. They'd been there since morning; the rain had pushed them back under an awning, like a herd of sheep. When the Killer Whale appeared, they hesitantly took three steps forward. The minister waved his hand wearily. Two servants appeared.

"Out! Get going!"

In a flash, they had pushed the masses of waiting people back and closed the gate. Courilof, gloomy and preoccupied, got into the carriage, gesturing for me to follow him. It was rather funny: he too got a bad reception that day . . . the Emperor was tired; the Empress was ill . . .

I waited for a long time in front of the palace, in the stifling heat of the enclosed little carriage. Then we retraced our steps back to the Iles.

He huddled in the corner, silently staring into space. Sometimes he would tell the driver to go faster by making a dry little clicking noise, but as soon as the horses began to gallop, he'd get annoyed and swear at the coachman. Then we'd slow down again. It was raining harder and harder. It's strange how well I understood the Killer Whale's "feelings." And still, it was difficult to guess the emotions that ran through him beneath his armour, his stony look. I sensed his emotions in a strange way, one that gave me both a feeling of satisfaction and a kind of contentment that was almost physical. Later on, when I escaped from prison in Siberia, I used to hunt for food along the road; as I stalked my prey, I remember sensing it quiver in the same way.

The heat, a steamy torrent, seemed to rise up from the earth. He was clearly dying to talk to me; but the poor fool was always afraid that a single look or gesture would be enough to give him away. "We're just slaves in fancy clothing," he finally said, bitterly.

I didn't reply, and he also fell silent, looked away to watch the waves of rain streaming down the windows. We'd gone past St. Petersburg's city limits. We took a large avenue lined with trees; their leaves were soaking wet and the raindrops fell from them noisily, with a sharp, metallic sound.

At one point, the horse shied. I glanced at Courilof. For a man who was usually absolutely in control of himself, every shout in the street, jolt, or the sound of glass shattering made him wince involuntarily. Almost immediately afterwards, his face would freeze into a look of icy calm. I felt something akin to pleasure in witnessing these nervous reactions, as they proved he was obsessed with the thought of being assassinated.

That day, he noticed nothing. He didn't stiffen; his body swayed with the carriage's movements as it was thrown to one side, veered off course by a stone. When I asked, "Did that hurt?" he seemed to awaken from a dream. I could see his pale, sagging face, his half-closed eyes.

"No," he said.

Then he shook his head.

"It's strange. I feel better. I feel less pain when my mind is on all these problems."

I said nothing.

"The higher a man's position," he sighed, "the heavier it seems the cross he must bear."

"But you're tired, aren't you?" I said. "Why don't you retire? Marguerite Eduardovna . . ."

He cut in. "I can't. This is my life."

He fell silent and we continued on our way home.

The idea of music along the riverbank had been abandoned. Courilof decided to have the entertainment in the Malachite Room, as Dahl had suggested. The Emperor and Empress had ended up vaguely agreeing to come, but it was possible they might cancel at any time. Nevertheless, the invitations were sent out.

The Malachite Room took up half of the first floor; it was

here that a stage was set up. A few days before the ball, I went in and found Courilof watching one of the rehearsals. A young woman was dressed as a shepherdess in the style of Louis XV; she was playing an antique instrument, a sort of bagpipe that made the sharp, shrill sound of a fife. All the furniture had been removed; all that remained was the enormous Venetian glass chandelier, its crystals chiming to echo the music.

Courilof listened, his wide, pale eyes almost popping out of his head. He paid his compliments to the musician, and finally the woman left. We stood alone in the middle of the stage. I noticed with surprise that the bare boards used to make the stage had been badly assembled. They looked as if they might collapse under the slightest weight. I pointed this out to Courilof. He looked through me, as though coming out of a trance, and said nothing.

"Look at how flimsy this is," I said again.

All of a sudden, he clenched his teeth; a look of blind fury came over his face. "Well, that's fine! Just fine! Lord! If only they would all go to hell! Disappear into a hole in the ground!" He pulled himself together but still seemed worried. "Don't take any notice of me, I'm not well, I'm nervous."

He walked away from me, went over to the window, looked outside for a long time without saying a word, then left the room.

CHAPTER 21

AS I RECALL, the ball was at the end of June.

That night, I went out for a walk through the Iles. I liked those clear nights. I could see the royal carriages, one after the other, driving down the wide avenues. I caught a glimpse of the most extraordinary faces through the carriage windows: women with thin, pinched features, covered in jewels, like religious relics, tiaras shimmering on their foreheads; men whose uniforms gleamed strangely, speckled with diamonds and gold. The odd light cast by the summer night made them look like ghosts from a dream.

Afterwards, when I was head of the Special Police, I remember I used to interrogate suspects on such nights; they were brought to me in groups and then executed at dawn. I can picture their pale faces, the evening light that fell on their features, their eyes staring into mine. Some of them were so exhausted that they seemed indifferent to everything; they answered my questions with a weary little sneer. Very few of them fought for their lives. They just allowed themselves to be taken away and massacred without saying a word. A revolution is such a slaughterhouse! Is it really worth it? Nothing's really worth the trouble; it's true, not even life.

I walked towards the gardens, opened the gate and immediately ran into Courilof. He had come outside to check on the police surrounding the house. Everywhere you turned was a policeman in civilian clothing hiding behind a tree.

"What are you doing out here, Monsieur Legrand? Come inside, you'll see how wonderful everything looks." He forced me to go back into the house. Through the open windows, I could see the dazzling lights in the Malachite Room shining down brightly on the women fluttering their fans; in the front row were the Emperor and the princes.

Courilof looked up and listened for a moment, frowning. "Can you hear that?" he said quietly. "Bach."

The calm, heavy music seemed to float very high above us. I listened with him. The famous R. was playing. I do not really like music, since I am not really interested in the arts in general. I only enjoy Bach and Haydn.

"Their Highnesses have arrived," Courilof said. "This is undoubtedly the first time you've seen them, isn't it? There's the Empress and, beside her, the Emperor himself. What venerable nobility shines from the faces of these absolute masters of our great Russia," he continued, adopting his usual solemn tone that simultaneously annoyed and touched me.

Through the bright glass partition, he pointed out Nicolas II; he was facing us, listening attentively. Once, during a slight pause in the music, I could distinctly hear the Emperor give a weary little cough; then I saw him raise his gloved hand to his lips and lower his head.

"Let me stay out here," I said to Courilof. "I can't breathe in these large reception rooms."

He left me and went back inside. The night was oppressively still, and every now and then there were flashes of lightning. I saw the crowd stand up; I heard the sound of footsteps and the clash of sabres against the parquet floor. The princes were going into the next room, where supper was being served. I kept walking back and forth beneath the windows. I saw the Emperor with a glass of champagne in his hand and Ina in a white dress. Marguerite Eduardovna was wearing a corsage of roses with a fan of diamonds pinned into her hair; there were many other people as well, a mass of strange faces.

I was having difficulty breathing; the air was absolutely still. As I turned the corner, I ran into one of the policemen; he had seen me talking to the minister and didn't bother me. All he did was follow me for a while along the path, absent-mindedly, out of habit. I offered him a cigarette, calling out to him. "You've got your work cut out for you tonight, haven't you?"

He frowned. "The house is well guarded," he said cautiously, hesitantly, in French; he had a heavy German accent.

He touched his hat and disappeared into the shadows.

It was strange to be walking through the garden like this, spied on by the police. At the time, I didn't often think about my own life. I existed in a kind of waking dream that was both lucid and confusing. On that night, for the first time, I thought about myself, about the death that awaited me. But truthfully, it was hard for me to care ... I remember thinking: "I have to get hold of some bombs, not a gun, so I can also be blown up." It was truly strange to be telling myself that the minister and I would probably die together ... I felt a burning sensation rise through my body. I find storms oppressive, and the heavy weather that comes just before them is even worse ... It was choking me. Once again I thought: "If I could just close my eyes, go to sleep." What a rotten life ... Incomprehensible. It's easy to kill people you don't know, like the men who were marched past me those nights in 1919, and afterwards ... And even they ...

I had interrogated them: "What's your name? Where were you born?" I'd look at their papers and passports; whether they were real or forged, they evoked the image of a life that was meaningful, almost fraternal. "You, the thief, the speculator, the dealer who provided the Imperial Army with worn-out leather boots, rotten food, you're not a bad person, you wanted the money, that's all. You lean towards me again, passionately, hopefully: 'Comrade, I have dollars ... Comrade, take pity on me; I've never hurt anyone; I have young children; take pity on me!' Tomorrow, when two men blow your brains out in some dark shed, will you even know what you died for?"

I remember the thugs in the White Army who hanged peasants by the thousands; they burned the villages they passed through so completely that the only thing left in the houses was the empty space where the stoves had been. As they were dying, they looked at me with their stunned, bloodshot eyes: "Superintendent, comrade, why, why are you making me suffer like this? I've never done anything wrong." It was ... farcical ... And it was the same with Courilof.

"Eliminate the unjust for the good of the majority." Why should we? And who is just? And how do people treat me? It is unbearable for a hunter to kill an animal he has looked after and fed. But all the same, as long as we are on this earth, we have to play the game. I killed Courilof. I sent men to their deaths, men who I realised, in a moment of lucidity, were like my brothers, like my very soul ...

I had a moment of madness that evening. It was another one of those stormy, oppressive nights. I abandoned the old, futile pile of papers and went down into the garden; for a long time, I paced up and down the small path, ten feet long, that leads to the wall and the road beyond. I was overwhelmed by thirst. Anger surged inside me, and I felt as if I were being strangled by a heavy, rough hand. In the morning, the rain finally came, and I was able to stretch out on my bed and fall asleep.

I'm coughing now, can't catch my breath. Not a single sound in the house. I like this irrevocable solitude.

And so, there you have it: one summer evening thirty years ago, I walked back and forth beneath Courilof's windows and watched that crowd of dazzling clowns, all of whom are now dead.

Time passed. It was time for the Emperor to leave. His carriage arrived. In the shadow of the trees, all the policemen moved forward, forming an invisible circle. I tried to see if I could hear anything: you could vaguely make out the sound of their breathing and see their feet brushing against the grass. The minister, bare-headed, accompanied the Emperor, as was the tradition; he held a large golden candelabra with lit candles, even though the night was perfectly clear. A respectful crowd bustled behind them.

As soon as the Emperor began to speak, there was absolute silence. I could clearly hear his hesitant little cough and his words: "Thank you. It was a wonderful ball."

He got into the carriage next to the Empress; she sat upright and stiff, mechanically nodding her sad, haughty head. She wore long white feathers in her hair and a wide necklace of various precious gemstones. They left.

Courilof was beaming. An eager crowd of people surrounded him, complimenting him, as if some part of His Royal Highness had remained glued to him. He pointed to the gardens.

"Ladies, would you enjoy walking beneath these arches?" he said, with the pompous tone he used on his best days.

He turned to Dahl and took his arm. They followed the crowd of people who were walking along the paths.

"I must congratulate you," Dahl said. "His Majesty was more than kind."

Courilof was walking on clouds. Soon the musicians, hidden by the shrubbery, began to play. Torches had been lit and set into the ground around the lawns; their flames cast a deep red glow. The reflected light on the deathly pale faces of Dahl and Courilof looked like shimmering blood; they had the same pale faces you find on the people of St. Petersburg who never see the sunshine, just the artificial light of their summer nights (they sleep during the day). It was rather appropriate, when you think about it.

Dahl took the minister's arm and squeezed it affectionately. It was then that I guessed the Killer Whale's end was near.

"I just knew that if Their Majesties got to know my wife a bit better," Courilof said, "they would realise that what they had been led to believe was incorrect." He smiled proudly. That's what this man was like. His mind was certainly not as impressive as he thought, but it was greater than I myself had first believed. Yet the moment everything was going well for him, he became confused. Success went to his head like wine.

I went back to my room. I opened the window, watching the carriages in the courtyard move off, one after the other. I listened to the sound of accordions playing in the stables until morning. I saw the light for a moment in Marguerite Eduardovna's bedroom, then everything went dark.

CHAPTER 22

A WEEK AFTER the ball, the Emperor sent for Courilof. Very
politely—for Emperor Nicolas was an enlightened sovereign
who, unlike his father, never displayed any brutality in his words
or deeds—he informed his minister that he must choose between
disgrace or divorce; he urged him to opt for the latter. But
Courilof refused to leave his wife; he even displayed a sense of
indignation in the matter that the Emperor found "tactless," as
he would later say. Courilof was relieved of his official duties.

I saw my Courilof return from St. Petersburg that day. His
face seemed as impassive as ever, just the tiniest bit greyer, the
corners of his mouth sagging slightly more. But he seemed perfectly calm and in control of himself; he smiled with an ironic,
resigned expression that surprised me.

"Now I'll be able to rest as long as I like, Monsieur Legrand,
my friend," he said as he walked past me.

His dishonour was meant to be kept secret for a while; but the
"upper circles" in St. Petersburg, as the court and its members
were referred to at the time, openly talked about it.

At first Courilof's composure surprised me. Later on,
I realised he hadn't actually understood the extent of his fall from
grace. He undoubtedly believed it would be temporary . . . or
perhaps his deep conviction that he had *behaved like a gentleman*,
as he liked to put it, tensing his lips and hissing in that particular
way I'd come to know so well, perhaps that was some consolation
to him . . . Nor was he unhappy to have spoken to his beloved
sovereign alone, for the first time in his life.

The rebels at court warmly congratulated him on his attitude; he thus enjoyed a brief popularity that deceived him and
made his head spin. But it was short-lived. Soon he was alone.
Forgotten. From my window, I started to watch him pace back
and forth across his room in the evening, for hours on end.

Gradually he became more irritable and miserable, locking himself away in his bedroom, all alone.

One day I went into his room. He was sitting at his desk; he was holding open a bronze box that contained a bundle of papers; he re-read them, then carefully folded them up, as if they were old love letters. They were all the telegrams he'd received when he'd been appointed Minister of Education; he always kept them with him, locked up in his desk.

When he saw me, he became a little flustered. I expected him to send me on my way with the same severe gesture he used to dismiss anyone who annoyed him, the regal turn of his head, as if to say, "What is it? What do you want?" accompanied by an icy, heavy look in his pale blue eyes. But all he did was sadly tense his lips.

"Vanity of vanities, Monsieur Legrand, everything on this earth is but ashes and vanity. One amuses oneself however one can at my age," he added, trying in vain to sound indifferent. "Honours are the baby rattles of the elderly."

He thought for a moment and closed the drawer. Finally he gestured to me, inviting me to sit down next to him. He talked to me about Bismarck, whom he'd known. "I met him; I went to visit the great man once; he was dismissed by an ungrateful ruler, like me . . . He lived alone, with his mastiff dogs . . . Being idle is deadly . . ."

He stopped for a moment, sighed: "Power is a delectable poison . . . To some people," he hastened to add, "to *other* people . . . As for me, well, I've always been philosophical."

He forced a slight, ironic smile, the way the dead Prince Nelrode used to do. But his wide, pale eyes stared into mine with a very human look of sadness and anxiety.

July finally came and went. I received my order to kill Courilof on 3 October. The Emperor of Germany was going to visit the Tsar that day. A performance was being given at the Marie Theatre. The bomb had to be thrown as they came outside, not in the theatre itself, to avoid any accidents; still, it had to be early enough for the public and foreign dignitaries to see the assassination happen before their very eyes.

I'd been called to St. Petersburg by Fanny. She was living in a kind of attic, above the dark canals of the Fontanka, in a room she shared with a family of workers.

I remember how hot it was that summer day and the blinding limestone dust that flew up from the scaffolding, lit up by the blazing sun. We were alone in her room. I told her I wanted to see one of the leaders of the Party. She didn't reply at first, then stared at me with her narrow, gleaming eyes.

"And just who would you like to see?" she finally asked.

I didn't know. I insisted.

"Your orders are to see no one."

I was getting annoyed and insisted again. We parted without having agreed on anything.

A few days passed; she called for me to come to her place again one evening. I crossed the rickety little wooden entrance, past the banister that led to her room; then a man opened her door, came towards me, and shook my hand. A small lamp, hanging on the wall, gave off such a dim light that all I could make out of him was a wide-brimmed hat. His voice was rather strange, dry and sarcastic. His careful economy with words convinced me that he was used to speaking in public.

"We can't go in," he said, shrugging lazily, wearily, in the direction of the room. "There's a woman asleep in there, ill or drunk. I'm ... " (He told me his name. This famous terrorist has since died, executed by the Soviets, whose bitter enemy he'd become in 1918.)

It was true; I could hear a woman moaning, interspersed with hiccoughs and groans.

"You wanted to speak to me," he continued.

And he didn't even lower his voice in that hallway full of drunks, beggars, prostitutes leaving to go to work, half-naked kids who rushed past like rats. They walked by, staring at us, and pushed us out of the way. The man leaned against the banister and looked down at the dark shaft of the stairwell. That was where Courilof's fate was to be decided.

I said I didn't want to kill the minister. He didn't protest, just sighed wearily, like Courilof did when his secretary came to ask for additional information about a letter he had to finish.

"All right, fine, we'll find someone else."

A drunk started singing in one of the filthy hovels. The man banged impatiently on the wall.

"So then . . . Shall we go downstairs?"

I stopped him again, and then . . . Ah! I can't remember what I said any more, but it felt like I was fighting for my brother's life.

"Why? What's the point? He's just a poor fool; if you get rid of him, the next one won't be any better, nor the one after."

"I know," he said, infuriated, "I know. It will start all over again; you know very well we're not killing a man, we're killing the regime."

I shrugged my shoulders. I felt a kind of embarrassment, as usual, afraid I might burst into the kind of pompous speech I so hated. But I simply said, "Do you want to punish someone who is guilty, or remove the cause of the trouble, the problem, someone you consider dangerous?"

He became more thoughtful. He half sat on the flimsy little banister, steadied himself and whistled softly.

"The latter, of course."

"He's finished. It's not been made official. But he's about to be replaced."

He swore in a low, muffled voice.

"Again! The animal's already been caught! And when will it be made official?"

I gestured that I didn't know.

"Listen," he said quickly, "the third of October is the date set. Remember that there are going to be strikes in all the universities in October. There will be riots. Many students will die if Courilof remains in power. If we get rid of him, we'll terrify his successor and save many lives that are far more valuable than that inhuman machine."

"What if he's resigned from office by October third?" I asked.

"Well, too bad then," he replied. "What can we do? He'll be left alone. Otherwise, you understand, whether it's you or someone else . . ."

He didn't finish. The drunk began singing again in a plaintive voice. Fanny crept into the hallway.

"Leave, now; the spy is coming."

We went downstairs together. The man walked quickly;

I could see he wanted to leave before me so I wouldn't be able to see his face, but I got ahead of him and quickly looked at him. He was a young man, but worn out, and with gentle eyes. He looked at me, surprised.

"Listen, in the end," I said rapidly, "it's a dirty business; don't you sometimes wish you could say to hell with it all and get out?"

I don't know why, but while I was looking at him, I felt something dramatic, something intense in our conversation.

He frowned. "No, I have no pity whatsoever," he said, responding to my thoughts rather than my words, as if he could read my mind. "Those people deserve no more pity than mad dogs."

I smiled in spite of myself, recognising Langenberg's words.

"You don't understand," he continued haughtily. "You emerged from your glass cage wrapped in cotton wool; you should have asked your father."

"It's got nothing to do with pity," I said. "It's more that we seem to lack a kind of sense of humour ... as do our enemies, for that matter ... Don't you think?"

He looked at me thoughtfully. "You have to make a choice, don't you? On October third!"

He said it again. I'd got the message and told him so. He smiled, nodding.

"You'll see; as soon as you have a bomb wrapped in your handkerchief or a gun in your trouser pocket and you see all those beaming people with their medals and fine decorations, the quiver that runs down your spine will be the ultimate reward. I've killed two of them."

He tapped his hat and disappeared. After he left me, I roamed the streets of St. Petersburg, the same three streets around the dark canal, until morning.

CHAPTER 23

ALMOST IMPERCEPTIBLY, Courilof changed, growing sombre and anxious. At this time of year, he and his wife normally went to their house in the Caucasus or in France. But this year, it didn't even occur to him to leave. I don't know what he was expecting to happen. He didn't even know himself. Probably he thought that the Emperor would change his mind . . . or that the world would grind to a halt since, he, Courilof, was no longer a minister.

Finally, towards the end of July, the Emperor's decree appeared, naming Dahl as successor to Courilof. He bore the blow without flinching, but he seemed to age very quickly. I noticed that his wife's presence weighed heavily on him. He was even more attentive and polite to her, but you could sense that she was a constant reminder to him of how he had sacrificed his career, and that memory was painful to him. The children, Ina and Ivan, were away—spending the summer somewhere in the Orel region with their aunt, as they did every year.

It seemed as if only my presence was bearable to the Killer Whale. I think it was because I walked very quietly, and he found my silence comforting. I have always walked as lightly and silently as possible.

The house had become as empty and hollow as an abandoned beehive. Quite naturally, no one came to see the disgraced minister any more, afraid of compromising themselves; but what astonished me was the surprise and hurt he seemed to feel because of this. In the morning, he would shout regally, "My post!" It echoed through the entire house.

The servant would bring a few letters. Courilof would eagerly look at them, then throw them down on his bed, riffle through them and sigh. His face remained impassive; only his fingers trembled slightly.

"No message from the Emperor? Nothing?"

As he asked, he blushed visibly, emphasising his icy expression even more. You could tell that the question itself was painful, but that he couldn't help asking it. I remember the blood inching slowly up his face, colouring his pale features, right up to his high forehead. He jumped every time the bell rang, every time he heard a carriage passing in the street.

The weather was hot and beautiful. Courilof often went out in the garden early, breathing in the perfume of the flowers, of the great lawns covered in a sea of grass, like a prairie. They were cut at this time of year; you could hear the hissing of the scythe and the peasants' voices carrying through the peaceful air.

"Cut down just like us, Monsieur Legrand, just like us!" He stopped; looked around him, over towards the gulf, pale grey beneath the blue sky.

"It's easier to breathe this pure air; it hasn't been polluted yet by the stench of men. Don't you agree, Monsieur Legrand?"

He stabbed a leaf with the end of his cane, then raised it up to the light, stopping to look at the grass and the shrubs without seeing them, his heart heavy. He started to say how much the singing birds delighted him, but then his face contorted with pain.

"That's enough; let's go back! I can't bear their chirping! The sun is making my head spin," he added, pointing to the pale northern sun reflected in the water.

It was the time of day when he used to report to the Emperor.

"*Cincinnatus . . . Let us begin to work our plough . . .*" Whenever he mentioned the Emperor or the Empress, the court or the ministers, he let out a short little snigger. As he stood beneath the stinging whip of adversity, this man—whom I had never known to be either spiritual or bitter—now voiced rather cruel and amusing verdicts on both people and things.

"Didn't you ever come across revolutionary immigrants in Switzerland?" he asked me once.

Fearing a trap, I replied: "No."

"Fanatics, cranks, villains!"

But, all in all, they scarcely interested him. What counted for him, for his sovereign, for Russia, were the plots of the grand dukes, the ministers, and, most especially, the conspiracies and schemes of Dahl and his cohorts. He was their victim; he called them "diabolical" and thought they were poisonous. He never spoke to me about it: I wasn't meant to know anything. I was nothing but an insignificant doctor, unworthy of sharing the destiny and misfortunes of the great men of this world. But in spite of himself, everything he said led back to what had happened to him.

My poor Courilof! I had never been as close to him, never understood him so well, despised him so much, felt as sorry for him as I did on those days, those nights. The pale, clear nights lasted twelve hours on the horizon, then began to darken, for it was August; in this climate it was already autumn, an arid, sad season everywhere, but especially here. I advised him to leave. I talked to him about Switzerland and a house in Vevey, a white house with a climbing red vine, like the Bauds' house . . . I drew the most idyllic pictures for him. In vain. He clung to his proximity to the Emperor, to his memories, to the illusion of power.

"Ministers, puppets," he repeated furiously, over and over again. "An Emperor? No, a saint! God preserve us from such saints on the throne! Everything in its proper place! As for the Empress!"

He stopped, pinching his lips into a scornful pout and sighed deeply. "What I need is something to do . . ."

He needed something else as well: the illusion of influencing people's fate. You never get tired of that; otherwise, you're finished . . . completely finished . . . I know that now.

"You're the only one who's remained faithful to this old, disgraced man," he said to me one day.

I made some vague reply. He sighed, then looked at me oddly, in that charming way of his.

"All in all," he remarked, "you're something of a mystery."

"Why?" I said.

It gave me a certain sense of pleasure to ask.

"Why?" he repeated slowly. "I don't know."

At that very moment, I knew that some doubt had crossed his mind. It was unbelievable to see how truly bizarre and obtuse these people were: they deported and imprisoned masses of innocent people and poor fools, but the really dangerous enemies of the regime slipped through their nets unharmed. Yes, at that moment, and for the first time, Courilof was suspicious. His uneasiness probably affected his reasoning. But without a doubt, he thought he had nothing left to fear; or perhaps he felt the same things towards me as I did towards him: understanding, curiosity, a vague kind of fraternity, pity, scorn... How could I know? Perhaps he wasn't thinking anything of the sort... He shrugged his shoulders slightly and said nothing.

We went back to the house to have lunch with Marguerite Eduardovna, the three of us sitting around a table that was meant for twenty. During the meal, he was so irritable it verged on madness. One day, he smashed one of the Sèvres vases that decorated the table; he threw it at the butler's head, I don't remember why now. It was pink, made of soft-paste porcelain, and it held the last small trembling roses of summer, yellow and almost faded, deliciously fragrant. When the butler had silently collected up all the debris, Courilof was ashamed; he gestured for him to go away. Then he shrugged his shoulders, looked at me and said: "We can be so childish!"

He sat motionless for a long time, his eyes lowered.

In the afternoon, he would go and lie down, spending long hours on his settee, reading. He called for stacks of books, armfuls of them, French novels whose pages he meticulously cut to pass the time. He would slip the blade between the pages, smooth them out, then cut them apart with little slicing movements. Lost in thought, he never made a sound. I often saw him staring into space with his wide, sad eyes, holding a large book open in front of him. Then he would look at the last page, sigh, and throw the book down.

"I'm bored," he said over and over again, "I'm so bored!"

He'd start pacing back and forth in his bedroom, a room filled with many icons. When his wife came in, his face would light up, but almost immediately, he'd look away and start wandering aimlessly from room to room again.

The few people who called to see him were sent away. He was reading the *Lives of the Saints*, I recall, and pretended it was some consolation to him. But since he was so attached to worldly possessions, to physical pleasures, he also dismissed religious books with a sigh.

"God will forgive me . . . We are all just poor sinners." He had pretensions of being European, so found his involuntary sighs more disconcerting than anyone else did.

There was only one thing he never tired of, one thing that he really loved. He gestured for me to sit down opposite him: he had some tea and lamps brought in. It already felt like autumn; a misty fog fell on to the Iles at dusk, dense and full of shadows. Then the Killer Whale would tell me about his past. For hours at a time, he would talk about himself: his services to the Monarchy, his family, his childhood, his opinions about the role of a great politician. But on the rare occasions he deigned to talk about men he'd known, he surprised me. He found a bitterly funny way of describing them. He talked about their petty intrigues, the misappropriation of public funds, their thefts and betrayals, so commonplace in the city and at court, a bizarre crowd who amused me.

I think it's because of Courilof that I was later able to give some good advice to the rulers of the time to help them manage things. This was when the glorious days of the Revolution were over and we had to deal with Europe and the growing demands of the people. He taught me more than he ever knew, my old enemy; and it was just the opposite of what he thought he was teaching me . . .

Often I wasn't even listening to what he said, just to his tone of voice, tinged with bitterness and venom; I watched his ghostly pale, haughty face, already marked by death and devoured by envy and ambition. A small mahogany table with two old-fashioned lamps and painted metal shades sat between us. Their flames burned peacefully in the dark. You could hear the policemen, ever present like me, even though they no longer had a minister to protect; they made their rounds beneath the windows, whispering softly as they passed each other in the night.

"Men . . . men," repeated Courilof. "Ministers, princes, what puppets they all are! True power lies in the hands of madmen or children, who don't even know they have it. The rest of humanity is chasing after shadows!"

That was exactly how he spoke: he was a man who lacked simplicity, but also managed to speak the truth.

Then came another silent dinner. Afterwards, Marguerite Eduardovna played the piano as we paced back and forth through the great reception room: the sparkling wooden floors reflected the lights from the chandeliers, all lit up for his solitary stroll. Sometimes, he would stop and shout in frustration: "Tomorrow I'm leaving!"

And the next day would be exactly the same.

CHAPTER 24

MEANWHILE, THE TROUBLES in the capital continued. From the universities, the problems spread to the factories where, in certain provinces, bloody battles broke out once more. Dahl didn't know how to deal with either the schools or the universities.

One evening, Courilof seemed more animated than usual. As he was saying good night to me, he added: "Don't go to St. Petersburg tomorrow: the students at the Imperial Secondary Schools intend to present a petition to the Emperor, who is currently at the Winter Palace, in support of the striking workers in the Poutilov factories."

"What's going to happen?" I asked.

He laughed curtly. "No one knows anything yet, and His Excellency"—he stressed the words sarcastically, as always when he mentioned his successor—"His Excellency knows even less than anyone. It will end quite simply. The commander at the palace will be caught off guard and will call in the troops. When that happens, power automatically passes to the colonel, and since there will be no lack of protestors to insult the army, the soldiers will be forced to open fire. That's what will happen," he said, forcing a little laugh. "That's where it will all end—with a minister like Baron Dahl who treats the children he's responsible for as if they were dogs!"

I said nothing.

"It could prove very damaging to him," Courilof murmured pensively.

I asked why, and Courilof started laughing again and patted me on the shoulder; his large hand was unusually strong.

"So you're interested in these events, are you? You don't understand? You really don't understand?" he repeated. (He seemed enormously amused.) "Do you think the Emperor will be pleased to see dead bodies underneath his windows? Such things are perfectly acceptable as long as they happen far from view . . ." (he suddenly frowned, no doubt recalling some inconvenient facts), "but not right in front of you, at your home. Do you know what Emperor Alexander I is supposed to have said? 'Princes sometimes like crime, but they rarely like criminals.' That's a good one, don't you think? And then of course there's the press; even though they are conveniently censored here, thank God, they still have some influence."

He went over to his wife and took her arm. "You see, my darling, personally, I am very happy not to be taking such risks, no longer having these problems," he said, in French, forcing his voice to sound light-hearted and indifferent. "Yes indeed, this has made me feel better! I admit I foolishly allowed myself to fall into a kind of depression. Next week we'll leave for Vevey, my darling. We shall cultivate our garden. Do you remember the sea gulls by the lake? Unless of course . . ."

And he drifted off, dreamily. "Those poor children!" he spat, thoughtful and grave. "Now there are truly innocent souls for whom *they* must answer before God."

He stood silent for a long time, sighed, then took Marguerite Eduardovna's hand. "Let's go upstairs, my dear."

Just then, the bell rang downstairs. He jumped; it was nearly midnight. A servant entered, saying there was a small group of men who didn't wish to give their names, asking to see him at once. His wife begged him not to let them in.

"They're anarchists, revolutionaries," she kept saying, anxiously.

"Let me go with you," I said to Courilof. "With the two of us and the servants within earshot, we'll be safe."

He agreed, doubtlessly to appease his wife: I knew how naturally calm and courageous he was. Still, he suspected something wasn't right and it made him curious. Whatever the reason, he agreed. The visitors were taken downstairs to the empty office. They apologised for having come so late at night, without having requested an audience. It was a delegation of teachers from the Imperial Secondary Schools; they were pale and shaking as they huddled by the door, afraid to come in, petrified by the heavy, fixed stare of the Killer Whale. As for my Courilof, he proudly stood up straight, as tall as a peacock. He let his hand drop on to the desk in his usual way; it was a large, powerful hand. It was white and freckled, adorned with a large gemstone ring, a garnet that caught the light and gleamed blood-red.

The teachers were old and frightened. They said they'd come to try to prevent something terrible from happening. The Minister of Education had refused to see them. A scornful little smile hovered over Courilof's lips . . . They had come to beg His Excellency to please warn Dahl, whom they believed was indebted to Courilof as his former colleague, his friend. (They had no idea that Dahl had stolen the post from Courilof; in the city, the official story was that Courilof had to retire for health reasons; the secrets of the gods were carefully guarded. The important people at the court knew every detail of what had happened, naturally, but the secondary schools teachers were hardly important people there.) Just as Courilof had said, a delegation of young people had decided to present a request to the Emperor, asking him to pardon the strikers who'd been deported. The teachers feared the children would be mistaken for strikers and shot. (Two years later, this is exactly what would happen to the workers led by G. in front of the Winter Palace.)

The longer he listened to them, the paler and more silent Courilof became. This man's silences had extraordinary power; he seemed frozen into a block of ice.

"What do you want me to do, gentlemen?" he finally said.

"Warn Baron Dahl. He'll listen to you. Or at least ask him to receive us. You will be preventing something awful, much loss of life."

They didn't realise that my Courilof was thinking of only one thing: how to seize the opportunity, offered to him by fate, to throw his successor into an impossible situation. He could first reclaim his job, then, later on when the moment was right, he would be hailed as the defender and saviour of the Monarchy. I felt I could read his mind. I don't know why, but I imagined he was quoting *deus ex machina* to himself, in Latin, as he liked to do.

"I cannot do it, gentlemen: what you are asking of me is quite improper. I have retired from public life, not because of my health, as you thought, but because the Emperor wished it. Go and see Baron Dahl yourself. Insist."

"But he refused to see us!"

"Well then, gentlemen, what can I do? . . . I am powerless."

They begged him. One of them was a pale old man in a black coat. Suddenly he leaned forward and (I can still picture it) grabbed Courilof's hand and kissed it.

"My son is one of the leaders, Your Excellency; please save my son!"

"You shouldn't have allowed him to get mixed up in this," said Courilof, his voice icy and sharp. "Go home and lock your son in."

The old man gestured in despair. "So you refuse?"

"Gentlemen, I cannot intervene, I repeat, it's got nothing to do with me."

Quietly they conferred with one another; then they began to all talk at once, imploring this motionless man.

"Their blood will be on your hands," one of them said, his voice shaking.

"It won't be the first time," said Courilof, smiling slightly. "Nor will it be the first time I've been held responsible for blood I haven't spilled."

They left.

The next day, before they reached the gates of the Winter Palace, the thirty young people were stopped by the army. As the army tried to disperse them, someone grabbed the reins of one of the horses. The Cossack felt his horse rear and thought he was being attacked; he fired. The youngsters responded by throwing stones; the crowd angrily took sides and a shower of stones fell against the bronze gates and the Imperial Eagles that decorated them. The colonel ordered his men to open fire. Fifteen people were killed: students and passers-by (amongst the first shot was the son of the elderly gentleman who had come to beg Courilof's help), and all right under the Emperor's windows. The scandal caused by the death of these fifteen victims would rid Courilof of Dahl and return him to his post as Minister of Education.

CHAPTER 25

NATURALLY, IT DIDN'T happen immediately; for a long time, even I knew nothing about it.

The following week, Courilof and his family left for the Caucasus, and I went with them.

Their house was not far from Kislovodsk, at the very edge of the city. From its large, circular wooden balcony, you could see the first foothills of the mountains. It was extremely beautiful, though arid and bare, with the occasional dark cypress tree surrounded by stones and water. In the garden, there were wild rose bushes in bloom; they had twisted branches, spiky thorns, and flowers whose perfume filled the evening air. Just like here in France, they grew in clusters, beneath the windows.

The air was too chilly for me; I couldn't stop coughing.

One day, Dahl arrived. He seemed perfectly calm. He told us he'd come to relax in the spa at Kislovodsk, take the waters of Kislovodsk, and that the moment he'd arrived, he'd immediately come to see "his dear friend." During the meal, he openly told all of us how he had been unfairly blamed for the events in August.

"Once again, 'they' found their scapegoat," he said, smiling. "And this time, it was yours truly."

(The expressions "they," "you know who," "those people," all meant the Imperial Family and the grand dukes. My Courilof often used these terms as well.)

"It's a sad story," Dahl added, shrugging his shoulders with indifference. Most likely it was feigned, for he too had the pleasure of gathering up the dead bodies at nightfall. I had noticed they were all stony-faced when it happened behind their backs; but when they actually saw the massacred children with their own eyes, touched them with their own hands, that was different. "If only I could have known what they were plotting . . . I heard the entire city knew what was going on, but *I*, well, I was the last to

know. That's always the way it is. So there you have it! The
Emperor considerately asked me to tender my resignation. His
Majesty, in his great kindness, deigned to promise me a post in
the senate and also asked my advice, even in my disgrace, about
who to eventually name as my successor. Moreover, to top off his
goodness, he kindly appointed my son secretary to the embassy
in Copenhagen. It's a city that doesn't maintain the same importance as in our day, Valerian Alexandrovitch, but the imperial
couple go there often enough to make the post desirable. We're
lucky to end up anywhere the sun spreads its rays, if you'll allow
me the metaphor."

He said no more, and changed the subject.

After lunch, the two former ministers went into Courilof's
office, where they remained for a long time. Froelich nudged me
to point out Irène Valerianovna's worried expression.

"I think that the old fox has come to negotiate his son's
marriage to Mademoiselle Ina," he whispered.

That evening, Dahl stayed for dinner; he was very happy and
several times before leaving, he kissed the young girl's hand. This
was very unlike him and clearly gave away his intentions. After
he'd gone, Courilof wanted to see Irène Valerianovna, but she'd
gone up to her room. It was the next morning, in front of me—
for they thought I knew no Russian—that Courilof spoke to his
daughter.

He complained of having been in pain all night long; when
his daughter came in to say good morning the next day, he asked
her to stay.

"Ina," he said solemnly. "Baron Dahl has done me the honour
of asking for your hand in marriage for his son. We had discussed
this last year . . ."

She cut in. "I know," she said quietly, "but I don't love him."

"There are serious considerations at stake, my child," said
Courilof in his haughtiest tone.

"I know Dahl doesn't just want my dowry for his son, and
that you . . ."

He blushed suddenly and banged his fist against the table in
anger. "That does not concern you. You will be married, rich,
and free. What else do you want?"

"That's it, isn't it?" she asked, ignoring what he'd said. "You want an alliance with the baron, don't you? He's promised to get you back your miserable post as minister if I agree, hasn't he? That's it, isn't it?"

"Yes," said Courilof. "You understand, you're not stupid. But why do you think I want the post?" he continued, and I could have sworn he was being sincere. "It's my cross to bear and will send me to an early grave, for I'm not well, not at all well, my child, but I must serve my Emperor, my country, and those unfortunate children being led to their downfall by the revolutionaries. I must serve them with all my strength and until I breathe my last. I must watch over them, punish them if necessary, but as a father would do, not as an enemy. Certainly not like Dahl, whose guilty negligence got them killed. And it is quite true that the baron promised to help me if you agree to this marriage. The Emperor holds him in great esteem; it is only public opinion following this unfortunate event that has forced him to distance himself from Dahl. Of course, Dahl has hardly behaved brilliantly," he continued, sounding disgusted, "but it is up to God to judge him . . . As far as I'm concerned, my conscience is clear. Moreover, Dahl comes from an honourable family that was often allied with ours in the past. It is natural to wish to increase one's worldly possessions by marrying wealth . . . and, my poor girl, as for love . . ."

He stopped: he'd been speaking French as he usually did when the conversation turned to higher or sensitive subjects. He frowned and turned towards me. "Please leave us, my dear Monsieur Legrand; I do apologise."

I went out.

That same evening, Courilof took his daughter's arm, and they strolled along an isolated little path where they could sit together. When they returned, he seemed happy; his face had taken on its normal solemn expression. His daughter, very pale, smiled sadly, ironically.

That night, I went out on the balcony. Irène Valerianovna was sitting very still, her head in her hands. The moon was very bright, and I could clearly see the young girl's white night-dress and her bare arms leaning on the hand-rail. She was crying.

I understood she had given her consent and that everything was going to change, which is exactly what happened.

Shortly afterwards, the engagement was made official. And finally one morning, his hands trembling, Courilof opened a package that I could see contained a small photograph of the Empress and two of her children, supreme proof of their reconciliation. Courilof hung the picture in a gold frame above his desk, just below the icon.

All that remained was to wait for a telegram from the Emperor informing Courilof that he was to be reinstated to the post of minister, assuming his improved health would henceforth allow him to resume his public duties. All of us were waiting for this telegram, in fact, and all with different emotions. It arrived in the middle of September. Courilof gathered everyone around and read it out loud to the whole family, made a large sign of the cross, and said, tears in his eyes:

"Once again the great burden of power falls upon my shoulders, but God will help me bear it."

CHAPTER 26

I FELT STRANGE: I was devastated, but at the same time, understood the intensely bitter joke destiny had played on us.

It was nearly time to go back; every day Courilof seemed
happier and in better health. The weather was beautiful, golden.
I had grown accustomed to the mountain air; at times, I felt a
kind of drowsiness and calm; while at other moments, I was so
tired of the world that I felt like smashing my head against the
rocks. Those beautiful red rocks; I remember them: they were
like the rocks here . . .

One evening I made my decision. I announced I was urgently
needed back in Switzerland. I would leave the next day; I said
I needed to speak to the minister.

After dinner (it was nearly eight o'clock and the sun was
setting) Courilof was in the habit of going for a walk before tea
was served later in the evening. He took the path in front of the
terrace and, from there, walked up a narrow road lined with
rocks. I went with him.

I remember the sound the stones made under our feet; they
were round and shiny and reddish beneath the setting sun. But
the sky was tinted violet, and under its mournful, dazzling light,
Courilof's face took on a strange expression.

There were waterfalls above; great torrents crashed down and
echoed off the rocks angrily. We walked past them, climbed
higher still, and it was there that I told him I had considered the
matter seriously and was leaving. I said I felt it was my duty as a
doctor to tell him he was undoubtedly more ill than he thought.
I believed he should take better care of himself, give up any
unnecessary activities; if he did, he would live longer.

He listened to me, his face impassive, without moving a
muscle. When I had finished, he stared at me calmly. I can still
picture that look.

"But my dear Monsieur Legrand, I am quite aware of my

condition. My father died of liver cancer, you know." He fell silent, sighing. "No good Christian fears death so long as he has fulfilled his duty here on earth," he said (and little by little, his sincere voice turned solemn and pompous again). "I intend to accomplish much in my few remaining years before sleeping in eternal peace."

I asked if I had understood him correctly, that he refused to give up his public duties, knowing what he now knew. I always suspected, I added, that he was aware of his condition, despite what that idiot Langenberg said; but did he realise that liver cancer progresses quickly, and that he had only months to live, a year at the most?

"Of course," he replied, shrugging his shoulders. "I willingly put myself in God's hands."

"I think that when a man is facing death, it is better to give up any work that could be harmful, in order to achieve peace of mind," I said.

He winced. "Harmful! Good Lord! My work is my only consolation! I am the holy guardian of the traditions of the Empire! I shall be able to say, just as Augustus did as he was dying: *Plaudicite amici, bene agi actum vitae!* Applaud friends, I have acted well in life!"

He could have gone on in the same vein for a long time. He had no regrets . . . I cut in. I tried to speak as simply and sarcastically as possible.

"Valerian Alexandrovitch, don't you think it's terrible? You know very well that what you did caused the deaths of innocent people, and will cause many more. I am not a politician, but I do wonder if that ever keeps you awake at night?"

He sat silently. The sun had set, so I could no longer see his face. Still, since I was very close to him, I saw how he tilted his head towards his shoulder. He looked like a dark block of stone.

"Every action, every battle, brings death. If we are on this earth, it is to act and destroy. But when one is acting for a higher cause . . ." He stopped and then said, "It isn't easy to live a good life." His voice had changed; it was softer and tinged with sadness. I think it was his frankness, these flashes of sincerity that made him so charming and yet so frustrating.

He stood up, calling over his shoulder, "Shall we go back?"

We retraced our steps in silence. It was very dark now, and we had to be careful of the stones and low brambles that got caught on our clothes. In front of the house, he shook my hand. "Good-bye, Monsieur Legrand. Have a good trip; we'll see each other again one day, I hope."

I said that anything was possible, and we parted.

Very early the following morning, I was awakened by the sound of footsteps and muffled voices in the garden. I leaned forward to look out of the window and through the wooden slats, I saw my Courilof with a policeman; he was easily recognisable in spite of his disguise. I remembered seeing this policeman on several occasions when he accompanied the minister to give his reports to the Emperor. I realised that Courilof was having me followed. As usual, he wasn't very clever about it; but it was the one and only moment during all the time I spent with him that I suddenly understood what it truly meant to hate. Seeing this powerful man, so confident, calmly standing in his garden, knowing that all he had to do was say the word and I would be tracked down, locked up, and hanged like an animal, made me understand how easy it can be to kill in cold blood. At that very moment, I could have happily held a gun to his head and pulled the trigger.

In the meantime, I had to get away, which I did. I openly took the train to St. Petersburg, followed by the policeman; in the middle of the night, I got off at one of the little mountain stations. From there, I made it to the Persian border. I remained in Persia for a few days; I exchanged my Swiss passport for the identity papers of a carpet salesman, given to me by some members of a revolutionary group in Tehran. Towards the end of September, I went back to Russia.

CHAPTER 27

I ARRIVED IN St. Petersburg and went straight to Fanny's place; she settled me into her room and then went out. I was tired, utterly exhausted. I threw myself down on the bed and immediately fell asleep.

I remember a dream I had, which is rare for me. My dream was very beautiful, very innocent; it seemed to rise up from the depths of an idyllic childhood, for I was young, handsome, and bursting with energy in a way I'd never really been. I stood in a meadow full of flowers bathed in sunlight; the most bizarre thing was that the children standing around me were Courilof, Prince Nelrode, Dahl, Schwann, and the stranger from Vevey. In the end, it turned into a painful, indescribably grotesque nightmare: their faces changed, becoming old and tired, yet they continued running and playing as before.

I woke up and saw Fanny come into the room, followed by a comrade I knew. But he didn't look as wonderfully calm as the first time we'd met: he seemed worried and annoyed. He warned me that the police had been alerted, they were already looking for me, and I was to take every precaution. I let him talk. I was so utterly frustrated by then that I felt I wanted to be done with him, as well as Courilof.

He looked at me oddly, and I'm convinced he had me followed from that day on, right up until the assassination. His men were better at it than Courilof's spies, but the minute I stepped out the door, I could sense them behind me.

October had arrived. It got dark early and it was relatively easy to slip away at a street corner. It hadn't started snowing yet, but the air had that icy heaviness peculiar to autumn in Russia; the lamps in the houses were lit from early morning. A misty, snowy fog rose up and sat low on the ground; the earth was frozen, hollow. A sad time . . . I spent hours on end stretched out on the bed, in the room Fanny had given up for me. I was coughing up blood; I had the smell and taste of blood in my mouth and on my skin.

I didn't see Fanny any more; it had been agreed that she would come to see me the night before the assassination to give the final order, since she was the one responsible for preparing the bombs and giving them to me. The comrade came to see me again, telling me the exact time to go through with it: eleven forty-five. There was no question of going inside the theatre itself, as it was by invitation only, so we'd have to wait at the entrance.

"If you hadn't been found out," he said bitterly, "it would have been so simple! Courilof would have got you a seat in the theatre and during the interval you could have gone into his box and shot him! All those months we tailed him, for what! Now, with these bloody bombs, you risk killing twenty innocent people for one Courilof."

"I don't give a damn," I replied.

Nothing had ever seemed as ridiculous to me as their false precautions. When he asked me: "What? If Courilof were in a carriage with his wife and children, you'd throw the bomb?" I said yes, and I thought I actually could have done it. What difference would it make? But I could see he didn't believe me.

"Well, comrade," he finally said, "that won't happen. He'll be alone with his servants."

They, apparently, didn't count.

"Well, good-bye then!" he said.

He left.

It happened the next evening. Fanny came with me. We were carrying bombs covered in shawls and wrapped in parcel paper. We didn't speak. We went and sat down in a brightly lit little square opposite the Marie Theatre. A long line of policemen and carriages waited in the street.

The square was empty. The sky was low and dark; a fine, light snow fluttered through the air, turning to rain as soon as it touched the ground. Tiny needles of icy rain that stung your face.

Fanny pointed to the parked carriages. "The court, the diplomatic corps, the German Embassy delegation, the ministers," she whispered with a kind of exultation.

The night was deadly long, terrible. Around eleven o'clock, the wind changed and a thick snow began to fall. We moved to another spot; we were frozen. Twice we walked around the little square.

Suddenly we found ourselves face to face with someone who'd emerged from the shadows to look at us. Fanny pressed herself against me and I kissed her. Thinking we were lovers, the policeman was reassured and disappeared. I held Fanny in my arms; she looked up at me, and I remember that, for the first time, I saw a tear in those cruel eyes.

I let go of her. We continued to walk in silence. I was coughing. Blood kept rushing into my mouth. I spat it out, then coughed again; blood trickled on to my hands. I wanted to lie down right there in the snow and die.

The carriages began to move forward. You could hear the sound of doors opening and banging shut inside the theatre, and the shrill whistles of the policemen.

I crossed the street. I was holding a bomb in my hand as if it were a flower. It was grotesque. I don't understand how no one noticed and arrested me. Fanny followed behind. We stopped close to the entrance, beneath the columns heavy with snow, between the rows of people.

The doors opened. Everyone came out. The Emperor, the Imperial Family, William II and his entourage had already left. I saw women in furs walk by, jewellery gleaming beneath their delicate mantillas dotted with snowflakes. There were generals whose spurs clattered against the frozen ground, and others as well, people I didn't know, the doddery old fools of the diplomatic corps, and still others . . . Courilof. He turned towards me; his face was old and pale; or was it just the light from the street-lamps that made his features seem so furrowed? He looked weary and defeated, with big dark circles under his eyes. I turned towards Fanny.

"I can't kill him," I said.

I felt her grab the bomb from me. She took two steps forward and threw it.

I remember a jumble of faces, hands, eyes, that swam around in front of me, then disappeared in explosion with the noise and light of hell itself. We weren't hurt, but our faces were cut, our clothes burnt, our hands covered in blood. I took Fanny's hand and we ran through the dark streets, ran like hunted animals. People were bumping into us, rushing in all directions. Several of them had ripped clothes and bloody hands, like us. An injured horse whinnied so horribly from pain that shivers ran down my spine. When we finally stopped, we were in the middle of a square, surrounded by an angry crowd. I knew we were finished. I felt relieved. It was there we were arrested.

Afterwards, Fanny and I found ourselves in a room next to the one where the dead bodies were piled up. We had guards, but amidst the confusion and horror, it hadn't occurred to them to separate us.

Fanny suddenly burst into tears. I felt sorry for her. I'd already said that I was the one who'd thrown the bomb, as that was only fair: if she hadn't grabbed it from my hands, I would have ended up throwing it. That . . . that was the easy part . . . And anyway, as I've already said, I was coughing up so much blood that I felt there was none left in my lungs; I was certain that if they just let me close my eyes and sit still, I would die; and I painfully, eagerly longed for that moment.

I went over to Fanny, put a cigarette in her hand and whispered:

"You have nothing to worry about."

She shook her head. "It's not that, it's not that . . . Dead! He's dead! Dead!"

"Who's dead?" I asked, confused.

"Courilof! He's dead! Dead! And I'm the one who killed him!"

Nevertheless, her instinct for survival remained strong within her.

When the policeman came closer, attracted by her cries, he heard her say again: "He's dead! And we're the ones who killed him!"

And so she was condemned to life in prison and I to be hanged.

But you should never count on death any more than you count on life. I'm still here . . . The devil alone knows why. Later on, Fanny escaped and took part in a second assassination. She was the one who killed P. in 1907 or 1908. She was caught, and this time, she hanged herself in her cell. As for me . . . Well, I've told my story. Life is absurd. Fortunately for me, at least, the show will soon be over.

ABOUT THE INTRODUCER

CLAIRE MESSUD is the award-winning author of four works of fiction: *When the World Was Steady*; *The Hunters*; *The Last Life*; and, most recently, *The Emperor's Children*.

CHINUA ACHEBE
Things Fall Apart

ISABEL ALLENDE
The House of the Spirits

GIORGIO BASSANI
The Garden of the Finzi-Continis

SIMONE DE BEAUVOIR
The Second Sex

SAMUEL BECKETT
Molloy, Malone Dies,
The Unnamable
(US only)

SAUL BELLOW
The Adventures of Augie March

JORGE LUIS BORGES
Ficciones

MIKHAIL BULGAKOV
The Master and Margarita

JAMES M. CAIN
The Postman Always Rings Twice
Double Indemnity
Mildred Pierce
Selected Stories
(1 vol. US only)

ITALO CALVINO
If on a winter's night a traveler

ALBERT CAMUS
The Outsider (UK)
The Stranger (US)
The Plague, The Fall,
Exile and the Kingdom,
and Selected Essays
(in 1 vol.)

WILLA CATHER
Death Comes for the Archbishop
My Ántonia
(US only)

RAYMOND CHANDLER
The novels (2 vols)
Collected Stories

JOSEPH CONRAD
Heart of Darkness
Lord Jim
Nostromo
The Secret Agent
Typhoon and Other Stories
Under Western Eyes
Victory

WILLIAM FAULKNER
The Sound and the Fury
(UK only)

F. SCOTT FITZGERALD
The Great Gatsby
This Side of Paradise
(UK only)

PENELOPE FITZGERALD
The Bookshop
The Gate of Angels
The Blue Flower
(in 1 vol.)
Offshore
Human Voices
The Beginning of Spring
(in 1 vol.)

FORD MADOX FORD
The Good Soldier
Parade's End

E. M. FORSTER
Howards End
A Passage to India

KAHLIL GIBRAN
The Collected Works

GÜNTER GRASS
The Tin Drum

GRAHAM GREENE
Brighton Rock
The Human Factor

DASHIELL HAMMETT
The Maltese Falcon
The Thin Man
Red Harvest
(in 1 vol.)
The Dain Curse
The Glass Key
and Selected Stories
(in 1 vol.)

This book is set in BEMBO which was cut
by the punch–cutter Francesco Griffo
for the Venetian printer-publisher
Aldus Manutius in early 1495
and first used in a pamphlet
by a young scholar
named Pietro
Bembo.